ETCHED IN BONE

A NOVEL OF THE OTHERS

ANNE BISHOP

ROC
New York

ROC

Published by Berkley

An imprint of Penguin Random House LLC

375 Hudson Street, New York, New York 10014

ROC with its colophon is a registered trademark of Penguin Random House LLC.

ISBN: 9780451474506

Roc hardcover edition / March 2017

Roc mass-market edition / February 2018

Printed in the United States of America

7   9   10   8   6

Cover illustration by Blake Morrow

Cover design by Adam Auerbach

For
Anne Sowards
and
Jennifer Jackson

And for
Ruth "the Ruthie" Stuart
You will be remembered.

ACKNOWLEDGMENTS

My thanks to Blair Boone for continuing to be my first reader and for all the information about animals, weapons, and many other things that I absorbed and transformed to suit the Others' world; to Debra Dixon for being second reader; to Doranna Durgin for maintaining the Web site; to Adrienne Roehrich for running the official fan page on Facebook; to Nadine Fallacaro for information about things medical; to Jennifer Crow for pep talks when needed; to Anne Sowards and Jennifer Jackson for the feedback that helps me write a better story; and to Pat Feidner for always being supportive and encouraging.

A special thanks to the following people who loaned their names to characters, knowing that the name would be the only connection between reality and fiction: Bobbie Barber, Elizabeth Bennefeld, Blair Boone, Kelley Burch, Douglas Burke, Starr Corcoran, Jennifer Crow, Lorna MacDonald Czarnota, Julie Czerneda, Roger Czerneda, Merri Lee Debany, Michael Debany, Mary Claire Eamer, Sarah Jane Elliott, Sarah Esposito, Chris Fallacaro, Dan Fallacaro, Mike Fallacaro, Nadine Fallacaro, James Alan Gardner, Mantovani "Monty" Gay, Julie Green, Lois Gresh, Ann Hergott, Lara Herrera, Robert Herrera, Danielle Hilborn, Heather Houghton, Pamela Ireland, Lorne Kates, Allison King, Jana Paniccia, Jennifer Margaret Seely, Denby "Skip" Stowe, Ruth Stuart, and John Wulf.

GEOGRAPHY

NAMID—THE WORLD

CONTINENTS/LANDMASSES
Afrikah
Australis
Brittania/Wild Brittania
Cel-Romano/Cel-Romano Alliance of Nations
Felidae
Fingerbone Islands
Storm Islands
Thaisia
Tokhar-Chin
Zelande

Great Lakes—Superior, Tala, Honon, Etu, and
   Tahki
Other lakes—Feather Lakes/Finger Lakes
River—Talulah/Talulah Falls
Mountains—Addirondak, Rocky
Cities and villages—Bennett, Endurance, Ferryman's
   Landing, Harmony, Hubb NE (aka Hubbney),
   Jerzy, Lakeside, Podunk, Prairie Gold, Ravendell,
   Shikago, Sparkletown, Sweetwater, Talulah Falls,
   Toland, Walnut Grove, Wheatfield

DAYS OF THE WEEK
Earthday
Moonsday
Sunday
Windsday
Thaisday
Firesday
Watersday

LAKESIDE

This map was created by a geographically challenged author who put in only the bits she needed for the story.

LAKESIDE COURTYARD

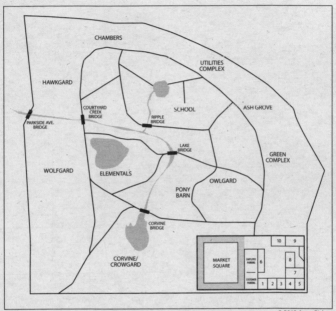

CHAMBERS

HAWKGARD

UTILITIES COMPLEX

ASH GROVE

SCHOOL

COURTYARD CREEK BRIDGE

RIPPLE BRIDGE

PARKSIDE AVE. BRIDGE

LAKE BRIDGE

WOLFGARD

ELEMENTALS

GREEN COMPLEX

PONY BARN

OWLGARD

CORVINE BRIDGE

CORVINE/ CROWGARD

MARKET SQUARE

EMPLOYEE PARKING

CUSTOMER PARKING

10 9

6   8

7

1 2 3 4 5

© 2012 Anne Bishop

1. Seamstress/Tailor & efficiency apartments
2. A Little Bite
3. Howling Good Reads
4. Run & Thump
5. Social Center
6. Garages
7. Earth Native & Henry's Studio
8. Liaison's Office
9. Consulate
10. Three Ps

PROLOGUE

End of Sumor

As they gathered in the wild country between Tala and Etu, two of the Great Lakes, their footsteps filled the land with a terrible silence.

They were Elders, primal forms of *terra indigene* who guarded the wild, pristine parts of the world. To the smaller forms of earth natives—shifters like the Wolf and Bear and Panther—they were known as Namid's teeth and claws.

Humans—those invasive two-legged predators—had made war against the *terra indigene*, killing the smaller shifters in the wild country that bordered Cel-Romano, a place that was on the other side of Ocean's domain. And here, in Thaisia, so many of the Wolfgard were killed that parts of the land were empty of their song.

As the humans in Thaisia and Cel-Romano celebrated their victory over the smaller forms of *terra indigene*, the Elementals and Namid's teeth and claws answered the call to war. They destroyed the invaders, then began the work of isolating and thinning the human herds in those two pieces of the world.

But now they faced a problem.

<Some of us will have to watch the humans,> said the

oldest male who had made the journey to this place. <Some of us will be poisoned by even that much contact.> A beat of silence as they considered taking over the task the smaller shifters had performed for many years. Then the question: <How much human will we keep?>

<Kill them all!> snarled another male. <That is what humans would do.>

<You would kill the sweet blood not-Wolf?> a female asked, shocked.

A heavy silence as they considered *that* question.

The sweet blood, the howling not-Wolf, had changed things in the Lakeside Courtyard—had even changed some of the *terra indigene* living in that Courtyard. She was not like the human enemies. She was not prey. She and her kind were Namid's creation, wondrous and terrible.

No, they could not kill the sweet blood not-Wolf, the one called Broomstick Girl in the stories that winged their way into the wild country and amused even the most dangerous forms of Elders.

Having agreed that killing all the humans in Thaisia wasn't the answer, they considered the problem as the sun set and the moon rose.

<If we allow some humans to remain, then what *kind* of human should we keep?> the eldest male finally asked.

A different question. A caught-in-thorny-vines, stuck-in-the-mud kind of question. Many of the smaller shifters who had survived the human attacks had withdrawn from human-occupied places, leaving the humans who lived there to the Elders' sharp mercy. Some returned to the wild country, retreating from any trace of humans, while others chose to resettle in towns that had been reclaimed—places that had buildings and human things but no longer had people.

But the Elders who guarded the wild country usually kept their distance from human places unless they came to those places as Namid's teeth and claws. They didn't study humans the way the smaller shifters did. The teaching stories told them there were different kinds of humans, but what made one human respectful of the land and the boundaries that had been set while another killed and left the meat, or tried to take away the homes of the feathered and furred? The HFL humans had made war on the *terra indigene*. Were there other kinds of humans who were enemies—kinds the Elders did not yet recognize?

If humans migrated to the reclaimed towns, would they fight with the shifters who were turning those places into homes for *terra indigene* who didn't want to completely abandon the human form? But earth natives didn't absorb just the form of another predator; they also absorbed aspects of that predator, traits that became woven into the shape. Were there human traits the *terra indigene* should not absorb? Where could they go to study humans closely enough to learn what could not be allowed to take root in the reclaimed towns?

As one, the Elders turned north and east, looking in the direction of Lakeside.

<That Courtyard was not abandoned, and it has a human pack,> the eldest male said.

It also had the Wolf and howling not-Wolf who intrigued so many of the Elders. Witnessing the stories that would flow into the wild country was worth the risk of human contamination.

All of them were curious, but only two Elders—a male and a female—were chosen to spend time on a small piece of land surrounded by humans. They had been in Lakeside before, when, as Namid's teeth and claws, they had roamed the fog-filled streets, hunting human prey.

Satisfied with their decision, most of the Elders returned to their pieces of the wild country, while the two selected for the task of studying the human pack began the journey to Lakeside.

CHAPTER 1

Windsday, Messis 1

Eager to join his friends for an early-morning run, Simon Wolfgard, leader of the Lakeside Courtyard, hurried toward the *terra indigene* Wolves who were using trees and shrubs for camouflage as they watched the paved road that looped the Courtyard. Actually, they were watching the man who was riding on the road at an easy pace.

<It's Kowalski,> Blair growled. It was a soft growl, but the human suddenly scanned the area as if his little ears had caught the sound.

<On a bicycle,> Nathan added.

<We gave him permission to ride on the paved roads,> Simon said, a little concerned about their focused attention on a human they knew fairly well.

Karl Kowalski was one of the human police officers who worked directly with the *terra indigene* to minimize conflicts between humans and Others. Because of that, he had been labeled a Wolf lover and had had his share of conflicts with other humans. The latest incident had happened the prior week when a car "accidentally" swerved and almost hit Kowalski while he was taking a bicycle ride before work. Because the *terra indigene* viewed that as a threat to a member of their human pack, Simon, Vladimir Sanguinati, and Henry Beargard—members of the Courtyard's Business Association—decided to allow the human pack to ride on the Courtyard's paved roads.

Simon had thought all the Wolves had been told about the Business Association's decision—especially Nathan, who was the watch Wolf at the Liaison's Office, and Blair, who was the Courtyard's dominant enforcer—but this was the first time any of the humans had ventured to ride on a road that still had Trespassers Will Be Eaten signs posted as a warning.

<*Bicycle*, Simon.> Blair's growl wasn't as soft this time.

Must have been loud enough for human ears, because Kowalski started to pedal a little faster.

Oh. Bicycle. Now Simon understood the real focus of the Wolves' attention, the reason for their excitement. Humans had ridden bicycles up to the Green Complex as well as a few other places in the Courtyard, and the Wolves had been intrigued by the two-wheeled vehicles. But those instances had been about transportation to or from a task. This could be something else.

<A game of chase?> Jane, the Wolfgard bodywalker, asked hopefully.

<Kowalski could be play-prey,> Nathan said.

<Does he know how to play chase?> Blair asked.

<He's a police officer,> Nathan replied. <He chases other humans all the time.>

<Doesn't mean he understands *our* game.> Simon thought Nathan's opinion of police work was skewed more toward hopeful than accurate. Still, they could offer to play. If Kowalski didn't accept, they would just enjoy a run. But . . . bicycle. Simon really wanted to chase one. <Let's find out.>

The Wolves charged up the road, Simon and Blair in the lead as they swiftly closed the distance between the pack and their play-prey. But would they have a game?

Kowalski looked back. His eyes widened—and he pedaled faster.

Yes!

<We don't catch, only chase,> Simon said.

<He's fast!> Jane surged ahead of the males, pulling up alongside the bicycle's back wheel in seconds.

<Don't grab the wheels,> Nathan said. <If you catch a tooth in the spokes you could break your jaw or worse.>

<I was listening when Officer Karl told the puppies about the dangers of biting wheels,> Jane snapped, clearly offended by Nathan's unwanted warning. She moved up a little more, now in position to play-bite Kowalski's calf.

Kowalski glanced at Jane and pedaled faster. Instead of going over the bridge that would take them into the Hawkgard section—and commit the human to the big loop within the Courtyard's three hundred acres—Kowalski turned onto the road that ran alongside the Elementals' lake, heading back toward the Green Complex.

The Wolves ran, maintaining their distance even when Kowalski slowed down while going up a rise. They took turns pacing the bicycle and pushing their prey to run and run. Or pedal and pedal. As they reached the intersection with the Courtyard's main road, Kowalski swung left toward the Green Complex instead of turning right toward the Market Square.

Most of the pack, having slowed to a trot as their prey tired, circled back toward the Wolfgard Complex. Nathan headed for the Market Square and the Liaison's Office, where he would keep track of the deliverymen and guard Meg Corbyn, the Courtyard's Human Liaison. Simon and Blair followed Kowalski until they reached the Green Complex. Then Blair continued on to the Utilities Complex while Simon dashed for the water trough in the common area that formed the open center of the Courtyard's only multispecies complex. He lapped water, then shifted to his human form and dunked his head, flinging water as he stood up and tossed his dark hair away from his face. He splashed his arms and chest, then grinned when Kowalski parked the bicycle and approached the trough warily.

"That was a great game of chase!" Simon said happily. "You understand how to be play-prey."

"I do?"

"Yes." Simon cocked his head, puzzled by the human's wariness. Hadn't they just played, had fun? "Want some water?"

"Thanks." Kowalski splashed water on his face and neck, then on his arms. But he didn't drink.

Simon pondered the not drinking for a moment. Humans were clever, invasive predators who had recently shown the *terra indigene* once again why they could never be fully trusted—not even by one another. But physically they were so much weaker than other kinds of predators. This not drinking, for example. Nothing wrong with the water in the trough. Someone had already drained yesterday's water, using it on the potted tree and other plants in the open area, and refilled the trough with fresh water for drinking and splashing. Humans would drink water pumped from the well if it was in a glass or a bucket or some other small container but couldn't drink the same water from a shared outdoor container?

It made him wonder how they had survived as a species long enough to become such a problem.

"So, who doesn't understand about play-prey?" Kowalski asked, rubbing a hand over his face.

"The female pack. Every time we invited them to play, they stopped riding their bicycles and asked if they could help." Simon spread his arms in a "what's that all about?" gesture. Then he pointed at Kowalski. "But you invited us to play, and we all had a good run."

Kowalski snorted a soft laugh. "Well, I sure had a good run."

"Since the females can't pedal as far or as fast as you, maybe they could play chase with the puppies." The pups would learn how to run as a pack without the risk of being kicked by real prey.

Simon studied Kowalski, who studied him in turn.

"I'll talk to Ruthie," Kowalski finally said.

They both heard the clink of glassware and looked toward the screened summer room below Meg Corbyn's apartment.

"Must be later than I realized," Kowalski said. "I'd better go home and get cleaned up for work."

Simon watched the man walk toward the bicycle—and the summer room. For a moment, it looked like Kowalski was going to go in and talk to Meg, and Simon felt his teeth lengthen to Wolf size as his lips pulled back in a silent snarl. But Kowalski just raised a hand in greeting, said, "Morning, Meg," and rode away.

Simon walked around the trough, then stopped suddenly when he realized he was naked in his human form. It had never mattered until Meg came to live in the Courtyard. But humans reacted in various ways to seeing one another without clothing, even when clothing wasn't needed for protection or warmth. Meg had adjusted pretty well to friends shifting to human form to give her a message or answer a question before shifting back to their preferred furred or feathered form, but it was different with him—maybe because their friendship was different from any other she had with humans or *terra indigene*.

Most nights, he slept with her in his Wolf form. They had their own apartments, but those places were connected by the summer room and a back upstairs hallway, and more and more it was becoming one den instead of two. But they weren't mates in the same way Kowalski and Ruthie were mates. Then again, *terra indigene* Wolves mated only once a year, when females came into season. Meg did the bleeding typical of human females, but she hadn't shown any physical interest in having a mate. Except . . .

She'd asked him to go skinny-dipping with her a couple of weeks ago. Both of them naked, in human form. She'd been nervous about being in the water with him, and she seemed scared after he'd kissed the scar along the right side of her jaw—a scar made by the cut that had saved the Wolfgard in Lakeside as well as many other Wolves throughout the Northeast Region and even beyond.

He'd kissed her before—on the forehead once or twice. But when he'd kissed that scar, he'd felt a flutter of change inside him, and in the days that followed he began to understand on some instinctive level that he wasn't quite the same as the rest of the Lakeside Wolfgard. Not anymore.

Maybe it wasn't just for Meg's sake that, after the kiss, he'd invited her to play a Wolf game despite their both looking human. Then she wasn't afraid anymore. And since then . . . Well, it wasn't lost on him that, in summer weather like this, human males wore next to nothing in and around their own dens and no one thought anything of it.

"It's hot upstairs," Meg said, not raising her voice because she didn't need to. His ears might look human, but he was still a Wolf and could hear her just fine. "I brought some food down here for breakfast."

"I'll take a quick shower and join you."

He hurried inside and up the stairs to the bathroom in his apartment. Washing his hair and body didn't take long, but he stood under the shower, enjoying the cool water falling over him as he thought about the complication that was Meg Corbyn.

He had brought her into the Courtyard, offering her the job of Human Liaison before discovering that she was a blood prophet, a *cassandra sangue*—a breed of human females who saw visions of the future when their skin was cut. She had escaped from the man who had owned her and used her, and Simon and the rest of the *terra indigene* in Lakeside had taken her in.

That sounded simple but it wasn't. Nothing about Meg was simple. She was the pebble dropped in a pond that was the Lakeside Courtyard, and the ripples of her presence had changed so many things, including the *terra indigene* who had befriended her. Because of Meg, the Courtyard's residents interacted with humans in ways that were unprecedented—or, at least, hadn't been considered in centuries. Because of Meg, the *terra indigene* throughout Thaisia had tried to save the rest of the blood prophets who had been tossed out like unwanted puppies by the humans who had owned them. Because of Meg, the Lakeside Courtyard had a human pack who provided an additional learning experience for *terra indigene* who had a human-centric education and needed to practice their skills with humans who wouldn't take advantage of mistakes.

Because of Meg, he had the uncomfortable feeling that a little bit of being human had become attached to and inseparable from his Wolf form.

Plenty of human females over the years had wanted to take a lusty walk on the wild side and have sex with one of the *terra indigene*. And plenty of *terra indigene* had been equally curious about having sex in their human form. But that was about pleasing the body for a night and walking away. Or, for the Sanguinati, it was about using lust as a lure in order to feed off the blood of their preferred prey.

Having sex was different from becoming someone's mate. Mating was serious business. It was about pack and family. Some forms of *terra indigene* mated for life; some did not. Even among the forms that usually mated for life, the bonds didn't always hold. Simon's sire, Elliot, never talked about why his mate had left him. And

Daphne, Simon's sister, had told them nothing about her mate or why she had shown up in Lakeside alone just days before her pup was born.

No, the mating bond didn't always last, and most of the time, the repercussions were small. A pack might break apart if the dominant pair split. Some might leave for other packs, even other parts of the continent. But ordinarily, a species wouldn't become extinct if a mating bond broke—and that could happen if his bond of friendship with Meg became something more but couldn't survive being something more, couldn't survive a physical mating. He knew it. Tess and Vlad and Henry knew it. Maybe some of the humans knew it. But he didn't think Meg knew it, wasn't sure she would be strong enough to carry that weight on top of what she had been asked to do already.

She had been hurt by the humans who had caged her and used her. Hurt in ways that made her fearful of the human male form. While he occasionally wondered if having sex with a human would feel different if the human was Meg, he wasn't willing to risk their friendship, wasn't willing to break the bond they already had. So he needed to be extra careful now for her sake, for his sake, for everyone's sake. How much human would the *terra indigene* keep? The Elders had asked that question without specifying if they meant human population, human inventions, or the intangible aspects of a form that were absorbed along with the physical shape if you lived too long in a particular skin.

Simon shut off the water and dried himself before pulling on a pair of denim cutoffs.

When the Elders had first asked that question, he thought they expected an answer in words. But after the recent war that had broken the Cel-Romano Alliance of Nations on the other side of the Atlantik, and the Elders' decision to thin, and isolate, the human herds in Thaisia, Simon understood that the answer would be shaped by what the Elders learned from the things that happened in and around the Lakeside Courtyard.

Meg fussed with the dishes on the small table in the summer room, but her mind was still replaying the image of Simon and Karl Kowalski standing by the water trough, talking. Simon had looked happy. Karl had had his back to the summer room, so she hadn't seen his face, but he'd seemed tense. She wondered why Karl would feel tense about something that pleased Simon so much. Then again, a Wolf and a human didn't often see things the same way.

But looking at them, their bodies communicating opposing emotions, she noticed the similarities. Unlike Henry Beargard, who was big and muscled even in human form, Simon and Karl had the strength and lean muscles of hunters who chased their prey—although she didn't think Karl usually had to run after the people he arrested. They both had dark hair, but Karl's was cut shorter than Simon's. The real difference, at first glance anyway, was the eyes. Karl's were brown, while Simon's were amber whether he was in human or Wolf form.

And when Karl left, she noticed the parts of Simon that weren't usually seen. She noticed—but she wasn't sure how she felt. Scared, yes, but also a little curious. She and Simon were friends, and she adored his nephew Sam. But more than that, they'd become partners who were committed to keeping the Courtyard—and the city of Lakeside—intact. And they were partners who were committed to helping the *cassandra sangue* survive in a world that was too full of sensation.

In the stories she'd read, people who were drawn to each other seemed to fight a lot or have misunderstandings or had sex and then broke up before eventually getting together. But those were humans, not a blood prophet and a Wolf. There were things that had been done to her in the compound that her body remembered but were veiled from her mind—things that made it much easier for her to be around Simon when he was in Wolf form. She knew in her heart that Simon would never do bad things to her like the men in the compound had done, but the furry Wolf still felt like a safer companion, despite the teeth and claws.

And yet, this time, seeing Simon without clothes . . . Scary, yes, but thinking about it made something flutter inside her, something that made her wonder what it would be like if they . . .

"You're upset."

Startled, Meg almost knocked over a glass of water. She hadn't heard Simon enter the summer room.

"No, I'm not." But looking at him, she was distracted by the male body that displayed everything but the scary bits, which were hidden by denim cutoffs. Then she remembered that she wasn't wearing anything except a thin cotton shift and panties. That hadn't seemed important when she'd put them on after her shower.

She was asking for it. Meg couldn't remember if she had read that phrase in a story or if it was part of a rememory—an image from an old prophecy. But she knew it was the excuse a man used in order to blame a girl when he forced her to have sex with him.

She hadn't given a thought to how little she was wearing, but if she was noticing Simon's body, was he also noticing hers? And if he was . . .

She was asking for it.

No! A human male might think that way, but Simon wouldn't, not even when he was in human form. Her brain knew that; it would make things easier for everyone if she could convince her body.

"Yes, you are." Simon stepped closer, and his amber eyes narrowed—but not before Meg saw the flickers of red that indicated anger. "You smell upset—and a little lusty. But mostly you smell upset." He snarled, showing fangs that definitely weren't human. "Did Kowalski upset you?"

"No." Her insides were feeling shaky, but her reply

was firm and definite. The last thing she wanted was for Simon to be angry with any of her human friends. "I was thinking of something that made me unhappy."

He stopped snarling and cocked his head, looking more baffled than angry. "Why would you do that?"

She stared at him. She didn't want to tell him what she'd been thinking about, which would be his next question, so she shrugged and changed the subject to one she knew would interest him: food. "I couldn't decide what to eat, so I brought a lot of stuff, including this." She picked up a container and a spoon, then hesitated.

"What is it?"

"Yogurt." She swallowed a spoonful and wondered why Merri Lee and Ruth said it was yummy. Was this an acquired taste? "Try some." She filled the spoon and held it out to Simon, wondering what he would do.

He leaned toward the spoon and sniffed. Then he ate the offering.

Meg held her breath, not sure if he would spit out the yogurt or swallow it.

He swallowed. Then he looked at the other food she'd brought down. "Why would you eat that when you could eat slices of bison?"

Since she couldn't honestly say she liked the taste of bison, she didn't see much difference. "Merri Lee and Ruth said yogurt is good for a person's innards, especially a girl's innards."

"Glad I'm not a girl," he muttered as he put a couple of bison slices on a plate before considering the rest of the available food.

Meg took another spoonful of yogurt before closing the container. There. She'd taken care of her innards for the day. She ate half the berries, then pushed the bowl toward Simon. She half hoped he'd refuse the offer, saying he had plenty of bison to eat, but he happily accepted his share of the berries without a word, leaving her to nibble on a slice of sharp cheese.

"You're not eating," Simon said a few minutes later.

"I've had enough for now." Which was true since she intended to dash over to A Little Bite before work and see what Nadine Fallacaro and Tess had available at the Courtyard's coffee shop.

They took the remaining food up to her apartment and washed the dishes before Simon went to his apartment to get dressed for work.

Meg stared at the clothes in her closet and considered what might be appropriate office wear for the person who was the Human Liaison and what was a practical way to dress on a hot, muggy day. She chose a pair of dark green shorts, a short-sleeve, rosy peach blouse, and a pair of sandals that looked nice and felt great.

After checking that the book she was currently reading was in her carry sack, Meg locked the front door of her apartment and went down the outside stairs to wait for Simon.

Lieutenant Crispin James Montgomery turned his head to look at Investigative Task Force Agent Greg O'Sullivan, who was sitting in the backseat of the patrol car. When O'Sullivan looked pointedly at the third man in the car, Monty turned his attention to his partner, Officer Karl Kowalski, who was driving them to a meeting with the new acting mayor and commissioner of police.

Kowalski was a vigorous man in his late twenties. A dedicated police officer, he believed that the best way to help the humans in Lakeside was to have a good working relationship with the *terra indigene*—a belief that had caused some personal problems with a landlord and created a rift between Karl and his parents and brother.

But after the slaughter of humans in some Midwest and Northwest towns in retaliation for the slaughter of the Wolfgard in those same areas; after the storms that raged across the continent of Thaisia and slammed into Lakeside; after the humans saw the briefest terrifying glimpse of the *terra indigene* who lived in, and guarded, the wild country, Monty wondered if Kowalski still believed there was any hope of humans surviving the force and fury of the Elementals and the *terra indigene* who were known as Namid's teeth and claws.

And he wondered what he would do if Kowalski and Michael Debany, the other officer on his team, wanted to work on another team or even transfer to another police station in Lakeside.

"Are you all right?" Monty asked. Was it pointless to ask with O'Sullivan in the car? The agent was doing his best to create a dialogue with Simon Wolfgard and the other members of the Courtyard's Business Association, but no one knew him well enough yet to consider him a personal friend.

Kowalski stopped behind a bus that was taking on passengers instead of changing lanes to go around. If they stayed behind the bus and waited at every stop, they would be late for the meeting.

Out of the corner of his eye, Monty saw O'Sullivan cover the watch on his left wrist, a silent message: *we can be late for the meeting.*

In looks, Monty and O'Sullivan were opposites. Greg O'Sullivan was in his early thirties. He had green eyes that were always filled with sharp intelligence, and his short dark hair was starting to thin at the top. On the job, he had a burning intensity and a face that made Monty think of a warrior who had chosen an austere life.

Monty, on the other hand, was the oldest of the three men, even though he wasn't forty yet. He had dark skin, brown eyes, and short curly black hair already showing some gray—and not all the lines on his face came from laughter. Not anymore.

"I took a bike ride in the Courtyard this morning and ended up playing a game of chase with some of the Wolves," Kowalski said. "I was the designated prey."

O'Sullivan leaned forward. "Are you all right?"

Kowalski glanced in the rearview mirror, then swung

around the bus when it signaled at the next stop. "More of a workout than I'd intended to take with it being so muggy. The Wolves didn't hurt me, if that's what you're asking. Didn't even try."

Monty and O'Sullivan waited.

"It was a game to them, and somehow I had signaled willingness to play. But, gods, seeing them around the Market Square . . . It's not that you forget how big they are, but I didn't really translate what their size means when they're hunting. When I saw them racing toward me, my instincts kicked in and I tried to outrun them. Couldn't, of course."

"Do you know what you did to join the game?" Monty asked quietly.

Kowalski focused on the traffic for a minute. "Simon said the girls stop and ask if they can help instead of accepting the invitation to play, so it could be as simple as me speeding up instead of stopping."

"Predator's instinct," O'Sullivan said. "If something runs, a predator will chase it."

"But they've never chased any of us before, and we ride bicycles up to the kitchen garden at the Green Complex all the time." The traffic light turned yellow. Kowalski braked instead of speeding up to slip through the intersection before the light turned red. "At first I thought the Wolves chasing me hadn't heard that we're allowed to ride on the paved roads. But I recognized Nathan and thought I recognized Simon. The roads are posted with Trespassers Will Be Eaten signs, and when I first saw them coming at me . . ." He blew out a breath and pressed the accelerator when the light turned green. "Just a game. Simon thought we'd had great fun. Bet the other Wolves did too."

"And you?" Monty asked.

"We look at the same things, but we don't see the same things. It made me realize how easy it can be to screw this up and send the wrong signal."

Monty looked out the window and wondered what

sort of signal the new mayor and police commissioner were going to send.

Meg opened the Liaison's Office, then glanced at the clock. Nathan was late, but Jake Crowgard was at his spot on the shoulder-high brick wall that separated the delivery area from the yard behind Henry's studio.

Just as well she had the office to herself for another minute or so.

Her arms tingled. It wasn't the pins-and-needles feeling that warned of the need to cut and speak prophecy. This was milder, more like a memo than a screeching alarm.

Opening a drawer, she lifted the lid of the wooden box Henry had made for her and looked at the backs of several decks of fortune-telling cards that she was learning to use to reveal prophecy instead of cutting her skin with the silver razor. Maybe today she would finally take all the cards out of the box and start discarding what wouldn't be needed to create the Trailblazer deck of prophecy cards.

She stirred the cards in a vague effort to shuffle them. Not that it mattered. When a question was asked, her hands would prickle, and the cards were chosen based on the severity of that feeling.

Meg closed her eyes so that she wouldn't influence her choice by recognizing the back of a particular deck. Placing her fingertips on the cards, she whispered, "What will the appointment of the new mayor mean to Lakeside?"

Nothing. Nothing. Her fingers brushed the cards while even the tingling faded away to nothing. Then a buzzing in the fingertips of her right hand. She brushed away the top cards until she reached the one that created the buzz. She picked up the card and opened her eyes—and knew the answer before she turned the card to see the image. The card had come from a children's game and had been mixed in with her prophecy cards.

But the images from the game had proved useful, even if the answers they provided were usually unwelcome.

What will the new mayor mean to Lakeside? A big question mark. Future undecided. Lakeside's future had been undecided ever since the *terra indigene* here realized the Elders' response to the Humans First and Last movement's actions was going to be very, very bad.

But she'd hoped for a different answer today.

She'd put the card back and started to close the box when she thought of another question. Lakeside was a human-controlled city, but the Courtyard belonged to the *terra indigene*. Any outbreak of hostility between humans and the Others could have terrible consequences in the wake of the recent conflicts.

Meg closed her eyes and placed her fingers on the cards again. When she'd first begun working with the decks, she had decided that a three-card draw would represent subject, action, and result. She didn't know whether that was the way other people used fortune-telling cards, but it seemed to be working for her.

"What is going to happen to my friends in the Courtyard?" She repeated the question over and over while she searched for the images that would provide the answer. When she'd selected the three that had produced the severest prickling, she took them to the big wooden sorting table and turned them over in the order she'd chosen them.

The first card had three images: train, bus, car. The second card had an explosion. The third card . . . the question mark. Future undecided.

That was not good.

She took a notebook out of a drawer, turned to a fresh page, then wrote down her questions and the cards she'd drawn as the answers.

She felt reluctant to put the cards away before she called someone to look at them and felt equally reluctant to tell anyone from the Business Association about this particular answer. Maybe one of her human friends?

Ruth Stuart lived across the street in the two-family house on Crowfield Avenue, and Merri Lee was moving into an apartment in one of the adjacent stone buildings the Courtyard had recently purchased to provide a place for their employees to live if they were turned away from human-owned rentals.

A knock on the doorway between the sorting room and the back room made her gasp. Then she relaxed when she saw Twyla Montgomery waiting to be acknowledged. The sorting room was usually out-of-bounds to humans except for a special few, and with so many new people visiting the Market Square, the boundary was being reinforced with snarls and sharp teeth.

"Good morning, Miss Twyla," Meg said.

She heard a scrambling in the front room and realized Nathan must have come in while she was using the cards.

"Good morning, Miss Meg." Twyla crossed the room and set a travel mug and container on the sorting table. "And good morning to you, Mr. Nathan. It's going to be a sticky day, and I don't envy you having to wear a fur coat, no matter how fine it looks."

Silence. Then Nathan acknowledged the words with a soft *arroo* and went back to the Wolf bed under one of the big windows in the front room.

Meg smiled. Twyla Montgomery was Lieutenant Montgomery's mother. A thin woman with dark skin that was beginning to sag with age, brown eyes that usually looked kind, and short, curly hair that was more tarnished silver than black. But Twyla also had a no-nonsense attitude and didn't take sass from anyone—a trait that made the Wolves keenly interested in observing her from a safe distance.

"Mr. Simon came into A Little Bite grumbling about yogurt and girl innards and how you don't like bison," Twyla said. "I thought he might have some kind of brain fever and was talking nonsense, but Miss Tess said you must not have eaten enough for breakfast, so she made an egg salad sandwich and a bit more for you." A pause. "You skimping on food, girl?"

"No, ma'am. I didn't eat much at home because I planned to pick up something when I got to work." When Twyla stared at her, Meg added, "I really don't like the taste of bison."

"I tried a slice the other day and can't say it appealed to me either. But I suspect if it was a choice between eating bison and going hungry, I'd like it just fine—and so would you."

Meg nodded. "If that was the choice, Simon might learn to like yogurt."

Twyla laughed. "You think so?"

Meg imagined being given a plate of rolled bison slices dipped in yogurt. Shuddering, she wondered if you could make a salad out of grass.

Twyla tapped a finger just above the three cards on the table. "What's this about? Or can't you say?"

"These are fortune-telling cards, but I call them prophecy cards. I'm trying to see if some of the *cassandra sangue* can use them to reveal prophecy instead of making a cut." A thousand cuts. It was said that was all a blood prophet had before the cut that killed her or drove her insane. Since most prophets didn't survive past their thirty-fifth birthday, Meg, at twenty-four, felt highly motivated to find an alternative to the razor.

"What do these tell you?" Twyla asked.

"I'm not sure. I asked what was going to happen to my friends in the Courtyard. These cards were the answer." Meg waited until the older woman came around to her side of the table. She pointed to each card. "Subject, action, result."

Twyla frowned at the train/bus/car card. "Does that mean travel or the transportation itself?"

"Could mean either. It was drawn as the subject, so that should mean the thing itself, but it could mean that one of these forms of transportation is bringing someone or something to Lakeside. The explosion, being the action card, could mean a 'call the bomb squad' kind of explosion or an emotionally explosive conflict between groups of people. So maybe a group of people traveling to Lakeside are going to cause some kind of trouble for the Courtyard. I'm getting pretty good at finding the cards that answer the question, but Merri Lee and I are still working on correctly interpreting them."

As she watched Twyla study the cards, the skin between her shoulder blades began to prickle.

"What does the question mark mean?" Twyla asked, sounding troubled.

"Future undecided. That was the same answer I drew when I asked about the city of Lakeside this morning." Meg studied the older woman. "You know what the cards mean, don't you?"

"I have a thought, but nothing I'd want to share. Not just yet." Twyla walked toward the back room.

"Thanks for bringing the food," Meg said.

Twyla turned to look at her. "You're welcome. Don't you be skimping on food. There's no need for that."

Meg heard the back door of the office close. Then she reached over her shoulder and scratched at her back. She liked Twyla Montgomery, and even the Others offered the older woman a trust they rarely gave someone they'd known for such a short time. That was the reason Meg felt uneasy now.

She just hoped Miss Twyla decided to share her thoughts about the cards before something bad happened.

Twyla polished the desks at the consulate—the building in the Courtyard that was the domain of Elliot Wolfgard. He was the Courtyard's public face, the *terra indigene* who talked to the mayor and the city council members, who attended political events, and who talked to the press. It hadn't taken her long to realize that

Elliot might be the urbane spokesWolf for the Courtyard, but Simon was the real leader.

"It never took the other humans this long to clean the desks," Elliot said.

Twyla jerked upright in surprise and turned to face him. She hadn't heard him come down from his office on the second floor.

At first glance, he could pass for the CEO of a successful company: expensive suits, thinning hair that was cut by someone who probably charged more than she usually made in a week, lean body that spoke of hours in a fitness place. Yes, he could pass for one, and she would bet plenty of CEOs and politicians had made the mistake of thinking that looking like them meant he thought like them. But the amber eyes belonged to a Wolf, and even if humans sometimes overlooked what he was, she was certain Elliot never did.

"I can see they didn't take that long to clean in here, which is why it's taking me longer than usual to give it a proper cleaning now," she replied.

Elliot studied her. She was getting used to that. The Crows who worked in the Market Square had more questions than a houseful of small children, and at least one of them joined her whenever she went into a store to buy anything, wanting to know why she chose one thing over another. The Wolves studied her, studied all the humans who were allowed some access to the stores in the Courtyard, but she noticed they watched her and Nadine Fallacaro and Katherine Debany, Officer Debany's mother, more than the younger women who were Meg Corbyn's female pack.

Who taught the young in a Wolf pack?

"Come over here," Elliot said. When she didn't move, he added, "Please."

He led her to the filing cabinets along one wall, then pointed to a stack of folders teetering on a small table tucked against the last cabinet. "Do you know how to file these the human way?"

She picked up a folder, looked at the designation on the tab, and chose the appropriate file drawer. Then she chose another drawer. And another.

She closed the drawers and turned to face him. "What sort of nonsense is this?"

"That's the human way to file papers."

"So you say."

A flicker of red, like a flash of lightning, filled Elliot's eyes. "What does that mean?"

"It means that whoever did this had his own system to find things but made it near impossible for anyone else to put his hand on the proper file, or the fool just shoved things into drawers and hoped he'd never be asked to find anything." She stepped forward to drop the folder on the teetering stack, and Elliot took a step back, watching her in a way that made her think he wanted to tear into someone's flesh and hers would do.

"Can you fix it?" he asked.

He seemed to be having some trouble pronouncing the words, and she wondered what was wrong with his mouth now when it had been fine a minute ago.

"Do you know how to work in a place like this?"

Everyone in the Courtyard had a job. Everyone in a Wolf pack had a position. And while not all the humans who were being allowed to share in the Courtyard's bounty had been assigned tasks, it had been clear that the Others expected all the newcomers to figure out what skills they could offer that would justify their being accepted.

Twyla considered what Elliot was saying. It would be a change from mopping floors and scrubbing toilets—although they needed someone to do that too. She didn't think many people bothered Elliot, so it would be calmer than working at one of the Market Square stores, and she could use a little calm in her day if she was going to help look after the children in the afternoons.

"I never learned about typing and computers and such," she finally said. "Answering the phone and filing—

that I can do for you. But only in the mornings when the children are having their lessons. I came to Lakeside to help Crispin take care of Lizzy, and that has to come first."

"Of course," Elliot said calmly, his pronunciation once more crisp. "We take care of our young." He paused before offering, "Sam is my grandson."

Twyla smiled. "He's a fine boy." She'd seen Sam around the Market Square, sometimes spending time with the other children but more often in the company of Meg Corbyn and a young Wolf named Skippy. The first time she'd seen him and noticed the gray eyes, she'd thought he was a human child with hair that was an odd mix of gold and gray. And she'd thought he was Meg's younger brother or a cousin. Then she'd seen Meg with a Wolf pup who had that same coloring.

"The Sierra listed computers and typing as some of her skills," Elliot said. "Maybe she could—"

"No."

The sharpness in her voice surprised her more than it surprised Elliot. But she'd had time to think about the prophecy cards Meg had drawn that morning. She didn't know how someone else would interpret those cards, but she knew what she had deduced from them about her family. It made her angry, and it made her heart ache, to realize Sierra had lied to Crispin when the girl insisted that she had no way of contacting their brother, Cyrus. If she had been honest, Crispin still wouldn't have paid for Cyrus's train fare to Lakeside the way he had for his mother, sister, and two nieces, but he would have called his brother and warned him to leave Toland before the storm hit.

Twyla looked at Elliot. Not the actual leader, but he had a significant position in the Courtyard and among the Wolves. She couldn't ask Crispin for help in confirming what she suspected. As a police officer, he had the means to find out, but it would create trouble between him and his little sister once he realized Sierra was in contact with Cyrus. "My Sierra is a good girl. She's smart, she's kind, she's a hard worker, and she loves her children. And most days and about most things, she can be trusted. But we all have our weaknesses, Mr. Elliot, and Sierra's weakness is her brother Cyrus. He twists her up and convinces her to do things she shouldn't do—things she knows are wrong." Twyla looked around the first floor of the consulate. "This is like a government office. Some things are everyday and don't matter, and some things are no one's business but yours. If Sierra worked here for you and Cyrus came by to pressure her into giving him information that would be worth selling, she might resist for a little while, but eventually she would give it to him and then try to justify why he should have it. That would cause trouble for her and for the rest of us."

"But the Cyrus isn't here," Elliot said.

"I think he might be on his way here." She went to one of the desks and wrote down the phone number for Howling Good Reads. She tore off the sheet and handed it to Elliot. "Sierra told me and Crispin that Cyrus hadn't left a number where we could contact him. I think she lied. I think she's called him a couple of times since we got here. Can't say if she made calls on other phones without permission, but when I saw her using the phone near the cash register on a day when Mr. Simon and Mr. Vlad weren't in the front of the store, she got flustered and claimed she was ordering pizza. I can tell you the children didn't have pizza for lunch that day." She hesitated. "The police have ways of checking calls made from a particular phone, but I can't ask Crispin to check this. Even if I'm wrong about her calling Cyrus since we arrived in Lakeside, the lie she told before we left Toland will create tension between her and Crispin."

Cyrus had always managed to create tension between his siblings, even when Crispin was standing up for Sierra.

"A lot of calls are made from the bookstore's phone," Elliot said.

"Most likely it would be a Toland phone number. One Mr. Simon and Mr. Vlad wouldn't recognize."

"All right." Elliot folded the paper and put it in his pocket. "If your pup isn't suitable, can you think of someone else who is?"

"Katherine Debany," Twyla replied. "She worked as a personal assistant. Probably knows how to run an office like this better than the rest of us combined. I know Pete Denby was asking her about working for him a couple of afternoons a week."

Elliot didn't ask why a skilled worker would be available, and Twyla didn't offer an explanation. Like her, Katherine had been dismissed because she wouldn't join the Humans First and Last movement in order to keep her job.

"Tell the Katherine to see me." Elliot headed for the stairs. His foot was on the first step when the phone rang. He looked back at her.

"You want me to answer that?" Twyla asked.

"Yes." Elliot headed upstairs. "Thank you."

Smiling, she picked up the phone. "Courtyard Consulate. Twyla speaking."

CHAPTER 2

Windsday, Messis 1

Monty took a seat at the conference table and wondered if anyone else was baffled about his presence at a meeting that included Lakeside's mayor and police commissioner, an ITF agent, and Captain Douglas Burke. He was just a lieutenant in charge of a two-man team.

He tried, unsuccessfully, to convince himself that the duties of that team had no relevance to his being there.

"Thank you for putting aside your important duties to speak with me."

Walter Chen, the new acting mayor, smiled at each man in turn. It was a gentle smile in keeping with the man's small stature and quiet voice. Deep lines spread from the corners of his brown eyes, and his black hair was carefully combed back from his face.

"We appreciate the opportunity to meet with you," Greg O'Sullivan replied. Then he nodded at the other man Monty didn't know.

"You know Police Commissioner Alvarez?" Chen asked, sounding a little surprised.

"We didn't work in the same precinct in Hubb NE,

but Agent O'Sullivan is related to Governor Hannigan, and I have the pleasure of being among the governor's friends," Alvarez replied. A handsome, robust man in his early fifties, he had flashing dark eyes and a headful of dark, wavy hair.

Monty glanced at Burke and wondered what his captain knew about the man.

"Please sit," Chen said. "Would you like coffee? Tea? We have black and green tea available. The green tea has come all the way from Tokhar-Chin and is sold at a small market in my neighborhood."

They all declined the offer of refreshments, took their seats, and waited for the mayor to begin.

But Chen seemed reluctant to begin. He gave them all another gentle smile.

Greg O'Sullivan leaned forward. "May I ask a question?"

"Please." Chen sounded relieved.

"Why were you and Commissioner Alvarez appointed to these positions?"

Alvarez looked at Chen, then addressed the other men around the table. "I support the governor, and I'm fresh blood. That's going to make every station chief in Lakeside unhappy since, under usual circumstances, one of them would have been selected to fill the position after Kurt Wallace's involuntary resignation. But circumstances aren't usual. This city is vital to the health of the entire Northeast Region, and the human government here can't afford to make any more mistakes. I didn't support the Humans First and Last movement. That's on record. I'm hoping that will weigh in our favor in the weeks ahead."

"Weigh in with whom?" Burke asked.

Alvarez smiled. "With the *terra indigene* in the Lakeside Courtyard—and beyond."

"I, too, did not support the Humans First and Last movement," Chen said. "Some businesses in my council district were damaged by HFL supporters, and there were a few physical altercations that convinced the merchants who participated in the open markets to stop bringing their carts."

A new police commissioner who supported the governor and hadn't supported the HFL, and a new acting mayor who had people in his neighborhood harassed and even hurt by the movement. Just like some of the businesses on Market Street. Nadine Fallacaro's bakery and café had burned to the ground. If Meg Corbyn hadn't felt a desperate need to make a cut, and if her warning hadn't been interpreted correctly, Nadine would have died in the fire.

"Mayor Chen and I also bring an additional benefit to our respective jobs," Alvarez said, looking at Burke. "He has family ties to people in Tokhar-Chin, and I have family ties to people living in the human areas of Felidae. We can receive news from those places and, hopefully, assist in continuing to trade with those parts of the world. Just as you, Captain Burke, have family connections in Brittania that have proved useful."

"I haven't heard from my cousin Shamus since early Sumor, but the assistance he provided to the *terra indigene* is a big reason ships are still permitted to travel between Thaisia and Brittania."

Alvarez looked at Burke, Monty, and O'Sullivan in turn. "There is a rumor that the three of you met an Elemental that commands the Atlantik Ocean."

"We did." O'Sullivan shuddered. "She—at least I had the impression of female—will permit Thaisian ships to travel to Brittania, Felidae, the Storm Islands, and Afrikah, but if we try to go to what is left of the Cel-Romano Alliance of Nations, she will destroy any Thaisian ship that touches her domain. That includes fishing vessels."

"Tokhar-Chin?" Chen asked.

"The Elemental who guards the Pacifik decides

about travel between Thaisia and Tokhar-Chin, but we have no reason to believe there is a conflict between the people there and the *terra indigene*."

Chen nodded. "So. We are living in a paper house, are we not? We have a city still governed by humans and land still under human control even if it is leased from the *terra indigene*."

"Who can refuse to renew a lease and evict the humans living on that land," Burke said. "The Others on the West Coast did it when there was trouble in Jerzy; they can do it here."

"But not all at once," Chen said. "The boundaries of the city weren't set by a single agreement. Neighborhoods were added as more people came to settle here. When troubles started between humans and Others, I checked the land leases for my district. I was dismayed to discover how few years are left on the current lease, and . . ." He stopped and seemed to struggle with what he was going to say. "Lakeside is a city made up of neighborhoods, and neighborhoods often contain families who came from a specific part of the world. The majority of families in my district came from Tokhar-Chin. There are neighborhoods of people from Felidae and Afrikah. I think those who came from Brittania are spread out among the neighborhoods made up of people whose ancestors had come from the Cel-Romano Alliance of Nations."

"That sounds about right," Burke said.

"When I looked at what the city pays for those land leases—information that was not hidden but also not easy to find—I had to wonder if government officials might forfeit the lease for one district in order to ensure there was enough money in the city's budget to pay the lease for what they considered a more worthy neighborhood."

Monty stared at Chen. Burke swore under his breath. O'Sullivan sat back and said, "Gods above and below. Was that seriously considered?"

"I do not know," Chen said softly. "At the time, I was one man on the city council and had little influence. Now?" He let the question hang.

Burke leaned forward. "There are four places situated at this end of Lake Etu within easy reach of each other: the city of Lakeside, the town of Talulah Falls, the village on Great Island, and a mixed community on River Road. Of those four places, Lakeside is the *only* one under human control. It's the only one where the human population can do what it pleases on the land it controls, whether that's farming or running factories or beating each other to death in the streets. At least, that's how it used to be. As long as we didn't interfere with the Others who were assigned to keep watch over our shenanigans, the rest of the *terra indigene* didn't step in. But that's no longer true. Humans did interfere with the *terra indigene* who were assigned to watch us. The Others were attacked and some were killed, and that enraged the residents of the wild country—the *terra indigene* that every cop who ever did a tour of duty in the wild country prayed he would never see. But *they* are on our doorstep now, and they are going to make sure we don't forget it."

"There is no safety in the dark," O'Sullivan said. "The actions of the people in the HFL movement erased the boundary between the human-controlled land and the wild country, and there is no going back."

Alvarez looked thoughtful. "No safety in the dark. Does that mean you're recommending a curfew that begins at sundown?"

"Within the city limits, I think people going to the movies or the theater or out to dinner won't be any more at risk than they'd been before when the only predators roaming the streets not only looked human but were human," Burke said. "But anyone foolish enough to leave the city limits after dark? That's just a gruesome way to commit suicide."

"Which begs the question," Alvarez said. "Are you recommending a curfew?"

Burke hesitated, then shook his head. "Unless there's a nightly slaughter, you won't convince the majority of people to be tucked in at home before dark, especially at this time of year. A request that all businesses close by ten or eleven p.m. would be better. That way most employees who work in the evenings would be home before midnight. The fewer people on the street, the easier it will be for us to handle calls for assistance instead of herding people who have more bravado than sense."

"Very well," Alvarez said. "That request can come from my office since the police will have to handle any trouble between people as well as any . . . results . . . of conflict with the *terra indigene*."

Any results of conflict. Monty looked at Alvarez and thought that was a diplomatic way of describing what the Elders had done to the humans who had been in their way as they raged through the city. The medical examiner was still trying to match body parts to the people listed as missing.

That much settled, the men went on to the next concern.

"Travel between regions is erratic. Even bringing in cargo over the Great Lakes is not without dangers," Chen said. "Lakeside has used household ration coupons for many months to discourage hoarding of perishable foods by allowing merchants to charge more for an item if it is not accompanied by a coupon. For the most part, people were sensible when it came to buying things like eggs and butter. Then we had shortages of things like flour—shortages caused by HFL supporters who were willing to let the people in Thaisia go without in order to sell to Cel-Romano for higher profits. Now when people see empty shelves because of shipping delays, they are not so sensible, are not able to believe the lack of a particular food is temporary. My office receives several calls every day, asking what I am going to do about the food shortages. People don't believe me when I tell them that, while some foods may not be available in abundant quantities, there is still a bounty of foods to eat. Therefore, an equitable distribution of food is vital but will also create hard feelings. The Others in the Courtyard may be blamed if a shop runs out of a particular item, especially if the Courtyard continues to receive supplies."

"Earth native trucks bring in goods from farms run by Intuits or Others, and the Others mostly buy products made in Intuit and Simple Life communities," Burke said. "Those aren't items that have ever been on the shelves in city shops."

"Anger and reason are rarely partners," Chen replied. "And do the Others not purchase things like gasoline for their vehicles?"

Monty sat quietly, but it took effort. Before the storms and the primal *terra indigene* who ripped their way through the city, Lakeside had had a population of approximately two hundred thousand people. What humans didn't consider, despite recent events, was that if people tried to stop deliveries, if they prevented the Others from buying gas for their vehicles, if they interfered with bringing in food that belonged to the Courtyard . . . From the Others' point of view, there were two hundred thousand meals within easy reach. And most of those meals would be easier to catch than the deer the Wolves hunted now.

"I've been reviewing the reports submitted by the station chiefs, including the monthly bills for supplies and utilities," Alvarez said. "The Chestnut Street station no longer pays the water tax that everyone else in Lakeside has to pay?"

"The water tax was lifted on that station and the Lakeside Hospital as thanks for our assistance when the Courtyard's Human Liaison was injured," Burke replied.

Alvarez and Chen looked at Burke, then at Monty, but neither man asked about Meg Corbyn. Did they know what she was?

"In that case, a courtesy for a courtesy," Alvarez said. "We expect there will be some gasoline shortages since getting anything across regional borders is an exercise in diplomacy these days, but I've already received a directive from the governor that the gas pumps connected to the municipal garages will have first rights to any gasoline that reaches the city since that's where the police cars, fire trucks, and ambulances fill up. Captain Burke, why don't you and Lieutenant Montgomery approach the Courtyard leaders and offer to let them fill their vehicles from that source?"

"That's generous," Burke said.

Alvarez smiled. "It's also practical. Our survival depends on the goodwill we can generate." His smile faded. "I don't think people have truly taken in how much was lost in recent weeks—or how much more we could lose if we're not very careful now." He focused on Burke. "As a young police officer, I, too, spent some time in a village located in the wild country. There was another village about an hour's drive away. One night there was trouble between humans and Others, and we were called to assist. I still wake up some nights with my heart pounding and my hands shaking because of what I saw in that village after the more aggressive forms of *terra indigene* retaliated. Whatever help you need to prevent that from happening here . . ." He stopped. "Or happening again, since I understand that some officers learned the same lessons you and I did."

O'Sullivan blew out a breath. "Governor Hannigan would like me to set up an official office for the Investigative Task Force here in the government building."

"But . . . ," Monty began, then stopped. O'Sullivan worked for the governor, and it wasn't his place to comment on O'Sullivan's decision—or the governor's order.

O'Sullivan nodded as if he'd heard the rest of Monty's protest. "Oh, I'm going to keep the desk in the consulate because it was offered and I don't want to lose that connection with the Courtyard. But I suspect I'll be dealing with some people who feel hostile toward the *terra indigene*, and it would be better to meet them on human ground."

"I can arrange that," Chen said. He studied O'Sullivan. "A foot in each camp. Not an easy place to be."

"No, it's not, but when the Wolfgard were attacked in the Midwest and Northwest, the governor responded to the information I provided fast enough to prevent similar attacks in the Northeast.

"That was a real danger?"

"We'll never know," Burke said. "But considering the way the Wolves in the Courtyard responded, I'd say the Wolfgard in the Northeast had been under a similar threat, but the attacks were successfully blocked before they could begin."

Chen seemed lost in thought. "We are lucky," he finally said. "So many places are isolated now. We don't even know yet how many places, how many people were lost. As Captain Burke pointed out, we are within reach of three other communities and are not so isolated. And we have working telephone and telegraph lines connecting many towns in the Northeast Region, so we have access to information instead of wondering if we alone survived." He looked at Burke and Monty. "Could you arrange a meeting with the leaders of the Courtyard? A goodwill visit?"

"I would like to be included in that, if possible," Alvarez said.

When Burke looked at him, Monty said, "I'll ask."

That ended the meeting. Burke gave O'Sullivan a lift to the Chestnut Street station while Monty and Kowalski headed back to the Courtyard.

"Let's patrol the neighborhood first," Monty said when the Courtyard was in sight.

Kowalski turned left on Crowfield Avenue and

passed the two-family house and apartment buildings that now belonged to the Courtyard.

"Anything I should know about?" Kowalski asked.

"Our new mayor wants to meet the leaders of the Courtyard."

Kowalski drove for a minute, saying nothing. Then, "As long as he doesn't ride a bicycle to the meeting, he should be fine with the Wolves."

"I wasn't worried about him meeting the Wolves. I was thinking about Tess." And what Chen and Alvarez might say when they met Meg Corbyn and saw the proof of what she was.

Officer Michael Debany
Chestnut Street Station
Lakeside, NER

Dear Michael,

You know how Mom and Dad look when they're having a very intense discussion, which really means they're having an argument about something? And how they can turn it off and speak normally to us as if nothing is happening, then go right back to being intense as soon as we leave the room? Well, I think I saw that kind of discussion yesterday between Jesse Walker and Tolya Sanguinati. I was riding past the general store in Bennett and saw them through the window. They saw me too. Jesse waved and Tolya smiled, and that's what made me think of Mom and Dad.

I'm not gossiping. I'm really not. It's just that Jesse is the leader of the Intuits who live in Prairie Gold and Tolya is in charge of Bennett, and having them mad at each other isn't good, especially since the rest of us don't know why they're at odds all of a sudden when they'd been working together so well.

Could you ask the Sanguinati in Lakeside if they've heard anything about this? I'm not trying to butt in. Okay, I am, but I like it here, and one of the houses was cleared out this week and available for new residents, and I was given first choice, so Buddy and I are moving in to our new place next week. It feels weird to choose furniture that belonged to people who were killed by the Elders, but people buy furniture and other things from estate sales all the time, and I guess this is sort of the same thing, except the whole town died and it *wasn't from old age or illness. So I'm trying to think of it like a town-wide estate sale, but I'm glad they cleared out the house before I saw it.*

I usually don't dwell on why there's a whole town empty of people. But it's like a friend telling you that their parents are getting a divorce and then coming home and catching your own parents in the middle of a heated argument. You tell yourself it won't happen to your family, and then you see it could be possible if people aren't careful about what they say and do.

I'm not sure I'll send this letter, because you'll be worried and want me to come home. But I'm fine here. I really am. And I wouldn't have said anything at all if I hadn't seen Jesse and Tolya at that moment.

Here's my new address. I'll probably be moved in by the time you get this letter, but even if I'm not, Bennett doesn't have a lot of residents yet, so the boardinghouse will hold my mail if you send it there.

Speaking of residents, a Wolf is our new sheriff. His name is Virgil Wolfgard, and he gives off an "I'm so dangerous I don't need a gun" vibe. Actually, it isn't a vibe because he really doesn't need a gun. He just shows his teeth and growls to encourage law and order. He calls me Barbara Ellen. So does Tolya. I don't know why. Everyone else calls me Barb.

And speaking of dangerous vibes, one of the Panthergard has taken possession of a small cabin just outside of town. There's a young guy, a human, living with him. I've seen them walking around the town square, but they've kept to themselves so far. We've all been told to give them space—no bringing over a casserole to welcome the new neighbors. Not that any of us are really cooking since meals at the boardinghouse and hotel are free for the residents but you have to buy food that you cook for yourself. So why make a sandwich when you can get a Mom-approved balanced meal made by someone else?

Have to go. Love and big hugs to Mom and Dad. And you too.

Barb

To: Vladimir Sanguinati and Simon Wolfgard, Urgent

Jesse Walker is unhappy and has threatened to withdraw her assistance in dealing with all the stores and houses in Bennett. She wants to know what we intend to do with the town and the other human places that the Elders cleansed and reclaimed. Are we intending to repopulate them with Intuits and *terra indigene*? Are some places going to be abandoned and allowed to decay? Are the humans who have come to Bennett just temporary help and muscle or will they be residents in the fullest sense, taking up a trade or working in the businesses? She wants to know if Bennett is going to be a real town or just a stage setting for humans getting off the train.

As Grandfather Erebus requested, the Sanguinati are now established here. We are in charge of the railway station, the bank, and the post office/telegraph office, and I am the acknowledged leader of the town. We have shifters from many gards who have come in and are willing to work here, but most have little direct experience in being around humans. Most of the Intuit youngsters who have come to Bennett have little direct experience in being around the *terra indigene*. Since the Elders are never far away, this is a concern.

That said, I think Jesse Walker has a point. Originally, the intention was to secure Bennett because it had the only train station for many miles and shouldn't be allowed to fall into the hands of humans who might be enemies of the *terra indigene*. To that end, I made note of the essential businesses we would have to keep. But if the town is going to be more than a handful of businesses that support the individuals working at the station, then we need to compromise and allow those who want to settle in a new place to come to Bennett—especially individuals who, like Barbara Ellen Debany, have a particular skill that we need here. We might even use Bennett as a posting station to send teams out to reclaim the other empty towns. But selecting the right humans is vital. We have plenty of young people who would stay if they had the opportunity to learn a trade. What we need now are adults who can run the other businesses.

Could the Lakeside Courtyard act as a filter and send applicants to Bennett? Enclosed is a list of professions and trades Jesse Walker feels should be filled, especially since the offices and businesses already exist. I do not think all these professional vacancies need to be filled immediately if a suitable candidate is not found, but I think an effort must be made if we want to build a mixed community here in the same way you are creating one near Lakeside.

—Tolya

P.S. Barbara Ellen is doing well. I have encouraged her to write to her family, and I was told by a Crow working in the post office that she did send a letter on Sumor 26, but she may not write as often as her family desires because she is busy making new friends and is equally busy taking care of all the house animals that were left behind. With so many pets, as she calls them, needing new homes—or at least new caretakers—she suggested giving a dog, cat, or bird to every new resident as a welcome gift. I am trying to discourage this idea without telling her that new *terra indigene* residents might think she was giving them an easy dinner.

CHAPTER 3

Thaisday, Messis 2

Out of sight of the females in the apartment, Simon paused at the open doorway and listened.

"That does it for this place," Eve Denby said. "This cream color isn't exciting, but it's a good neutral, and doing all the apartments in the same color sure makes it easier."

"Personal touches will add the color," Twyla Montgomery said. "Besides, I don't think any of the tenants are going to want to go out and spend the money right now to buy different paint and do this work again on their own."

"You got that right. My instructions were to clean and paint and make sure everything was in working order. The plumbing works. So does the electricity. And may the gods bless them, the Others purchased new appliances for all the apartments, including a washer and dryer installed in each of the basements of the two stone apartment buildings as well as the two-family."

"One washer and dryer shared by the folks living in four units? You planning to assign laundry days for each unit?"

"If it comes to that. I'm thinking more of a sign-up sheet to reserve the washers and dryers if someone wants or needs a particular time or day. Besides, there are coin-operated machines in the Courtyard's social center, as well as a launderette in the Bird Park Plaza. Tenants can enjoy cooperation and convenience, or they can take their laundry elsewhere."

Simon thought that sounded fair. A laundry pecking order. Not that dissimilar to feeding on a deer—the dominant members of the pack had first choice. It would be interesting to see how the females taking up residence in the apartments sorted out their dominance.

While this talk about laundry was interesting, up to a point, he had a reason for coming over to the apartment building before going into the meeting to talk about the e-mail he and Vlad had received from Tolya Sanguinati.

He stepped into the apartment and waited for the two females to notice him.

"Mr. Wolfgard." Eve wiped her paint-smeared hands on a rag. "Give it a day for the paint to dry, and Sierra and her girls can move in."

"Kitchen is clean, cupboards and floor, and the dishes and the rest are put away," Twyla added. "It was thoughtful of you to supply the basics."

Simon shrugged. The Business Association had had a lengthy discussion about how much they should provide to their tenants. In the end, the decision was based on the humans who would be living in those dens. Ruthie and Karl Kowalski had already lived together in a different place before being driven out, so they hadn't needed much beyond the appliances when they moved into the top floor of the two-family house that sat between the two stone apartment buildings. But Merri Lee hadn't had anything of her own but clothing, books, and personal items, and Nadine Fallacaro had been burned out of her den and lost everything but a couple of boxes of business papers. So he and Henry and Vlad had gone to the Bird Park Plaza with Ruthie and Eve Denby to purchase basics: glasses, silverware, cooking utensils, four-place settings of dishes, pots and pans, bed linens, and bath towels. They purchased the basics for each of the eight apartments, even though only four were about to be occupied.

Maybe five. That was the reason he had come over here—to get an answer about the fifth apartment.

He looked at Twyla. "Have you decided which den you want?" Lieutenant Montgomery had taken a ground-floor apartment in the building to the right of the two-family house. Sierra Montgomery and her pups had been assigned a second-floor apartment on the opposite side of the building—at Montgomery's request. Nadine Fallacaro and Merri Lee had taken the ground-floor apartments of the other stone building.

There had been some hesitation in agreeing to have two females residing in a building that had no male occupants, but they were across the street from the Courtyard, where there were plenty of sharp-toothed males who would respond to a call for help, and two of the males who were residing in the other buildings now owned by the Courtyard were police officers. Three if they counted Michael Debany, who wasn't quite living with Merri Lee yet but was around enough to be counted as male protection.

This not quite living with a female was being watched with great interest by most of the Courtyard's residents. Until now, the Others had never interacted so closely with humans as to be able to observe mating rituals.

And Simon had more reason than the rest to observe those rituals. He found it encouraging that his living arrangement with Meg was so similar to Debany's arrangement with Merri Lee because it meant a Wolf's behavior didn't have to change in order to be viewed as human.

"If you don't need me, I'll clean these brushes," Eve said.

Simon moved away from the door and the freshly painted walls. The paint wasn't overwhelmingly stinky since the women had opened the windows, but he didn't want to be in the apartment longer than necessary.

"Well now," Twyla said when they were alone. "I wanted to talk to you about that. I was wondering if any of the efficiency apartments above the seamstress/tailor's shop are available."

He studied the older woman, confused. "Don't you want to live with your pack?"

She smiled, showing him the denture teeth—something he still wanted someone to explain. "When an adult Wolf gets tired of having puppies chewing on her tail, what does she do?"

"She gets up and leaves."

"Exactly. I love my children and grandchildren, but I don't want to be around them every minute of the day."

He couldn't picture Lieutenant Montgomery pestering Miss Twyla enough to get nipped, but he'd seen the Sierra sometimes revert to juvenile behavior around her mother, despite having two pups of her own.

"These apartments all have porches and real kitchens," he pointed out.

"And an extra bedroom that I don't need." The smile she gave him now didn't show teeth, but it was warmer somehow. "I'll be spending plenty of time over at Crispin's apartment, looking after Lizzy when he's working. But he needs time on his own with his daughter, and she needs time with him. And Sierra needs to stand on her own without me being a crutch. An efficiency apartment lets me be close by if I'm needed but not right on top of my children. Not much housekeeping with a small place, and I'm happy about that. And there is the Market Square. Plenty of places there to sit and enjoy an evening. I can select a book from the library, pick up a meal at Meat-n-Greens, and spend an hour reading outside."

She could do all those things if she lived in one of these apartments, but she seemed certain she wanted a small den.

That meant all the efficiency apartments would be full, since one was going to be the classroom for the human pups, Henry still wanted to keep the one he used when he worked late in his studio and didn't want to go back to the Green Complex, and they'd agreed to let Chris Fallacaro have one since he didn't want to live with Nadine, despite her being a relative.

Which left him with the problem of what to do with Emily Faire, the young Intuit woman they had hired to work part-time as a nurse practitioner in the Market Square medical office. Now that Dr. Lorenzo was away from Lakeside so much, doing his work for the task force that was gathering information about the *cassandra sangue*, they needed someone trustworthy to look after Meg when she made a cut. The Business Association had intended to let the Emily use one of the efficiency apartments; now they would need to find another place for her to live. There were rooms above the social center, but those had been used for sexual liaisons and didn't have anything beyond a bed, a lamp, and a table. The *terra indigene* had been clearing out those rooms, using the frames from the single beds to provide beds for the human children—although the parents of those children insisted on purchasing new box springs and mattresses. Since any scents on the mattresses had faded to the point that even the Wolves couldn't pick up anything, it was doubtful human noses could either, but it had been important to the adult humans, so the Business Association had made the extra purchases.

<Simon?> Vlad called, using the *terra indigene* form of communication. <We need you at Howling Good Reads.>

<Problem?>

<Looks like it. Officer Debany is upset. Something about a letter from his sister.>

"I have to go," Simon told Twyla. "You can use the efficiency apartment that Meg had when she first came to the Courtyard. You know which one that is?"

"The only one unoccupied?" Twyla replied.

"Yes." He hurried down the stairs and out the door. He hesitated at the curb and considered if he should walk up to the light at the corner or just dash across the street. Crowfield Avenue had enough traffic at this time of day to make going up to the light prudent, so he did. Then he hurried to Howling Good Reads to find Blair and Vlad facing Michael Debany.

Vlad glanced at Simon, then gestured toward Debany. "There is a concern."

<Which makes no sense,> Blair added.

"What's the problem?" Simon asked, focusing on Debany, who was in uniform. Which included a gun. Fortunately for the human, he was waving a piece of paper and not the gun.

"The problem is my sister, Bee."

"Barbara Ellen," Vlad clarified. "Went to Bennett as the vet-in-training to take care of the small animals that were found in the houses."

"She's been away from home barely a month, and she says she's moving in with some guy named Buddy," Debany said. Normally an even-tempered male, he sounded snappish.

Simon pondered the information, trying to sort out why this was a problem. "Don't you want your sister to find a mate and have puppies?"

"Someday. Not now. And not with a guy she hasn't mentioned to anyone in the family until now. What do we know about him? What does he do for a living? Where did he come from?"

"Do you need to know these things because you can't give him a good sniff and decide if you like him?"

"I need to know because she's my kid sister and she's living in a town hundreds of miles away in a different region of Thaisia so I can't even call her to find out what's going on. I need to know because I'm a cop and I've seen the bad things that can happen to vulnerable young women. And because Bee shouldn't be shacking up with a guy."

"Aren't you shacking up with Merri Lee?" Vlad asked.

"That's different."

"How?" Simon asked. "Barbara Ellen and Merri Lee are about the same age."

"That's beside the point. It's different."

"Why? Because Merri Lee doesn't have a brother to growl and snap at you when you go to her den to mate?"

"We could growl and snap," Blair said, sounding more than willing to oblige.

All the anger drained out of Debany. He gave them a pleading look. "She's my kid sister. Isn't there someone in Bennett you could ask about this Buddy guy? She's moving in with him, and she didn't even mention his last name."

"We'll see what we can do," Simon said.

Debany folded the paper, put it in his breast pocket, and left.

"Are we going to help him?" Blair asked.

Simon nodded. "Pack is important to him, like it's important to us."

"Tolya mentioned Barbara Ellen in his e-mail but said nothing about this Buddy," Vlad said. "I'll send him a telegram and use the special communications network the Intuits set up between regions. We should have an answer by tomorrow."

Tess walked through the archway that connected A Little Bite with Howling Good Reads. Her hair was still brown but starting to curl, a sign that she wasn't upset—yet—but wasn't calm. "Steve Ferryman just pulled in for the meeting."

"For a town so far away, the citizens of Bennett are certainly giving us plenty to do," Vlad said.

Tess gave them a sharp smile. "Hopefully we can return the favor."

"Mama? Are you up here?"

Hearing the agitation in Sierra's voice, Twyla took a deep breath and let it out in a sigh. She wasn't looking forward to this talk. "Back here." When her daughter walked into the second of the two bedrooms, she kept her voice calm, conversational. "The other bedroom has the door to the porch. Better if you have that one and put Bonnie and Carrie in here."

"I heard Ruth and Merri Lee talking about jobs that needed to be filled in the Courtyard, including a secretarial position in the consulate, so I went over to talk to Elliot Wolfgard. Why did you tell him not to hire me? It's a good job, Mama, and I'm qualified for it."

"You have the typing skills and the rest that's needed for an office," Twyla agreed. "But if you're thinking you'd get paid more for that job than working at the coffee shop or the library or helping clean shops and offices, then you'd be wrong. Everyone who lives in the Courtyard is expected to do a job according to their abilities, so everyone is paid the same hourly rate, except, maybe, the folks who actually run the businesses. I heard you might get a cash bonus in your pay envelope if the Business Association is pleased with your work, but that's the only difference in pay."

She could see by Sierra's expression that the girl hadn't taken in that difference between working for the Others and working for a human company.

"That's beside the point," Sierra said, rallying. "Why did you tell him not to hire me?"

"Because you lied to me," Twyla replied quietly. Seeing the guilty look on Sierra's face, she nodded, feeling her heart grow heavy with sorrow but also heated by a touch of anger. "And you cheated the Others who sheltered us during that storm."

"I didn't!"

"You told me you didn't know how to reach Cyrus, that he didn't leave a phone number. You told Crispin the same thing. Mr. Simon and Mr. Vlad were quite clear that local calls could be made on the telephones in the stores, but we were expected to make long-distance calls on our mobile phones or use pay phones—or receive permission before making a call. I heard you making a call, child. Heard how many numbers you pressed and knew it wasn't a local call."

"I can't afford to buy time on my mobile phone right now," Sierra said. "And it was just a phone call. The Others can afford it."

"And that's just the kind of thing Cyrus says to justify taking what isn't his," Twyla snapped. "And hearing you saying what he would say is exactly the reason I told Mr. Elliot not to hire you. You think I don't know why you lost at least two good jobs? You think I don't know that Cyrus came around and talked you into doing something you knew was wrong? Maybe you said no the first time he asked. Maybe even the second. But you've always listened to him more than you've listened to your daddy and me. He's like a poison to you, getting what he wants and leaving you with the consequences. Cyrus doesn't suffer when you lose a good job. He may be inconvenienced because one of his sources temporarily dries up, but he doesn't suffer. The ones who pay are you and your children. Do you ever think about your girls when he comes calling, wanting you to steal supplies or tell him some confidential information that he can use to his advantage? He's buying drugs and booze and ignoring his own wife and children while you're struggling to scrape up enough money to put a meal in front of your girls."

"Jimmy is my brother. We're supposed to help family," Sierra cried.

Twyla had never understood why so many people, including her children, couldn't be satisfied with the name they were given. But her husband, James, had started it in their own family by calling their firstborn CJ instead of Crispin James. That had lasted all through the boy's schooling until he went to the police academy. Then he became Monty to his friends and colleagues. Cyrus James, on the other hand, had decided on Jimmy as his preferred name from the moment he could talk. And Sierra had ended up being called Sissy by her brothers, a word Twyla suspected meant something different for each boy—for one a term of affection, for the other a term of derision.

"Aren't your own children also family, Sierra?" Twyla asked quietly. "Don't you owe them at least as much loyalty as you show the brother who has never done a single thing for you?"

"He did a lot, gave up a lot."

"It's best if we don't have that discussion." She had fought that battle all the years Sierra was growing up, had felt the frustration of knowing Cyrus had somehow gotten under Sierra's skin so deep that nothing she or James or Crispin had been able to do or say could dislodge Cyrus's influence. Away from him, the girl was bright, loving, a good mother, and a steady employee. But everything Sierra knew about right and wrong collapsed when Cyrus showed up.

"You betrayed your employers," Twyla continued. "You've lied more than once to me or Crispin or your daddy when he was still alive. Most of the time you're not a liar or a cheat. But I suspect you've told Cyrus enough about the Courtyard that he's on his way here, thinking to get a handout."

She studied her daughter. Sierra had been two years old when she and James adopted her. Crispin had been twelve, Cyrus nine. One boy had embraced having a little sister; the other boy had resented her from the day she'd come into their home. Maybe it was human nature to want to please the person who rejects you, who wants you to prove you deserve to be loved. Maybe. But no matter what Sierra did or how much she gave, Cyrus would never love his little sister. It was a hard truth for a mother to admit, but Cyrus James Montgomery had never loved anyone but himself.

"You're a grown woman," Twyla said, feeling tired. "If this was just another job, I would have left the decision between you and Mr. Elliot about whether he wanted you to work for him. But this isn't just another job. Mr. Elliot deals with the mayor and the rest of the city's government. I reckon there's plenty of information that might be worth some money to the wrong people. Cyrus would know that, and it never takes him long to find the wrong people. And it wouldn't take him long to apply whatever hold he has on you to do wrong for him. But this time, girl, you wouldn't just lose a job and a place to live; you wouldn't just be taking food away from your children. The Others have their own way of dealing with betrayal, and it's harsher than receiving a pink slip."

"CJ wasn't being fair," Sierra said. "He could have sent Jimmy the train fare if he'd wanted to, but Jimmy had to flee Toland on his own."

Twyla noticed there was no mention of Cyrus's wife or children. "He's on his way here?"

Sierra hesitated, then nodded.

"Where's he going to stay, especially if he does have his family with him?" She would never admit it to Sierra, or Crispin when he heard about her choice, but this was one reason she wanted the efficiency apartment. She could turn down Cyrus and his wife, Sandee, but if she had a spare bedroom, it would be hard to refuse giving the grandchildren a place to sleep. And Cyrus wouldn't hesitate to use his children as the wedge to get as much from her as he could. Which wasn't much, considering how little she had right now, but it still soured the day knowing that his children paid for his schemes because helping them meant helping him continue to do wrong, and that she would not do.

"Not all the apartments are occupied," Sierra said in a small voice. "And we don't have to pay . . ."

"That's what you told him? You've got a place rent free? Child, what are you using for a brain these days?"

"The Others said we could live here. They've even given us some furniture and stuff."

"They're not giving you those things. They're providing some furnishings that stay with the apartment. Those things are not for you to do with as you please. And living in those buildings isn't free. Crispin doesn't work in the Courtyard, so he pays rent like he would to any other landlord. For the folks who do work in the Courtyard, the rent is deducted from the pay up front—something you should think about if you're going to live here."

Sierra stared at her, her mouth hanging open.

"Well." Twyla sighed. "You'd best decide quick if you want to find a job at a local business and pay rent same as Crispin or if you're going to work in the Courtyard doing whatever you're assigned to do."

Sierra walked out of the room. A few moments later, Twyla heard the apartment door close.

It wasn't surprising that the girl hadn't taken it all in when the terms of employment were explained. They'd been told about working in the Courtyard shortly after the storm came through last month—the storm and the terror that had followed in its wake.

The terror hadn't gone away. Not completely. No one said anything, but Twyla knew it by the way Eve and Pete Denby kept a sharp eye on their children, by the way Crispin called to check on her and Lizzy and Sierra a couple of times a day despite being with them each evening. She knew it by the way the Crows flew over to see what was happening at the apartments—curious about the humans, sure, but also watchful for what might whisper past the buildings unseen. She knew by the way the Wolves howled at night.

And she didn't need to hear Meg Corbyn speak

prophecy to know what would happen to the humans in this city if the Wolves stopped howling.

She needed to tell Crispin about this as soon as possible. And she needed to warn Meg about Cyrus. A lot of folks now were aware of what it meant when a girl had evenly spaced scars. Cyrus would look at Meg and see his ticket to wealth beyond measure. He wouldn't consider that she might be treasured by someone else for very different reasons.

If he found an opportunity and acted on it, he might get them all killed.

Steve Ferryman handed Tolya's letter back to Simon. "Are you limiting the potential settlers to Intuits and *terra indigene*?"

"Who else did you have in mind?" Simon asked.

"Simple Life folk." Steve looked at Henry, Tess, Vlad, and Elliot before focusing on Simon. "I hadn't realized they were following what was happening in the Midwest so closely until James Gardner asked Roger Czerneda about who was going to resettle the empty towns. Simple Life families have the same challenges as any human group—limited space and opportunities for their children. There are folks on Great Island who are interested in resettling. A few Simple Life youngsters are going to resettle in the River Road Community and are happy about having their own place that still isn't far from home and family. But others . . ." He sat back. "I have a feeling some of the Simple Life folk don't want to abandon their way of life altogether, but they're looking to expand what is available to them. The Intuit way of life is somewhere between Simple Life and what most people living in Lakeside would consider the necessities of life."

"Do any of the Simple Life youngsters know about livestock? About cattle?" Henry asked.

Steve nodded. "Dairy cows. Horses. Some sheep and goats. Chickens."

Simon scratched behind one ear. None of the humans on the ranches between Prairie Gold and Bennett had survived the Elders' wrath. But not all the houses and outbuildings had been destroyed, and the animals were still out there. The Intuits who worked on the Prairie Gold ranch couldn't handle all the livestock, but Simple Life humans occupying the empty ranches might not provoke the Elders into another attack. "We'll consider them."

"How do you want to do this?" Steve asked. "Hold a job fair?"

They all stared at him.

"You mean have a hoard of humans descend on us looking for work?" Vlad finally asked.

Steve winced. "Not exactly. Well, sort of. If I can have a copy of the list of desired skills, I'll ask Lois Greene, the editor of the *Great Island Reporter*, to print a special page with the information, and I'll see it's distributed to the Simple Life folk as well as the Intuits in Ferryman's Landing." He blew out a breath. "You should know I've been receiving some queries from Intuit settlements in the Midwest asking if the *terra indigene* are going to allow the empty towns to be resettled. Obviously they can't come here for a personal interview, but it's something for the *terra indigene* leaders to think about."

"None of those places will be human only or human controlled," Simon said. "Not anymore."

"I think everyone who is inquiring realizes that 'empty' means empty of humans, not empty of everyone," Steve replied.

"I want to hear more about this job fair," Tess said. "Telling the Intuits and Simple Life folk about potential work in Bennett is one thing, but word will spread to the humans out there, and what do we do with the mob who thinks they're entitled to work whether they're qualified or not—or whether the *terra indigene* want them?"

"We're not going to advertise it beyond Great Island," Steve said.

"Humans will notice that many humans are gathering at the Courtyard," Henry said. "Some will be curious and join them, will find out why they're there and apply for work."

"The people who have approached me have been thinking about this for a while," Steve said. "Maybe they've been wanting a change for a lot longer but didn't see how to make it happen. And maybe this is an opportunity for some of your people too. Is there anyone here who is able to run a business but will remain subordinate if he or she stays in Lakeside?"

Simon sat up, thinking hard about the question and about the Courtyard residents. There was at least one who fit that description.

"I'll specify that this job fair is about taking a job in Bennett, and that the interview here is a preliminary one. The final decision will be made by the leaders in Bennett, so there is the possibility that a person will be sent back to Great Island if they aren't suitable."

"Or if they're uncomfortable when they get there," Vlad said.

Young Intuits had already traveled to Bennett to help clean up the town—organizing food supplies and discarding food that had gone bad being some of the first things that had been done. Some of those youngsters, mostly male, had remained in Bennett hoping to find other kinds of work. Some had expressed interest in going on to the next town that needed cleanup and had been reassigned. Others had returned to Great Island, unnerved by the feel of the Elders who were watching the town.

"The Sanguinati control Bennett for the most part, but the new sheriff is a Wolf," Simon said. "It might be helpful if we could find some kind of human to be his deputy."

"I can package up résumés and send them to you,"

Steve said. "You can review them and invite the people you want to interview."

Simon shook his head. "We won't be able to tell enough from paper to decide if we're going to send them on to Bennett for Tolya to look at."

"Then spread the job fair over several days, each day being given to a specific kind of work."

Vlad nodded approvingly. "One day for farm and ranch workers and the support people like cooks and such. Another day for shops, and another for professionals with the medical and legal skills Jesse Walker felt should be included."

Simon looked at Steve. "How soon can you get the humans gathered?"

"A couple of days after the job list is distributed. I'll talk to Lois Greene as soon as I get back to Ferryman's Landing. And we'll arrange for buses to transport the people from Great Island."

"Then interviews will begin next Moonsday," Simon said. "We'll start with the humans who want to work on the farms and ranches."

Steve pushed back from the conference table. Then he hesitated and looked at Simon. "I'd like to say hello to Meg, let her know how the young *cassandra sangue* are doing and our progress on building the campus for them. We broke ground on the residential building."

Simon struggled to keep his teeth human-shaped and reminded himself that Steve wasn't a rival.

Besides, Nathan would be in the Liaison's Office keeping watch over Meg.

"Meg would like that," he said. Then it was his turn to hesitate. "And Jean?" Jean and Meg had been friends in the compound where they'd been held and trained and used. Jean was physically and mentally damaged and only marginally sane. But she saw things the other blood prophets didn't see.

"She's Jean." Steve thought for a moment. "She has some trouble with the farm animals—even within the routines of caring for them, there can be too much that's different—but she is managing to help Lorna Gardner work in the family's kitchen garden. Things may bloom and vegetables may grow larger overnight, but they don't move around, so Jean can handle the change. Lorna says sometimes Jean will sit and watch a zucchini plant for hours. Lorna doesn't know why she does that or what she sees that the rest of us don't, but it gives Jean some peace."

<I need to speak with all of you except Ferryman,> Elliot said, using the *terra indigene* form of communication.

"I'll walk you out," Vlad said, leaving the conference room with Steve. He returned a minute later and resumed his seat.

Elliot told them about his conversation with Twyla Montgomery. "She wouldn't have spoken against her own pup without good reason."

"Lieutenant Montgomery is careful when he deals with us," Henry said. "He would not have brought someone into the Courtyard who might cause trouble for Lizzy or the police pack."

"Kid sister," Simon said, thinking of Officer Debany's reaction to Barbara Ellen's news that she was moving in with the Buddy. "Montgomery wouldn't have kept the Sierra from shelter in the face of the storm that hit Lakeside. And the Sierra and Miss Twyla had been living in Toland, which took a harder hit."

"But he didn't try to save his brother," Elliot said.

"Maybe he couldn't. Or maybe he realized the brother was a danger to the whole pack."

"And if the brother shows up here and looks to be a danger to us?" Tess asked. Red streaks appeared in her hair as it began to coil.

"We'll deal with him," Vlad replied.

"And if he looks to be a danger to Meg?"

Simon snarled, revealing Wolf-size fangs. Fur sprang up on his chest and shoulders.

Tess studied Simon, then Vlad. "All right, then."

"Miss Twyla said the humans who had worked for us at the consulate had not done their jobs well—an opinion I agree with," Elliot said. "But we need some support staff, especially since Agent O'Sullivan is also working out of the consulate, so I would like to approach Katherine Debany, Officer Debany's mother. Miss Twyla thinks she would be a good worker and has the necessary skills."

"I'll speak with Grandfather Erebus and see if any of the Sanguinati would like to learn office work," Vlad offered.

"And I'll talk to Nadine and see if we can provide baked goods and sandwiches during the job fair without shorting our own humans," Tess said.

That much decided, they separated to go to their own work. But Tess, Henry, Vlad, and Simon all walked down the access way, and every one of them glanced at the newly constructed screen that allowed Meg to keep one of the side doors open without fighting off bugs all day. They didn't stop, didn't stare, but they all listened to the tone of Steve's voice as he talked to Meg.

Satisfied that there was no need to interfere, Simon continued on to the back door of Howling Good Reads.

"Are you going to talk to John?" Vlad asked.

"Yes. He would be a good fit for running the bookstore in Bennett. He's worked with humans and gets along with them. He could teach youngsters, both human and *terra indigene*, about running a bookstore. And it would be good to have another Wolf there—one not as quick to bite as Virgil."

"So, you know Bennett's new sheriff?"

"I do." And that was why personality would count as much as skill when choosing a potential deputy for the Wolf.

Considering the number of Hawks who had perched on the apartment's porch railing and the Crows who had settled for spots on the roof or in nearby trees, Monty wasn't sure how private his talk with his mother had been, but he didn't care. Most likely, Jimmy was on his way to Lakeside right now, thinking the Courtyard would provide free room and board. But short of wasting police resources to locate a man who, in the eyes of the law, hadn't committed a crime—at least recently—there was no way to find Jimmy before he reached the city.

Gods. He didn't know if Simon or Vlad had any experience dealing with that kind of manipulative personality—someone who didn't do a damn thing for anyone unless it was the only way to get something for himself. He didn't know if they had any experience with a human who had a cunning street intelligence and an absolute conviction that no action of his should have any consequences *for him*. And if there were consequences, that human would dismiss them as insignificant the moment he had slipped away or the next scheme popped into his head.

Just the thought of Jimmy being here, surrounded by cops, Wolves, and Sanguinati, made Monty shiver. And Tess. He didn't want to think about what would happen if Cyrus James Montgomery tried some scam on Tess. Or what would happen if Jimmy so much as approached Meg Corbyn.

But it looked like he was going to have to deal with his brother. Mama wasn't going to put up with nonsense, but standing up against Jimmy's wheedling, schemes, and outright lies took a toll on her; it always had, even when Jimmy was little and his lies and schemes didn't have serious repercussions. And unlike Sierra, Mama understood you couldn't be careless around the Others.

Before he turned personal business into a professional concern, there was one person Monty wanted to see.

Having crossed at the intersection of Crowfield Avenue and Main Street, Monty noticed the For Sale sign on the Stag and Hare, the tavern across the street from the Courtyard—the tavern that had provided refuge for HFL supporters and other schemers. Had the owner been among those who had died when the Elders swept through the city? Or was the man selling the place with the intention of buying another tavern in a different part of Lakeside?

Opening the front door of the Liaison's Office, Monty nodded to Nathan, who watched him but didn't challenge.

"Lieutenant." Meg came out of the sorting room and stood at the counter. "You just caught me. I was about to close up for the midday break."

"Could you give me a couple of minutes before you go?" he asked.

"Of course." Meg opened the go-through so that Monty could join her in the sorting room. She closed the Private door partway—the most privacy a human male could have around Meg.

"There's something I need to know," Monty said. He raised a hand as if she'd reached for her silver razor. "It's not crucial enough to ask for a cut. I had hoped the cards might provide some guidance."

Meg studied him, and he studied her. He saw her desire to grab at the excuse to make a cut, to feel the euphoria that came from speaking prophecy. He saw her struggle with the knowledge of how Simon Wolfgard and her friends, both *terra indigene* and human, would react to her making a cut when she'd managed to hold her addiction at bay for several weeks.

"I could try the cards," Meg finally said. She opened a drawer and removed a carved wooden box. She opened the box, removed the stacks of cards, and spread them over the sorting table. Then she placed her hands just above the cards. "What is your question?"

"What will happen if Cyrus James Montgomery, aka Jimmy, comes to Lakeside? Speak, prophet, and I will listen." He wasn't sure if those words were needed when

Meg used the cards, but it was part of the ritual of prophecy when she used the razor, so he said the words.

Meg closed her eyes. Monty waited. Then her hands moved as if she was searching for something by touch. She chose one card, but she frowned and her right hand kept moving over the cards scattered on the table. Finally she chose a second card and sighed, as if freed from a discomfort.

Meg turned the cards over so they could see the answer.

The first card showed an explosion. The second card was a hooded figure holding a scythe.

"I drew that card yesterday." Meg pointed to the explosion. "I asked a question about Lakeside, and that was the action card."

Monty had learned enough about how Meg used the prophecy cards to know she usually selected one card for a simple answer to a question and three cards for a complex answer requiring subject, action, and result. He suspected drawing two cards was unusual. "When you selected the cards yesterday, what was the subject card that preceded the explosion?"

"A travel card—train/bus/car. The action card was the explosion."

"And the result?"

"Future undecided." She looked troubled.

Monty felt equally troubled. "Thank you, Meg."

"Miss Twyla came by this morning. She mentioned him too. Cyrus James. She said I should stay away from him because of what I am."

"Unfortunately, that's true. Jimmy would try to use your . . . talent . . . for his own benefit. If you obliged him even once, the next thing you know, he would be bringing friends around and pressuring you into reading the cards for them—or making a cut if the cards weren't providing a satisfactory answer."

Meg looked alarmed. "Bringing strangers into the Courtyard would be dangerous and cause trouble."

"Yes, it would." Jimmy had a knack for starting something, squeezing what he could from it, and then walking away just before things went sour and escalated into real trouble. Starting something that involved Meg wouldn't be trouble; it would be lethal.

Meg put the cards back into the box, forming stacks that fit the space but not trying to put the decks together. "I'd better close up. I'm meeting Simon for lunch."

Monty waited for her to lock up, then walked with her to the back door of A Little Bite. Simon wasn't there yet, and Monty felt relieved. He wasn't ready to have a chat with Wolfgard yet.

First he would talk to Kowalski and Debany, would be honest with them about the potential damage his brother could do if—or when—Jimmy arrived in Lakeside. Then he would talk to Captain Burke and Agent O'Sullivan, would tell them about the cards Meg had drawn in answer to his question. And finally he would talk to Simon about the brother who obeyed the law only when it suited him. Of course, human law didn't apply in the Courtyard, and Monty already knew the hard choice he would make—would have to make—if the Wolves went after Jimmy.

To: Tolya Sanguinati, Urgent

Officer Debany is concerned because Barbara Ellen is moving into a house with a male named Buddy. Do you know him? Is he a suitable mate for her? Please reply as soon as possible.

—Vlad

To: Vladimir Sanguinati, Urgent

Buddy is a suitable roommate for Barbara Ellen, but he is not a suitable mate. Buddy is a parakeet.

—Tolya

Dear Meg,

These are sketches of my friend Amy Wolfgard. Whenever I'm outside drawing, she tries to steal my pencils. I thought she was going to chew on them, like Wolves chew on twigs to clean their teeth. Then, just this week, she shifted to (mostly) human form, and I discovered she'd been trying to indicate her interest in what I was doing. She wants to draw too, and trying to take a pencil was her request for me to play, to share. I want to show her how to draw, but I don't know how. I can't explain what I'm doing or how she can do the same thing. No one taught me; I just hold a pencil and things get drawn on the paper.

Grace Wolfgard went down to the Intuit village here at Sweetwater to see if their little bookstore had any books about how to draw, but they didn't. Jackson and some Intuit men even went farther down the road to Endurance, the human town. What's left of the human town.

Where do the people who survived the Elders go if they want to leave the place where they live now? Jackson said the people in Endurance were fools for packing up their cars and sneaking off in the middle of the night. He said they should have left at dawn and traveled during the daylight hours because all the humans had been warned that there is no safety in the dark. But some of the people didn't listen, and now the Ravens and Eagles are flying over the roads and telling the Wolves and Intuits where to find the cars—and what's left of the bodies.

The people who remained in the town are going to stay. They told Jackson and some of the Intuits that this was never a kind place to humans, but they would endure as their ancestors endured. That's what I overheard Jackson tell Grace.

Nothing feels different in the terra indigene settlement. Well, Jackson and Grace have decided all the youngsters should have some book learning. They've hired an Intuit teacher to come up to the settlement to teach everyone who wants to learn how to read and write and do sums. So every morning, the Wolves haul a rolling blackboard to a shady spot, and youngsters from all the gards— Eagles, Ravens, Hawks, Wolves, even one of the Panthers—gather to listen to the teacher. Most don't shift to a human form; I don't think most of them have ever tried. But we all listen. Grace said that even if this is simple for me and something I learned before, I need to pay attention because I need to set an example for the rest of the youngsters about how to behave during school. I think I'm doing a good job most of the time, but sometimes when I'm listening to the teacher I slide to a different place where I still hear her voice but it's far away. And then I blink and there's a drawing filling a page of my notebook and everyone is watching me, including the teacher. But no one says anything. No one threatens to cut off my fingers like they did when we lived in the compound. Jackson just comes over to where we're having class and removes the drawing from my notebook, and the teacher starts talking again.

Grace says the young cassandra sangue who are living with the Intuits are doing well. They have structured days that include schooling and chores appropriate for their age. They also get to experience a little bit of new every day. So do I. The land around our settlement is the same and different every day. I like it.

Could you look in your bookstore and see if there is a book to teach someone how to draw? I'll pay for it, once I figure out how to do that.

*Your friend,
Hope Wolfsong*

CHAPTER 4

Moonsday, Messis 6

John Wolfgard looked at Vlad, then focused on Simon. "Are you sure?"

"We're sure," Simon replied. "You know how to run a bookstore, and you know how to work with humans. And having another Wolf in Bennett would be a good thing." He studied the other Wolf before adding, "I'm not telling you that you have to go. It's your choice. There are only two other Wolves there right now, so it will be a small pack for hunting prey."

"But you won't have to depend on what you catch being the only food available," Vlad said. "Bennett has plenty of food for the next few months or more."

John thought for a moment. "Is one of the other Wolves dominant?"

"Virgil," Simon said. He'd wondered how Virgil and Tolya had confirmed which of them was the dominant predator. Since Tolya was still in charge of the town and, as sheriff, Virgil technically worked for him, the Wolf must have realized instinctively how deadly the Sanguinati could be.

"When do I leave?" John asked.

"As soon as possible. They need to get the stores up and running again. I'll write the travel letter this evening."

"Perhaps John should hold off catching the train for a day or two," Vlad said. "It will be easier if a group travels together, especially if there are Simple Life folk among Bennett's prospective new residents."

Simon nodded. The first day of the job fair would begin in a couple of hours—the farm and ranch workers. He hoped there would be a few humans suitable to send out to help the residents of Bennett and Prairie Gold.

When John left to pack his belongings and consider his new assignment, Simon let out a sigh. The good-natured Wolf had been a great help during the years when Howling Good Reads was open to the general public. But now the Courtyard stores would serve a different, more enclosed purpose, and John's easy temper would be more valuable to Tolya in a place where neither humans nor *terra indigene* had had much contact with one another.

"That takes care of John," Simon said. "You can take the lead with our next employee."

Vlad gave him a sour look. "So I get to handle the exploding fluffball? Why?"

"Because you do it so well. And I'll be right behind you."

Vlad muttered a nasty comment that Simon pretended not to hear.

"Assistant manager? Really?" Merri Lee's smile showed a lot of teeth. Since she was human, they were small teeth and not intimidating in any way.

"Yes, really," Vlad replied, giving her a warm smile that *didn't* show his teeth. Somehow revealing fangs seemed like one-upmanship.

Merri Lee's smile faded. "But what about Meg? The work I do with Meg?"

"Simon and I understand that some flexibility is required since you can't predict when Meg will need your assistance. However, for the time needed to work on *The Blood Prophets Guide*, perhaps you could work with Meg after the midday break, before she makes her deliveries? Ruthie would also be available then since the human young have school in the mornings and are watched by other adults in the afternoons."

Merri Lee nodded. "We could work that out."

"Either Simon or I will be in the store most of the time, so you won't be completely on your own."

"Okay." She gave them another beaming smile. "This is great. Really great. When do I start? Can I order books?"

A happy fluffball could be as unnerving as an angry fluffball. "You can make recommendations, but for the time being, Simon or I will approve the final list to send to the publishers." Based on the timidly reported news about the condition of the remaining human-controlled cities throughout Thaisia, getting books out of the publishers in Toland might be problematic. Simon had sent letters to all the Intuit and *terra indigene* publishers he knew about in the Northeast, Southeast, and High North. Until they heard back, they couldn't say what would fill the bookstore's shelves.

"Can I run over to the Liaison's Office and tell Meg? I guess I should ask Tess, since I'm working at A Little Bite today." Merri Lee darted through the archway, shouting, "Tess! I've been promoted!"

"Do you think Tess will mind?" Vlad asked. When they'd considered who could become their full-time employee after John left, Merri Lee had been the obvious choice because she'd already been putting some hours in at the store and could handle the *terra indigene* who came in—even the Wolves from the Addirondak packs who came to Lakeside for a few days for just that kind of controlled interaction with humans.

But they hadn't considered that Tess might not be pleased to lose her best human employee.

On the other hand, the color of her hair and the amount of curl were clear indications of Tess's mood. If it was any color except brown when she learned about Merri Lee's promotion, he and Simon would find work to do in some other part of the Courtyard until she calmed down.

"She'll still have Julia Hawkgard working with her, as well as Nadine Fallacaro," Simon said. "And she'll have the Sierra to wait on customers and do other work."

"Not the same thing."

Simon didn't want to agree, but finally, reluctantly, he said, "No, it's not."

They tensed when Tess suddenly appeared in the archway, her hair solid green and coiling. "You don't get Merri Lee until the job fair is done. After that, the *whole* Business Association will discuss the reassignment of human employees." She left as suddenly as she'd appeared.

Vlad stared at the empty archway. For years they had worked with Tess without knowing what she was, beyond that she was a deadly form of *terra indigene*. Knowing she was one of the rare forms—a Harvester, a Plague Rider—didn't make working with her easier. She was one of Namid's fiercest predators—not as lethal as the Elementals or the Elders, but more than a match for most of the shifter forms.

"That went pretty well," Simon said. He looked out HGR's big front windows. "Come on. We'd better get ready for the humans. They're starting to arrive."

"This would be more enjoyable if we could eat a few of them." Vlad shook his head. Even potential employees had to be considered nonedible. "Forget I said that."

"I'll collect the first batch of applications and bring them upstairs for us to review," Simon said.

Vlad went upstairs to HGR's office and wondered how he and Simon would select potential employees when their own knowledge of the job consisted of herd cattle, ride horses, and don't piss off the Elders and get eaten.

"Tess? Do you have a minute?"

Tess turned her head toward Nadine Fallacaro but didn't look at the woman. When A Little Bite had served any human who came in for a cup of coffee and a sandwich or pastry, it had been easy to take tiny sips of their life energy. Not enough to damage them, not even enough to be noticed by the humans, especially in the morning, when the caffeine from the coffee would mask the little extra bit of fatigue. With all the other kinds of food available, those sips had been enough to sustain her, if not satisfy her.

But the coffee shop wasn't open to the general public anymore, and those sips had to be taken much more carefully since she knew every person she fed on and didn't want them to be harmed. She didn't sip from Nadine in the morning for the same reason she didn't take any life energy from the police officers—they needed that energy to remain alert and safe while they worked.

She wondered if any of the human parents realized why the children's energy so conveniently waned just before bedtime. She wondered if Simon, Vlad, and Henry knew—or cared, since she wasn't feeding on any of the *terra indigene* young.

"Am I going to be annoyed?" Tess asked.

"I think this might be advantageous for both of us." Nadine held out a letter.

That would be nice if it were true, Tess thought as she read the letter. "I don't understand. We get our supplies from Intuit and *terra indigene* farms."

"The Courtyard does; that's true. But those places send you an agreed-upon amount to provide for the *terra indigene* who are here, not for all the humans you're now permitting to shop at the Market Square stores. If you use the supplies so that I can make things for A Little Bite, you won't have any left to use anywhere else."

That was true enough. More quantity restrictions were going into effect throughout the Northeast Region—probably the whole of Thaisia—because of delays when shipping foodstuffs from one region to another. Shops received a guaranteed amount of rationed items based on the number of households that were registered with those shops. Since the Courtyard residents didn't receive ration books, it was unclear if they would be able to purchase anything in human stores.

"I went to the post office branch that used to deliver my mail," Nadine said. "I listed the Courtyard as the new address for my bakery as well as my personal address. Because so many of the bakeries in Lakeside burned the night mine was torched, a bakery that existed previously is still considered a viable commercial business even if the owner is running it out of his home kitchen. As part of the fair-distribution restrictions in effect, supplies are being reduced by a third of a bakery's previous usage. For most people, that's going to mean a loaf of bread will cost the same but be a smaller loaf in order to supply all the registered customers. And that means families like the MacDonalds and Debanys, and your tenants in the apartments, will want to buy what they can through the Courtyard. The supplies I'll receive will handle any baked goods those families may want, as well as being able to supply A Little Bite."

"So you'll use the kitchen here, but I'll buy the baked goods like I did when you were located in a separate place?"

"Yes. You'll pay me so my business will continue to operate as a business. I'll purchase my own supplies, pay rent for my apartment, and buy things from the Market Square shops."

It sounded like a way to complicate something that

should be a straightforward exchange, but if Nadine needed to do that in order to follow human rules and keep her business, Tess could work with that.

"As an individual, I'm going to register at shops in the Bird Park Plaza in order to purchase rationed supplies. I think all the human households should do that, since we have that option. That way, if we run out of something before the next earth native delivery, there will still be a way to purchase things."

Tess considered everything that had been said. Nadine had thought about this. Had Eve Denby or Twyla Montgomery been thinking about this too? What about Meg's female pack?

"All right, we'll try it. Do you need to put up a sign or something?"

"I thought we could put up a sign for the bakery near the coffee shop's back door. After all, that's where the supplies would be delivered."

And not advertising the bakery where the sign could be seen by humans driving on Crowfield Avenue was practical, since none of the Courtyard shops were open to the general public anymore.

Tess felt her hair relaxing out of its coils. "Anything else?"

"I heard Twyla Montgomery wants to use one of the efficiency apartments. Since the other three efficiencies are already taken, that doesn't leave any place for Emily Faire to live when she starts work at the medical office here. I'll have an extra bedroom when I move into my apartment. Emily is welcome to use it."

"I'll let her know." Tess watched a group of young men wearing white shirts, dark trousers with suspenders, and straw hats walk past the coffee shop's windows and go into Howling Good Reads. "Looks like the first job fair applicants have shown up. They'll be herded in here to fill out applications and wait."

"What do you think? Should we offer muffins and sandwiches?"

Tess nodded. Fresh faces, here for only a day. While she served them food and drink, she could sip a little life energy from each of them.

Preoccupied with the humans who suddenly swarmed the Courtyard's cluster of buildings, the smaller shifters didn't notice the odd silence, didn't catch the wild scent in the air.

The Elementals who were watching the swarm did notice those things but said nothing.

The lack of concern for a swarm both puzzled and intrigued the two Elders who had slipped into the Courtyard at first light—and confirmed that Lakeside was the right place to watch how different kinds of humans acted around earth natives. After they had watched long enough, they would share what they had learned—and the Elders in this part of the world would decide what kind of humans would be allowed to survive in Thaisia.

Simon wondered how the Simple Life folk on Great Island had spread the word to other communities so quickly. Maybe Simple Life communities had one telephone for emergencies and someone had called other communities in the Northeast Region to tell them there was potential work for anyone who wanted to resettle in the Midwest? However they had done it, the young men who had made the trip to Great Island and then traveled on a bus to Lakeside for these interviews had come from several communities around the Feather Lakes and Addirondak Mountains. There were even a few from a community in the High North on the other side of Lake Tahki.

Two dozen men who had lived and worked around animals. They were familiar with dairy cows, not the beef cattle that were raised in the Midwest Region, but they could ride a horse and knew how to mend fences and work around a farm. They all had older brothers who would inherit the family farms, so this was a chance for them to make a new beginning, to establish something for themselves.

Nothing smelled off about any of these men. Nothing raised his hackles. Nothing about them troubled Vlad either. They were ready, even eager, to work—and to have an adventure.

There was nothing wrong with the five women who also applied to work on ranches, although they, unlike the men, had questions. Did the ranches have a dairy cow to supply milk? Were there chickens for eggs and meat? Were there any sheep to supply wool for spinning and weaving? What about goats?

How was he supposed to know? Whatever had been there that hadn't run away or been eaten would be there when they arrived. As for supplies and whatever else was required, they would work that out with the residents of Bennett and Prairie Gold.

"Not bad for our first day," Vlad said when all the happy humans climbed into the bus to go back to Great Island and pack their belongings and inform their families that they were headed to the western edge of the Midwest. "Twenty-four men to work on the ranches and deal with the horses and cattle, and five women who will tend the ranch houses and cook."

"Four women," Simon said, locking HGR's front door with a relieved sigh. "I don't think the youngest female wanted to keep house or whatever humans call it. She kept talking about being able to ride a horse and how she had learned to lasso animals by practicing on the dairy cows and the goats."

"Well, Tolya will have to work that out." Vlad laughed. "He might end up with his own exploding fluffball." He stopped laughing. "I never considered that Simple Life humans would have exploding fluffballs."

Simon thought about the smile Merri Lee had given

them earlier in the day when they told her about her promotion and the smile that lit up the Simple Life woman's face when he said she could travel to Bennett for the final interview. Yep. Exploding fluffball. "That one is going to herd something, whether it has two legs or four. Better for Tolya and everyone else if they give her some cows to keep her busy—and happy."

"I wonder if her family was thinking the same thing," Vlad said dryly.

Amused—and glad they could no longer make a direct telephone call to, or receive one from, Bennett—Simon went upstairs to meet with the rest of the Business Association and discuss how they would feed the human pack.

Meg bit into her beef burger and chewed slowly, enjoying the flavor along with the novelty of eating at Meat-n-Greens with Simon and Sam in their human forms. They ate plenty of meals together, but it was usually at her apartment or in the summer room, not in the closest thing the Courtyard had to a human-style restaurant. This was new, and Simon wasn't the only one who was watching her for any sign that this new experience—and the number of humans who were also venturing in for some food—was causing distress.

There had been distress earlier in the day. She'd endured the pins-and-needles feeling that came in waves along with the people coming to the job fair, hoping to build a future for themselves in another part of Thaisia. She'd been tempted to go into the bathroom and make a tiny cut on a toe, but Nathan would scent even that much blood and raise a howling protest. That would bring Simon, who would feel angry with the strangers and shut down the fair.

She'd been given a chance at a new life. She didn't want to be the one who stopped other people from having the same chance. So she'd struggled with the craving to cut, telling herself it wouldn't help anyone because she wouldn't be able to ask anyone to listen when she spoke prophecy.

In the end, Nathan had made the decision for her by shifting to his human form and taking up a position in the doorway between the front room and sorting room. The deliverymen could see her working away in the sorting room, but it was Nathan who dealt with them and signed for the packages, giving her that much distance from actual contact.

It was enough—along with the Wolf eyes that watched every twitch she made and breath she took—to get her through the day. She'd left the office early to make her deliveries, getting back to the Green Complex long before the rest of the residents finished their workday. She'd sat in the summer room, doing nothing but listening to the birds chirping as they went about their own day in a part of the Courtyard that was, for the moment, free of Hawks.

By the time Simon got home, she was calm and ready to pick up Sam at the Wolfgard Complex so that the three of them could have this dinner together.

Meg felt prickles come and go as friends came in, but no one's presence produced the painful buzz that might compel her to make a cut. Eating at Meat-n-Greens wasn't a new experience that might overwhelm her. She'd been here with Ruth and Merri Lee. She'd even come in by herself for a meal. It was the experience of being here with Sam and Simon that was new—and that made her happy.

"Meg? You want a bite of my bison burger?" Sam held out his barely cooked burger. "It's really good."

A Wolf offering to share food wasn't a small gesture, but . . . "No, thank you, Sam. I have my own burger."

"But yours is *beef*," Sam protested, as if she'd been given inferior meat.

"I like beef better than bison," Meg assured him.

Sam looked stunned. "Why?"

"Enough, pup," Simon said. "Let Meg eat her burger in peace."

But Sam wasn't done exploring her food choices. "What about deer? Do you like deer better than beef?"

No, she didn't, but she was getting used to it, just as she was getting used to chops on the menu coming from other animals as well as pigs, and being served freshly caught duck or goose instead of chicken when the meat was listed as "poultry." She hadn't, to her knowledge, eaten elk, moose, or horse. She was pretty sure horse wasn't a meat offered in the Courtyard anymore, which made her wonder who ate the horsemeat now.

"Meg?" Just a hint of concern in Simon's voice.

Meg set her burger on her plate and picked up her fork to eat some of her salad. "I like deer meat, but I like beef better."

Sam ate a couple of bites of his burger. Then he turned to Simon. "Maybe Meg doesn't like eating deer because she doesn't get any of the best parts. Maybe you could give her some of the heart or—"

Meg's fork clunked on the plate. She swallowed hard to keep her suddenly queasy stomach from doing something that would ruin everyone's meal.

Simon's hand came down on Sam's head so fast, the boy didn't have time to flinch let alone avoid his uncle. Not a slap or a grab, just the weight of the leader's hand giving a warning, keeping a youngster from causing trouble.

Meg heard nothing, but she was sure plenty was being said between them using the *terra indigene* form of communication. Then Simon removed his hand, discipline completed.

Looking thoroughly chastised, Sam sat with his head bowed, his lower lip quivering, and his hands in his lap.

Meg looked at Simon, who resumed eating his meal as if nothing had happened. She wanted to mimic Simon's move, put her own hand on Sam's head, run her fingers through hair that was a mix of gold and Wolf gray. Whether it was fur or hair, the coloring made him distinctive. According to Jane, the Wolfgard bodywalker, the fur would change as Sam matured, becoming more of a gray shot with gold—better coloring for a hunter.

Privately, Meg hoped Sam would retain more of the gold color in his human form. All the girls would have crushes on him—as long as he didn't talk about his meat preferences.

Anxious looks from Sam. A different kind of look from Simon. More of a question: had Sam ruined her enjoyment of the meal?

Since she didn't want this to be the only time they ate together like this, she picked up her burger and took another bite, hoping her stomach had settled. She swallowed and nudged Sam. "Eat your burger. And your salad."

The chastised look faded. Sam gave her a happy-puppy grin and attacked his meal with enthusiasm.

Simon focused on his own food, seeming to ignore both of them. But the one time he looked at Meg, his amber eyes were filled with amusement.

Relieved that he wasn't angry with Sam, and a little bit curious about what had been said that she hadn't heard, Meg watched a couple of the Addirondak Wolves approach the counter where Michael Debany and Merri Lee were studying the menu board for the day's offerings. She couldn't hear them, but it was obvious that the humans were explaining how to place an order, pay for their meal, and receive a number that they would put on their table when they sat down. When the meal was ready, whoever was serving tables that day would bring the food over.

"Prickles?" Simon said so softly Meg barely heard him.

But she saw the way he watched her, and she considered the question. Wolves and humans interacting. She rubbed her foot against her calf. Was that a tingle or just an itch?

Meg shook her head and turned her attention back to her meal. No, there was no danger in the Courtyard. At least, not tonight.

As they walked out of Meat-n-Greens, Simon caught the back of Sam's shirt. "Meg and I are going to walk around the Market Square. If you stay out of trouble, we'll all have a scoop of ice cream before we go home."

Letting out a happy *arroo*, Sam raced away from them, heading straight for Nathan and Blair, who looked less than happy about the number of humans shopping in the Market Square that evening.

Watching Sam's bouncing enthusiasm, Simon linked his fingers with Meg's and they headed in the other direction. Since Blair led the hunt when the pack needed meat, Simon didn't want to hear the dominant enforcer's opinion of a human who preferred beef over venison. Beef had to be brought in from the farms that supplied the Courtyard; venison was available on the hoof right here.

But Simon wondered if he would be the only Wolf who would have a quiet word with Boone Hawkgard to make sure Meg received her share of any beef that came into the butcher shop.

"You eat hearts?" Meg asked as they wandered around the Market Square looking at the stores.

"If I tell you, will you throw up?"

"No."

He studied her and finally decided she wouldn't. "I'm the leader of the Courtyard and the dominant Wolf of the pack here. When we bring down game, I have first choice of the heart and liver. When I've had as much as I want of those meats, Elliot and Blair take the rest."

"What about lungs?"

She wasn't looking at him, but she sounded interested in an "I just found a big spider in my shoe" sort of way.

"We're Wolves, Meg. We eat most everything on a

deer. Even bones. Although a lot of times we don't eat the smaller ones as they are because they could splinter and get stuck in someone's throat. So we grind them up with a rock before eating them."

"Why eat bones?"

"The nanny in the pack where I grew up always said you eat strong bones to make strong bones."

"We drink milk to make strong bones."

"After a pup is weaned, there's not a lot of milk in the wild country."

Meg said nothing for a moment. "Has Sam eaten a heart?"

"He's displaying his dominance in the puppy pack," Simon replied. It thrilled him that Sam had come so far in just a few months, that the pup he'd had to keep in a cage after Daphne's death was not only playing with the other pups but showing the strength and personality of a Wolf who could lead a pack. "So, yes, I've allowed him to have a taste of a deer heart." He waited a beat. "Humans eat animal hearts and livers too."

Meg stopped walking. Her gray eyes were filled with alarm. "You're not going to make me eat heart or liver, are you?"

"I wouldn't make you eat anything you didn't want." Besides, the hearts and livers of their prey weren't items that would be offered in the butcher shop. Those delicacies belonged to the Wolves.

He just hoped he'd made it clear to Sam that Meg wouldn't appreciate the gift of a piece of deer heart or liver. Or lungs. Or brains. Or tongue.

He was pretty sure she wouldn't appreciate any of those things even if they came from a cow.

"You promise?"

"You don't have to eat them. And I promise I won't try to sneak any of them on your plate and trick you into eating them." He looked at her and laughed. "You get finicky about bits of meat, but you'll eat that yogurt stuff?"

"One has nothing to do with the other," Meg muttered.

But she didn't sound sure, which made him laugh again. He'd choose eating brains over yogurt any day.

Most of the human pack was in the Market Square this evening. Ruthie held a string bag, but she wasn't carrying food. It looked like she had a couple of books from the library and maybe a movie from Music and Movies. Kowalski came out of Chocolates and Cream carrying a small container. They paused for a moment to talk to Merri Lee and Debany before leaving the Market Square.

"Do you want to join them?" Simon asked, tipping his head to indicate the exploding fluffball and Debany.

"No. Since they have permission to be in the Market Square, Michael's parents are going to join them and celebrate Merri Lee's promotion." Meg looked around. "We're going to have some food restrictions, aren't we?"

"Nothing anyone needs to howl about." *You won't go hungry. Neither will Sam.* "We may not always have foods that come from outside the Courtyard, and there will be limits on how much the humans can purchase from the stores here, but we'll be all right."

Sam raced back to them. "Can we have ice cream now?"

"When Meg and I reach Chocolates and Cream, we'll get ice-cream cones."

"Skippy is here. Can he have one too?"

Simon was about to refuse. The juvenile Wolf with the skippy brain wouldn't be able to hold a cone.

"They could put Skippy's scoop of ice cream in a bowl," Meg said.

That settled it. Sam *arrooed*, and Skippy hurried to join them.

The ice cream was made in an Intuit community that had branched out from the original dairy farm that the *terra indigene* had permitted within their land. Other Intuit families had joined the dairy farmers, bringing skills that made use of the supply of milk. Some of those humans made cheeses. And one family made ice cream. Once a week, the refrigerated truck made the trip to Lakeside, followed by a van. Once a week, the Courtyard received ice cream and a selection of cheese in exchange for manufactured items the Intuits wanted—or for money if the trade that week wasn't an equal exchange.

After considering the humans who were connected to the Courtyard, Simon had asked for a larger supply of ice cream—enough so that everyone could have one scoop each week as a treat. He wasn't sure they would receive more. Cows produced only so much milk, and the ice-cream makers were dependent on the supplies they received. Still, he'd asked. He also knew asking for any additional food might not matter if the manufactured items the Courtyard brokered for *terra indigene* settlements and Intuit communities in the wild country were no longer available.

Those were problems for another day. This evening, they had ice cream.

Sam got a scoop of chocolate; Simon chose strawberry. Meg wanted vanilla, and Skippy was given a scoop of vanilla in a bowl, which Simon carried outside since he was the one among them whom the juvenile Wolf wouldn't dare try to knock over in order to get the treat.

They chose a bench where they could observe the comings and goings of everyone else who had ventured into the Market Square. Simon put the bowl on the ground and watched it scooting this way and that in response to Skippy's enthusiastic licking.

Then the bowl headed toward them. Meg made a V with her feet and the bowl scooted into the space.

Skippy looked up, growling that someone else was

claiming his treat. Simon bared his teeth and noticed Sam doing the same thing. But Skippy paid no attention to them; his eyes were focused on Meg.

"I'll hold the bowl for you," she said.

The growling stopped. Skippy licked the ice cream and seemed surprised that it didn't try to run away. He flopped down in front of Meg, his forelegs bracketing her feet, and happily licked his treat.

Simon turned his attention to his own cone, catching the drips. Sam was also focused on his cone. Then Meg sucked in a breath, and they looked at her.

"Ice-cream tongue," she said.

Sam looked at Skippy, who gave Meg's ankle a lick before turning back to the last bit of ice cream. He looked at Simon and grinned.

Simon flashed a grin at the pup and then looked away before Meg noticed. She had a special relationship with Sam. Because she was a *cassandra sangue*, she didn't feel like prey, didn't smell like prey. That had confused all of them when she'd first come to work for the Courtyard—especially him. But that difference had sparked Sam's curiosity, had drawn the pup out of the trauma of his mother's death. Meg was like a big sister who was wise and brainless at the same time.

It was a good match for Sam's puppy brain as long as there was an adult Wolf close by to make sure they didn't get into *too* much trouble.

When they'd finished the cones, Simon returned the bowl to Chocolates and Cream. As he came out of the shop, he saw Lieutenant Montgomery and all the members of his pack, along with the Denbys.

"Coming for some ice cream?" Simon asked.

"If that's all right," Montgomery said.

Simon nodded, pleased that Montgomery understood that making room for a different kind of pack required adjustments for everyone involved. "There are several flavors this week." He looked at the oldest female in that pack. "Miss Twyla."

"Mr. Simon." Twyla nodded her head. "It's a fine night."

It would have been finer if he'd been wearing fur instead of jeans and a shirt. Speaking of fur . . . Simon squinted. Meg stood there with her hands over her eyes. Behind her was a pile of discarded clothes and a furry Wolf pup.

Sam had had enough of the human form.

The pup gave Meg's knee a lick, making her squeak loudly enough to draw the attention of all the Wolves and Sanguinati in the square.

"I have to go," Simon said, seeing Blair and Nathan heading toward Meg.

Montgomery tried but couldn't quite keep a straight face. Miss Twyla didn't even try. The Denbys and the Sierra had glanced at Meg and Sam, then herded all the human children into the shop, sufficiently distracting them.

By the time Simon returned to Meg, Vlad had joined them, but Sam and Skippy had scampered off to sniff all the new and interesting scents.

<Do not lift your leg in the Market Square.> Simon's order was fast enough to stop Sam but not fast enough to stop Skippy.

"We're heading back to the Wolfgard Complex," Blair said. "We can take those two with us."

"If you want to shed your clothes and shift to Wolf, I can drop off all the clothing on my way home," Vlad offered.

"Meg and I will walk home, so you can take her BOW," Simon said.

"We're walking?" Meg said.

"It's a nice night." And happily, they had all discovered that the sweet blood of the *cassandra sangue*, while alluring to the *terra indigene*, repelled biting insects. Probably some instinct told the bugs that Meg's blood was lethal to them.

Nathan and Blair left the Market Square to discreetly shift into Wolf form. The two Wolves collected Sam and Skippy while Vlad collected the clothing and headed out in Meg's Box on Wheels.

That much settled, Simon smiled and turned back to Meg, looking forward to some time alone with her after a busy day full of human strangers. Then his smile faded and he looked to see who had caught her attention.

Lieutenant Montgomery. Miss Twyla. And, mostly, the Sierra, who was just coming out of the shop with an ice-cream cone, followed by her two daughters and Lizzy. Simon watched Meg watching the Montgomery pack and rubbing her right arm as if there was something buzzing under her skin.

"Let's go home, Meg." He took her hand and led her out of the Market Square, feeling the tension in her. He wanted to run, wanted to pull her away from the humans as fast as possible. But if she tripped, a scrape would be as bad as a cut with the razor. Worse, because a scrape might not leave a scar that would indicate that the skin had already been used for prophecy.

Eventually Meg relaxed and began to notice the small amount human eyes could see by moonlight.

"Something's coming," Meg whispered.

"We already knew that. You already drew the prophecy cards that warned us."

And her reaction tonight confirmed that the threat to the Courtyard and the city of Lakeside was connected to Montgomery and his pack.

"No." She pointed. "Something's coming."

He'd been focused on her, on the threat she'd seen coming toward Lakeside, and hadn't taken in the potential threat coming right at them now.

Not a threat, he decided as his fingers tightened on Meg's, then relaxed. This was just another Courtyard resident enjoying a fine summer night.

Air rode by on Mist—not the barrel-bodied, chubby-legged pony but the elegant, and dangerous, steed. The Elemental smiled at them as she passed, and Mist . . . misted.

Meg laughed as water droplets cooled warm skin.

Simon smiled, enjoying the pleasant sensation produced by the water—and by Meg's laughter.

CHAPTER 5

Windsday, Messis 8

Simon kept glancing at Meg as he drove the BOW toward the Market Square. Her hands were closed into tight fists and she stared straight ahead, not talking, not even paying attention to the land. If he hadn't been convinced already that she shouldn't spend the day around a crowd of strangers, he was certain of it now.

She had endured the first day of the job fair when it had been the Simple Life folk, and she had seemed to fully recover by the next morning. But she'd lasted only until noon on the second day of the job fair. Nathan had warned him about the itchy restlessness that had plagued Meg throughout the morning and kept the watch Wolf alert for the slightest hint of blood. That had made Simon, Vlad, and Tess look more closely at the humans crowded into A Little Bite and realize that humans from Lakeside were mixed in with the Intuits and Simple Life folk. Some came in because they saw other people inside the coffee shop and were curious—or simply wanted to buy a cup of coffee. Some came looking for work but backed out fast when they learned where they would be sent—and who would watch their every breath once they left Lakeside.

Those additional humans seemed to be the tipping point for Meg, overloading her ability to endure the futures of so many people prickling and buzzing under her skin. That was why Simon had already decided she wouldn't go to the Liaison's Office today—and already knew that she couldn't be left alone with the silver razor.

He slowed down as they reached the fork in the Courtyard's main road. Going straight would take them to the Market Square. Going to the right would take them to the Pony Barn. He saw a handful of ponies standing near the fork. Jester must have told them Meg was going to spend the morning with them and they were waiting for her.

"Stop." Meg's voice was barely audible, even to his Wolf-sharp hearing.

"We're almost—"

"Stop the BOW!" Her voice rose in a wail. "Stop!"

She opened the door and tried to leap from the BOW.

Simon grabbed her arm to keep her inside and stomped on the brakes. "Meg, wait."

She flailed at him, screaming and trying to scratch. The attack surprised him so much, he let go of her arm. Then she was out of the BOW and running back toward the Green Complex.

He threw the BOW into PARK, flung himself out the door, and ran after her.

Jenni Crowgard flew over him, then turned and flew back to him. <What's wrong with our Meg?>

<We have to stop her before she gets hurt.> Running in a blind panic, she could trip and fall.

She had a head start, but he was fast enough to catch her—and the ponies were even faster. Thunder got ahead of her and turned, blocking her path. She ran into him and bounced off his side, right into Simon's arms.

"I can't," she gasped.

"I know," he replied, holding her against him, the only comfort he knew how to give just then. "I know."

He heard Jenni still cawing a warning, heard Crows

responding—and heard a couple of Wolves respond as well.

<We're all right,> he told Jenni. Then he looked around and tried not to tense, tried not to show that he knew he was in the middle of a dangerous potential explosion. The ponies surrounded them, some of them so close Simon could feel their breath—and worry about those clompy pony hooves being so close to Meg's feet.

"Meg." He said her name as both warning and plea when the smoke that had been rushing toward them shifted into Nyx and Grandfather Erebus, who was the leader of the Sanguinati and doted on Meg. Having the Sanguinati wanting an explanation was bad enough. But most of the Elementals who lived in the Courtyard were also there.

"Did the humans upset our Meg?" Fire asked.

Not a question he wanted to answer.

As if unaware of everyone around them, Meg started finger combing Thunder's forelock. That seemed to calm her.

"Did they?" Erebus asked, his dry-leaves voice producing a skitter of fear down Simon's spine.

"What's all the howling about?" Jester asked. He had patches of fur on his torso and arms, indicating his haste in shifting to his human form after running up from the Pony Barn. Fortunately, enough of the Coyote was hidden by Mist's body that Meg wouldn't notice he was naked. "Doesn't Meg want to spend the morning with us at the Pony Barn?"

Damn Coyote, Simon thought when all the ponies tried to crowd in a bit more as if to encourage the correct answer.

"What?" Meg said.

Thunder licked her chin.

"You. Me. The ponies. All of us being sensible and staying away from the chaos in the Market Square," Jester said. "Simon already made arrangements for the mail to be brought there so you can sort it and the ponies can make the deliveries." He looked at Simon. "Didn't you tell her?"

Meg twisted in Simon's arms in order to look at him. "What?"

"Stupid human books," he growled. "It was supposed to be a nice surprise. Human females are supposed to like nice surprises." On the other hand, he'd been concerned about Meg's reaction to the job fair and only skimmed a couple of the kissy books they still had in stock, so he might have missed the part that would have told him that this was what usually happened when a male tried to give a female a nice surprise.

"Oh." Meg petted Lightning's nose. "We were going to the Pony Barn?"

"Yes. I was going to drop you off before going to Howling Good Reads to deal with the last group of humans." He really wanted someone unsuitable to show up today and give him an excuse to take a bite or two.

"Caw?"

<Meg is fine,> he said. Hopefully Jenni would pass along that message.

"I would like to go to the Pony Barn," Meg said.

"Good," Simon replied.

<Wolfgard,> Erebus said, his voice sounding too courteous.

"Can you walk back to the BOW and pick up your carry sack?" Simon asked Meg.

She blinked. Her eyes widened as she finally took in who had reacted to her panicked flight. She nodded.

Jester shifted to his Coyote form and quickly got out of the way of all the hooves as the ponies sorted themselves into two lines.

"Sorry," she said under her breath.

He gave her waist a light squeeze to tell her he'd heard her. Then he let her go and watched as the Elementals, led by Fire and Summer, and the ponies escorted Meg to the BOW and then on to the Pony Barn.

Jester looked at Simon. <Meg will be fine.> He ran,

passing Meg and her escorts in order to reach the Pony Barn first.

Simon turned to Erebus and noticed Blair standing by the side of the road, watching Meg. Then the dominant enforcer shifted to human and joined Simon and the Sanguinati.

"Why is the sweet blood so upset today?" Erebus asked.

Before Simon could decide the best way to respond, Blair said, "I was wondering the same thing. Why *is* Meg more upset today?"

"Overload," Simon replied. But was that all of it? "There were humans other than Intuit and Simple Life who came in yesterday. Vlad and I didn't recommend any of them to go on to Bennett. We wouldn't have hired them, so we weren't going to send them to Tolya to cause problems for him. But word about the job fair has spread beyond the preferred employees, so there are bound to be humans today looking for work."

Having human employees wasn't necessarily a bad thing. Barbara Ellen Debany was human, and Tolya was pleased with her as an employee and new resident of Bennett.

"Vladimir said he found unknown humans in the stock room yesterday," Erebus said.

Vlad hadn't told him that. But that explained why HGR's comanager wanted the back door of the store locked during the day. Humans could be as curious as Crows, so an unlocked door could be the next best thing to an invitation to come in and look around.

"Nathan ran off a human who had been sneaking toward the Market Square, but the man escaped through the door between the customer parking lot and the employee parking lot," Blair said.

He hadn't been told about that either. As the Courtyard's leader, he should have been told. Then again, he was handling the interviews of the humans Vlad felt had potential—or weren't obviously unsuitable—so

Vlad and Blair probably felt he didn't need to know about things they'd already dealt with.

"I'm going to put up sawhorses to make it harder for someone to sneak down the access way, and Nathan and Jake Crowgard will handle the Liaison's Office," Blair continued. "Marie Hawkgard is going to watch the door between the parking lots. Any human trying to get in that way will get whatever she feels like giving."

Marie's talons would certainly make an impression.

"And I'm going to keep watch around the consulate," Nyx said. "Like a tourist guide, directing humans to where they're supposed to be—and away from where they shouldn't go."

And feeding on every one of them.

For a moment, Simon envied the Sanguinati's ability to feed so subtly that the prey didn't know anything had happened. If a Wolf tore off a chunk of meat, it was pretty obvious.

Damn. He needed something to eat before he started talking to all those humans.

"The question was not answered, Wolfgard," Erebus said. "Why is the sweet blood so upset today?"

Simon thought about Meg and the prophecy cards that indicated trouble was coming. But what if the trouble was already here and had no connection to Lieutenant Montgomery's pack, despite Montgomery's concerns about his brother?

Theral MacDonald took care of the medical office in the Market Square and was part of Meg's female pack. She had run away from her abusive mate, but a couple of disturbing packages had been sent to her here at the Courtyard—proof that the bad male knew where to find her. Unfortunately, the *terra indigene* hadn't found him.

It would be so easy for a potential enemy to mingle with the rest of the humans who had a legitimate reason to be in the Courtyard today.

<Jenni?> he called, scanning the trees until he spot-

ted the Crow. <Are you and Starr going to be working at Sparkles and Junk today?>

<Maybe.>

<I'd like you to keep watch around the Market Square even if you don't open the shop.>

She stared at him, then flew off.

Now Simon looked at Blair and Erebus. "I'd like a few Sanguinati in smoke form in the Market Square and a couple in human form in A Little Bite and Howling Good Reads. Unless Jane is needed in the Wolfgard Complex, have her spend the day with Theral in the medical office."

"You think that Jack Fillmore might try for Theral?" Blair asked, flickers of red appearing in his amber eyes.

"It's possible he was the human Nathan ran off yesterday," Simon replied. "With so many unknown humans milling around, it would be a good time for it."

"You think that is what the sweet blood is feeling?" Erebus asked.

Simon shrugged. "Trouble might try to hide among the humans at the job fair today. That could be the future that is buzzing under Meg's skin."

They parted. Erebus and Nyx shifted back to smoke. She headed for the Market Square while Erebus returned to the Chambers to select the Sanguinati he wanted guarding the stores—and the Courtyard's residents. Blair headed back to the Utilities Complex to pick up the sawhorses. And Simon hurried back to the BOW to get to Howling Good Reads and select the professionals who were suited to life in a Midwest town ruled by the *terra indigene* and surrounded by Namid's teeth and claws.

Meg watched Jester as he made a pad of blankets to cover a hay bale. Once he was satisfied, he invited her to sit.

Feeling embarrassed about causing a scene, and wondering how much trouble she'd made for the humans who were coming to the Courtyard today, she gave Jester a wobbly smile when he squatted in front of her.

"This is what I'm wondering," he said.

Did he know his ears were still Coyote-shaped and furry?

"You've lived in the Courtyard for several months now, and you've been learning all kinds of things during that time. So why are you dumber now than you used to be?"

Meg stiffened. "Jester! That's not a nice thing to say, even as a joke."

"I'm not joking."

She studied his face, his eyes, and realized he really wasn't joking, wasn't saying something to create a bit of mischief. Jester being completely serious made her uneasy.

"Humans talk about having a role model, someone they can learn from," Jester continued. "You know who I think you've been using as a role model lately?"

"Ruth or Merri Lee?"

He shook his head. "Skippy."

Meg stared at the Coyote. "But Skippy . . ."

"Has a skippy brain and has trouble holding on to parts of what he's learned, which is why youngsters like him don't usually survive in the wild country. If Skippy chases a deer and gets knocked down and bruised, he should learn that deer could hurt him if he isn't careful. But what his brain understands is *that* particular deer could hurt him, so he goes out the next morning and chases a different deer—and gets knocked down again. And maybe this time the injury is serious because he's still healing from the previous day's bumps and bruises.

"When the Elementals and Elders struck Lakeside a few weeks ago, you knew you couldn't stay near the humans who were offered shelter around the Market Square. You came to the Pony Barn—a place where you wouldn't have to deal with humans and also wouldn't be alone. You showed sense, Meg. Then Simon and

Vlad do this job fair to help Tolya find the workers he needs in Bennett, and what do you do? You spend the whole first day working in the Liaison's Office—a place you already knew wasn't safe for you when there are so many strangers around—and get knocked over by the pressure of being close to so many potential futures. And those were Simple Life folk, who should have been the easiest humans to deal with. So what do you do on the second day of the fair? You go into the office and get knocked over harder and faster. But you were still going to open the office today. Why?"

Put that way, it did sound pretty dumb.

"All my friends could do their jobs, even with the job fair going on," Meg mumbled, not meeting his eyes. "I didn't want to be different."

Jester looked bewildered. "But you are different."

"I don't want to be the one who can't cope with something that is easy for everyone else to do."

"How do you know it's easy?"

She leaned toward him until they were almost nose to nose. "They're in the Market Square, doing their jobs."

"They're not going to cut themselves to release some of the hornet's nest of prophecies that are buzzing under the skin. They may wonder what the future holds for those humans, but they're not going to hurt themselves to find out." Jester leaned back a little. "You don't want to be different? I understand that. I'm the only Coyote here in a Courtyard controlled by Wolves. It's not dangerous for me to be here like it would be for a regular coyote to tangle with a pack of wolves, but I am alone here."

"Do you wish it was different, that there was someone else like you? Or that you could be like another group of *terra indigene*, fit in with them better?"

"Being the only one can have advantages. Looking after the ponies and dealing with the girls at the lake isn't without risk, and I might not have taken that risk if there had been other Coyotegard here to work with as part of a pack. I probably wouldn't have lived in the

Green Complex with Wolves and Sanguinati and a Grizzly, not to mention Tess. But I am the only Coyote in this Courtyard, and I get to poke my nose in all kinds of things my kind usually wouldn't see."

"You're even more curious than the Crowgard," Meg said.

"You say that like it's a bad thing."

She laughed.

Jester thought for a moment. "What would have happened in Lakeside these past few months if you hadn't been different from the other humans who work here?"

Meg shifted on the hay bale as she considered the question. Regular humans had worked in the compound where she'd lived. But she wouldn't have been one of them, wouldn't have taken a job where other people, where *children*, were treated like property. Would she? "I probably wouldn't have traveled to Lakeside if I hadn't run away from the Controller and followed the visions that showed me how to escape. I—" *wouldn't have met Sam . . . or Simon.*

"Simon opened a few of the stores to humans and had human employees for several years before you arrived. They were considered nonedible, but we still saw them as prey. If you, the human who was not prey, hadn't come along looking for a job, Simon, Vlad, Henry, and Tess wouldn't have changed the way they thought of the human employees—and some of those humans might have died in the blizzard last Febros. If the females working here hadn't become your friends, hadn't become a human pack the Wolfgard and Sanguinati decided to protect, those humans wouldn't have been sheltered here when the Elders came through the city. If you weren't here, Simon and Lieutenant Montgomery wouldn't have had a particular reason to work together, and Montgomery wouldn't have had a way to prove he was a trustworthy human. If you weren't here, Nathan would have stayed with the Addirondak Wolfgard for the full time he was supposed to be away from the Courtyard, and Lizzy might not have reached Lakeside because Nathan wouldn't have been on the train to protect her." Jester stood up. "All those things happened because you're different, Meg. Don't be so quick to want to be like everyone else. Crows and Hawks and Owls can fly. I can't. I don't need to jump off a cliff to prove it to myself. Why do you?"

Jester headed for the doors. Then he stopped. "What would you have told another *cassandra sangue* if she'd pushed herself like you have these past couple of days? Being the Trailblazer means being a role model for the other girls. You should think about that."

He walked outside. Meg sat on the hay bale, listening to Jester talking to the ponies.

What would she have told another blood prophet, especially a young girl who hadn't been cut yet and had a chance of escaping the addiction to cutting? She would have told the girl not to go to the office, not to push when she was already feeling uncomfortable. She would have told her to respect her limitations as well as her abilities.

She hadn't done any of those things for herself.

In the beginning, she hadn't cared that she was different. She was alive and free, and, thinking she had only a few weeks to live, she'd thrown herself into experiencing as much as she could. But she'd misinterpreted the prophecy and hadn't died—or her future had changed because Simon and several other *terra indigene* had saved her. In the beginning, she'd had only a small window into the lives of the humans who became her friends. Now, with some of them living across the street from the Courtyard, she saw more of what it meant to have a human life with friends and family. Some of it was bad, but most of it was good. She saw people doing things that overwhelmed her, and she envied their ability—and she didn't think any of them felt envious of her abilities.

Had she been trying to prove she could be different from and yet the same as other humans?

Being different didn't mean she couldn't fit in. She'd been learning to fit in with the Others since the night she stumbled into Howling Good Reads looking for a job. And now she'd stumbled again by reaching for something she wasn't even sure she wanted instead of looking at what she already had with Simon and Sam and the rest of her friends in the Courtyard.

All right, so she couldn't fly. But she was the one who could tell her friends when to stay on the ground because there was a storm coming.

Simon read through Jana Paniccia's résumé a second time and decided not to ask how she'd heard about the job fair.

He set the résumé aside and studied the Jana. Taller than most of the female pack, but not as tall as the males in the police pack. Brown hair, brown eyes. Looked vigorous and healthy. Smelled clean.

She'd been nothing but polite since she'd sat across the desk from him for the last part of the job interview, but she reminded him of a small predator who believed it was larger and fiercer than anything around it—and managed to make larger predators believe it too.

"You want to work for the police?" he asked.

"No." One of her hands smoothed her skirt, the first sign of nerves she'd shown. But her eyes showed a hint of anger, not nerves. "I don't want to be a dispatcher or a secretary. I don't want to work *for* the police; I want to be a police officer. They let me attend the academy, let me pay for all the classes and training, let me believe I could be hired for the job. I put up with all the crude comments about wanting to grow a pair of balls. I spent hours at the shooting range to learn to be proficient with firearms. I took more self-defense classes than any of my male classmates. I bought extra books about the law and law enforcement and studied them on my own. I passed all my courses and graduated in the top five percent of my class, but I still can't be a serving police officer because I have breasts instead of balls."

Simon waited for her to regain control of her emotions. Obviously he'd stomped on her tail by asking what he'd thought was a simple opening question. And he wondered just how much teasing she had received—and why human males would train a female to shoot a gun and then tease her into being angry enough to shoot them.

"I'm sorry for speaking so crudely," the Jana finally said.

But not for being angry, Simon thought. "You want to be a police officer."

"Yes." She pointed at the paperwork. "You can see that I'm qualified."

"You realize the job is in a town in the Midwest, which is under the *terra indigene*'s control?"

The Jana nodded.

"The new sheriff is a Wolf. You would be working as one of his deputies." Maybe Virgil's only deputy. "You understand that?"

She nodded again.

"Before we send you to Bennett to talk with Tolya Sanguinati and Virgil Wolfgard, I want the police here to confirm your skills." She didn't look happy about that, so he added, "Can you ride a horse?"

The anger vanished from her face and her eyes brightened. "I could be a mounted deputy?"

What was it with human females and horses? "That would be something to discuss with Tolya and Virgil." He noticed that she hadn't said she knew how to ride a horse, but that would be Tolya's problem if he wanted her to stay.

He and Vlad had agreed it was best to send all the job candidates on two trains so that no one would be traveling alone. He'd have to nip a few people to get the Jana on the second train.

"Your skills will be reviewed tomorrow," Simon said. "If everyone agrees, you can catch the train the day after. Will that be a problem?" Humans always seemed to need considerable time to leave a den.

"Not a problem. I can fit my clothes and personal items into two suitcases. That and three boxes of books are everything I own."

He wondered if that had always been true. He looked at her résumé again. Nothing about her family pack. But she was here in the Courtyard looking to work in a place far from the Northeast. Maybe her family pack had supported the Humans First and Last movement and she'd been driven out because she hadn't. No way to know, and it really didn't matter. But there was one other thing on the résumé that caught his eye because so few of the humans had mentioned other skills beyond the professional ones.

"Writing is your hobby?" he asked. "What kind of writing?"

"Fiction, mostly. I've sold a few short stories to magazines, but lately I've been writing . . . observations."

Simon tried to keep his ears from shifting to Wolf to show interest. Officer Debany grumbled about the lack of news from his sister. With so many humans migrating to Bennett, other families would be grumbling as well. Maybe having someone like the Jana writing observations, whatever those were, that could be published in the Courtyard's newsletter or Great Island's newspaper would make the humans who were left behind feel easier about the ones who were leaving. Something to discuss with Vlad before passing on the information to Tolya.

Saying nothing more about the writing, they agreed upon a time the next morning when she would come to the Courtyard.

The moment Vlad confirmed that the Jana had left

Howling Good Reads, Simon placed a call to Captain Burke, asking him to come to the Courtyard.

Douglas Burke read the résumé and transcript a second time before handing it back to Simon Wolfgard. He owed the leader of this Courtyard, but there were some things he couldn't do.

"We need to know if the Jana is really qualified to be a police officer," Simon said.

"On paper, she's certainly qualified." Burke sighed. "Whether it's fair or not, women aren't hired for positions as serving officers. They are not on the street."

"That's your rule, not ours," Simon replied. "In a pack, males are the enforcers because they're bigger and stronger. But females are important in a hunt because they're lighter and faster. They can run the prey until it tires, and then the males bring it down."

"That may be, but I still can't hire her." Although if the Others were so set on having a female police officer working with them, maybe the new mayor and police commissioner would be willing to bend the rules, which would set a precedent for other women who wanted to go into active police work. Hiring Ms. Paniccia also would solve the problem of finding a partner for Officer Debany.

Simon growled softly, as if warning off a rival. "*We* want to hire the Jana to go to Bennett and be a deputy. We want *you* to confirm she's properly trained to do the fighting and hunting." He paused, then added, "But you don't have to test if she can ride a horse. Someone in Bennett will do that."

Well, damn. "Let me see that transcript again." If she were a man, he'd definitely want her as one of his patrol officers. "What about the sheriff? Will he have a problem with a female deputy?"

"Virgil will have more of a problem with her being human, but Tolya thinks they need a human to help keep the peace."

"Does Virgil have any training in law enforcement?"

"He was a dominant enforcer. He knows how to kill."

Struck by a tone in Simon's voice, Burke studied the Wolf. Had Virgil lost family members when the Humans First and Last movement killed so many of the Wolfgard? Wasn't a question he could ask, but he had the feeling Virgil Wolfgard had never had the tolerance for humans that Simon did.

Suddenly he could see the value of having a human female police officer to balance a male Wolf's aggressive reaction when it came to humans disturbing the peace.

"When do you need to know?" Burke asked.

"Can you test her tomorrow? If she qualifies, she can go with the others who are leaving on the train the day after."

"I'll meet her here and take her to the firing range. We'll go on from there."

"Barbara Ellen will need a roommate besides Buddy. The Jana could live with her."

"About Buddy." Michael Debany had been rattled after receiving the news about his sister's living arrangements, and Burke kept a close eye on officers who were rattled for any reason.

Simon opened a desk drawer, removed a piece of paper, and handed it to him. "Vlad asked. Tolya replied. We told Debany."

Burke read the message and laughed. Well, that explained why Debany had looked a bit sheepish these past few days whenever anyone asked about his sister.

"Once the Jana arrives in Bennett, Barbara Ellen will have a roommate with a gun. She will be safe from unwanted males, so Officer Debany doesn't need to worry anymore."

It sounded like an attempt to reassure, and it made him curious. "Would you want Meg to have a roommate with a gun?"

Simon looked puzzled. "Why would Meg need one? She has me when she's home and Nathan is the watch Wolf when she's in the Liaison's Office. And if someone defeated the Wolves, they would have to deal with Vlad and Henry and Tess and the girls at the lake."

The slightest change in Wolfgard's eyes, in his stance, made Burke realize Simon had been wearing the persona of the bookstore owner for these interviews—and had, for the most part, maintained that persona while talking to him about Jana Paniccia. Until now.

"We'll keep Meg safe," Simon said. "And Theral."

Burke stiffened. "Has Jack Fillmore tried to see her?"

"Some humans were sniffing around where they shouldn't have been. They were driven off before they caused trouble. We don't have the scent of that Jack Fillmore, so I can't say if he was one of them. But Theral doesn't need a roommate with a gun. Not in the Courtyard."

Message received. "I heard that Katherine Debany will be working for Elliot Wolfgard."

"Yes. She starts tomorrow. Miss Twyla will also work there in the mornings, helping with the files." Simon smiled, showing a canine that was a little too long to be human. "They both looked at the files this morning. Elliot said he's never heard a human say so much by just saying *tsk*."

"A skill some women perfect." Burke pushed out of the chair. "We'll see you and Ms. Paniccia tomorrow morning."

He went downstairs and spent a few minutes looking at the books on the display table, finally selecting a thriller by a *terra indigene* author and a story by a human author that was set in a frontier town from a hundred years ago. He had a feeling that living in Bennett was going to be somewhere between the two.

He paid for the books, then returned to the Chestnut Street station to inform Lieutenant Montgomery that he and his team would be helping to review the qualifications of a young woman who was going to wear a badge, carry a gun . . . and ride a horse.

Late that night, an odd silence followed the Elders' path as they moved through the Courtyard unseen.

They prowled around the denning place where the Wolf and Grizzly and other *terra indigene* lived. Where the howling not-Wolf lived. They spent time learning the scents of the humans who did not leave proper markers around the patch of turned earth but were present often enough that their scent rubbed off on the ground and on the plants. Then they moved on to the buildings across from the Courtyard, identifying the dens of the humans the Elementals had told them belonged to the not-Wolf's pack. Standing on their hind legs, they had looked in the upstairs windows of one den with mingled male and female scents. Was the female in season? That was interesting, but the male suddenly sat up as if he could sense their presence. A hunter in the human pack?

They returned to the Courtyard before the human became too uneasy and sounded an alarm. Even so, they heard a door open, saw the male come out to the open part of the den and look around. He would not see them. Could not see them since they were in their true form. But he'd known something was out there in the dark, watching him—watching his mate. Not many humans sensed their presence. That made this human different from others of his kind. Different, a hunter, but not seen as a threat by the smaller shifters. That was interesting too.

They circled the building that was the not-Wolf's other den—the place where they had found the tasties hidden inside a tough shell. The female pushed at the door, curious about what they might find in the den this time. Then they heard a human stirring upstairs, caught the scent of metal and oil when the door above them opened—a scent they associated with a human weapon.

Another hunter in the human pack?

So easy to grab the male from his high perch and crush him in their jaws, tear open the soft belly with their claws.

Then a Wolf howled. Had the first human hunter sounded an alarm after all?

It was a single voice, but it would be enough to wake the pack. Both packs.

Disappointed that they hadn't found the tasties, they still felt pleased by the reaction of both kinds of hunters to a potential threat. Retreating to the spot in the Courtyard that they had chosen for their resting place, they considered what they had learned—and decided it was time to let the Wolf and Grizzly know they were there.

Dear Douglas,

I hope this finds you well. Brittania survived the recent storms, which only gave our island a glancing blow on their way to Cel-Romano. The savage retaliation against the Cel-Romano Alliance of Nations for the deaths of so many shifters and the attempt to seize some of the wild country and bring it under human control has caused plenty of sleepless nights for everyone here in Brittania— especially government officials and those of us in law enforcement. It has made me grateful that I was able to spend a little time in the Lakeside Courtyard when I visited you in Juin. Having some knowledge of how to work with the Others has been a tremendous help.

Everything we've heard about Cel-Romano is just scraps of information coming from people who live in fishing and farming settlements in the wild country and have traded goods with Brittania for generations. And their information comes from rumors from border villages that were spared the full force of the attacks.

According to the rumors, every factory that built the weapons that were used against the shifters was destroyed. In that, the Others were merciless, and in some cases, an entire city was laid to waste. There is rumored to be a wealth of salvage in those places—metals, tires, tools, even money; it's also rumored that few who go in to grab whatever they can carry survive the predators who have staked out those broken cities as their hunting grounds. Salvagers who enter as healthy men come out dying of some kind of plague, if they come out at all.

Many villages and towns were left untouched. There is limited fuel for motor vehicles because fuel depots are now surrounded by wild country, and only humans who have dealt fairly with the Others in the past have any chance of being allowed access to the fuel.

Cel-Romano used to be the largest area of unbroken human-controlled land in the world, encompassing all the land around the Mediterran Sea as well as the land around the western and southern shores of the Black Sea. Now each nation is divided from the rest by broad veins of wild country. It's said the land doesn't look different— there are still roads and human farms and villages—but it feels different. Dangerous. The people who live on the farms and in the villages claim they are safe enough during the day, but strangers trying to cross that land rarely survive. And no one is safe in the dark.

Electronic communication in Cel-Romano is limited or nonexistent. In fact, smaller villages are more likely to have working telephones than what's left of the industrial cities. But service is erratic since many of the telephone lines running through the new veins of wild country were torn down and can't be repaired.

That is the information that has reached us. Best guess from what I can piece together? Veins of the wild country will continue to spread throughout Cel-Romano, isolating people on smaller and smaller pieces of land. Some communities will survive, may even thrive, while other places will wither until they, and the people who lived there, are nothing more than a memory or cautionary tale.

Take care, Douglas. I hope Lakeside is one of the places in your part of the world that continues to survive and thrive. I'll stay in touch as best I can.

—*Shady*

CHAPTER 6

Thaisday, Messis 9

Meg put her carry sack in the back of the BOW, then stepped back and smiled at Simon. "I want to walk to work."

"But I need to get to the office early today."

"Which is why you need to drive the BOW." Okay, that wasn't quite true. Even in human form, Simon could easily walk to the Market Square and get to Howling Good Reads in plenty of time for his early meetings. But he couldn't get there on time if he kept to *her* walking pace. "I want to look at the garden and see what vegetables we can pick, and I just want to move this morning."

He sighed, a sound that held so much disappointment that Meg almost relented. She enjoyed going into work with Simon, liked the companionship. But she didn't want to go to the Liaison's Office early—and she didn't want anyone with her as she approached the Market Square, just in case whatever had triggered her distress yesterday was still there. The job fair was over, so she should be fine, but Simon would be unhappy if she had another panic attack, and she didn't want him distracted from helping the remaining people who were waiting for a decision about whether they were going to Bennett.

"I'll be fine, Simon." When he continued to stand beside the BOW, she added, "I'll let you know as soon as I reach the office."

What would Merri Lee or Ruth do to convince a male to go along with her plan?

Meg walked up to Simon, went up on her toes, and licked his cheek. Okay, Merri or Ruth would have given him a human kiss, but judging by the surprised and pleased look in his eyes, he didn't care about that.

He ran a hand over her short black hair and gave her a light scritch behind her ear. Then he got into the BOW and drove away.

Feeling independent and competent and free, Meg left the Green Complex and walked on the grass to reach the big kitchen garden. Along with the Green Complex's residents, she and her human friends had been harvesting vegetables for the past few weeks. They'd picked a bit of this and that during Sumor, but now it seemed there were all kinds of vegetables that needed to be picked every day—and whether it was true or not, it *felt* like she was picking zucchini every day. The peppers were growing and almost ready, and there would be fresh corn soon. It was fun to come out here and see what was flowering and what was getting ripe and . . .

What was that?

White and red. And a patch of brown over there. And . . .

A couple of days ago, she had startled a young rabbit grazing near the garden. She hadn't meant to; she just hadn't seen it. But when it moved, it had dragged a hind leg. Had it been hit by a car? The complexes weren't built that close to the city's streets, but animals did cross the streets looking for food. Julia Hawkgard told her dead prey was often found on the grass beside Parkside Avenue—animals that had been moving from the park to the Courtyard or the Courtyard to the park. But Parkside Avenue was on the other side of the Courtyard. An injured rabbit wouldn't cross all that land.

Meg approached cautiously, her stomach already doing little flips.

White bone stripped of muscle but still connected with ligaments—and still attached to a furred foot. The patch of brown turned out to be a hunk of fur. And the red . . . Was that the bunny's backbone?

Meg backed up and screamed when she hit something.

Big hands held her up. Henry's voice rumbled above her head. "It's just a rabbit, Meg."

"Someone ate the bunny."

"No one in the Green Complex. Not all the hunters who look for food in the Courtyard are *terra indigene*."

"Do you think Simon . . . ?" He ate bunnies. So did Sam. So did all her neighbors except maybe Tess and Vlad, and she wasn't sure they hadn't. Even she had eaten rabbit a few times. But it had been cooked. And nothing on her plate had looked like *that*.

"None of your friends ate the rabbit," Henry said.

"How do you know?"

"They wouldn't have left bones and scraps where you or the female pack would find them." He put his arm around her shoulders and led her away from the garden.

"He had an injured leg," Meg said when they reached the Courtyard's main road and started walking toward the Market Square.

"That made him easy prey." They walked in silence for a minute before Henry said, "Why did Simon leave you behind?"

"I wanted to walk to work. Wanted the extra time to approach the Market Square." Meg sighed. "If I'd gone with Simon, I wouldn't have seen the bunny, the . . . backbone." Seeing the leg bones hadn't been so bad, but the image of the backbone would stay with her.

"All meat hopped or ran or flew before it became meat," Henry said. "That is the way of things."

She nodded. That was the way of things. But the raw truth was a little harder to accept.

Shit, fuck, damn, Simon thought when Henry told him about Meg's discovery. "Better tell whoever is cooking at Meat-n-Greens today not to put rabbit on the menu board."

"I already did," Henry said. "But that one looked like it was eaten where it was caught."

When she saw an injured bunny, Meg's feelings would have gone all gooey. A Wolf, seeing the same thing, would have grabbed the quick meal and taken it to the Wolfgard Complex for the pups or eaten it himself.

"I will go back and dispose of the bones and scraps," Henry said. "You should find something to distract our Meg so she doesn't spend the day thinking about the rabbit."

"There's not . . ." Simon looked at the box that had been picked up at the train station early that morning. "I might have something to distract her." Of course, he hadn't done more than glance at the books Jesse Walker had sent for his review and had no idea if they were exciting mystery-thrillers with lots of chasing or scary stories. Well, if the books scared Meg and she kicked him because of bad dreams, he couldn't snarl at anyone but himself.

Simon picked up the box and left the office, pausing long enough to tell Vlad he was going to the Liaison's Office.

The back door of the Liaison's Office was locked. He'd expected that. What he hadn't expected was to hear a footstep on the stairs above him and see Greg O'Sullivan looking down at him, a hand on the service weapon the ITF agent carried.

"Mr. Wolfgard." O'Sullivan's hand moved away from the weapon. He came down the stairs, his steps quick and light. "Didn't know it was you."

Simon watched the agent. Nadine Fallacaro and Eve Denby both said the second room above the office was similar to a hotel room, with the perk of a small fridge to hold cold drinks or snacks. O'Sullivan had been happy to become the tenant, saying it was more secure than a regular hotel room, and he could leave personal items there when he needed to travel back to Hubbney and report to Governor Hannigan. "Were you expecting someone else?"

"No, but I'd heard that, during the job fair, a few people had been poking around where they didn't belong—and I thought I heard someone testing the back door late last night. Just wanted to make sure no one was trying to bother Ms. Corbyn."

A different kind of watch Wolf, Simon decided as he studied O'Sullivan. Not an unattached male sniffing around his Meg, but a member of the larger pack committed to protecting the territory that sheltered all of them—which meant O'Sullivan needed to be warned about the Courtyard's guests.

Simon hadn't seen them, had been too busy dealing with humans to even sense their presence or catch their scent. But Kowalski had called Blair last night, and after the dominant enforcer had sniffed the ground around Kowalski and Ruthie's den this morning, Blair told Simon that two of the Elders had returned to Lakeside. That was the reason he had asked Henry to delay going to the Market Square—so that Meg wouldn't be walking alone. And that was why Henry had been there when Meg found the bunny backbone.

He wasn't ready to discuss that with the humans, so he changed the subject. "Katherine Debany is starting her new job at the consulate."

"I met her yesterday," O'Sullivan said. "And Miss Twyla." He rubbed the back of his neck. "Made me feel like I was being scrutinized by two strict but affectionate aunts. I checked all the drawers in the desk I'm using to make sure there wasn't anything there that might get me into trouble. I have a feeling those two have heard the 'it isn't mine' defense too many times to believe it."

The ITF agent had struck Simon as intense and distant, focused on his job and more of a lone wolf. Now he saw a glimpse of the juvenile the man had been. "Older females are good for a pack."

O'Sullivan smiled and made a noncommittal sound before heading to A Little Bite for breakfast.

Simon unlocked the back door of the Liaison's Office, walked in, and heard something make a rhythmic *slap, slap, slap* on wood. "Meg?"

<She is restless,> Nathan reported from his spot in the front room. <And she's angry at the mail.>

Meg slapped another letter on the sorting room table. Simon approached the table cautiously and set the box on a corner. "Meg?"

"I don't want to be a bunny! Bunnies get eaten!"

"Sooner or later, everything gets eaten," he countered.

She growled at him. She looked as ferocious as a puppy. He wanted to give her a couple of licks and find a toy. If they could play for a few minutes, she would forget about the bunny.

No, she wouldn't. Meg wasn't a puppy, and she didn't forget something once she'd seen it. At least, she didn't forget something she'd seen unless it was veiled by the euphoria that was produced by cutting.

He didn't like that thought, so he picked up the box and put it in front of her. "When you're done with the mail, I need a favor."

Meg frowned at the box. "A favor?"

"Jesse Walker sent me some books that we don't sell at Howling Good Reads."

It was a shame Meg couldn't prick her ears to show interest. It certainly looked like she wanted to.

"Crowgard cozies?" she asked.

"More thriller than cozy, I think." Simon tapped the

box. "Jesse Walker says Intuits like the stories, but I'd like to know if you think the stories would appeal to the *terra indigene* and the human pack."

"So I'm like a book reviewer for the store?"

He nodded, watching her. It suddenly occurred to him that this was a new thing, something not part of Meg's routine. Would it upset her? No, she looked intrigued.

Meg set the box aside. "I have to finish sorting the mail first." She blinked at him. "Aren't you supposed to be working?"

He glanced at the clock. He was late for his meeting with Captain Burke.

Giving the tip of her nose a quick lick, Simon walked out of the sorting room. He looked back when he reached the door. Meg was sorting the mail, but she kept glancing at the box.

Feeling lighter, as if they'd had a few minutes of playtime, he wondered how many pieces of mail the ponies would have to redeliver because he'd found the right distraction.

Sitting in A Little Bite with Jana Paniccia, Monty smiled at the young woman. Early that morning, Captain Burke had taken her to the firing range to review her skill with the weapons commonly used by the police. Kowalski and Debany had been tagged to test her hand-to-hand and self-defense skills. And he and Burke had reviewed her transcript. Now, while Simon Wolfgard was listening to Burke's opinion of Ms. Paniccia's ability to serve as a deputy, Monty was here to talk—and to listen.

"Waiting is always hard," he said. And the hardest part for him, for Burke, even for Kowalski and Debany, was wondering if they were sending a young—and female—officer too far into the unknown, where her new boss would either accept her or eat her.

"It's brutal." Jana glanced toward the archway leading into Howling Good Reads.

"Going to Bennett is a big decision. It won't be like anything you've known. It certainly won't be like living in Lakeside." While that was certainly true, Monty wondered if the town would be run like a Courtyard with a larger business district.

"I know. But it's a place ripe with possibilities." Jana laughed a little. "I loved stories about the frontier and the sheriff squaring off against villains who wanted to take over a town that was the only human place for hundreds of miles. My favorite stories usually had a feisty woman who was held captive and whacked one of the villains with a frying pan and escaped in time to warn the sheriff."

"You wanted to be the feisty woman?"

"Well, no. I wanted to be the sheriff, and in my versions of the stories, the feisty woman was my sister or cousin. Sometimes the captive was a brother who had never done anything else with a frying pan in his life, and sometimes it was a brother who wanted to own a restaurant someday and really did know his way around a kitchen."

"But you wanted to wear the badge and carry the gun?"

Jana nodded. Then she sucked in a breath as Simon Wolfgard and Captain Burke approached the table.

Simon held out two envelopes. "Your travel letter and your pass for the train fare are in the first envelope. You need to show the pass and letter when you board the train at Lakeside and again when the train stops at the station closest to the regional boundary between the Northeast and Midwest. That's the only way you'll be allowed to cross to another region. The second envelope has a letter to Tolya Sanguinati, which includes the résumé you gave me. It also includes the address of the house where you'll live if Tolya feels you are suitable to be a deputy in Bennett. Barbara Ellen, Officer Debany's sister, is willing to share the house with another female. As the houses are cleaned up and made available, Tolya wants permanent residents to move out of the hotel to make room for temporary workers and travelers. If you don't like the house or don't want to share, you can stay at the hotel for a while."

"Having a housemate would be great," Jana said, gripping both envelopes.

"The train leaves tomorrow morning. We'll pick you up in our van so there will be room for everything you want to bring with you."

"Thank you." Jana sniffed. "I'll be ready."

Simon studied her face. "Your eyes are watering and your nose is runny. Are you sick?"

She shook her head. "Just really happy."

He studied her face a little longer, then walked away.

Monty handed her the paper napkins that were on the table. She wiped her eyes and blew her nose.

"Congratulations, Deputy Paniccia." Burke held out his hand.

Jana stood up and shook his hand. "Thank you, sir, but I don't have the job yet."

"I'm confident that you will. Let us know how you're getting on."

"I will."

Burke stepped away from the table. Monty pushed his chair back, ready to return to his duties. When Jenni Crowgard rushed up to the table, both men hesitated.

"Are you going to Bennett?" Jenni asked. "Do you have a pen pal? The Ruthie explained what that is. I could be your Crowgard pen pal and send you news from Lakeside."

Lots of emotion invested in this, Monty thought as he watched feathers appear in Jenni's long black hair.

Jana stared at the feathers, then, with effort, focused on Jenni's face. "Yes, I'm going to Bennett. I promised to write to Merri Lee, but I don't have any Crowgard pen pals, so I would enjoy writing to you."

Jenni set an index card on the table. "This is me. When you get to Bennett, you can send me your address." She dashed out of the coffee shop.

Jana stared down the hallway that led to the back door, then looked at Monty and Burke.

"For the Crowgard, information is a form of currency," Monty said, smiling. "I got the impression from things I've overheard lately that having a pen pal and receiving postcards from another region in Thaisia has become a bit of a status symbol."

"Is having a human for a pen pal more or less of a status symbol?" Jana asked.

"More, I think."

"Communicating with one of the Lakeside Crowgard won't hurt your status either," Burke said quietly. "Especially since plenty of individuals in Bennett and Prairie Gold already have ties to this Courtyard."

Jana gave them a brilliant smile. "I'd better get home and make sure everything is ready for my trip tomorrow."

"Have your mail forwarded to the Bennett post office," Monty said.

"Will do."

Tess joined them, giving Monty and Burke no more than a glance before focusing on Jana. "You ready to go?"

"I am."

"Our minivan can take you home. It's in the access way. The driver's name is Harry."

"Thanks." Jana hurried out the back way.

"Well," Tess said. "I hope we're done with all the excitement for . . . a . . . while." As she looked toward the archway, her hair changed to red-streaked green and began coiling. "The job fair is over."

"Didn't come for a job."

The familiar male voice—a voice Monty had hoped he wouldn't hear in person, despite what Meg had seen in the prophecy cards and what his mother had told him—was like a hammer blow to the chest.

"Came to see family." A gesture to the woman and two children behind him. "Was told there was a place we could stay." The smile aimed at Monty wasn't sincere, unless you counted the hint of meanness. "Hey, CJ."

"Lieutenant?" Burke's voice was barely audible but a warning nonetheless. "You know him?"

"My brother. Cyrus James Montgomery. Jimmy."

Burke took a step toward the archway. "Sir, you need to leave. Now."

Monty glanced at Tess and felt a wave of dizziness. Something wrong with her face. Something . . .

He looked away and waited for the dizziness to pass. Hoped it would pass.

A squeal from the archway. Then Jimmy's wife and children were pushing into the coffee shop, and Henry Beargard stood in the archway, blocking escape.

Monty looked at Jimmy, who was still trying to hold on to his cockiness.

"Whether or not he leaves isn't your decision, Captain," Tess said. "He's in the Courtyard. The Wolfgard will decide what happens to him now."

CHAPTER 7

Thaisday, Messis 9

Watched by the ponies, Meg stood at the sorting room's side door and flipped through the envelopes going to the Sanguinati. Smiling self-consciously, she removed a letter that belonged in the Hawkgard mail, then put the rest in Thunder's baskets.

Thunder circled to the end of the line since Meg didn't hand out the day's treat until she'd dealt with all the mail. Lightning stepped up to receive the letters he would deliver.

Hawkgard Complex. Wolfgard Complex. Crowgard and Owlgard. Pony Barn. Utilities Complex. Even the Green Complex, which meant someone from the Business Association had to return to the complex, empty the baskets, and put the mail in the slots in the mail room. It would have been easier to take that mail with her when she went home, but most days *all* the ponies living in the Courtyard showed up to receive mail, and they all expected to be able to deliver something somewhere despite there being more ponies than mail drops. That was the reason she now had a pony deliver mail to the Market Square shops, and why she had the ponies making other kinds of deliveries if she didn't have any mail to put in the basket. The girls at the lake didn't receive mail or catalogs, so Meg now split the books requested from the library. A pony took a couple of books in the morning and she took the rest when she made her afternoon deliveries. Ever since the Elders came through Lakeside and the Courtyard last month, dispensing their primal form of justice, it had been made clear to Meg that the girls expected to see her when she made her afternoon rounds, even if she had nothing to deliver. Same with Mr. Erebus. Whether she had anything for him or not, she stopped at his home in the Chambers, stood on one side of the gate in the black, wrought-iron fence, and chatted with the old Sanguinati for a few minutes.

With the Elementals and Mr. Erebus, her stopping wasn't about physical deliveries. It was about letting them see she was all right—and about sharing news that wasn't written down.

When she gave the last pony, Whirlpool, the books Summer and Earth had requested, and everyone had received their treat of carrot chunks, Meg went into the bathroom to wash her hands. Mail all sorted. No packages to shelve for the afternoon deliveries. Just that box of books from Jesse Walker. Unless a delivery arrived, she didn't have anything she had to do until the midday break. She could select one of the books and read a chapter or two.

Why was she holding her left elbow up to the mirror?

Frowning, Meg gingerly rubbed the skin, then looked closer. No cut or injury of any kind. Not that she could see anyway. The skin didn't hurt when she rubbed it. But the elbow hurt, faintly. And the skin prickled, faintly.

Leaving the bathroom, she went through the sorting room, glanced at the box, and almost shrugged off the odd feeling in her elbow. If she said something, she might cause who knew how much upset. But if she said nothing and the odd feeling was a forewarning of trouble . . .

She opened the drawer that contained the wooden box of prophecy cards. She put the box on the counter, opened the lid, and placed her fingertips on the cards. Probably wouldn't get an accurate answer if she didn't spread the cards out on the table. If she left them in the box, it would be harder to find the correct one. It was time to look at all of them and start discarding the ones with images that could be represented by a single card when the Trailblazer deck was created.

And how many times was she going to say she should do it before she actually started doing it?

Hadn't she seen an article in a magazine recently about how to stop procrastinating? Maybe she should find that article and read it again.

For now, she would ask a question and select a card as the answer.

Why is my elbow hurting? Why is my elbow hurting? Why . . .

Her left hand tingled. The fingers buzzed. Didn't have to search far to find the card. She held it up, turned it over.

Explosion. She'd drawn that card when she had asked about her friends in the Courtyard—and when Lieutenant Montgomery asked about his brother, Cyrus, aka Jimmy.

Meg put the cards away, then pressed her hand against the pocket of her capris, feeling the shape of the silver razor. But the buzzing, prickling, tingling feeling was gone, giving her no indication of where she should cut to find this particular prophecy.

Her elbow hurt again, but not in a way that indicated prophecy.

Disturbed, Meg stepped up to the counter in the front room. "Nathan? Could you look at something for me?"

No leisurely stretch and yawn. He was across the

room and had his forelegs on the counter before she had time to blink.

She held up her elbow. "Can you see anything wrong with my elbow? It feels . . . odd . . . but I don't see a scrape."

He sniffed her arm from wrist to shoulder, then gave the outside of her elbow a more thorough sniff. He licked the skin. They both waited to see if he would react to a trace of blood so small it couldn't be found any other way. He gave the skin a dismissive "you're fine" lick and started to turn away. Then he growled, startling her. Was he reacting to something on her skin after all?

She didn't know what to think when he rushed to the front door and shifted a front paw enough to have fingers that could turn the simple lock. Frightened by his inexplicable behavior, Meg backed away from the counter, bumping her shoulder against the doorframe.

Returning to the counter, Nathan shifted to human form. "Let me see that arm again."

Not her friend. Not the office's watch Wolf. This was Nathan as a Courtyard enforcer.

"Meg."

The snarled word was a warning. If Nathan was this angry about what she'd thought was a small question, she didn't want to consider how Blair would react.

I'm not a bunny. I'm not a bunny. I'm not . . .

She kept repeating that as she eased forward and held up her elbow.

His hands gently closed on either side of her elbow. He bent his head and studied the skin, sniffed it, gave it another lick before releasing her.

"Nothing." He sounded calmer but also puzzled.

The counter hid him below the waist, so she refused to consider what anyone pulling up for a delivery could see through the glass door.

Meg blinked. Thought. Nothing about her had upset him—but *something* had. "What happened?"

"Uninvited male visitor. Tess said to lock the door and stand guard until Simon decides what to do about that male."

That sounded bad. The image of the bunny's backbone popped into her head, making her queasy.

Nathan twisted around and focused on one of the front windows. Nyx looked back at them, nodded, then glided across the delivery area to the consulate.

Jake Crowgard landed on his favorite spot on the brick wall and cawed, letting everyone know that he, too, was watching.

"You're safe, Meg," Nathan said. "Nothing will hurt you."

Her heart pounded so fast she felt dizzy. "Someone is here looking for me?"

"No." He cocked his head, as if listening to something—or someone. "No, not looking for you." He studied her elbow. "But if that keeps hurting, you let Simon know. Or Henry."

Explosion. A physical explosion or an emotional one? Considering how many times she'd drawn that card lately, it could be either—or both.

She didn't know why her elbow hurt, but she knew it would be pointless to make a cut now. The events she'd seen prophesied in the cards had already begun.

Something had changed in the Courtyard. Air carried the scent of anger. Earth reported that the Wolves were in motion, moving to guard the vulnerable in their pack. All because of the male who had just arrived with his mate and young. The Wolfgard and human packs hadn't reacted like this to the swarms of humans who had come and gone—the humans who were migrating to other parts of Thaisia. Why was this one male considered a threat to so many when he could be killed so easily? What made him different from the rest of the humans?

This was the reason they had come to Lakeside. This was the kind of human they needed to observe before the migrating humans returned to the places Namid's teeth and claws had reclaimed for the *terra indigene*. And they needed to make sure that male remained within reach of the Courtyard.

<Wolf!>

Mostly hidden behind Henry's large human form, Simon studied the human herd that had gathered in A Little Bite. Strange how the addition of one human could change his way of looking at them, change them from a pack back to a herd. Back to prey.

Maybe that wasn't so strange. Meg's arrival in the Courtyard had changed all kinds of things, including changing female employees from nonedible prey to a female pack that was approached with some degree of caution. And with the female pack came the connection to the police pack. So a single person could create a lot of changes.

Nicholas Scratch, the spokesman for the Humans First and Last movement, was another example of a human who had set many things in motion. But the ripples Scratch created had ended with many Wolves and humans dying and Thaisia being broken into pieces to keep the humans more isolated.

Now he was looking at another human he instinctively knew had the potential to cause trouble for the *terra indigene*. But how? This male was related to Miss Twyla and Lieutenant Montgomery, who were good humans, but both had been concerned about what might happen if this member of their family pack arrived in Lakeside. And Meg had seen trouble when she'd drawn cards to reveal prophecy. Not just trouble; an explosion, which was *not* a small thing.

And yet, he couldn't see the threat, couldn't explain why he wanted to drive this male away from Meg and Sam and everyone else in the Courtyard. So he watched as Miss Twyla and the Sierra entered the coffee shop, followed by Kowalski and Debany, who were in uniform. Miss Twyla looked stern, ready to snap at a misbehaving pup. The Sierra, on the other hand, looked ready to roll over and offer her belly in submission.

Was this a fight for dominance of the Montgomery pack between Lieutenant Montgomery and this newcomer, Cyrus Jimmy? Leaving the pups out of it for the moment, Simon considered the two sides. He was sure Miss Twyla sided with the lieutenant, but the newcomer had a matc. That left the Sierra. Lieutenant Montgomery would be the better leader, but Simon had a feeling the Sierra wanted the petting and approval of that Cyrus.

Would other humans here want his approval?

Simon looked at Nadine Fallacaro. She wouldn't. She was indicating clearly that she wanted to drive that Cyrus out of her territory. Good. And Kowalski and Debany weren't pretending they had come in for food or coffee. They were watching, waiting for orders. Pack enforcers. That, too, was good.

<What do you want to do with the intruder?> Henry asked.

Vlad, in smoke form, drifted to the other side of the Grizzly. <We can't kill him in the coffee shop. He is family to the lieutenant. It might cause trouble with the police pack.>

<Maybe. I don't think Captain Burke would object too much if I swatted the intruder and snapped his neck.>

Vlad shifted to human form. <Simon? What do you say?>

<Wolf!>

He'd been expecting this summons ever since Blair told him that *they* had returned, but Simon still flinched at the sound of that voice.

<Simon?> Vlad said, studying him intently.

<I'll be back,> he told Vlad. <Don't let that Cyrus leave.>

Going to HGR's stock room, he stripped off his clothes and hung them on the row of pegs installed near the back door. Then he stepped outside, shifted to Wolf, and ran toward the odd silence near the Market Square.

It didn't take him long to find the two Elders. Their presence made him uneasy, but it didn't surprise him that they had returned. After all, their curiosity about his relationship with Meg was the biggest reason they had not already exterminated all the humans living in Thaisia. Was it that curiosity that had drawn them back to the Courtyard so soon? Or something else?

<Wolf.>

They shifted from their true form and took on the shapes of other predators. The male stood upright, his furred body vaguely human. But he was huge, with powerful limbs and big claws that could score glass and tear through flesh, and he had a head that belonged to some ancient predator. Perhaps being upright wasn't an attempt to look human. Perhaps it was simply one of the ancient forms no one remembered. The female was some kind of feline, but she was much bigger than Henry in his Grizzly form.

Were these the Elders who had been here during the storm that ripped through Lakeside? Were they the ones who had consumed the Wolf cookies Meg kept at the office for Nathan and Skippy?

<We watched the migrating job-fair humans,> the male said.

<How did you know about the job fair?> Simon asked. Elders preferred to have little or no contact with anything connected with the human species. And when they did have contact, their intentions usually were not benevolent.

A light wind ruffled his fur.

<The Crows told us about the job fair, and we told the Elders when they wondered about the human swarm,> Air replied.

Simon couldn't see her—she hadn't chosen to take a visible form—but he could hear her just fine. And he wondered what it meant that the girls at the lake had been aware of the job fair. Under the best circumstances, humans drawing the attention of the Elders or the Elementals was a bad idea. Or a good idea, since the humans rarely survived.

<Another male has arrived,> the male said.

Simon bared his teeth. <That male will not stay long in the Courtyard—or in Lakeside.>

<He will,> the female said.

Simon tensed. <He is a bad kind of human. We don't want him here.>

<Why is he bad?>

There was something *wrong* with Lieutenant Montgomery's sibling. He knew it. Vlad knew it. Henry and Tess knew it. But could any of them explain it?

<Can he make war on the *terra indigene*?> the male growled.

<No,> Simon replied reluctantly. <I don't think this male is a big human predator—not like that Nicholas Scratch and the humans who followed him. But the humans who know this male believe he will cause trouble.>

<For them,> the female said. <Not for us.>

<For us too,> Simon argued.

<How?>

He tried to think of something big enough to be considered a reason to get rid of that Cyrus but small enough that the Elders wouldn't attack *all* the humans in the Courtyard. <I don't know.> A hard thing to admit.

<We must know,> the male said. <We must understand what makes this male a not-war-but-trouble human predator.>

<Why?> Simon asked, curious about their persistence.

<The smaller earth natives have left many human places unguarded,> the male said. <Now some of Namid's teeth and claws must stay close enough to those places to keep watch. We must recognize the difference between a good human and a bad human. We must know what is a threat to the *terra indigene* and cannot be allowed to survive.>

<If this male is a threat to your pack, then his kind

of human will be a threat to *terra indigene* in other places,> the female said. <The Elders will not allow humans to migrate through the wild country and den in the reclaimed places if we cannot recognize the ones that are dangerous. You saw many humans that are not members of your pack and did not howl the Song of Battle. We must learn why this one is bad, why he should be driven away.>

<What if he isn't close by for you to watch?> Simon asked, feeling a trap close around him.

<We are not done thinning the human herds,> the male replied. <If we can't recognize good humans from bad, we will kill *all* the humans who try to migrate through the wild country. We will do this to protect the land and the earth natives who survived the human attacks.>

Simon whined softly. The first group of humans from the job fair were already on their way to Bennett. If the Elders stopped all migrations, the train with the Simple Life humans aboard wouldn't survive to reach Bennett. And the professionals who were supposed to take the train tomorrow would never leave Lakeside.

He wasn't supposed to be responsible for more than the Courtyard in Lakeside, but the Elders were going to decide about every human place in Thaisia based on what they learned here.

How much human would the *terra indigene* keep? He knew it was risky to let that Cyrus stay so close to his Meg. But if Simon told her what was at stake, Meg would insist on taking the risk. She wouldn't want to be the one who stopped a human like the Jana Paniccia from having a choice about the work she could do and where she could live. He couldn't ask Meg to carry that weight, not when she was the Trailblazer who was looking for ways to help the rest of the *cassandra sangue* survive.

But he was still the leader of this Courtyard. If he was going to do this for the Elders, it would be on his terms. He wasn't going to take unnecessary risks with Meg or Sam or the rest of his pack. His *whole* pack.

<We can let that male and his mate and young stay in one of the human dens across the street.> Simon pointed a front paw at the stone apartment buildings. <And we can allow him to shop in the Market Square so that you can watch how he acts around other humans—and around us. But in return, you must promise to help us guard the human female pack.>

He felt the Elders swell with anger. They were Namid's teeth and claws. They were not used to having anything but the world telling them what to do.

Then Air said, <That is fair. Whatever trouble this male causes will distract the Courtyard's enforcers, so others of us must help keep watch.>

Earth joined her sister, took on human form, and smiled at Simon. <We will help too, even though our Meg comes to visit us almost every day.>

<Meg?> the female said.

<The sweet blood howling not-Wolf,> Simon replied.

<Broomstick Girl,> Air added, referring to the song Charlie Crowgard had written about Meg and Merri Lee protecting Skippy from a bad human named Phineas Jones.

<We will help watch,> the male said.

Were they a little too interested in watching Meg? He'd have to warn Nathan to check for the Elders' scent around the Liaison's Office.

<One other thing,> Simon said. <Some of the humans who are migrating to Bennett left Lakeside this morning. Some are leaving tomorrow. You will tell the rest of the Elders that these humans are migrating with our permission and will not be harmed. The Lakeside Courtyard won't help you unless you promise.>

He felt a terrible silence surround him, but he held his ground. He was leader here; they were guests. Not that such things mattered to Namid's teeth and claws.

<That is fair,> Air said again.

<We are Elders,> the male snarled. <We decide.>

Earth smiled. <We could wake up Winter and see what she thinks.>

Wake up Winter during the last month of Summer's reign? Wake up Winter and tell her the Elders wanted something that might pose a threat to Meg? Even the thought of how that Elemental would respond made Simon shiver.

Apparently the threat impressed the Elders too.

<We will allow this migration to Bennett,> the female said.

Having reached that much of an agreement, Simon hurried back to Howling Good Reads and whatever drama was taking place between Montgomery and that Cyrus. He wasn't happy about this arrangement with Namid's teeth and claws, but if the survival of the humans migrating to other parts of Thaisia depended on what the Elders learned over the next few days, he'd rather have them watch the female and police packs here than humans elsewhere.

"What are you doing here, Jimmy?" Monty asked. Gods, this was the worst possible place to have a family reunion. Bad enough to have his men witnessing this contretemps, but he didn't want to speculate about what Burke was thinking. And he didn't want to consider what the *terra indigene* thought about Jimmy showing up here with Sandee and the kids, Clarence and Fanny.

Jimmy had never done an honest day's work in his life, preferring shady deals and manipulating people, but had managed to stay out of jail for the most part. Communication with Toland was spotty at best, and he didn't think any cop from Lakeside would get much help from the Toland police force. Despite that, Monty didn't think it would take Burke more than a day to pull enough strings to have a copy of Jimmy's rap sheet. And if Burke couldn't pull those strings, ITF Agent Greg O'Sullivan, nephew of Governor Hannigan, certainly could.

"Came to see family, like I said." Jimmy's smile widened as Twyla approached the table. "Mama. As pretty as ever." He wrapped his arms around her and gave her a smacking kiss on the cheek. "Stand up, boy. Let your grandma have that seat."

"I want a cookie," Clarence said, eyeing the baked goods in the display case.

"I want a cookie too," Fanny said.

"We should all have something," Sandee said when Nadine approached the table. "I'll have a diet soda and a piece of pie. What kind of pie you got today?"

"Sit down, Mama." Jimmy resumed his seat. "CJ's a big shot now, so he can treat."

Monty watched the way Nadine looked at Jimmy and Sandee. Members of the HFL movement had burned her business and home to the ground and had intended to kill her in that fire. She should have received counseling. Instead she'd thrown herself into working with Tess, and there had been too many other crises to deal with since the fire, so he hadn't thought about how well she had handled the trauma. Seeing the look in her eyes now, he braced to block an attack.

And then there was Tess. After that wave of dizziness, he didn't dare look at her face, but looking toward her shoulder, he could see the red hair coiling.

"Sure," Monty told Nadine. "My treat."

"This time," Tess said, her voice strangely harsh.

"No pie today," Nadine said. "Have some cherry fruit tarts—and one raspberry tart left. No soda of any kind. No diet foods of any kind."

"Well," Sandee huffed. "What kind of place is this that you don't sell diet?"

Tess laughed, a terrible sound. "You whine about not having a diet drink but you want to eat pie?"

"How about a cookie and a serving of milk for the children?" Monty suggested.

"I want—," Clarence began.

"If you don't want what is offered, you don't have to eat it," Twyla said. "But you don't get anything else."

"House rules, Mama?" Jimmy didn't raise his voice, but his anger came through loud and clear. "You don't have a say about my kids."

"Cookie and milk or cookie and water," Tess said, threads of black appearing in her hair. "This is my shop, and those are the choices *I'm* offering."

She walked away. After a moment, Nadine went with her.

"Hey, you didn't take my order," Jimmy protested.

"If you value your life, don't push her," Monty whispered.

Sierra moved closer to the table but didn't join them.

"Why are you here, Jimmy?" Monty asked again.

"You don't care, so why are you asking? You warned Mama and Sissy to get out of Toland, even paid their way. But not a fucking word to me, CJ."

"I was told there was no way to reach you," Monty replied quietly, not looking at his sister. "No one had a working phone number."

"You could have found me if you'd wanted to."

"You would have wanted me to locate you through the Toland police?"

No answer.

"Got out of Toland before everything shut down," Jimmy said conversationally, turning toward Twyla. "Thought we could stay in Hubbney, but too many people were scrambling for a place there." Now he looked at Monty. "Heard you could put us up while I figure out what to do."

When Monty didn't say anything, Jimmy looked at their sister, and that look accused her of lying to him. Had Sissy lied or just misrepresented the living arrangements because she hadn't understood the situation?

"Jimmy could stay with me," Sissy said.

Twyla turned to look at her. "Child, you've got two single beds for the girls and a single bed for yourself. You've got a kitchen table and four chairs. So I guess Cyrus, Sandee, and the children could sleep on your living room floor, but that's about all you have to offer right now."

The look in Jimmy's eyes was so ugly, Monty wondered if he'd escalated to physical abuse once Sissy had left home. Elayne hadn't wanted to spend time with his family, so his time with Sissy had been limited to an occasional lunch or times when Lizzy had visited Grandma Twyla and Sissy was there with her girls. When she was with Mama or with him, Sissy was the strong, bright girl he remembered. But her response to Jimmy's presence wasn't healthy.

"What about you, Mama?" Jimmy turned to Twyla.

"I have an efficiency apartment. One room with a single bed."

Now Jimmy turned to Monty, rage in his eyes.

No pretense now of coming to see family. Most likely, the storm that had struck Toland wasn't the only reason Jimmy needed to leave that city. But he'd come to Lakeside expecting free room and board. He hadn't considered how little help Sissy would be able to give him.

No one else within hearing of this little drama had said a thing until Captain Burke broke the silence.

"Lieutenant. Your brother—"

"Will stay here." Simon Wolfgard walked into A Little Bite, flanked by Vlad and Henry.

Seeing Jimmy's eyes widen, Monty turned in his seat. Wolfgard looked human but couldn't pass for human. This was a leader staring down an enemy, and there was no doubt in Monty's mind that a wrong move now would start a slaughter.

"Mr. Wolfgard." Monty kept his voice quiet and courteous. "This is my brother, Cyrus James Montgomery. Jimmy."

"I know who he is," Simon growled.

Since Simon continued to stare at Jimmy, Monty glanced at Burke, who met his eyes. The message in those fierce blue eyes was clear: *keep it smooth, Lieutenant.*

Never easy to do when Jimmy was tangled up in something.

Simon dropped a single key on the table. He handed a second key to Monty, his amber eyes never leaving Jimmy's face. "You can use the apartment above Lieutenant Montgomery's during your visit. We have rules. There are consequences if you break them. The apartments belong to the Courtyard. You do not let other humans into the building without our permission. We do not permit drugs on our land. If we find them in your den or smell them on your body or clothes, you, your mate, and your pups will be driven out of our territory— and our territory, where you're concerned, is the city of Lakeside. Lieutenant Montgomery, as police, has a key to your apartment. So do I. We will check the apartment whenever we choose."

"The key to the outer door?" Monty asked quietly.

"Not necessary. The door will be open during the day. It will be locked at dusk. The guard has a key and will open the outside door for anyone who has permission to enter the building. Anyone else is a trespasser."

Remembering the Trespassers Will Be Eaten signs posted on the Courtyard roads, Monty shivered.

"You will be allowed to purchase food and merchandise from the stores in the Market Square but no more than we allow for a family pack," Simon continued.

"This is like a fucking house arrest," Jimmy said.

"Yes. Except you're not confined to the den."

"And if I don't agree?"

"We will drive you to the train station now and purchase four tickets to whatever human town you choose within the Northeast Region. You either stay where we can watch you, or you leave."

"And if I decide to stay somewhere else in Lakeside?"

Gods, Jimmy, stop arguing with him. He's not a human you can bully.

"We'll hunt you down and kill you. And then we'll allow your mate to leave with her pups."

Jimmy looked sick and, finally, truly scared. Monty doubted the fear would last more than a minute after Simon walked away—with Jimmy it never did—but for the moment, Cyrus James Montgomery appreciated that he'd put himself in a situation that was dangerous, even potentially deadly.

Simon leaned down, bared his teeth to reveal fangs that weren't even close to human, and said, "If you go near Meg, I will snap your bones, tear open your belly, and eat your liver while you're still alive."

Wolfgard left the coffee shop, followed by Henry, Vlad, and Tess.

Stunned silence. Even Burke seemed frozen by the threat.

Nadine walked over to the table and set down glasses of water. "You still want the food?"

Monty forced a smile. "Not right now. Thank you."

Burke stepped forward. "If you want to leave, I'll check the train schedule to find out if there's a train this afternoon and where it's heading. If you don't want to spend the night on a train after it stops for the travel curfew, you'll have to choose a town that's no more than four or five hours away. Otherwise you'll have to stay overnight and head out at first light."

Jimmy ignored Burke and focused on Sissy. "What the fuck did you pull me into?"

"Sierra didn't pull you into anything, Cyrus," Twyla said. "Maybe she didn't understand as well as she should have that we were going to be surrounded by police officers and *terra indigene*, but coming here was your choice." She drew in a deep breath and let it out slowly. "This place is all right for me, and for Sierra and her girls. But it's not a good place for you, Cyrus. You chose long ago the kind of life you wanted, and nothing I ever said could change that. But you're my son, so I want you to hear me. This isn't a good place for you. Pick another town. Make a new start for yourself and your family. There's always room for a man willing to do an honest day's work."

"Honest day's work," Jimmy sneered. "The only thing an honest day's work ever got Daddy was a heart attack."

"That's not true."

"Well, thanks to Sissy, I hauled my wife and children here, passing up better opportunities. Now I'm stuck, so I guess I'll have to stay until I can sort things out."

Since there were no human-controlled towns between Hubbney and Lakeside, Jimmy hadn't passed up anything. But Monty was sure his brother, being Jimmy, now believed he had passed up something better by coming to Lakeside.

Monty rose. "In that case, let's go across the street and get you settled. Where's your luggage?"

Jimmy waved a hand toward the archway. "Left it in that other store."

"We'll carry it over, Lieutenant," Kowalski said.

Kowalski and Debany stiffened in response to the look Jimmy gave them. "You going to search through our things while you're being helpful?"

"That won't be necessary," Burke replied, giving Jimmy his fiercest smile. "I'm sure the Wolves have already gone through your luggage and removed anything that doesn't meet with their approval." He walked to the front door of A Little Bite and pushed it open. "Shall we?"

Monty led the way, feeling Jimmy's fury like claws scratching his back. Things had gone wrong between them while they were still children—long before he'd chosen a career with the police and Jimmy had chosen . . . other pursuits. There was more at stake now than a family rift. If Jimmy screwed up the relationship the humans here had been building with the Others . . .

Monty looked at Burke as he walked out of the coffee shop and wondered if it was Simon Wolfgard or his captain who posed the biggest threat to his brother.

"I'm not sure what's going on, but the children are safer where they are. No. It's better if you keep an eye on things over there."

Vlad glanced toward the checkout counter as he followed Simon, Henry, and Tess toward the stairs leading to HGR's office. Merri Lee froze, the store phone pressed to one ear and her mobile phone pressed to the other. Must be talking to Ruthie and Eve Denby.

"Good advice," he said quietly, then hurried up the stairs. He hadn't realized how angry he was until he closed the door. Then he strode up to Simon and gave the Wolf a shove.

"Are you sure about this?" Vlad demanded.

Simon snarled at him. "No, I'm not sure. I do know there's a fight for dominance going on, but I don't think Montgomery understands that."

"That Cyrus knows it," Henry rumbled.

"He wants control of that pack, wants to drive Montgomery out," Simon said. "His mate will go with him. So will the Sierra. And Miss Twyla might go to try to protect the Sierra and her pups."

"Families do split sometimes during a fight for dominance," Vlad said. "But when that happens, they don't both stay in the same territory."

"Montgomery and the Lizzy will be the ones who stay," Henry said. "If Montgomery is driven away from that family pack, the rest of them will be banned from the Courtyard."

"Not Miss Twyla," Simon said. "Elliot almost likes her."

Vlad studied Simon. "That Cyrus will bring trouble here. He'll be close to the vulnerable among us." What would Grandfather Erebus say about a hostile male being that close to Meg? "Why should we let him stay? Why are you giving in?"

Simon growled. "Two of the Elders returned to the Courtyard when we were all distracted by the job fair. They've decided that Cyrus needs to stay where they can watch him."

"Blessed Thaisia," Henry rumbled. "Why?"

Simon kept his eyes on Vlad. "Unless the Elders can understand why one human like that Cyrus can be a threat to a whole pack of humans—or us—they won't allow *any* humans to migrate through the wild country to reach other towns."

"So we risk the humans we trust for the Elders' benefit?" Tess said.

No answer. Finally Simon said, "They agreed to help protect the female pack. And they agreed to let the humans from the job fair travel through the wild country unharmed."

Human cities were ideal hunting grounds for the Sanguinati, so they rarely brushed up against the Elders. But he understood now the choice Simon had made about letting that Cyrus stay—save the Lakeside Courtyard from what would hopefully be nothing more than an annoying inconvenience or let Tolya and the town of Bennett fall along with Prairie Gold, the Intuit village that depended on the train station for its supplies. And how many other places, other people, could have fallen if Simon hadn't made that choice?

"Well," Vlad said. "If that Cyrus draws out others like himself, he may be of some use to us."

The coils in Tess's hair relaxed a little. "Bait? For who?"

"For that Jack Fillmore, the male who hurt Theral MacDonald and is still hunting her," Vlad replied.

They let the words settle and grow weight.

"That Cyrus lived in Toland. Would Stavros know about him?" Simon asked.

"Since he's still alive, my guess is he wasn't important enough to draw the problem solver's attention," Vlad replied. "But I can ask."

"Ask."

"Nyx is willing to work around the consulate, freeing Elliot to deal with the mayor and other government officials. She'll make sure no one enters the consulate who shouldn't." And he would talk to Grandfather Erebus about assigning more Sanguinati to spend time around the Market Square.

"Good," Simon said. "Tell her that includes the Sierra and that Cyrus's mate."

"I'd like the upstairs offices here to be off-limits as well."

Simon nodded. "I don't want that Cyrus or his mate working in any of our stores. And they're to be watched whenever they're in the Market Square."

"Are you hoping that Cyrus will do something so that you can justify killing him without causing trouble with the police or the Elders?" Tess asked.

"Aren't you?" Vlad looked at her shoulder, relieved to see green streaks in her hair. Their resident Harvester was calming down.

"We'll do our best to protect our friends and deal with our enemies," Simon said.

"I'd like the Sierra to put in her work hours at A Little Bite," Tess said. "I can watch her there."

"Divide the time with library work," Henry said. "I think it's a place that holds little interest for that Cyrus."

Simon agreed and Vlad had no objections, so they all returned to their work. But the enemy was among them now, and so were the Elders, so none of them let down their guard.

Exhausted from the emotional bomb of Jimmy's arrival, Monty stopped at Captain Burke's office before clocking out and going home. He wanted to spend time with Lizzy, maybe take a walk while he listened to her chatter about her day—which was more entertaining now that there were fewer complaints about her having to spend the mornings in school despite its being summer. She and Sarah Denby were teaching some of the *terra indigene* how to play human games such as hopscotch, and it wasn't just the youngsters who wanted to learn. Apparently, Jenni and Starr Crowgard were fascinated by the game and played with the children whenever they could.

Crows were nimble and had excellent balance.

Monty knocked on the doorframe of Burke's office and walked in.

"Busy day," Burke said. "Your brother and his family get settled in?"

"I'm not sure what my sister told him, but the accommodations were a shock."

"I'm sure they were." Burke folded his hands on his desk. "You know I'm going to make some calls about him, find out whether he's just a nuisance or a potential threat."

"Yes, sir. Given the restrictions on the living arrangements, I don't expect Jimmy to stay long. He was looking for a free ride and easy pickings. He won't find either of those things here."

"He'll go too far one day, and it will cost him more than a few days in jail."

"I know."

"Is he going to take your sister down with him?"

Monty rubbed the back of his neck, trying to ease the sore, tense muscles. "Gods, I hope not. She's a different person when she's away from him, but I think there's a lot Mama didn't tell me when it comes to Sissy."

"Families are complicated, and family loyalty can push a person into making difficult, even imprudent, choices." Burke paused. "My men are a kind of family, and I'll do whatever it takes to protect them. And that includes you. You're a good man, Monty, and you're doing good work here—important work that has an impact on every person living in Lakeside. I'll keep out of it as long as your brother remains nothing more than a nuisance, but I won't let him become a threat."

"Sir?" Monty said, alarmed.

"Are you worried that I'll take Cyrus for a long ride?"

A long ride meant taking someone deep into the wild country and leaving him there without food, without water, without shoes. Technically it wasn't a death sentence because there was the slimmest chance of reaching a human settlement and being given the opportunity to start over. In reality it was a form of execution.

"No, sir, I'm not worried."

Burke gave him a chilling smile. "Well, you should be."

CHAPTER 8

Firesday, Messis 10

Jimmy stepped out on the apartment's porch, wanting to inflict a world of hurt on somebody. But there were too many people already awake, and some of those people were cops. And one of those cops was his brother.

Caw!

And if being around cops wasn't bad enough, there were too many fucking *things* watching him, keeping tabs on every ass scratch and fart.

A bit of mellow weed would have smoothed things out, but the fucking freaking Others had found not only Sandee's stash of pills but the weed he'd carefully hidden in a secret compartment in the suitcase. *Nobody* should have found that hiding place. But his stash was gone, and the compartment had been slashed by a claw or something.

This was all Sissy's fault. Stupid bitch. Yeah, she'd told him that she was going with Mama and her girls to visit CJ in Lakeside. But she hadn't pushed hard enough to get him included, and he couldn't squeeze anything out of her, not with Mama holding the train tickets and the available cash. And, yeah, once she'd reached Lakeside, Sissy had called to warn him to get out of Toland, that something bad was going to go down. And maybe she'd called him in time for him to get one of the last trains out of Toland before the storm shut everything down. But he'd had to pay for his own tickets, with Sandee clinging to him so tight he couldn't shake her. Weighing him down with her snot-nosed brats. Gods. The way she put out when she needed something, he wasn't sure those kids were his, so why should he use the stash of money *he* needed in order to buy clothes and food for them?

After getting out of Toland—he heard on the news later that entire blocks in some neighborhoods were nothing but rubble—he got bogged down around Hubbney, unable to find transportation to a town large enough to have the kind of business opportunities he preferred. In the end, Lakeside was the largest city he could reach. He would have preferred Shikago, even knew some people there, but he couldn't afford the train fare or, gods, even the bus fare, since the ticket prices had doubled after the travel restrictions were put in place. As it was, he had to scrimp and save for weeks before he could buy the bus tickets to Lakeside and then had to wait a while longer to reach the top of the travel list. And during that time he'd had to smile and pretend to be grateful for the work that allowed him to eat watery soup and hard bread.

At first he'd thought he could set up in Hubbney, maybe meet up with acquaintances and do a little business, but the handouts ended after the first week. With all the storm damage, there was plenty of grunt work to be had, and every physically able adult had to show a work chit in order to get a meal at the reduced price for displaced persons. The chits could also be used to buy food from the nearest grocery store—and they could be exchanged for money. But Sandee gobbled up as much food as the two kids put together and then whined about there being no one to watch the kids when he told her he wasn't feeding her anymore. If she wanted to eat, she could work too.

Since she was coming back to the flop with money instead of chits, he had a good idea what kind of work she was doing. Fine with him. These days, she was the body he banged when he couldn't find better.

Should have gone back to Toland, where he knew the players, knew the games, knew whose back to scratch and who was weak enough that he could lean on them to get something. But he was in Lakeside because Sissy had led him on, let him believe CJ had somehow greased some wheels and set her and Mama up with a place to stay and food for the taking. But there was no food for the taking, and while he wasn't paying anything to stay there, the apartment wasn't any better than the flop they'd had in Hubbney. The freaks had found another bed and brought it up yesterday afternoon. Single beds for a man who had a woman. And bedsprings that squeaked every time he moved. How was he even supposed to hump his woman, knowing there were cops—and worse—listening?

Sissy's fault. All of it. Well, she could do a little something to make it up to him. She surely could.

Jimmy went inside, letting the screen door slam. The sound woke Sandee, who jerked up in bed.

"What's going on? Jimmy? Where are you going?"

"Out."

"Out? Where? Baby, let me put some clothes on, and I'll go with you."

He left the apartment while she was still scrambling to find something to wear that didn't stink since she'd been "too busy" to wash any clothes. He wasn't concerned about his own clothes. If Sandee didn't look after him properly, he'd boot her ass out and let Sissy look after him.

Maybe he should do that anyway.

When a break came in the morning traffic, Jimmy hustled across Crowfield Avenue and went into A Little Bite to let Sissy provide him with a decent breakfast.

While Nadine filled the display case with fresh baked goods, Tess wrote the day's offerings on the menu board.

"We received extra eggs yesterday, so I made quiche for the breakfast crowd and figured I'd use the rest of the eggs to make egg salad for sandwiches later in the day," Nadine said.

"I'll add them as specials," Tess replied. "Save a piece of quiche for Meg. She dashed out this morning without eating an adequate breakfast."

"Why was she in such a hurry to reach the office? Some kind of special delivery?"

"She's reading a book, which she left at the office because she went to the Quiet Mind class last evening. But she had stopped at an exciting part and wanted to read more before work."

Nadine raised her eyebrows. "And there were no comments at home?"

Tess smiled. "Simon doesn't know how to complain about it since he asked her to review the book."

Nadine laughed softly. "Maybe I'll walk the piece of quiche over to the Liaison's Office and see for myself what Meg finds so interesting."

Tess looked at the Sierra, who was moving a broom around but didn't seem to be doing much actual work. Her smile faded. "Hold off for a few minutes. I'll be back."

Howling Good Reads wasn't open yet, but the lattice door that separated the two shops wasn't latched. Going in, she went to the checkout counter, picked up the phone, and called the Market Square bank. The Business Association had an account with a human regional bank, but the Market Square bank was a private institution run by the Sanguinati. It was the place where all the Courtyard businesses recorded the amount of credit employees could use in the stores here. Pay was always split between Courtyard credit and money that could be used in human places.

When Miss Twyla arrived with the Sierra and the pups, Simon and the rest of the Business Association had been prepared to give them food and shelter for a few days simply because they were Lieutenant Montgomery's family, and the Courtyard had offered the best protection against the storm and the Elders' wrath. But Miss Twyla had insisted on working for her keep and had insisted that the Sierra do the same. No pay had been involved. But after it became clear their visit was actually a permanent move, Simon had held by the Courtyard's basic rule: anyone who lived off the land's bounty had to do a job that supported the Courtyard. Humans like the police pack didn't officially work in the Courtyard, didn't receive a pay envelope like an employee, but the interaction they provided was valued, which was why the police directly involved with the Courtyard were allowed to purchase things in the stores.

"Market Square Bank," a male voice said.

"This is Tess. How much credit does Sierra Montgomery have available?"

While she waited for the information, she looked out the window and saw that Cyrus waiting to cross the street. Her hair turned green with broad red streaks and started to coil.

The banker returned to the phone. "How much credit do you want to allow that she hasn't yet earned?"

Tess watched that Cyrus cross the street as she considered the question. All the children received half their daily milk ration as part of their midmorning snack on school days, courtesy of the Courtyard. When they had decided how much rent to charge for the apartments, the Business Association had taken into account that the Sierra was a lone female who had to feed two pups, so they had agreed to charge her less than their other tenants. They had done those things because, while the Sierra wasn't a dominant female like Miss Twyla and hadn't earned the same respect, she had started out as a good, reliable worker.

She'd sulked a bit about their decision not to let her work at the consulate, and showed her displeasure by not doing her assigned work as well as she'd done it before. They were used to that behavior in humans, and she would have improved or been fired. But since the arrival of that Cyrus yesterday, the Sierra acted like a different person—someone none of the *terra indigene* would have trusted if she hadn't been connected to Montgomery and Miss Twyla.

"Basic meals for herself and her pups at A Little Bite and Meat-n-Greens," Tess said in answer to the banker's question. "She has to pay cash for everything else, including food for anyone else, until she has a credit balance again." She heard his hesitation. "Get Simon's and Vlad's approval before you send a message to all the stores, but let them know I'm going to hold to it in my shop."

"Vlad just came in. I'll tell him. If he agrees, I'll tell all the stores."

Tess hung up and stood to one side of the archway, watching the Sierra and that Cyrus, who had taken a seat.

"We've got quiche with seasonal fruit this morning," the Sierra said. "And we have fresh muffins and some pastries left over from yesterday."

"I'm not eating that shit," that Cyrus replied. "I'll have some bacon with scrambled eggs and fried potatoes and buttered toast. And coffee."

"We don't make that kind of breakfast," the Sierra whined. "It's a coffee shop, Jimmy."

"You got the fixings here. You can go in the kitchen and make it for me." That Cyrus leaned toward the Sierra, who cowered but didn't have enough sense to walk away. "You owe me, Sissy. You lied to me about the situation here, so you owe me. Now, get your ass in the kitchen and cook me up some breakfast."

Nadine stepped into the front room. "My kitchen is off-limits to everyone but Tess."

Tess glanced at Nadine. Then she considered the knife in Nadine's hand and the weirdly calm fury in the woman's eyes.

Shit. <Henry, I need you here *now*.>

Her hair turned red with threads of black as she

strode into the coffee shop, a predator to be reckoned with. "This coffee shop works the same way as any other in the city. You order the food, you pay for the food, and then you take it with you or eat it here." She stayed focused on that Cyrus, struggling to stay in control while the threads of black in her hair turned into streaks—a warning that she was getting closer and closer to her true nature. She wanted to blacken his organs, turn them into festering slush. She wanted to make it rain inside his skull while she harvested his life energy. She didn't care if she damaged the Sierra, but she didn't want to hurt Nadine, so she had to stay in control, had to avoid taking that last step toward her true nature.

"Sissy can pay," that Cyrus said.

"She's tapped out," Tess snapped. "So unless you have cash for the food, get out."

That Cyrus rose, knocking the chair over. "Who do you think you are?"

She didn't want to tell him. She wanted to show him.

"Tess?" Merri Lee's voice from the archway. "Should I call the police?"

"Human law doesn't apply here," Henry growled, coming in from the back door.

She knew by the expression on that Cyrus's face that Henry didn't look completely human.

That Cyrus looked at all of them, then headed for the front door. Pausing as he pushed the door open, he hawked and spat on the coffee shop's floor.

Feeling Henry move to block Nadine, and hoping Merri Lee had enough sense to hide, Tess shouted, "Hey!" In that moment when Cyrus looked toward her, her hair turned black with a few threads of red and she looked away before he saw more than the tiniest glimpse of what she was. He clutched at his chest, staggered out the door, and almost stumbled in front of an oncoming car before righting himself.

It didn't feel like she had harvested enough life to

damage him permanently, but that brief look at her should weaken him for a day.

The human mask wasn't sufficiently in place, so Tess avoided looking at anyone—and hoped none of them were looking at her. <Are Nadine and Merri Lee all right?> she asked Henry as she headed for the hallway.

<Vlad pulled Merri Lee into HGR so she wouldn't see, and I blocked Nadine and the Sierra,> he replied.

<We'll finish this,> Simon said. <You need some quiet time.>

Startled, Tess almost looked up. When had the Wolfgard arrived?

<Nadine needs quiet time too,> she said.

<She'll get it. Julia Hawkgard is here. She'll take care of customers. Merri Lee can help and take things out of the oven.>

<I'll go upstairs.> She had an office up there that she'd turned into a cozy nest where she could rest and still keep an eye on the shop during the day.

Keeping her eyes lowered, Tess went upstairs. Once she was safely alone, she looked in the mirror that hung on one wall. Black hair streaked with red, the coils beginning to relax. A face that, once again, looked human.

She had managed to contain her true nature—or enough of it.

She wondered if she was the only one regretting her self-control.

Simon had come in too late to see the start of the fracas, but he was going to put a stop to this part of the trouble.

Hearing Vlad's angry hiss, he glanced toward the archway in time to see Merri Lee elbow the Sanguinati in the ribs and break free.

Great. Now they had to deal with one of the exploding fluffballs as well as . . .

"By all the gods, what is wrong with you?" Nadine snarled as she turned on the Sierra, her hand tightening on the knife handle.

That. <Call Lieutenant Montgomery,> he told Vlad.

<Already did,> Vlad replied.

Montgomery and Kowalski came in through the front door, avoided the gob on the floor, and scanned the room, taking in the people and their positions. A young woman hustled in behind them, then froze just inside the door.

"Mr. Wolfgard . . . ," Montgomery began.

Nadine swung toward Montgomery. "I have things to say!"

"You can say all of them after you give me the knife," Henry said.

She looked at the fur-covered hand clamped around her wrist. She blinked and offered no resistance when Henry took the knife.

Simon wondered if she even knew she'd been holding it.

"Now," Henry rumbled as he released Nadine and stepped back, "say what needs to be said."

Nadine turned back to the Sierra. "How long are you going to pander to that man?"

"He's my brother!" The Sierra's voice cracked. She looked at Montgomery. "We're supposed to help family."

"You're supposed to help him lie, cheat, steal?" Nadine demanded. "Or does he remain above it while you become the liar, the cheat, the thief?"

"No! It's not like that!"

"He wants a full breakfast, so you're going to use the supplies here? Were you even going to offer to pay for them, or were you hoping no one would notice missing supplies when we keep track of every egg and stick of butter? And after he'd eaten his fill here, would he have persuaded you to fill up a bag with food to take with him? Would you have paid for it or pretended that you didn't know who took the breakfast sandwiches and pastries?"

The Sierra started to cry. "Jimmy doesn't have any money to buy food."

"He had money yesterday when he went to the Stag and Hare," Nadine snapped. "Unless he makes friends awfully fast, he had to pay for his drinks and food there." She looked disgusted. "Yesterday you took home dinner for three people. Did you end up splitting it seven ways because he claimed he didn't have money?" Her disgust deepened. "Or did he get half the food because he's the man and the rest of you split what was left?"

Simon frowned. That wasn't right. The Sierra and her pups should have eaten their fill first since she was the one who had done the work for the food. But larger predators did steal food from smaller ones. Maybe that's how it had always worked in the Montgomery pack, with that Cyrus waiting until the Sierra brought home food and then taking it away from her.

He studied Montgomery and saw a grim expression on the lieutenant's face—and sadness in the man's dark eyes.

Anger in Kowalski's face—and in Merri Lee's. Who had caused the anger? That Cyrus or the Sierra, or both?

"I owe him!" the Sierra shouted.

"For what?" Nadine shouted back.

"He never had enough because Mama and Daddy adopted me. My first mother didn't want to keep me, tossed me out like trash. And trash isn't entitled to anything."

Simon heard a soft, pained sigh. Looking over his shoulder, he saw Miss Twyla—saw tears running down her face.

"You owe him because the resources for two children had to be divided three ways?" Nadine said. "Well, if that's how you want to count it, Jimmy owes his brother half of everything he gets because Monty is the oldest child, right? So when Jimmy arrived, Monty only got half of what he would have had if Jimmy hadn't been born. And somehow he managed to survive just fine without taking and taking and taking."

"Cyrus said that to you?" Miss Twyla stepped forward. "He said you were trash? And you never said a thing to your daddy or me? Child, we shielded you as best we could from Cyrus's childish meanness, but we couldn't help with what you kept secret."

"You made him leave and he blamed me," the Sierra said, crying.

"When he was eighteen, we told him he had to find another place to live."

"Because of me."

Miss Twyla nodded. "That was part of it. Childish meanness was turning into a harder kind of meanness. Along with the lying and scheming, that wasn't something your daddy and I could live with anymore. We couldn't change Cyrus, and we were concerned about you, about the way you sometimes acted like you'd taken a beating."

Shocked, Montgomery turned to the Sierra. "Did Jimmy hit you?"

"No!" She shook her head. "No, he didn't do that."

"No, he didn't," Miss Twyla agreed. "I looked for bruises because I wondered—and I would have told you, Crispin, if I'd noticed any." She sighed. "But words can beat down a person as surely as fists, and I hadn't known about the things Cyrus was saying when I wasn't around to hear him and put a stop to it."

"He hurt your heart, bullied you into doing things for him just like he tried to do now, and you kept coming back for another serving of hurt instead of slamming the door in his face," Nadine said.

Simon studied the Sierra. He'd seen this behavior once before when he'd attended the *terra indigene* college to learn how to work in, and run, a Courtyard. A young female Wolf had been besotted with one of the males. She did everything she could to win his approval— brought him food, brought him gifts. The male had paid attention when he wanted something, made promises to become her mate if she could do just one more thing. Other males, Simon included, had tried to befriend her, but she ignored them—just like the Sierra ignored the brother who didn't put a price on his love.

The young female died trying to bring down prey that was too big for a lone Wolf to handle because the male had told her that would prove her love for him. The male was expelled from the college but stayed on the fringes of the college's land, fully expecting to be allowed to return. Then he disappeared and was never seen again.

Simon had never caught a whiff of an Elder's primal scent—a scent he remembered from the time he'd run with the juvenile pack in the Northwest—but he had wondered if the instructors had killed the male to prevent more trouble, or if something larger and less merciful had passed judgment.

Now, comparing the Sierra with that young female Wolf, Simon had a better appreciation of why the Elders wanted to see what happened when a male like that Cyrus entered a successful working pack of humans. The man hadn't been in Lakeside a full day and the pack was already fighting among themselves.

He stepped forward, drawing everyone's attention.

"There are two Montgomery packs," he said. "One pack is Lieutenant Montgomery and Lizzy. The other pack is that Cyrus, his mate, and their two pups. While they came from the same family, they are now separate packs, are adversaries. That means the other pack members can be loyal to one or the other but not both. The rest of the family now must consider what each pack has to offer." He looked at Miss Twyla. This would hurt her, and he was sorry for that. "Choose."

She stared at him, the tears still flowing. Then she took tissues out of her pocket and wiped her eyes and nose.

"Guess I always knew it would come down to this, but I can't choose between my children. Not that way." Miss Twyla straightened her shoulders. "Crispin asked me to come here and help him with Lizzy, and I'd like to keep on doing that. But even if I have to turn away from one of my children, I don't want to turn away from any of my grandchildren."

"You have to choose," Simon said with regret.

She nodded. "I choose your pack, Mr. Simon."

"What?" Simon gave Montgomery a look that said, *Does she know what she's doing?*

"Mama?" Montgomery's look at Simon said, *She knows.*

"I've put my hand to different kinds of work over the years, Crispin," Miss Twyla said quietly. "There is plenty of work to be had, and I could find a job in this city. But this Courtyard feels more like the neighborhoods your daddy and I lived in when we were newlyweds and when you and Cyrus were young—a place where people looked out for each other. Haven't lived in a place like that for the past few years, and I've missed that. I've done what I could for all of you, but my children are grown, so I'm making a choice for myself first."

"All right, Mama." Montgomery didn't sound happy. "If this is what you want."

Simon looked at the Sierra. "Now you. Choose." He held up a hand and noticed the patches of fur on the back. Damn. What else didn't look completely human? "Understand the choice you have to make."

"I know the choice," the Sierra said bitterly. "I have to choose between Jimmy and CJ."

"No, *you* have to choose between that Cyrus and your pups."

He heard several gasps. He suspected those had come from all the females in the room, including the female still standing just inside the door.

"If that Cyrus is so important to you that you'll crawl for his approval, that's your choice. But your pups would be the lowest members of that pack, considered orphans if that's what he wanted, and pups in that position don't often survive if food is hard to find. Odds are one or both of your pups would die of hunger. So if you want that Cyrus, you can live as another female in his pack. But your pups won't go with you. They'll be transferred to another pack that will be able to care for them."

"You can't take my children!" the Sierra cried.

"Yes, we can. And we will. Or you can swear to the members of the Courtyard who are here and to the human witnesses that you will not give that Cyrus food or money that you need for your pups. No excuses." Simon bared his teeth. "And know this: if you steal from us, we take a hand the first time. The second time we take a lot more."

"CJ?" The Sierra turned to the brother who gave his love.

Montgomery shook his head. "Sissy, if you want to find another job and another place to live that isn't under Mr. Wolfgard's jurisdiction, you can do that. But I'm guessing you'd have to do it soon."

"We would give her a week," Simon said. "Then we would drive her out of our territory."

"Even if you found a place you could afford and work to support you and the girls, who would stay with them?" Montgomery continued, then added when the Sierra slid a look at Miss Twyla, "Mama has a job and her own bills to pay."

"That's right," Miss Twyla said. "If you and the girls are here, I'll help you look after them, same as I'm helping Crispin. But if you leave, maybe you'd best think of going a long ways away from all of us. Maybe one of those towns out west that need good workers. And if you leave and have any sense at all, you won't tell Cyrus where you're going."

Sobbing, the Sierra fell into one of the chairs.

"For you, being around that man is like drinking a glass of poison every day," Nadine said. "Maybe it just makes you sick, makes you weak, makes you forget who you really are and what you really want. But if you keep drinking, sooner or later, the poison will kill you."

Simon wondered if Nadine had drunk that kind of poison when she was young. If she had, she'd also stopped drinking it. So had Theral MacDonald. She'd run away from an abusive mate. That Jack Fillmore was still sniffing around, still a threat, but Theral wasn't crawling back to him. So there was a chance the Sierra would make a good choice for herself and her pups if she had a little time to think.

"We'll all meet back here in one hour," Simon told her. "You'll give us your answer then."

The Sierra ran out of the coffee shop, brushing past the female, who looked at them with big eyes and said, "Is it always so dramatic here?"

"Who are you?" Simon snarled. He wasn't close enough to catch her scent, but her voice sounded vaguely familiar.

"Emily Faire. The nurse practitioner who is going to be working here? I have a letter from Mr. Ferryman for Mr. Wolfgard."

Simon nodded, remembering where he'd seen her before. She had been in attendance as the healer when Meg made the cut and saw the possible future for the River Road Community.

He looked at Vlad. <You weren't much help.>

<Why should both of us wear a target?> Vlad replied. <Besides, I was keeping track of the fluffball to make sure she didn't grab a teakettle and hit someone.>

For the *terra indigene,* Merri Lee would always be the Teakettle Woman from Charlie Crowgard's song about Teakettle Woman and Broomstick Girl.

"Come up to the office and we'll discuss your employment," Simon told Emily Faire. Then he pointed to Nadine. "This is Nadine Fallacaro. You'll have a room in her apartment on the days you're working here."

"Really?" Emily Faire didn't sound enthusiastic. She probably wondered how often Nadine attacked other females with a knife.

They hadn't seen this behavior in the woman until now, but Simon was wondering the same thing.

Nadine sighed. "I'll show you the apartment when you're ready." Her eyes widened. "Gods! I forgot about the muffins. Didn't even hear the timer."

"I took care of them," Tess said, stepping in from the hallway. Her hair was green and curling. She wasn't calm, but she was safe enough to be around the rest of them.

Simon walked past Montgomery on his way to HGR's office.

"Simon," Montgomery said quietly. "Would you really take Sierra's girls away from her?"

"Yes."

"Away from all of us?"

A good man, Simon thought. Intelligent and courteous. A man who had been trying to work with him from the first day they met. A man who understood loyalty. A man who had been separated from his own pup for a few months and wouldn't willingly do that again.

A man who cared.

"If it came to that, the pups would be close enough that you and Miss Twyla could visit them," Simon said.

"But Sierra couldn't see them?"

"No." He waited, but Montgomery didn't say anything more. "One hour, Lieutenant."

Simon and Vlad went upstairs to talk with Emily Faire about the terms of her employment. Since their original idea was for her to divide her time between the Courtyard and the River Road Community, they offered her one of the duplexes in the community, thinking that, being an Intuit from Great Island, she would want to live as close to her kind as possible. But she surprised them and asked if there was an inexpensive apartment in Lakeside that she could rent because she had a feeling she was needed here full-time and that someone else would be more suited to run the little clinic in the River Road Community.

Yes, they had an apartment she could rent, if she wanted her own den instead of a room with Nadine, but they didn't have much furniture to offer.

Vlad took her across the street to show her the available apartments in the building where Nadine and Merri Lee resided. Simon watched them from the office window.

So, Emily Faire had a feeling she was needed here full-time? Why? Did that feeling have something to do with that Cyrus or the Elders? Or did she just want to learn more about the *terra indigene* and Meg and living around them was a way to do that? A new addition to the Courtyard. She hadn't seemed overly excited while witnessing the scene in the coffee shop, so maybe they wouldn't be adding another exploding fluffball to the female pack.

That was a problem for another day. Right now, he wanted to shake off the drama and go for a quick run before he had to deal with whatever problems the Sierra's decision would cause.

Maybe he could pester Meg for a few minutes before going for a run. The pester game couldn't last more than a couple of minutes before it stopped being fun for Meg. If she was still reading that book, she'd growl at him for interrupting her. He'd bring a snack from A Little Bite to distract her. She must be hungry by now.

He stripped off his clothes, shifted to Wolf, and went downstairs and through the archway to the coffee shop. Then he considered who could be approached and decided that Tess, while more dangerous than Nadine, was the better-known threat.

"We were just packing up a piece of quiche and a couple of other things for Meg," Tess said. Then she looked at Nadine. "Guess you're not going to have a chance to ask Meg about that book."

Nadine gave Simon a look that made him very glad he could run faster than she could.

Tess gave him one of the insulated sacks she used to deliver food in the Market Square and opened the back door for him. When he looked back, he noticed her hair was brown and wavy.

How nice that Nadine amused one of them.

He trotted to the back of the Liaison's Office and faced a locked door. Of course, he didn't have a key tucked in his fur, so he put the sack on the ground in front of the door and moved to the back room's small window, which was open to let in fresh air.

"Arrooooo!"

Meg rushed into the back room and looked around until she spotted him at the window. "Simon?"

He grinned at her, showing a lot of healthy teeth.

He returned to the door and had the sack in his teeth before she turned the lock and opened the door. He brushed past her and went into the sorting room. Standing on his hind legs, he set the sack on the big wooden table and eyed the book that was held open with a rough purple rock that looked like a mountain range.

As Meg joined him, she reached up and gave him a scritch behind one ear. Almost made him forget about playing the pester game.

"Look what Jenni brought me to use as a paperweight." Meg held up the rock. "It's amethyst. Isn't it pretty?"

It was a rough purple rock.

"She showed me a split geode that would also make a good paperweight. I'm bargaining with her to buy the geode and the amethyst."

Crows had that look in their eyes when they spotted a coveted shiny. To distract Meg before they ended up with a den full of rocks, Simon nudged the sack with his nose.

"What did you bring?" Meg set the rock back down on the book and opened the sack. "Oh! Quiche and . . . this is for you."

Simon caught the beef scent before she pulled the treat out of the sack. Wolf cookie! He'd smelled the beef but thought it was some of the food for Meg.

"There's another cookie in here. Must be for Nathan."

Why? But she was already walking into the front room, and Nathan, having heard, was already waiting for her at the counter.

"I'm enjoying this book," Meg said, returning to the sorting table. "It's exciting. I had to read a couple of chapters like this"—she put one hand over her eyes, then moved her fingers to see between them—"but I didn't mind. Is it okay if Ruth and Merri Lee read it too so we can all give you a review?"

This wasn't happy Meg. This was brittle cheerfulness. This was Meg trying not to show she was scared.

Simon carefully placed a paw on her shoulder.

No pretend happy or cheerful now.

"Jenni said there was trouble at A Little Bite, but she didn't know what happened except that it upset Tess. And Ruth called to say I should stay in the office until everyone settled down. Simon?" She touched his face. "Do you need answers?"

"Roo," he replied sternly. No silver razor. No cuts.

Her fingers combed through his fur as she studied him. "You're sure?"

He licked her chin. She tasted better than the cookie, so he licked her again.

Her entire body sighed, and she felt more like his Meg again.

She gave him a hug and said, "You'd better get back to work. I'll let you out. Thanks for bringing the quiche and other food."

He was outside staring at the closed door before he realized Meg hadn't given him a chance to play the pester game. That was so unfair, but at least he'd gotten a cookie, a scritch, a hug, and a couple of licks out of it.

He could live with that kind of unfair.

"Want some orange juice?" Pete Denby asked, going to the small fridge in his office.

"Sure," Monty replied. It would probably burn a hole in his stomach, but he appreciated the offer of a drink that might not be in the Northeast grocery stores much longer since it, like the oranges, came from the Southeast and West Coast regions.

Pete poured two glasses and handed one to Monty before taking his chair behind the desk. "Do you know what's going on?"

Monty told Pete what he'd seen and what he'd pieced together—and the choice his little sister had to make in an hour.

"Gods, what a choice," Pete said softly.

"It shouldn't be a choice."

"You're a cop. You know addiction doesn't just come in the form of a pill or syringe. From the sound of it, your sister is addicted to your brother's particular form of abuse." Pete leaned forward. "Do you know why Simon Wolfgard is letting your brother stay? Or why your brother is staying?"

"I can't guess Simon's motives, but Jimmy is staying because the use of the apartment is free, and he came here expecting a handout. But the Sanguinati guard the building's outer door and will keep tabs on everything and everyone."

"So Cyrus can't harass Sierra in the hallway or try to push into her apartment to discuss things without someone coming to her defense even if you're not home."

Monty nodded. "Jimmy wasn't expecting the kind of scrutiny he's under now. Even if Sissy had told him flat out, he'd still think he could get around being in close proximity to cops and Wolves." He sighed. "Whatever Jimmy thought, my sister is in a bind."

Pete said nothing. Then: "Did you come here because you needed a sounding board or were you looking for an opinion?"

"What do you think of my mother's decision?"

"Smart move. No 'you took his side' accusations when things go sour, which you know they will. There is an unsavory part to any city, and I don't think it will take your brother long to find Lakeside's underbelly."

"You haven't even met him yet."

"I live next door, so I saw enough when you got him and his family settled in. I know Eve brought them a bag of groceries, on Simon's orders, so that they would have food for the first day or so."

Monty sat up. "No one mentioned that." He and Kowalski had picked up pizzas from Hot Crust, and he'd brought one up for Jimmy's family and one for Sissy and the girls, while he, Lizzy, and Mama had the third. But if he'd understood Nadine's accusation, Sissy had also brought home dinner last night and shared the food with Jimmy's family. Had she held on to the pizza, or had that, too, become part of Jimmy's larder?

"If you were me, what would you do?" Monty asked.

"Does your sister-in-law have any skills?"

Monty looked at Pete.

"Any skills that wouldn't require you to arrest her?" Pete qualified.

"I don't think so. As long as I've known her, she's never held a job."

"Regardless, if I were you, I'd start researching towns that are looking for workers, a place where the rent doesn't cost more than your month's pay. Start looking for your sister-in-law and the kids."

"Three tickets out of town. And where is Jimmy?"

"In the morgue, if you're lucky. If you're not lucky, he'll be one of those humans who disappear without a trace."

Or some identification will be left at the cairn in Lakeside Park and the police will fill out a DLU form, Monty thought. A Deceased, Location Unknown form was needed in order for a family to receive a death certificate. It was the way the Lakeside Police Department acknowledged that a person had been killed, and most likely eaten, by the *terra indigene* and no body would be found.

"Your brother is a powder keg, Monty," Pete continued. "Don't let him take you down with him." He hesitated. "Do you want me to come with you when your sister makes her choice?"

"As an attorney, what would you tell her?"

"To do what it takes to keep her children. And that means staying away from Cyrus."

"When I first came to Lakeside, Simon kept his nephew Sam in a cage to keep the pup safe. It upset all the Wolves and it hurt him every day, but he did it." Monty looked at Pete. "So I know he won't hesitate to take those girls away from Sissy if he believes she'll allow them to be mistreated."

"If he does take them, do you think he'll ever give them back?"

Not while Jimmy is alive. But Monty didn't say that. "Thanks for the talk and the orange juice."

"I might not have the orange juice the next time, but as an attorney or a friend, I'm here if you need to talk."

As Monty walked down the outside stairs, he heard a car driving up the access way to the employee parking lot. Captain Burke's black sedan. He should have called his captain, because Pete was right: Jimmy was a powder keg waiting for a match. Apparently someone else had made the call.

Packs and loyalty. Police and family. And consequences no matter what choice he made.

As Burke came around the corner, heading for the back door of Howling Good Reads, Monty hurried to meet him and give his report.

CHAPTER 9

Firesday, Messis 10

"Meg?" Following the sound of Merri Lee's voice, Meg went to the back room of the Liaison's Office and opened the door for her friend. Then she noticed Sierra standing nearby.

Merri Lee stepped inside. She spoke so quietly Meg could barely hear her. "Could you use the cards to answer a couple of questions?"

Meg glanced at Sierra. "What's going on?"

"Simon says Sierra has to choose between her children and her brother Cyrus. She's asked all of us, except Ruth, who's still in the schoolroom with the children, and we've all told her the same thing: Simon will take her girls, will drive her out of the Courtyard if she chooses to be part of Cyrus's pack. But it's like she's lost her brains and won't believe this can happen. I finally said we'd ask you to look at the cards as the final input before she makes her decision."

Meg nodded. Merri Lee gestured to Sierra, and the three of them went into the sorting room.

Nathan was at the front counter, taking notice of who was in the sorting room with Meg.

"Private consultation," she said, and closed the Private door almost all the way. The Wolf, with his keen hearing, would still know everything that was said, but the illusion of privacy was for Sierra's sake.

She took the wooden box out of the drawer, set it on the table, and removed all the cards, spreading them out. Pins and needles filled her breasts, made her nipples burn. Made her grateful she didn't have to use the razor on that part of her body.

"No!" she snapped as Sierra reached for one of the cards.

"Having someone else handling the cards interferes with Meg's ability to find the answers to people's questions," Merri Lee explained, moving Sierra's hand away from the cards.

"This is absurd," Sierra said angrily. "He has no right to say that I'm unfit to take care of my girls."

Meg's hands buzzed. "What is your question?"

Before Sierra responded, Merri Lee said, "Two questions. The first is, what will happen to Bonnie and Carrie if they are separated from their mother?"

Meg closed her eyes and silently repeated the question. Her fingers brushed the cards until one card produced a painful buzz in her left hand. She opened her eyes and turned the card so they could all see the answer.

"Future undecided," she said, feeling troubled.

"What does that mean?" Sierra demanded.

"It means they could be fine and have a good life, or things could go badly for them," Merri Lee replied. "But right now, there is no clear answer."

Meg put the card facedown and set it to one side. "Second question."

"What will happen to Sierra if she continues to allow her brother to pressure her into doing things she knows are wrong?"

Meg sucked in a breath. She could have sworn she'd just felt the silver razor's kiss against her skin. She followed the buzz, partially distracted by the icy pins-and-needles feeling in her left wrist—the exact spot where she thought she'd felt the razor.

She found the card that buzzed with the answer to the question, turned it over, and stepped back from the table before opening her eyes.

Merri Lee looked pale. And Sierra? Fascinated? Horrified? Meg didn't want to spend her energy trying to recall a training image that matched Sierra's expression, especially after she looked at the card she'd drawn for the young woman's future.

Hooded figure holding a scythe.

"Death," Merri Lee whispered. "Cyrus will push and push until something happens that kills you. You keep saying you owe him. You said it to me, to Theral, to Eve, even to Mrs. Debany, trying to get *anyone* to agree with you that you owe him. We all told you the same thing: just because you believed what he told you when you were a little girl doesn't make it true. But we're not talking about him getting more than his share of a treat because you gave up part of yours. Not anymore. You're an adult and you're going to lose a lot more than a cookie. It's time to stop wrecking your life while you still have one."

Sierra ran out the back door, sobbing.

"Go after her," Meg said.

"Are you all right?" Merri Lee asked.

She nodded. "I need to think about some things."

She waited until she was sure Merri Lee was gone. Then she brushed her fingers against the cards and asked a question of her own.

Why is Simon allowing Cyrus Montgomery to stay around the Courtyard?

Cyrus being Lieutenant Montgomery's brother wasn't enough. There had to be another reason.

Strictly speaking, her question didn't lend itself to prophecy, and she wasn't certain she'd be guided to an answer. Then her fingers burned. She picked up the card, opened her eyes, and turned it over. She dropped the card faceup on top of the rest.

Meg stared at the card. Stared and stared as she thought about children and mothers and safe places to build a life.

She picked up the phone and called Steve Ferryman. And then she called Simon.

"You're buying the Stag and Hare?" Simon cocked his head and studied Captain Burke. "Why are you telling me? The *terra indigene* don't drink alcohol." At least, not from a glass. The Sanguinati had been known to get a little tipsy when they fed on someone who had been consuming alcohol. And Wolves and other shifters could be affected by drugs or other substances in a human's blood. But going to a tavern wasn't something the Others did by choice, because humans pumped up on liquid courage could be dangerous.

"The Stag and Hare also serves food. Pub grub." Burke smiled. "It will provide a place in the neighborhood where everyone could mingle. The place has a large-screen television. Customers come in to watch sporting events. Another kind of experience for your people, and a safe place for mine."

"For the Wolf lovers." Simon suddenly understood. It had never been safe for someone like him to go into that kind of place. But it wasn't safe for a human like Kowalski or Debany to go into a drinking den either. Not anymore.

"Why are you telling me?" Simon asked again.

"Customers of the Stag and Hare have caused you some trouble in the past."

True, but the last humans who crossed the street intending to cause trouble had been killed by the Elders, and their intestines had ended up festooning the nearby trees.

Maybe that was the reason the tavern was for sale?

"The other reason I'm telling you is because I wanted to float an idea," Burke said. "I'm wondering if an Intuit from Great Island would be interested in managing the tavern. I'm wondering if one of the Sanguinati would be interested in learning to tend bar. Some of the wait-staff will stay because they want the jobs. I think the cook will stay for the same reason. There's an apartment as well as a small office on the second floor. The apartment would be part of the manager's salary if he wanted to live there."

"A business that is a mixed community."

Burke nodded. "Having a manager who has a feeling about trouble before it starts would benefit all of us."

"You want me to talk to Vlad and to Steve Ferryman."

"I do."

Simon studied the police captain. "You know what happened here?"

"Lieutenant Montgomery told me. I'd like to stay and hear the decision, if that's all right with you."

Before Simon could answer, the phone rang. "Howling Good Reads." He shot to his feet. "Meg? What . . . ? Are you . . . ? I'll be right there."

Burke also rose. "Problem?"

"Not yet." Simon rushed for the door, then stopped when he realized he'd almost left Burke, a human, alone in HGR's office—something he wouldn't have considered doing a few months ago.

Burke met him at the door, then went out ahead of him, hurrying down the stairs to get out of the way. Simon brushed past the man and rushed to the Liaison's Office to find out why Meg needed to see him so urgently before the Sierra made a choice.

"I already called Steve Ferryman," Meg said when Simon ran into the sorting room.

<Simon?> Nathan planted his forelegs on the front counter and stared at the Wolfgard leader through the Private doorway.

<Was there trouble here?> Simon asked.

<No. Some growling when Meg used the prophecy cards, but it was mostly Merri Lee who did the growling, and she wasn't growling at Meg.>

The wooden box with the carved lid that Henry had made to hold the prophecy cards was on the table. Three cards were on the table, facedown.

Meg waited until Simon stood next to her. "Merri Lee asked two questions on Sierra's behalf. What will happen to Bonnie and Carrie if they are separated from their mother?" She turned the big question mark card. "What will happen to Sierra if she continues to allow her brother to pressure her into doing things she knows are wrong?" She turned over the second card.

He bared his teeth. "Death."

"My question: why are you allowing Cyrus to stay around the Courtyard?" She turned over the card that represented something terrible and dangerous—something most humans thought was a fantastical, make-believe creature and most *terra indigene*, while knowing such forms existed, had never seen. "Your decision has something to do with them, doesn't it? The Elders are coming back to the Courtyard."

Simon stared at her as his ears became Wolf-shaped and fur suddenly covered his shoulders and chest. "They're already here."

"What do they want?"

"To observe. To learn."

"They don't want you to send Cyrus away?"

"Not yet." He hesitated, trying to think of how to explain. "The human pack connected to the Courtyard is as big now as some of the human settlements in the wild country. The humans here were working well together and working well with us. Then that Cyrus walks in and humans are suddenly fighting among themselves. The Elders want to know why one human can sour an entire pack. If they can't learn the reason by observing the humans connected to the Courtyard, they won't allow humans to migrate to any of the reclaimed places. They won't allow humans to migrate at all."

Simon touched Meg's shoulder, wanting contact for a moment. "And I want to understand too, Meg. Humans who cause this kind of trouble usually stay away from us. They certainly wouldn't be trying to work with us. Not that that Cyrus is offering to do any kind of work." He paused. "It feels like it should be a fight for dominance, but Montgomery doesn't seem to understand that."

"A fight for dominance would decide who is the leader of the human pack?" Meg asked.

He nodded.

"Then it wouldn't be Lieutenant Montgomery who would fight Cyrus; it would be Captain Burke."

Simon blinked. He'd been thinking of a dispute within a family pack, but Meg was right. Now that the conflict had spilled over to the rest of the human pack, that Cyrus would have to defeat Burke in order to claim dominance over the rest of them.

Suddenly he was looking forward to watching their next meeting.

Meg lifted her chin. At first he thought she was inviting him to give her a lick. Then he remembered that, in the kissy books, females did the chin lifting as a challenge or to indicate defiance. Since he didn't know what Meg was challenging or defying, he just waited.

"If we have to let Cyrus stay, then I want you and Steve Ferryman to figure out a way to relocate Sierra and her daughters to Great Island."

"She's human, Meg. Ferryman's Landing is an Intuit village."

"But Roger Czerneda isn't an Intuit, and Steve hired him as the village's full-time police officer."

"That was different."

"Yes. Officer Czerneda doesn't need to be in a place that is beyond someone's reach." Meg looked into his eyes. "Being in the Courtyard put me beyond the Controller's reach, beyond the reach of the human laws he would have used to get me back under his ownership. The Courtyard is a safe place for Theral because it puts her beyond the reach of Jack Fillmore. But it's not a safe enough place for Sierra because Cyrus is here, because he exerts a kind of ownership over her, and as long as she is within reach, she'll remain weak where he is concerned." She rested her hand on his. "Simon, Sierra's daughters need her."

Simon turned his hand in order to hold hers. "I don't think the Sierra's pups will survive if she's allowed to keep them."

Whether the Sierra's pups survived would matter to Meg—especially after the discovery that the humans who "owned" blood prophets had been killing the girls' unwanted puppies.

"I've been thinking about my friend Jean, who was brought to the compound when she was a small child," Meg said. "She had a mother, a father, and a brother. She never forgot she'd had a family once or that she'd been taken from them. If we start breaking up families because we decide something bad might happen to the children, are we any better than the Controller or the other men like him? In the beginning, they had claimed they were taking children away from their families for the children's own good." She paused, then added, "Give Sierra a second chance."

"Coming to Lakeside was a second chance," he argued, "and what did the Sierra do? Called that Cyrus and told him where to find her."

"Then call this a last chance. One last chance to break free from Cyrus's hold and build a life for herself and her daughters."

"What if she doesn't want to break free?"

Meg looked so sad, he wondered if she was thinking about the *cassandra sangue* who had chosen to stay in the compounds. They chose to remain a commodity that would be used up in exchange for someone taking care of them so they wouldn't have to take care of themselves.

"Then that's her choice." She sighed.

"It's also Steve Ferryman's choice, as well as the *terra indigene* on Great Island. No one settles on the island without their consent." Simon ran a hand over Meg's head. "Your hair is growing. It doesn't look like puppy fuzz anymore."

Might not look like puppy fuzz anymore, but he couldn't resist petting it whenever he thought she wouldn't growl at him.

<Police car just arrived,> Nathan reported. <It isn't howling, but all the lights are flashing.>

Meg and Simon stepped into the front room just as the passenger door opened and a dark-haired man got out.

"What did you tell Steve Ferryman?" Simon asked.

"That we needed to talk to him and that it was urgent," Meg replied. "But it's time for that meeting, and it's better if I stay here."

Trying not to look too happy when they had serious things to discuss, Simon vaulted over the counter and went out to greet the mayor of Ferryman's Landing.

"You got here in a hurry." He smiled as he walked up to where the Intuit waited by the patrol car. The sharp look he received from Steve Ferryman told him that his ears hadn't shifted all the way back to human yet.

"Meg said it was urgent," Steve replied. "What happened? You don't usually look this pleased to see me."

Meg said "we." We were talking and we were deciding. Partners in running the Courtyard. And that means you're not a serious rival anymore.

Not that Steve Ferryman had ever presented himself to Meg as a potential mate. But Ferryman was human and didn't have to adapt to things that weren't a natural part of himself.

"Do you mind if Officer Czerneda pulls into the employee parking lot?" Steve asked.

"No, but if he wants food, he'll need to go to

Meat-n-Greens. There is a discussion going on in the coffee shop. That's part of the reason you're here."

Steve gave Simon a long look. "I'm here as the mayor of Ferryman's Landing?"

"Yes."

They waited until Roger Czerneda drove the car down the access way before they headed for A Little Bite. Simon told Steve about the Sierra and the choice she had to make. He told Steve about the two cards Meg had drawn in answer to the questions about the Sierra and her pups, and about Meg's concern for the girls if the Sierra died.

He hadn't equated the girls with his nephew Sam. What would have happened to Sam if Daphne had died anywhere else but the Lakeside Courtyard? Simon had reached his sister moments after she died, had been there to take the traumatized pup back to the Wolfgard Complex, where he and Elliot had done everything they could to take care of Sam.

Just as Lieutenant Montgomery and Miss Twyla would take care of the Sierra's pups if they were orphaned. But would that be true of a human pack if the Sierra lived somewhere else?

"I'll listen," Steve said. "I can't promise to do more than that."

"Captain Burke also wants to talk to you."

"If Burke wants Roger to transfer to his police station, forget it," Steve growled.

Simon grinned, appreciating the human's possessiveness of his own pack. "He bought the Stag and Hare and thinks having an Intuit as a manager would be a good idea."

Steve stopped at the back door of A Little Bite. "How would you feel about that?"

"Emily Faire claimed one of the apartments for her den, so the Intuits are already overlapping our territory."

"One young woman is hardly an invasion."

"The female pack was the invasion," Simon grumbled. "Exploding fluffballs. Bunnies with teeth."

Steve burst out laughing. "I enjoy talking to you, Wolfgard. You face challenges that make my mayoral duties look easy."

<Simon?> Vlad called. <It's time.>

Simon opened the door to the coffee shop and went in first as a courtesy to his guest. If Tess and Nadine were still in a dangerous mood, he could warn Steve, who would have a chance to run away.

The coffee shop was so full of witnesses, Simon almost felt sorry for the Sierra. Tess's hair was red and green coils, but he didn't spot any threads of black. Nadine's hair didn't give any warning of mood, but Simon noticed that Henry stood behind the woman, ready to grab her if she tried to spring on the Sierra. Vlad was in the archway, keeping an eye on Merri Lee and the rest of the female pack. The police pack was there. So were Elliot and Miss Twyla, as well as Agent O'Sullivan. In fact, about the only humans who weren't there to witness the Sierra's decision were Ruthie, who was watching the human pups, Meg, and . . .

<Where is Eve Denby?> Simon asked Vlad.

<That Cyrus was feeling so poorly, Eve drove him and his mate to the Lakeside Hospital. She isn't back yet. That Cyrus's pups are with the rest of the human puppy pack.>

Since dumping two extra pups on Ruthie in the middle of schooltime was Vlad's doing, Simon hoped she didn't snarl at *him* about it.

The Sierra stood in the center of the room, looking small and weak. She should have been an auntie helping to raise the dominant pair's puppies. In fact, that was how that Cyrus seemed to treat her—as someone who was expected to help him raise his pups. That would have been fine if she hadn't had pups of her own. But even by pack standards, it wasn't right to expect her to hunt and provide food for all of them while the other two adults did nothing understandably useful.

Simon stood in front of the Sierra. "Have you made a choice?"

The Sierra wrapped her arms around herself. "I want to keep my girls. And I don't want to die." The words were a pleading cry for help.

Wondering if he could mention moving her and her pups to Great Island, Simon glanced at Steve Ferryman and was surprised by the hard, grim look on the man's face. Clearly, the Sierra wouldn't be going to Ferryman's Landing.

"Last chance, Sierra Montgomery," Simon said. "If you want to keep your pups, you will stay away from that Cyrus."

Fear. And relief. Someone besides that Cyrus had determined the Sierra's place within a pack. Right now, she didn't care that the decision had been made by a Wolf.

The Sierra began to cry. Miss Twyla put her arms around the other female and led her pup out of A Little Bite.

The rest of the humans slunk out of the coffee shop, except Burke and Steve Ferryman. Montgomery would have held his ground, but a look from Burke sent the lieutenant away—proof that Burke was the dominant male of the human pack.

"You wanted me to consider having Sierra Montgomery relocate to Great Island?" Steve asked.

"Yes."

"Was that your idea?"

Simon shook his head, baffled by the scent of anger surrounding the man. "It was Meg's."

"Then we'll talk to Meg." Steve headed for the back door, then looked over his shoulder at Burke. "I understand you want to talk before I go."

"If it's convenient," Burke replied, making no move to leave.

Steve looked at Simon. "I'll meet you at the Liaison's Office."

Wondering where Tess and Nadine were, Simon focused on the police captain.

Burke gave him a fierce-friendly smile. "I read an article a few years ago about how hunters in some parts of the world use a tethered goat to bring predators into the open. I'm just wondering what kind of predators you're looking to snare with bait like Cyrus Montgomery."

Sometimes Burke was too smart. But drawing out other predators like that Jack Fillmore would be a side benefit. The Elders weren't watching to see what other kinds of predators were drawn to that Cyrus so much as how the other humans responded to a predator who was also a bottom feeder.

"Having Cyrus here puts a strain on Monty, not to mention the strain on Twyla and Sierra," Burke continued. "Is there a reason to do that?"

Simon considered what he could—should—say to Captain Douglas Burke, dominant male of the human pack.

"This isn't my choice." Before Burke could respond, Simon said, "Did you fix the door on the police station? Replace the glass that had been scored by Namid's teeth and claws?"

Burke paled. "No. I convinced the station chief that it was a valuable reminder of why the police and local government need to work with the Lakeside Courtyard."

"The tethered goat? Not my choice."

"They're here?" Burke asked.

Simon nodded.

"Does Monty know about your . . . guests?"

"None of the humans know." Except Meg, but she'd figured it out for herself. "Captain . . . what the Elders learn from observing that Cyrus and the rest of the human pack here will affect the decisions they make about every human in Thaisia."

"Well," Burke said eventually. "I'll do what I can to

help Lieutenant Montgomery and his men keep things smooth." He gestured toward the archway. "Mind if I browse while you have your meeting with Mr. Ferryman?"

"Go ahead. We have some new thrillers by *terra indigene* authors." There was also a new book about the Wolf Team, but Simon didn't think that would interest Burke. Besides, the handful of copies he'd ordered for the store were already bought, and there was a long waiting list for the copy in the Market Square library—and some of the names on the waiting list belonged to humans.

Leaving Burke to deal with Merri Lee, their teakettle-wielding exploding fluffball of an assistant manager, Simon bolted out the back door of A Little Bite and wondered what Steve Ferryman wanted to say to Meg.

"No," Steve said.

Frightened by the ferocity in that one word, Meg moved closer to Simon, who bared his teeth and snarled at the Intuit.

"Why?" she asked. "Sierra needs a safe place to live."

"Not in Ferryman's Landing. And not on the island. I watched her, Meg. I listened to her. And I had a feeling—a very bad feeling—that she would cause serious trouble for my people if I permitted her to relocate to Great Island."

She hadn't been prepared for an argument, hadn't considered that Steve would put one of his *feelings* ahead of one of her prophecies, even if her prediction of the future had come from using the prophecy cards.

"She needs a safe place," Meg insisted.

"Then you and Simon and her cop brother should help her relocate somewhere far away."

Simon had narrowed his eyes at Steve and growled softly, but he wasn't adding anything to her argument—which made her wonder if he actually agreed with Steve. Which made her angry.

"Give me one good reason for not allowing Sierra to live on Great Island," Meg snapped.

"I can give you five," Steve snapped back. "Six if you count Jean."

She swayed as if he'd given her a hard slap.

Steve rammed his fingers through his hair. "I'm not saying Sierra would go after the girls and try to do them deliberate harm. I didn't get *that* feeling. But everyone who lives in Ferryman's Landing knows about the girls. Almost every business in the village is involved in building the new campus, and Lois Greene has begun printing a progress report in the *Great Island Reporter*. That we're taking care of young blood prophets isn't a secret—gods, I'm the one who sends out *The Blood Prophets Guide* e-mails—but there aren't many people beyond Intuits and *terra indigene* who know about the girls in our care." He hesitated, then looked directly at Simon. "Stavros Sanguinati knows. He dropped by to introduce himself, being the new leader in Talulah Falls. He said I could call him if I needed his kind of help."

Meg looked at Steve, then at Simon. "What kind of help?" She'd met Stavros. He reminded her of Vlad, only more intense.

"Stavros was the Toland Courtyard's problem solver," Simon replied, focused on Steve. "He doesn't offer his kind of help lightly."

Steve nodded. "That was my impression."

The skin around Meg's spine buzzed. The pins-and-needles feeling prickled the skin above her collarbone. She wanted to cut, wanted to feel the relief and release. Wanted the euphoria that came from speaking prophecy. She'd been good for weeks and weeks, using the cards instead of the razor. Cards that might provide answers but not the pleasure.

"Meg?"

Simon's hand, warm on the back of her neck.

"Sierra and Cyrus," she said softly. "It's like me and the razor, isn't it?"

She didn't hear the snarl; she felt the rumble of it through his hand.

"There's no need for that," Steve said, sounding upset.

No need except wanting something that harmed her and would eventually kill her.

She took the wooden box out of the drawer and spread the prophecy cards over the sorting room table. "Ask the question."

Steve looked confused—or perhaps just unwilling.

"What would happen if the Sierra moved to Great Island?" Simon said. "Speak, prophet, and we will listen."

Meg closed her eyes and let her fingers brush over the cards until she found the one that made her fingers burn, made her spine buzz and the skin around her collarbone prickle. She turned the card over before opening her eyes.

Hooded figure holding a scythe.

"Death," Simon said grimly.

"We don't know who will die," Meg said.

"It doesn't matter," Steve replied. "It might be Sierra or one of the young blood prophets. It might be an Intuit or one of the *terra indigene*. If she lives among us, she'll bring death."

"Because she won't be able to resist her own kind of razor," Meg said. Hadn't she been receiving that message in one form or another from Ruth and Merri Lee and Theral? "Sooner or later, Sierra would call Cyrus or leave some kind of clue of where to find her."

"I'm no counselor, but that sounds about right," Steve said. "Until she chooses not to make that call, there is no safe place for her to live, and I can't agree to something that will put our most vulnerable citizens at risk."

Meg nodded. You couldn't help someone who didn't want help. That was a hard, and bitter, life lesson.

"Well," Steve said after an awkward silence. "I'd better go hear what Captain Burke has in mind." He reached across the table and touched Meg's hand. "Sorry I couldn't help." Giving Simon a nod, he left the Liaison's Office.

Meg gathered up the cards and returned them to the box. "Whatever the Elders expect to learn from all this, I hope it's worth it."

A moment's hesitation. Then she felt the heat from Simon's body as he moved close to her, felt his lips press lightly against her temple, giving her the oddest sensation of pleasure.

"I hope so too," he said.

Simon found Lieutenant Montgomery in Meat-n-Greens, drinking ice water and pretending to eat a small bowl of cottage cheese.

"Why?" Taking a seat opposite Montgomery, Simon pointed at the bowl. "Do you like that cheese?"

Montgomery gave him a weary smile. "Not really, but I felt like I should purchase something if I was going to sit here, and the cottage cheese is something cold to eat on a hot day." He fiddled with the spoon. "I brought this trouble to your door. I'm sorry."

"You wanted to protect your mother and sister, get them to a safer place," Simon countered. "I encouraged you."

"I didn't expect Jimmy. His being here changes things."

Simon waited. He couldn't force that Cyrus away from the Courtyard, but the Elders hadn't said anything about Montgomery sending the other human away.

"Eve Denby called me from Lakeside Hospital. Seems Jimmy had some sort of attack—shortness of breath, heart feeling wonky." Monty stared at the bowl of cottage cheese. "Someone here expressing . . . displeasure?"

"Yes." No point denying it, even if he wouldn't confirm it was Tess the Harvester, the Plague Rider, who had taken some of that Cyrus's life energy.

"Anyone else hurt?" Monty asked.

"No." He knew what he would want as a Wolf, but

he wasn't sure what a human would want. "We could move the Sierra and her pups to the other apartment building. I won't move that Cyrus over there, not with three females living there alone." All right, Officer De-bany was almost living with Merri Lee in her den, but he wasn't there all the time to discourage anything that Cyrus might decide to do.

"I'd prefer having my sister in the same building as me," Monty said. He pushed the bowl of cottage cheese to one side, then drank some water. "Why did you put Jimmy and his family on the second floor?"

"He can't fly. We didn't think he would be inclined to use the porch to sneak out or in if he had to climb to the second floor. And even if he tried, we would see him before he reached the ground."

Monty's smile was fleeting but genuine. "You got that right. But he would have even less contact with Sissy—with Sierra—if he had no reason to be on the second floor."

As Simon considered that, he pulled the bowl of cot-tage cheese to his side of the table and ate a spoonful. He liked cheese and happily purchased his share when a delivery came from an earth native dairy farm. But no matter what they called it, this just wasn't his idea of cheese. He'd thought he didn't like it because he was a Wolf. Maybe it was because he was male, since Meg and the female pack chose to eat it.

"That Cyrus and his mate are still at the hospital, and his pups are in the schoolroom with Ruthie," Simon said. "We could move all of their possessions to the other downstairs apartment in your building and have Chris Fallacaro swap the locks so the key we gave that Cyrus would work on the other apartment." When Montgomery hesitated, he added, "If you don't want to look at their things, I could ask Jenni and Starr to pack up their belongings."

"No offense to the Crowgard, but I think it would be better if I did the packing," Monty said.

"Well, you're not likely to lose any shinies while taking the belongings down the stairs." Simon smiled. "I'll help you." The Wolves had looked in the suitcases when that Cyrus arrived, but it wouldn't hurt to see if the human had brought in anything that wasn't allowed.

"Thank you. I'll check with Captain Burke about taking some personal time for this."

Steve Ferryman and Roger Czerneda had left the Courtyard, but Burke was still in Howling Good Reads. He looked amused as he held up the two books he'd selected—a thriller by Alan Wolfgard and a book Merri Lee referred to as a Crowgard cozy, with an amateur sleuth who had a habit of picking up more than clues while investigating a murder.

"This is the other one," Merri Lee said as she returned to the front of the bookstore. She handed Burke a book that, from the look of it, had been read a few times already. "Jesse Walker from Prairie Gold sent it to us. You can take it as a loaner. It's a mystery-thriller series with a human investigator who receives assistance from a couple of *terra indigene* acquaintances. I gather the author is pretty popular among the Intuit communities but is unknown anywhere else."

"Was that in the box of books Jesse Walker sent to HGR?" Simon's chest and shoulders furred a little in annoyance. Until he and Vlad decided whether to order copies for the store, those books were supposed to be a distraction for Meg, not be handed out to other humans.

"Jesse sent two copies of that one," Merri Lee replied, showing her teeth.

Simon pretended the teeth were displayed in a smile. The female pack was upset because of the Sierra, and he really didn't want to tangle with any of them. At least, not over a book.

"I have all the information you or Vlad would need to order new copies of the series," Merri Lee said.

"Good. Fine. Lieutenant Montgomery and I will be

across the street. Vlad should be around if you need help with anything."

"Problem across the street?" Burke asked.

Simon went over to the display table to give Montgomery the illusion of privacy while talking with the captain, and to give himself a moment to digest the changes that had occurred since the Elementals and Elders had retaliated against the Humans First and Last movement, altering so many things in Thaisia—not to mention the savage destruction of so much of the Cel-Romano Alliance of Nations on the other side of the Atlantik.

On the one paw, he felt relieved that the Courtyard wasn't faltering while his attention was pulled in so many directions. On the other paw, it felt weird not to know what was going on in his own store. Were the rest of the Business Association members feeling the same way? Maybe not Henry, who spent his time in human form carving totems and sculptures from wood. But Tess was more volatile lately.

He looked at the books on the display table. He wanted to arrange a few things as a substitute for lifting a leg and marking territory. He and Vlad had made Merri Lee their assistant manager in order to free up their time to deal with larger concerns and to take over John Wolfgard's duties now that John had left to run the bookstore in Bennett, but he hadn't expected her to mark the store as her territory so quickly.

We're sharing, he reminded himself as he went upstairs to fetch the spare key to that Cyrus's apartment and call Chris Fallacaro to meet them at the apartment and swap the locks.

Montgomery waited for him at the bottom of the stairs. "We should get this done. Eve Denby called me again. She's at the Bird Park Plaza right now, doing a bit of scouting for Meg, but she'll be back at the hospital in an hour to pick up Jimmy and Sandee since the doctors wanted to keep an eye on him a bit longer. They've decided this is a variation of that mysterious malady that has cropped up a few times in recent months. That being the case, once he's released, the only cure is rest."

They went into the apartment that Cyrus and his family were using and found the suitcases.

Simon looked around the adults' bedroom and covered his nose with his hand. What had that Sandee rolled in to smell this stinky?

"Gods above and below," Montgomery muttered. "Jimmy was raised better than this."

"You smell it too?"

"Yes, I smell it. I'm surprised the station hasn't received complaints from nearby houses about a bad odor." Montgomery looked at Simon. "This must be a lot worse for you."

"We roll on dead fish." Simon lowered his hand and took a quick sniff. "This is a lot more pungent. More like skunk spray."

Montgomery laughed, a quick sound muzzled to a chuckle. "Let's toss it all in the suitcases and leave the suitcases on the porch. I'll talk to Eve and my mother about how to fumigate this apartment."

"I'll pack up the puppies' things," Simon said, heading for the other bedroom. The pups' clothes didn't smell as bad, but they didn't smell clean either.

Why would parents turn their offspring into scent markers for predators? Or was being stinky off-putting enough to discourage the human kind of predator?

He didn't want Montgomery to think he was suggesting the man stink up Lizzy, so he would ask Kowalski or Debany. It seemed a silly way to protect the young, which was exactly why humans might do it.

The locks were swapped, the suitcases were packed and on the porch of the downstairs apartment across from Montgomery's, and the Sanguinati who was keeping watch had been told who could, and couldn't, go upstairs to the Sierra's den.

It wasn't said, but it was understood, that if that

Cyrus or his mate tried to see the Sierra, they would need another trip to the hospital for a sudden loss of blood.

Meg moved the kneepad, then resumed weeding the next section of the kitchen garden. She wanted to do something simple—a task that had an instant visible reward, that had no gray areas, no emotional turmoil. At least, not for her. If weeds had feelings, they might take a different view of her plunging her gardening tool into the ground around them and ripping them out, roots and all. But they weren't voicing opinions or arguing with her, so she dug and ripped with homicidal cheer.

No one believed the solicitous excuses that Simon and Monty had made for moving Cyrus and his family to the apartment across from Monty's, especially after Cyrus was barred from going upstairs to talk to Sierra. When Simon told Sandee that she couldn't go into the Courtyard until she washed her clothes and stopped smelling like skunk spray, she shrieked loudly enough to be heard by people at the end of the next block. Combined with Sierra's drama and Steve Ferryman's opposition to Sierra's living on Great Island, Sandee's reaction became the one thing too many, depleting Meg's ability to cope with the feelings and futures of the people around her.

She would do a bit more weeding, then take a cool shower. Simon and Sam would be home by then, and they would make a salad and warm up the already-cooked meatloaf she'd picked up at Meat-n-Greens for sandwiches. Then she intended to do nothing but sit in the summer room and read. Maybe even sleep there tonight.

"Arroo!"

Meg waved as Sam raced toward her, looking hot and dusty but happy. Of course he was happy. He hadn't been touched by all the trouble caused by pesky humans—and she had a copy of the new Wolf Team book for him.

"Hello, Sam!" She dropped her weeding tool and hugged him. "Did you have a good day?"

He *arrooed* and licked and made her laugh. She smiled at Simon when he trotted over to join them.

"Give me a few more minutes to finish this section; then we'll go home and have dinner," she said.

She picked up her tool and dug around one of the zucchini plants and pulled out a gray wad. But when she turned the wad over, she realized she had snagged a white puff of a tail.

Simon heard Meg yelp and saw Sam snatch something from the end of her weeding tool. The pup bounced forward, then darted back, clearly inviting her to play. Meg didn't look like she wanted to play, but Sam wasn't taking the hint.

<Come on, pup. I'll play with you,> he said.

<But Meg found the toy. She should play too,> Sam protested, the bit of white fur dangling from his mouth.

<She isn't going to want to play with a bunny tail.>

<Why not?>

Simon pounced on the pup, rolling him over and pretending to grab for the toy. Sam scrambled to get away, and the two of them ran around while Meg cautiously lifted the zucchini leaves to make sure there weren't any other surprises. Somewhere along the way, Sam dropped the bunny tail and Simon didn't pick it up, figuring he could find it and bury it later. They ran and played a few minutes more before Simon trotted over to the water pump, shifted his front paws into furry hands, and pumped some water for both of them.

More interested in playing in the water than drinking it, Sam was thoroughly wet when he ran to Meg and jumped on her back, his belly fur soaking her cotton shirt. She squeaked and shrieked, and Sam slid off her back as she scrambled to her feet.

"I'm going home now." She stomped toward their apartments.

<Is Meg angry with me?> Sam asked.

<Not really. Acting upset about getting wet is part of the Squeaky Dance game,> Simon replied.

He lapped a little more water, which seemed a lot colder than the hot, humid air. Making sure his front paws were back to proper Wolf form, in case he needed to run, he caught up to Meg, timed his move, and swiped his tongue along the back of her knee.

Another satisfying squeak accompanied the prancy steps of the Squeaky Dance before Meg returned to a stride that would put some distance between her and wet Wolves.

<See, pup?> Simon said as he and Sam watched Meg hurry toward her den. <You don't need another toy in order to play with a human friend.>

CHAPTER 10

"I know, I know." Eve hauled more art supplies out of the carry sacks she'd brought into the sorting room. "I got carried away. But I wasn't sure what you wanted, and I can return anything that hasn't been opened or used."

Meg stared at all the items piled on the table. She'd asked Eve to look for a how-to-draw book and a set of pencils for Hope's friend Amy Wolfgard. It looked like Eve had done that, but what was she supposed to do with the rest of the supplies?

Eve studied Meg, then returned a couple of items to the carry sacks. "Too much?"

"How did you pay for all this?" Meg asked.

Eve winced. "I used my house money. It didn't occur to me that I wouldn't be reimbursed for the supplies you wanted to keep."

"You have the receipt?" Meg studied the itemized list Eve provided. Did the Others already know about drawing and painting? They knew about telling stories and making music. Since Hope's friend was interested in drawing, maybe there were Courtyard residents who would be interested in the art supplies. Something to ask Henry.

Meg selected a book of basic drawing instructions and a book about drawing the natural world—animals and landscapes. She added two sketchbooks, a box of colored pencils, graphite pencils, a sharpener, and an eraser.

Eve set a wood box on the table. It had a simple hook lock and a handle. "Figured you would want something to hold the pencils and other supplies. This was the least expensive artist box available."

Meg put it with the rest of her selections and added it to the tally. "I'll go to the bank in the Market Square during my midday break and get the money to pay for these items. And I'll talk to Simon about how to pay you for the rest."

"You're paying for these?" Eve sounded surprised— and a little unhappy. "If I'd known that, I would have asked how much you wanted to spend before I started buying things."

"I hadn't thought about setting a purchase limit," Meg replied. "I'm doing this for Hope, so I should pay for it." She paused to savor the feeling of buying something for a friend, the excitement of spending money this way, the anticipation of Hope's pleasure when the box of supplies arrived.

Eve returned everything else to the carry sacks and set them to one side. "Okay to leave them here?"

Meg tensed, anticipating the anxiety that came from a change in the room. Then she realized that this was just another kind of delivery, and she coped with deliveries all the time. "That's fine."

Eve rummaged in the sacks and put one last item on the table. "Catalog from the art store in the Bird Park Plaza. I'm happy to go to the store for you when I'm out shopping, but this way you could order supplies and ask Harry to pick them up when he makes his deliveries."

Harry had worked for Everywhere Delivery until

the company changed its name to Everywhere Human Delivery. Now he worked for the Courtyard, picking up anything the *terra indigene* ordered from businesses in Lakeside. There weren't a lot of things to be picked up, and there weren't a lot of other deliveries being made. Some of that was simply because the Business Association had ordered and stored everything they could before the Elementals and Elders shook the continent. And some of that was because everyone, humans and Others, was trying to figure out what businesses still existed and had merchandise to sell. You couldn't phone a company outside of the region where you lived, and not receiving a reply to a letter could mean a sack of mail was sitting in a railway station somewhere and a response would come eventually—or it could mean there was no one left in that town to send a reply.

"I'll find out what to do with the rest of the supplies," Meg promised, tucking the receipt under the new geode paperweight she'd purchased from Jenni Crowgard.

Eve smiled. "Then I'll leave them with you and get to work."

Meg called Henry, figuring that, as a sculptor, he would be the most interested member of the Business Association when it came to art supplies. And he was interested. She just hadn't expected him to walk out of the Liaison's Office with charcoal sticks, graphite pencils, the other sharpener and eraser, and a sketchbook—and a slip of paper that told him what he owed Eve Denby.

Before she had a chance to call, not only had word reached Simon and Vlad that she had something new and interesting, but Jake Crowgard had spread the news to the rest of the *terra indigene* in the Courtyard, and a steady stream of Crows, Hawks, Owls, and Wolves showed up to look at what was available.

By the time Meg closed the office for her midday break, all the art supplies were gone and she felt exhausted and overwhelmed—partly because she had ended up warning everyone away from the supplies she'd selected for Hope. She'd even leaned over them and growled a couple of times, which amused Vlad more than it did Simon.

No telling how long the interest in this kind of art would last, but for the moment, the Others were excited about exploring something new.

Monty didn't break the silence that had filled the car ever since he and Kowalski headed out to patrol some of the streets in the Chestnut Street station's district. Jimmy had recovered sufficiently from his inexplicable weakness and had gone off that morning "to explore his options."

Monty knew all about his brother's options. What he needed to know was if Jimmy's presence was splintering his relationship with his men, his captain . . . and Simon Wolfgard.

Only one way to find out.

"Something you want to tell me?" he asked.

"Don't want to," Kowalski replied after a moment. "But have to, I guess. And it's better if you're the one who talks to Commander Gresh."

Monty sat up straighter. "Why do I need to talk to the commander of the bomb squad?"

"He and his family are among the humans Simon Wolfgard is allowing to shop in the Market Square and buy food items as well as other goods."

"Captain Burke is also included among those humans. Is that a problem?"

Kowalski breathed out, an audible sound. "With everyone putting in extra hours since that storm in early Sumor, shopping in the Market Square has been handy, you know? You come home from work, do some chores, buy some ground meat from the Courtyard's butcher shop and a couple of rolls from A Little Bite, and have burgers with a salad or some of the vegetables from your share of the Green Complex garden. You buy eggs there because it's easier than standing in line in the grocery store or butcher shop in the Bird Park Plaza and finding out the person ahead of you bought the last dozen—and then having to break up a fight between the woman who bought the last dozen and a woman trying to take them in order to bake her kid a birthday cake. And broken eggs end up on the floor, along with the women, and you, being an officer of the law, have to sort it out and arrest one or both."

"You had to do that?"

"I broke up a fight like that a couple of days ago—after the eggs hit the floor and things really got nasty—but I was off duty at the time, so Officer Hilborn made the arrest."

"Gods," Monty muttered. Had his preoccupation with his own family distracted him so much that he hadn't been aware of what was going on? "Are we going to have to quell riots?"

"If we do, it's because people aren't using the same sense and neighborly kindness they would have shown each other a few months ago," Kowalski replied. "Before the Humans First and Last movement got everyone thinking that any time a shop runs out of something it's a shortage and people are going to starve if they don't hoard whatever they can grab off the shelves, those women might have fought over a dozen eggs. People do stupid things all the time. But more likely they would have been passing acquaintances—women who didn't know each other outside of chatting in the shops while waiting their turn, but still people who would know a bit about each other. Instead of fighting over the eggs, they would have split the dozen so that the woman could bake a birthday cake for her kid. That's what people would have done. That's what most are still doing."

"New people have run to the remaining human-controlled cities, looking for work and a place to live.

They'll be trying to buy rationed goods at the shops too, so it stands to reason that supplies won't always match the demand for a while."

"That concern about supply and demand isn't limited to the human shops."

Monty considered his partner's body language. Kowalski was circling around something. "Just say it, Karl."

"If we're not careful, we may not be welcome in the Market Square stores much longer, and that's going to make it harder on all of us."

Monty sighed. "This is about Jimmy?"

"It's about all of us. As for family . . ." Kowalski let out a bitter laugh. "Ruthie's mother, the woman who loudly declared that her daughter was dead and called my Ruthie trash, rang her this morning and wanted Ruthie to buy her a ham—five or six pounds would do. After all, the freaks had plenty of meat and could just catch more if they ran out. When Ruthie said she couldn't buy that much meat even if a ham was available . . ." He drove for a minute in silence. "I could hear her screaming at Ruthie halfway across the room, so I took the phone and hung up on the bitch."

"I'm sorry, Karl. For you and for Ruth."

"Yeah, well. Personally, I hope that bridge is burned for good. Not sure what that says about me, but I hope it is."

"You love your wife and don't want to see her hurt." Monty studied his partner, an uneasy feeling corseting his ribs. Even before the storm and the difficulty of transporting food and other goods between the regions, it was less expensive to buy food in the Courtyard than in other stores in the city. With prices going up even more, and with some food items in short supply, would there be pressure from friends and family on those who had access to the Courtyard to supply them with food as well?

Was selling food under the table one of those options Jimmy was exploring? Gods.

"I'm piecing this together from things the girls over-heard or were told by Nadine, who has more informa-tion about raw food supplies than the rest of us since her bakery is now operating within A Little Bite," Ko-walski continued. "When Simon Wolfgard made the apartment residents part of the Courtyard and, there-fore, among the beings who could eat the food produced within the Courtyard or brought in from the farms that supply the Courtyard, the Others figured out they would need an extra fifty pounds of meat per week to provide for their tenants. Someone figured out that amounted to twenty-four ounces of meat for each human—roughly four good-size burgers or a small roast or meat for a stew. And that means the Wolves now have to bring down two deer each week instead of one because the quantity of beef and pork being sent to the Courtyard from earth native farms hasn't changed."

"And a pack isn't successful at every hunt."

"The deer herd has been self-sustaining because the Wolves won't kill a fawn unless it's already injured. But how long will that be true if more deer are killed than reproduce?"

Now Monty understood why he would have to talk to Louis Gresh. Every purchase of meat from the Mar-ket Square butcher shop was putting pressure on the Wolfgard. Regardless of whether the Wolves preferred eating deer or moose over beef, some members of their pack—mainly Meg Corbyn—preferred beef and pork. The day Meg went hungry because some other human had bought the last pound of meat or the last dozen eggs was the day there would be a significant change in the relationship between the humans in Lakeside and the *terra indigene*—and that change would not be good.

"You have any thoughts about this?" he asked.

"Now that the mayor has implemented the fair-distribution act so that each butcher shop receives a percentage of the meat coming in from another region, twenty-four ounces is the per-person, per-week limit a registered customer can reserve at a butcher shop," Kowalski replied. "The kind of meat doesn't matter. That's the total."

"A significant change for most households—except for the few of us who can buy that amount from two sources."

Kowalski nodded. "The girls talked it over, and they're going to purchase what they can from the human stores because we can buy rationed goods and the Others can't. The *terra indigene* can buy pizzas at Hot Crust or eat at the Saucy Plate, but they can't go into a butcher shop and buy a roast. So the girls are thinking that if we sell half the meat ration to the Courtyard each week—and by 'sell' I mean receiving a credit equal to the amount we paid for the meat—we can buy a sandwich at A Little Bite or have a meal at Meat-n-Greens without putting a squeeze on the Others. Nadine is going to float the idea to Tess."

"I'll talk to my mother. She may have some ideas. Even during lean times, she made sure we ate pretty well." Monty thought for a moment, then looked at Kowalski, fighting not to smile. "Or is my mama one of the girls?"

Kowalski blushed and concentrated on his driving.

"There is the creek running through the Courtyard. Maybe a few of us should try to catch some fish." Were there places along the shore of Lake Etu where people went to fish? He'd never been interested in the activity, but it was another source of food.

A weighted silence. Finally, Kowalski said, "We're not going far enough into the Courtyard to reach the creeks. Won't be for a while."

Surprised, Monty turned toward his partner. "Why? I thought you and Michael were riding your bicycles along the Courtyard roads. Did you have a problem with the Wolfgard who are guests here?"

"Not with them, no. I'm not an Intuit, but I am a cop. Michael and I both have a feeling that there are other guests in the Courtyard right now, guests no one mentions—at least not to any of us."

Elders. Even the word made Monty shiver. Gods above and below, had *they* returned to the Courtyard?

Monty's mobile phone rang. "Montgomery." He listened for a minute, then hung up. "That was the captain. He and I are expected at the mayor's office in thirty minutes."

"Trouble?" Kowalski asked.

"Only the type and degree are in question." After a moment, Monty added quietly, "Your idea of adding what we can to the communal pot is a good one. It's better for everyone if it doesn't look like we expect the Wolfgard to hunt for us. Better yet if we bring what meat we can to the table."

Stopped at a red light, Kowalski looked at Monty and nodded.

They didn't need the words. There had been no need to fill out a DLU form lately, or check the cairn where keys and wallets might be left when nothing else remained of a missing person. But if the *terra indigene* were squeezed out of eating their usual prey, they would go hunting outside the Courtyard for a different kind of meat.

Jimmy sat at a table in the Stag and Hare, eating a handful of chicken wings and nursing a beer as he eavesdropped on the men in a nearby booth.

"Price of everything is going up," one man complained. "The only thing staying the same is the paycheck."

"Price is going up, and the quantity is going down," his companion said. He lifted half his sandwich, then dropped it on the plate, looking disgusted. "I bought this same lunch special last week, and the sandwich had twice the meat as this one."

"Know what you mean. I went to the Saucy Plate yesterday. Piece of lasagna smaller than my hand, a few greens and a slice of tomato as the salad, one roll, and one fucking pat of butter. One. Charged me ten dollars. And a second roll with butter is now an extra item."

"Mayor says he's working with the governor to keep the lines of transportation open within the Northeast."

"We need the lines open to the rest of the regions. That's what we need."

"They're open for those who have the money to grease the right palms. Bet the mayor and the governor aren't feeding their kids watery soup made out of cheap cuts of meat."

"Bet the fucking Others aren't going hungry either."

A moment of uneasy silence. Then the men focused on their meals.

Jimmy looked at the chicken bones on his plate. Didn't even begin to fill the hole in his belly. And one beer didn't relax him the way mellow weed did—if he could find a source here in Lakeside. The freaks might growl about anyone enjoying a bit of weed on their property, but CJ wouldn't let the freaks toss him out for a bit of weed, not when it meant tossing Sandee and the kids out too. With Mama looking on, Lieutenant Crispin James Montgomery would smooth things over, and the brats knew how to play sentimental suckers like Mama and their uncle CJ.

Finding a source of weed would have to wait. Right now, he needed to scout around the Courtyard a little bit and see if he could turn men bitching about food into a business opportunity. Dropping enough money on the table to cover the bill, Jimmy headed for the door.

As he walked out of the Stag and Hare, he realized the blond-haired man who had been sitting at the bar, also nursing a beer, had been watching him in the mirror behind the bar the whole time.

The meeting at the mayor's office included Acting Mayor Walter Chen, Police Commissioner Raymond Alvarez, and ITF Agent Greg O'Sullivan, as well as Monty and Captain Burke.

"I received a phone call from Governor Hannigan this morning," Chen said. "Based on the news reports, it sounds like we have some serious shortages of certain foods, and Commissioner Alvarez tells me the increase in break-ins that target butcher shops and small neighborhood grocery stores seems to reflect that. But it's my opinion, and the governor agrees, that the *terra indigene* have not curtailed the transport of food to such a degree that food cannot be purchased. Could shops be attempting to create 'luxury items' as a way to increase prices? Your thoughts?"

Everyone looked at O'Sullivan, then at Burke, but it was Alvarez who answered. "I sent men to every human farm that supplies food to Lakeside to find out the status of the family and the farm. The savagery of the storms that slammed into the city didn't last much beyond the city limits, so the farms dealt with minor damage to crops and buildings, but no loss of life among the people or livestock. The cluster of stores that supply the farms reported running low on things like sugar and coffee, and they're hoping to get resupplied before they run out, but it's pretty much business as usual for them. Same with the farmers. They're still bringing meat, dairy, eggs, and produce to market."

"My impression is animals from the Midwest Region are slower to arrive at cities like Shikago, whose meat-packing plants supply much of the meat for the Northeast Region," Burke said. "Grain is also arriving in smaller quantities, but those things *are* crossing regional boundaries. Same with the foods grown in the Southeast Region. The farmers may not be exporting as much out of their region because they're being encouraged to sell within their region first."

"One difference in supply and demand may be the number of people who have temporarily swelled the population of Lakeside and other human-controlled cities in the Northeast," O'Sullivan said. "A lot of people fled from Toland before and after the storm. Some went back to their homes, either permanently or to salvage what they could. Many are looking to find work and settle someplace else. Problem is, there are significantly fewer human-controlled places than there were a month ago. There are two college towns in the Finger Lakes area. Around them are small towns, farms, vineyards and wineries, and wild country. All those places, including the college towns, are semi-isolated now—even more so than they used to be. People can come and go, and goods are delivered to stores. The phones don't always work beyond the local area—and phone lines that would connect the Finger Lakes area with Toland are brought down with such regularity, the phone company has stopped trying to repair them. But people who have skills that would benefit one of those small towns, or can work at the colleges, would be able to relocate there." He smiled tightly. "I don't think there are many people who have tried to resettle in an area controlled by the *terra indigene*—especially people who aren't used to such sharp scrutiny."

"What about the Others in the Courtyard?" Chen asked. "Are they experiencing shortages?"

Monty held himself still, but no one else spoke—because they were waiting for him. "Not everything is as plentiful as it was," he said carefully. "But that's because the Lakeside Courtyard has allowed some police officers to purchase goods, including food, at their stores. And the tenants in the apartment buildings the Business Association purchased are also permitted to buy food in the Courtyard."

"They are trying to feed more people from the same bowl of rice?" Chen said.

"Yes, sir. That was brought to my attention a short while ago." The lack of criticism for his failure to spot the potential trouble earlier was its own form of censure. "A suggestion has been made that if the humans want to continue eating in the Courtyard in order to interact with the *terra indigene*, then all the tenants in the apartments should offer part of their weekly meat ration to be used at the coffee shop or the restaurant in the Market Square. That way the humans are helping the Wolves feed all the residents."

"Do you think they'll agree to this?"

Monty smiled. "I don't think the Business Association will argue with the female pack."

"Which brings up a point Elliot Wolfgard asked to be addressed." O'Sullivan took a folded piece of paper out of his inside jacket pocket and handed it to Walter Chen. "To sign up for a ration book, a person needs to go to the government office that is handling the distribution and show a place of residence and employment, as well as provide a list of the people to be included if it's a ration book for a family—and to show proof so that someone can't claim to have four children when they really have two."

"Or they can receive the books at their place of employment," Chen said. "For example, all police officers and staff working at the Chestnut Street station will receive their ration books at the station."

"The accounting department at each station will be responsible for distribution," Alvarez said, looking at Burke and Monty.

O'Sullivan pointed to the paper he'd given to Chen. "These people are employed by the Courtyard. Being human, they're entitled to receive a ration book. Mr. Wolfgard did not want them penalized for not working for a human employer."

"The consul is very thorough," Chen said with approval. "I'll personally make sure these names are correctly recorded. They will receive their books at the Courtyard?"

"Yes. The consulate will distribute the ration books."

Chen stared at one name before looking at O'Sullivan.

"She's human," O'Sullivan said quietly. "She's entitled to rationed goods, same as anyone else."

Monty tensed. Elliot had added Meg's name to a list that would become a record in the mayor's office?

"Knowing where she is doesn't mean being able to reach her," Burke said so softly his voice barely carried. "Her being included sets a precedent for the other girls. They all face enough challenges without being forced to depend on someone else for food."

Monty wasn't sure how Steve Ferryman listed the five young *cassandra sangue* who lived in the Intuit village, or Jean, who lived with a Simple Life family. Were Intuits and Simple Life folk even included to receive ration books? Did they need them? Something to ask, but not here and not now.

"I'll speak with all the station chiefs and make sure they're aware that price gouging should be reported," Alvarez said. "Since people have to register at shops, the owners shouldn't be allowed to take advantage of what, hopefully, will be a temporary situation."

"One last thing, Lieutenant." Chen picked up a carry bag from the floor beside his chair and set it in front of Monty with a gentle smile. "Rice. It's a staple food in my neighborhood. I offer it as a small token of goodwill to our neighbors in the Lakeside Courtyard."

"I'll make sure they receive it," Monty said.

He, Burke, and O'Sullivan walked out together. O'Sullivan stopped the other men before they reached their cars.

"Lieutenant, you should know that Elliot Wolfgard included your mother and sister as employees and tenants of the Courtyard. He was precise about saying your brother was neither an employee nor a tenant, that his position in Lakeside was that of a temporary visitor and he couldn't claim the apartment as a place of residence."

"Is Cyrus looking for work or another place to live?" Burke asked.

Monty shook his head. "As far as I know, his official residence is still listed as somewhere in Toland."

"Then you, and he, should be aware that the ration

book for him and his family will be issued out of To-land," O'Sullivan said. "If he wants rationed goods, he'll have to return to Toland and pick up the ration book in person or provide the proper authorities with his new permanent address."

Jimmy wasn't going to do without. Jimmy never did. Not for long, anyway. But Monty couldn't see his brother going back to Toland just for a ration book.

"You need a lift back to the Courtyard?" Burke asked O'Sullivan.

"No, but thanks. I still have some work to do at the office here. I just wanted a private moment to let you know about Cyrus."

"I appreciate that," Monty said.

After asking Kowalski to deliver the rice to the Court-yard and continue patrolling, Monty went back to the station with Burke.

"Do the Others think there are shortages?" Burke asked. "Or do they just enjoy what's available?"

"They tend to eat what is in season," Monty replied. "And the supplies that come in from the earth native farms differ from week to week."

"You let me know what the women want to do about sharing the meat ration. I'll participate."

Monty studied his captain. "But you don't usually eat in the Courtyard."

Burke said nothing until they pulled into the station's lot. "I think I should for a while, don't you?"

"I'll take one of those lasagnas," Jimmy said. He wasn't sure what kind of freak ran the Market Square butcher shop. Wasn't one of the Wolves, because the freak had brown feathers in its hair.

"Four pieces of lasagna is ten dollars. The dish is an extra five. You bring back the dish, we refund the five." The freak pulled out a ledger, opened it to a flagged page, and made a notation.

"What's that?" Jimmy asked.

The freak didn't answer. He set aside the ledger and sealed the package of lasagna just as Sierra walked into the shop.

Jimmy smiled, pleased that she hesitated when she saw him. Bitch should hesitate. Bitch had a lot to make up for.

"Hey there, Sissy," he said pleasantly. "Did you have a good day at work?"

"Yes, I did." She approached the counter, still watching him, trying to assess his mood. As she should. Then she turned to the freak. "Hi, Boone. I'd like a package of lasagna."

Brown eyes stared at her. "That's four pieces."

"My mama is having dinner with me and the girls."

More marks on the ledger. Shit. The freaks were keeping tabs on what was bought and how much? Well, he'd just have to figure out how to get around that in order to assure his customers that he could deliver a steady supply and quantity of meat.

Jimmy slanted a glance at Sissy. Wouldn't be that hard, with a little help from someone who owed him.

He waited for her, walked out of the shop with her. Once they were outside, where there was bound to be something watching them, he closed his hand on her carry sack. "Let me carry that for you."

"It's all right," she said hurriedly. "I can . . ."

Cross me on this, and you will pay.

She read the threat in his look and released her hold on the sack. "Thanks, Jimmy."

Gods, the bitch even thanked him. Could it get any better?

They walked through the Market Square's open area. They walked through the employee parking lot to the wooden door that opened onto what had been the customer parking lot when some of the stores had been open to the general public. And they dashed across Crowfield Avenue to the apartment building.

The building's outside door wasn't locked at this

time of day, but the bloodsucker on guard would be nearby. While Sissy opened the door and blocked the view of anyone inside, Jimmy slipped her carry sack into his own. Nothing suspicious about consolidating packages.

He had his apartment door key in his hand and was turning toward the apartment when she started to reach for her carry sack, then stopped, confused—and a little frightened.

"Jimmy . . ."

"That's all right, Sissy." His smile and friendly voice were at odds with the look in his eyes. The look was a warning to Sissy. The rest was playing to the unseen audience. Here was the kindly brother bailing out his little sister again—and providing a reason for any sniffling and whining the bitch might do. "You can pay me back whenever you get the money." Next time he squeezed her for a little cash, the dumb-ass bloodsucker would confirm that she owed him money. How good was that?

Pleased with himself, Jimmy walked into his apartment and shut the door in Sissy's face.

Sandee met him in the kitchen, looking disheveled and pouty. Gods, what had he ever seen in her?

"Here." He pulled one of the lasagna dishes out of the carry sack. "Dinner. I get half. You and the brats can have the rest."

"That's not enough," Sandee whined. Her eyes fixed on the second lasagna when he put it in the fridge. "And you got another one."

"That's business," he snapped. "If I see so much as a spoonful of it missing, you'll end up with broken fingers and a few missing teeth." He rounded on Clarence and Fanny, who stood in the kitchen doorway. "And that goes for you too."

"Don't you be talking to your children like that," Sandee protested.

"Who says they're mine? Got no proof they're mine."

"Jimmy," she whispered, her eyes filling with tears.

"If you want to do that shit, do it somewhere else," he snapped. "If you want to eat, get this heated up."

Sandee sniffled and brushed at her eyes, then picked up the lasagna, busying herself at the counter. The kids slunk away, which was fine with him. He settled at the kitchen table and watched Sandee struggle to remove the simple clips that held the cover to the dish. He didn't trust her. She'd gobble up some of the food cold and then try to split the rest.

That ledger at the butcher shop was going to be a problem. But he'd find a way around it.

Heading to the grocery store in the Market Square to pick up some greens for a salad to go with the lasagna Sierra had picked up for dinner, Twyla saw her daughter dash into the butcher shop, not even having the courtesy to thank Vladimir when he opened the door for her.

Taught her better manners than that, Twyla thought. Then something about the girl's movements made her uneasy, and she hurried to the butcher shop and stepped inside.

". . . wasn't paying attention and I tripped over one of the girls' toys and dumped the lasagna on the floor. Couldn't salvage any of it." Sierra gave Boone Hawkgard a brittle smile. "So I need to buy another one."

"Don't have any more," Boone said.

Sierra looked at the dishes of lasagna still in the case. "But . . ."

"Those are reserved."

"But my girls and my mama won't have anything to eat if I don't get another one."

"Don't have any more," Boone insisted. "The dishes I've got left are reserved."

Twyla listened to her daughter, but she watched Vladimir—and knew by the look on his face that Sierra was lying about what had happened to the food she'd bought. Knew he'd contacted the guard at the apartment building. Could guess what had happened.

And she knew what she had to do to try to protect Bonnie and Carrie.

She slipped out of the shop and hurried to Howling Good Reads, catching Simon as he walked out the back door.

"Mr. Simon," Twyla said, hurrying toward him. "Could I have a word with you in private?"

Some change in him, as if he sensed that being human wasn't going to be enough. He looked toward the Liaison's Office and raised a hand.

Meg waved at Twyla, then smiled at Simon and pointed toward the Market Square.

"Miss Meg shouldn't be going to the Market Square just yet. And not by herself," Twyla said.

Nathan, who had been trotting off for home, suddenly spun around and charged at Meg, backing her up against the office door.

"Hey!" she protested.

"Wait for me," Simon called.

Meg looked at Simon, then at Nathan, and nodded.

At least Miss Meg wouldn't get tangled up in whatever drama was going to take place.

Simon unlocked HGR's back door and held it open for her.

Sighing, Twyla went inside.

<Vlad?> Simon called. <What's going on in the Market Square?>

The Sanguinati had offered to pick up the dish of lasagna after Meg had invited him and Nyx to join her and Simon for dinner. Nyx didn't usually participate in human-style meals, and Meg was excited that she had accepted the invitation.

<The Sierra tried to lie to Boone Hawkgard in order to purchase a second dish of lasagna.> Vlad

paused. <The Sierra just rushed out of the shop. Lieutenant Montgomery isn't home yet, so I expect she'll be running to her mother for help. Anything you want me to do?>

<Pick up our meal and escort Meg home. Nathan's got her pinned to the back door of the Liaison's Office.>

Simon turned his attention to Miss Twyla.

"You gave Sierra a chance, and she messed up," Miss Twyla said. "If you say that's the end of it, then that's the end of it."

"What do you want me to say?" He wasn't sure what she wanted from him.

"Among your kind, if a parent doesn't bring home food, what happens?" she asked.

"The pups go hungry. If they're hungry for too long, they'll die."

She nodded. "I know for a fact that Sierra has a little food in her apartment—some peanut butter and crackers. Maybe a bit more tucked in the cupboards. But she doesn't have enough to make a meal, and peanut butter on crackers isn't lasagna."

Simon cocked his head. "You want the Sierra's puppies to go hungry?"

"Yes. I don't want anyone to help her this time. Not me, not you, not the neighbors who will want to help, and especially not Crispin. He'll want to help his nieces, and Sierra knows that. As long as someone helps her girls, Sierra won't stand up to Cyrus. I'm sure Mr. Vlad knows, as I do, that Cyrus somehow ended up with the lasagna she bought."

"It could cause trouble if I bite Lieutenant Montgomery to stop him from helping."

She smiled. "Hopefully Crispin is smart enough not to need a bite to see reason." Her smile faded. "I shouldn't have asked for help."

"You're part of my pack." By accepting her choice, he'd closed that door on his own tail. Besides, this was just the kind of confrontation the Elders wanted to ob-serve in order to see how a human like that Cyrus could cause so much trouble.

"I'll give the lieutenant enough reasons not to help the Sierra," he said. "You should be scarce this evening."

"No, Mr. Simon. Sierra needs to see that not helping her isn't your decision alone. You may dote on your young, but I bet you Wolves understand about tough love. So do I."

Simon sighed. "The female pack will be unhappy." And he didn't think anyone except that Cyrus and his mate was going to enjoy the lasagna tonight.

Miss Twyla touched his arm. "I don't think they'll be unhappy with you."

She walked out of Howling Good Reads. Simon waited a moment before locking up.

<Simon?> Vlad called. <Meg was starting to prickle, so I told her why there might be trouble tonight. She and Nyx decided to postpone the lasagna dinner until tomorrow. See if Tess still has anything you and Meg can eat tonight.>

<Where is Meg now?>

<She's calling the female pack. I think most of our tenants are going to be looking for a different meal tonight.>

Growling softly, Simon went into A Little Bite and heard Nadine Fallacaro on the phone. Heard the growl in *her* voice and hesitated.

"You did the right thing," Nadine said. "No point spoiling a good meal. Eve Denby just got home. I'll call her and let her know. You want someone to bring your box of cards to your apartment? No? Okay, if I see him . . . Oh, he's here. I'll tell him." She hung up.

"We're not eating lasagna tonight," Simon said.

"Pick what you want from the display case," Nadine said. "I have to call Eve." She turned her back on him as she dialed the Denbys' number.

As he chose food for himself and Meg, he listened to Nadine and felt sorry for himself and Montgomery. It sounded like the female pack was going to gather in the Market Square this evening, and he and Montgomery—and the Sierra—were going to be smack in the middle of a showdown.

CHAPTER 11

Watersday, Messis 11

Monty tensed as he listened to Pete's hearty voice. "We're driving up to Ferryman's Landing to eat at Bursting Burgers. Special treat for the kids. Henry Beargard said there would be no objections to us going up there. Okay if we take Lizzy?"

"It's fine with me if she wants to go." It wasn't lost on him that he wasn't included in the invitation.

"Better if she comes with us." A warning, carefully worded.

Monty looked at Kowalski, who was talking on his mobile phone, his face set in hard lines.

"We'll be back before bedtime," Pete said.

Translation: whatever trouble was in the Courtyard would be settled by then—one way or another.

Kowalski ended his call at the same time that Monty hung up and Burke approached Monty's desk.

"Might not be the best night to have dinner in the Courtyard," Monty said quietly. "Sounds like there's some trouble."

Burke smiled. "Should be interesting."

"'Interesting' isn't the word for it," Kowalski muttered as he and Monty accepted a ride from the captain.

Burke pulled into the customer parking lot instead of going into the Courtyard and parking in the employee lot. The wooden door between the two lots was usually unlocked while stores were open, allowing the tenants easy access to the Market Square.

Unlocked didn't mean unguarded, but the door wasn't usually guarded by a Wolf in human form—and certainly not Simon Wolfgard. But he was the one waiting for them when Burke parked the car.

The three men got out. Burke walked beside him. Kowalski remained a couple of steps behind. Watching their backs or distancing himself because he knew more than he'd said about what was happening here?

"Lieutenant," Simon said.

Barely a look and nod to Burke before the Wolf focused on him again.

"Is there a problem?" Monty asked, keeping his voice calm with difficulty. Lizzy was with Eve and Pete. Out of the way. Safe. But what about the other children? What about his mother and sister?

Simon stepped up to him and bared his teeth, revealing Wolf-size fangs. "If *anyone* helps the Sierra feed her pups tonight, those pups will be gone by morning. And 'anyone' includes you, Lieutenant. Especially you."

Stunned, Monty said nothing when Simon walked away. He turned to Kowalski. "What do you know?"

"Nadine showed the *terra indigene* who work at Meat-n-Greens how to make lasagna. Special dish. Lots of ingredients. Limited quantity. Some of the lasagna was sold at the butcher shop in dishes that held four servings. The rest is being served tonight at Meat-n-Greens. I know that much because Ruthie told me we were splitting a dish with Merri and Michael. The weekly twenty-four-ounce per-person limit on meat purchased in the Courtyard is now in effect, and the meat in each piece of lasagna counted toward that limit." Kowalski waved a hand toward the door Simon had left open. "This? Something to do with Sierra lying to Boone

Hawkgard when she tried to purchase a second dish of lasagna."

Gods. Well, he could guess why she'd tried to buy more than her share of a limited food. "I'll talk to her."

"Maybe you should talk to your mother first," Burke suggested, tipping his head to indicate the woman standing at the far end of the employee parking lot, watching them. "She was here." He turned to Kowalski. "And you're off duty, Officer."

Kowalski looked at Monty, then at Burke. "You sure, sir?"

"I am sure," Burke replied.

Kowalski walked up to the light at the corner to cross the street instead of trying to dodge the traffic on Crowfield Avenue.

"Excuse me," Monty murmured, leaving Burke to join his mother.

Twyla said nothing, just walked around the garages that formed one side of the open area behind some of the stores—and led to the back stairs of the efficiency apartments. She stopped at the foot of the stairs.

"We can go up if you feel the need," Twyla said.

"But you don't." His father had taught him many things, but his mother had taught him the value of courtesy. She'd taught him to respect the feelings of others. And both his parents had taught him to stand up for himself without beating down someone else. Did she sometimes snap at her children when they pushed too hard or annoyed her too much? Sure. Every parent did on occasion. But true anger was rare, even toward Jimmy—and that's what Monty saw in her now.

"It's easy to say we're helping Sierra in order to help the girls," Twyla said.

"It's easy because it's true," Monty replied quietly.

"Not this time, Crispin. Helping her keep on this way . . . That's called enabling, isn't it?"

He almost teased her about reading psychology magazines, but she wasn't in a mood or a mind for teasing.

"What do you want me to do?"

"Mr. Simon is doing what needs doing—doing what I asked him to do. So I want you to support him."

Monty let his breath out in a long sigh. "Maybe I shouldn't have encouraged Sissy to come here with you."

"What could she have done in Toland alone with two young girls, especially after that storm hit? No, Crispin. You did right by her—and me—when you helped us come to Lakeside. Now give your sister a harder kind of help."

He kissed his mother's cheek. "The Denbys have taken Lizzy with them to Ferryman's Landing. Want to have dinner with me at Meat-n-Greens?"

He wanted to go home and change clothes, but he didn't want to get waylaid by Sissy—and he sure didn't want to talk to Jimmy, who was somehow at the heart of this mess.

He got only half of what he wanted, because Sissy was in the Market Square facing off with Simon.

"It's just a stupid piece of lasagna!" Sissy screamed.

"It's food," Simon snapped. "You already took your share. You don't get more. Not from the Courtyard."

"But my girls are hungry!"

"Then go to a human store and buy food there!"

"I can't afford to buy another meal tonight, not with what *you* pay me!"

"That was uncalled for," Twyla whispered, shaking her head. "Girl shouldn't be mouthing off like that when she knows it's her fault."

"You don't like what we pay, then find another job," Simon snarled, showing fangs.

Monty scanned the crowd gathering around Sissy and Simon. Most of the women who worked in the Courtyard were present, except Katherine Debany and Elizabeth Bennefeld, the massage therapist. Among the *terra indigene* females were Tess, whose hair was red and coiling, Nyx Sanguinati . . . and Fire, who watched Monty's sister with frightening intensity.

Simon started to walk away, carrying one of the insulated sacks from A Little Bite.

"I hope you choke on that food!" Sissy yelled.

An odd and terrible silence suddenly filled the Market Square.

Simon turned to face her. For just a moment, the Wolf looked frightened, but Monty couldn't tell if the fear was for himself or Sissy.

"You're fired," Simon said. "Find a job among the humans."

"I second that," Vlad said, stepping out of the crowd.

"I agree," Henry rumbled, also stepping forward.

"Yes," Tess hissed.

Simon walked away. The Others moved aside for him.

Gods, Sissy, Monty thought. Her words were stupid and childish under the best conditions. A human boss would have fired her too. She didn't realize how lucky she was that Simon didn't do more than that.

Monty touched his mother's shoulder. "I'll take Sissy back to her place. Why don't you go into Meat-n-Greens? I'll join you as soon as I can."

Twyla shook her head. "I'll go sit in the library for a bit. Need a little time to settle."

He didn't want to leave her alone. Seeing Sissy hurting like this was hard on her too. But when he looked past his mother, he saw Elliot Wolfgard, who met his eyes and nodded.

Twyla was part of the Wolfgard pack now. The Wolves would watch over her.

Monty hurried over to where Sierra stood crying, a little girl alone on the playground, unable—or unwilling—to do anything to help herself.

"Come on, Sissy." Monty put his arm around her shoulders. "I'll take you home."

The Sanguinati on duty gave them a curious look but said nothing as Monty led his sister upstairs to her apartment. The girls were home, unsupervised, which produced a flicker of annoyance until he realized the

Others wouldn't see anything odd about leaving young alone in the den when there were adults nearby.

"Mommy?" Carrie said when they walked in.

"Play quietly for a little while," Monty said, leading Sissy to her bedroom. He closed the door and sat on the bed next to her. Then he grabbed the box of tissues off the nightstand and handed it to her, letting her cry until she was ready to talk to him.

"CJ," she began, looking at him with eyes that had always melted his heart. "CJ, it was just a stupid dish of lasagna. There was plenty. They were just being mean."

He shook his head. "One piece per person. That's not unreasonable."

"But my girls aren't going to have anything to eat. I don't have even a full glass of milk left to split between them."

"They'll be hungry," he said sympathetically. "Tomorrow you can buy more food." Maybe. He wasn't sure what would be open on Earthday except for A Little Bite. "I can't give you any food tonight, Sissy."

"You could give me the key to your place, and I could slip down and pick up a few things from the fridge and cupboards." She gave him a wobbly smile. "I wouldn't take much, CJ. Just enough for the girls."

"I can't do that. If I help you, the Others will take the girls." If he helped her after Simon warned him not to, would the *terra indigene* even tell him where they relocated the girls? "They aren't bluffing, Sissy. You act like they are, but they're not."

"CJ . . ."

Gods, this was killing him. Would making a sandwich for the girls really be so bad? If he was dealing with other humans, maybe not. But the Others wouldn't see it that way. "I can't help you."

"Won't help me." Sissy pulled away from him. "Because I'm not really family."

Monty stared at her. "What does that mean? Is that more of Jimmy's crap?"

"It isn't crap if it's true."

"For a smart girl who did so well at school, I swear, Sissy, sometimes you can be stupid." When he tried to hug her, she sprang up, putting as much distance as she could between them.

Sighing, Monty pushed to his feet. "Look, I still have a one-bedroom apartment near Market Street. That area of the city has had some trouble, but you and the girls could stay there for a few days if you wanted to get away from Jimmy while he's in Lakeside." He'd been planning to talk to the landlady about dissolving the lease to free himself of that expense. He didn't think she'd hold him to it since rents had doubled in the past few weeks with the influx of people looking for jobs in a human-controlled city. But if Sissy wanted to take over the lease, he would talk to the landlady about paying the difference in water usage for three people instead of one.

"I'll take care of myself *and* my girls. I don't need your help."

The bitterness in her voice stung him. "I'll see you in the morning."

She didn't respond, so he walked out, smiling at Carrie and Bonnie as he left. He stopped at his apartment long enough to change into casual clothes and collect his mail. Returning to the Courtyard to have dinner with his mother, he thought about Sierra—not as a big brother but as a cop. If he'd done that before, would he have spotted the signs of trouble when they were all living in Toland? Well, he'd spotted enough of the signs, but would he have acted on them?

He thought about Sierra as a young woman with her first job, struggling to pay the rent on a tiny box of an apartment but proud to have her own place. Except . . . had she struggled financially because her job didn't pay quite enough, which is what she'd told him when he'd treat her for lunch, or because Jimmy had been coming around every few weeks and squeezing her for money?

And later, when the man who had fathered her children took off for good, had he accepted the excuses for the lost jobs or the final notices on utilities because he truly believed them or because his life with Elayne and raising his own little girl was his own excuse for not asking hard questions?

And now it had come to this: Sissy feeling betrayed, feeling like an outsider, because her family loved her enough not to help her continue on this path.

Meg slipped off her sandals and rubbed one calf with the bottom of her foot to try to relieve the pins-and-needles feeling.

"You're not eating," Simon growled, "and you're itchy."

She'd eaten just enough not to feel empty, but she wasn't enjoying the food. "I'm mad at Sierra for spoiling the nice dinner we were going to have, and I feel bad about feeling that way."

"Why? The whole female pack feels that way." Simon cocked his head. "Do you want to go bite the Sierra?"

"Yes!"

He narrowed his eyes and leaned back a bit, as if worried that she might bite *him*, and that made her smile.

"Not for real," she amended. Then she clenched her hands. For the past couple of weeks, she'd put the silver folding razor in a dresser drawer when she got home. That made it easy to find if she really needed to cut to see a prophecy, but she no longer carried it with her all the time. Right now, sitting here in the summer room with Simon, the razor felt too far away. And yet, she really didn't want to make a cut. Not for Sierra.

"Vlad is still in the Market Square," Simon said. "So are Henry and Tess. Do you want them to bring back the box of prophecy cards?"

She thought for a moment, then shook her head.

But what if something bad happened, something her warning would have stopped?

What if the something was actually a good thing?

"I think something is going to happen tonight," Meg said.

Simon took a bite of his sandwich and studied her as she raised her leg and rubbed the calf, trying to relieve the prickles.

"Blair and I will go back to the Market Square and keep watch," he finally said. "Nothing bad will happen to the Sierra and her pups."

The prickles faded. Her words had been vague but, apparently, they had been enough. Or had the prickles faded because Simon promised to keep watch?

What did that mean for herself, for the other blood prophets, if a vague warning sometimes could be enough because someone really listened?

Simon picked up her sandwich and held it in front of her mouth. "If you're going to bite something, bite this."

She did. And because her teeth scraped one of his fingers when she bit down, she had to hold her own sandwich for the rest of the meal.

In Wolf form, Simon trotted back to the Market Square. Allison Owlgard, Vlad, Blair, and Elliot were already in position to watch the Sierra's apartment and the area around the building. If Meg hadn't been itchy, none of them would have been out there watching a human they didn't like.

The Wolves had been keenly aware of the odd silence filling the Market Square since the Sierra had challenged him. Did the Elders understand that firing her was a human way of asserting his dominance as the leader of the Courtyard? Maybe he should tell them to make sure they understood this kind of dominance since they might see it in other places where humans lived.

<Anything?> he asked when he joined Blair and Elliot in the shadows of the customer parking lot.

<Montgomery is still awake and sitting on the

porch,> Blair reported. <Vlad said the Sierra is awake too. That Cyrus and his mate haven't left their den this evening. A little while ago, they were either fighting or mating—he couldn't tell which—but there are no sounds coming from them now.>

<Simon?>

<Jester?> The Coyote was supposed to be at the Green Complex, asleep in his own den.

<The girls at the lake want to know why you asked Nyx to watch over Meg tonight.>

A breeze suddenly ruffled his fur. Blair and Elliot looked at him in surprise.

<I promised Meg we would watch the Sierra tonight, but she was itchy earlier and I didn't want her to be alone,> he told Jester.

<Ah. I can sleep on Meg's porch.>

With all the windows open to let in the cooler night air, Jester would be able to hear if Meg got up in the night—or opened a dresser drawer. He would alert Nyx, if she didn't understand the significance of that sound. <Thanks.>

Nothing else to do, so Simon and the others settled down to keep watch.

Shortly after daybreak, before most of the humans were awake, a taxi pulled up in front of the stone apartment building.

The Wolves and the Sanguinati watched the Sierra carry luggage to the curb, watched the taxi driver quietly load the carryalls into the trunk. They watched her lead her pups to the taxi and tuck them in the backseat. They watched her return to the building just long enough to close the outer door very quietly.

They watched the taxi drive away.

<Can you follow her, find out where she goes?> Simon asked Air when she ruffled his fur.

<Why?>

<So I can tell Meg what happened to the Sierra. So

she knows why she was itchy.> And to tell Montgomery and Miss Twyla, but that wouldn't be important to the Elementals.

<I will follow.>

Lights were on in Nadine's den. In a few minutes, she would come over to A Little Bite to start her baking.

Kowalski stepped out on the top porch of the two-family house across the street, yawning and rubbing his head but looking around in a way that made Simon think the human wasn't as sleepy as he appeared. Had Kowalski heard the taxi and come out to investigate? Or did he do this every morning?

Kowalski spotted the Wolves who were watching him and froze. After a moment, he raised a hand in greeting.

Simon raised a front paw in acknowledgment but didn't add a friendly *arroo*. No reason to wake up everyone yet.

Vlad, in smoke form, flowed across Crowfield Avenue and joined the Wolves.

<Montgomery is awake,> he said.

Quiet voices in Miss Twyla's efficiency apartment. Simon eased to the edge of the parking lot and cocked his head. Radio. Maybe television. Ah. Weather report. As if a human knew more about weather than the girls at the lake.

Time to go home and catch a quick nap. He had a feeling there would be a lot of howling from the humans today.

Dear Douglas,

Here in Brittania, it's business as usual, which, for us humans, feels surreal. Fishing boats go out and bring back a catch. Hunters trade some goods in order to enter the wild country and bring back a deer or two to sell at market. While we aren't receiving the same quantities of foodstuffs from Thaisia, ships are coming in to our harbors with needed cargo, the manifest carrying both the signature and seal of the harbormaster overseeing the point of origin as well as the signature of the terra indigene assigned to approve any shipment of food. We're even receiving shipments from the human territories in Afrikah and Felidae, as well as merchandise from Tokhar-Chin. No one mentions Cel-Romano. It's like there is a big hole in the world that we're all working around as it fills in and takes a different shape.

Some Cel-Romano refugees have made it to coastal villages on the continent—human places that were established in the wild country outside the Alliance of Nations and have been allowed to exist for generations. The refugees call the war the Destruction of Cel-Romano and the Alliance of Nations. The Others I've talked to call it the Thwarted Human Invasion of the Wild Country. A truth seen through different eyes. The invaders were not only stopped; they were hamstrung so that they will have no time for anything but survival.

While that is true of the cities with factories that made the weapons of war, the country villages, especially those along the original border between Cel-Romano and the wild country, celebrated the return of most of their sons and are living much as they had before the war. There is more wariness, more concern about provoking an attack, but the same can be said for the people in Brittania who deal with the Others.

Recently I met one of the terra indigene who is considered a historian and scholar. I can't tell you what kind he is because I only saw him in his human form and he didn't offer a name that indicated his form or gard. He showed me a map he claimed was five hundred years old. The map showed human places I'd never heard of—places that had once been great civilizations, until humans forgot the world wasn't theirs to claim. He told me remnants of those civilizations still exist, with statues that were great works of art standing sentinel in pastures. The surviving people live in isolated communities on the land that wasn't reclaimed by the wild country, coming together for major celebrations that provide an opportunity to trade merchandise and arrange marriages. They live simply, and few humans in other parts of the world even know of their existence anymore.

I think he showed me the map so I would understand that the land that had once been the largest human-controlled area in the world is gone forever. The people who still live in Cel-Romano will adapt to a simpler way of life or fade away as many did before them.

Business as usual, but nothing will be the same. I think you, better than I, understand that.

—Shady

CHAPTER 12

Moonsday, Messis 13

As he started up the stairs to Sissy's apartment, Monty nodded to the Sanguinati who stood watch in the building's front hall.

Yesterday his mother had shown up early, asking him to take her to the neighborhood Universal Temple, saying they should all spend a little time on Earthday thanking the guardian spirits for their blessings and asking them for the strength to meet coming challenges. When he suggested they take Sissy and the girls with them, Twyla told him to let Sierra have some room to think. She'd been a bit sharp with him, which had made him wonder if she'd spoken to Sissy that morning and already knew the response to that suggestion.

After visiting the temple, he had taken Twyla and Lizzy out for lunch. They met up with the Denbys, who also wanted a day away from the Courtyard. All of them went to a beach on Lake Etu where the children could look for shells and play at the water's edge. They picked up pizzas from Hot Crust on the way home and spent the evening at the Denby residence playing board games.

There were no lights on in Sissy's apartment when Monty watched Twyla cross Crowfield Avenue and go up to her efficiency apartment above the seamstress/tailor's shop. He heard no footsteps overhead while Lizzy got ready for bed. But he hadn't thought much about it since it was the girls' bedtime and Sissy might have turned in early too. His mama had told him that morning that Sissy didn't need anything. He had taken that to mean she had come to some arrangement with Tess and Nadine to supply Sissy and the girls with some food before all the Courtyard shops closed for Earthday.

But this was a new week, a new beginning. He had followed Simon's orders and not given Sissy any food on Watersday, and he'd stayed away from the Courtyard most of yesterday. But the "no food" command didn't apply now, so there was no reason he couldn't buy breakfast for Sissy and his nieces before he went to work. Maybe, having been given a day to herself to consider her actions and the serious consequences, Sissy would really talk to him about what kept happening between her and Jimmy. Or if she wouldn't talk to him, maybe he could convince her to talk to Theral MacDonald, who had gotten away from an abusive relationship.

He raised his hand to knock on Sissy's door, then realized the door was ajar, as if someone had stepped out for a moment.

Monty pushed the door open a little ways. "Sissy?"

No answer. No sounds.

Monty pushed the door open all the way and wished he had his gun. He stepped inside, cautious, listening. "Sissy?"

No sign of struggle. What was left of a package of crackers sat on the kitchen table, along with an open jar of peanut butter. Crumbs on the dishes, milk residue in the glasses. Was this from last night or early this

morning? Had he misunderstood and Sissy had been
left for a whole day without food?

He looked in the bedrooms. No one there. He checked
the bathroom. Then he checked closets and drawers and
the medicine chest.

And then he rushed back down the stairs.

"My sister," he said, wondering if the Sanguinati
could sense how fast his heart was beating. "Did you
see her last night or this morning?"

"I saw her just after daybreak on Earthday," the Sanguinati replied. "She and her young left in a yellow taxi.
They had luggage."

"Didn't you try to stop her?"

"Why would I?"

A grown woman leaving with her own children. No
reason for anyone to stop her. After all, the Sanguinati
was there to prevent anyone who wasn't authorized from
entering the building, not to detain someone who lived
there. "I don't suppose she said anything about where
she was going?"

"No, but you could ask Vlad or Simon. They kept
watch that night. They might know more."

"Thank you. I will." Monty returned to his apartment. Pulling aside the sheer curtains, he studied the
Courtyard stores across the street. No lights on in Howling Good Reads. No lights in the front part of A Little
Bite, but Nadine would be there by now, making the
breads and pastries that would be offered for breakfast.

He checked his watch, then pulled out his mobile
phone. He would call Captain Burke and . . . tell him what?
This wasn't a manhunt where every minute counted. No
crime had been committed—at least none he knew about.

But his sister had packed up and left without a word
to anyone.

He looked across the street to the efficiency apartment his mother had chosen to make her home.

Maybe Sissy *had* told someone. Maybe that explained
his mama's sharpness until they were away from the

Courtyard—until he wouldn't have reason to notice Sissy's absence for a full day.

Monty reined in his impatience when he saw the untouched food on Lizzy's plate. Breakfast had turned into a weird little power struggle, with Lizzy dawdling and dawdling until he pushed back hard because being late meant missing the bus and having to spend money on a taxi in order to get to the station reasonably close to the start of his shift. Burke was willing to give him more leeway than other officers because the constant interaction with the Courtyard was like being on call 24/7, but it wasn't fair to other officers and certainly wasn't fair to Kowalski, who was his partner and would wait for him.

He didn't have time for power struggles this morning. Lizzy hadn't touched the two slices of the peach he'd cut up to share between them, and the half slice of toast had a single bite out of the soft middle.

This morning he wasn't going to cajole or scold.

He picked up Lizzy's dish, put the peach slices into a container, which went in the fridge, and dumped the toast into the sealed bucket that held scraps that would be used as food for the critters the *terra indigene* ate.

He poured the rest of her milk down the drain and heard her shocked "Daddy!" as he rinsed the dishes and left them in the sink—and was glad his mother wouldn't see them.

He fetched his service weapon from the gun safe in his bedroom. Lizzy was still sitting at the table. At least she was dressed for the day. "Let's go. You need to stay with Miss Eve until it's time for school."

"I have to brush my teeth," Lizzy protested.

"You're out of time, so you'll just have to go to school with stinky breath and fuzzy teeth." Monty walked to the door and opened it. "Let's go."

Lizzy slid off the chair and clutched Grr Bear as a column of smoke flowed through the open door. The Sanguinati's head, chest, and arms shifted to human form; the rest of him remained smoke.

"Do you want me to stay with the young one until an appropriate human comes to fetch her?" he asked.

"Appropriate human" meaning someone who wasn't Jimmy or Sandee.

No reason to think the Sanguinati would hurt Lizzy—or feed on her. He wouldn't have hesitated if Vlad had made the offer, but he didn't feel comfortable leaving his girl alone with someone he didn't know well, human or not.

Lizzy settled things by rushing over to him and grabbing his hand. "Grr Bear and I want to go with Daddy."

The Sanguinati nodded, shifted back into a column of smoke, and returned to his position at the foot of the stairs, guarding nothing.

Monty locked the door but left the screened windows open. Providing intruders with easy access to one's residence was not what the police department recommended, but he knew the Hawkgard and Crowgard made use of the porch railings and the shade as they kept an eye on the activity in the Courtyard apartments—and watched for small furry meals.

He hustled Lizzy across the yards and up the porch steps. Pete Denby met him at the door, a question in his eyes.

"Hi, Monty," Eve said too brightly as she joined her husband. "Lizzy, Miss Ruth hasn't gone to the schoolroom yet, so why don't you come in? Sarah is just finishing her breakfast."

"Daddy poured my milk down the drain," Lizzy announced as she and Grr Bear went inside.

"I should put a sign around my neck," Monty muttered.

Pete forced a smile. "Don't bother."

They both heard the *caws* as Crows winged back to the Courtyard.

Kowalski came around the side of the two-family house, dressed for work. "Lieutenant?"

"Call me if I can help," Pete said.

"I will."

Unspoken warnings from Pete and Eve. Did they know something about Sierra's disappearance, or had they observed something this morning that made them cautious? Monty went down the steps and met Kowalski on the walkway. "Karl, you should go to the station, see if there is anything we need to know before we start the day's shift."

"Should I look for anything in particular?"

Monty hesitated, but only for a moment. "A yellow taxi picked up my sister and her girls around daybreak on Earthday. I might need to talk to the driver after I speak to my mother."

"I can make some calls, but you might want to ask Simon first. I didn't see the taxi, but I saw him in the customer parking lot that morning. He might have seen something." Kowalski hesitated. "If Sierra had been coerced in any way, I think the whole neighborhood would have known about it."

"I know." Simon might be upset with Sissy, but he wouldn't have allowed her to be taken against her will.

"I'd better get moving if I'm going to catch the bus," Kowalski said.

Monty saw the lights go on in Howling Good Reads and A Little Bite. "Tell Captain Burke I'll be in after I see a Wolf about a girl."

Simon didn't flip the Closed sign, but he unlocked HGR's front door before returning to the counter where he'd begun sorting the book requests from the *terra indigene* settlements the Courtyard supplied with human goods. According to Toland publishers, an entire warehouse of stock had been destroyed in the storm, and shipments of paper had been reduced by half.

No reason to doubt the statements, and he wasn't about to accept damaged goods. Which meant he really needed to see what Intuit and *terra indigene* publishing companies might have available. He looked up as Lieutenant Montgomery walked into the store.

Before he dealt with books, he had to deal with Montgomery's pack.

"My sister left yesterday morning," Montgomery said. The hand he set on the counter kept trying to curl into a fist.

Tension, not aggression, Simon decided. "Yes. She and her pups left in a taxi."

"Did you notice the license plate by any chance? Did anyone overhear where she was going?"

"She bought tickets for a bus that was going east."

"Do you know where?"

"Not yet." Simon studied Montgomery, who looked a bit . . . trampled. "Meg was itchy because of the Sierra, so we kept watch on Watersday night. I asked Air and her kin to follow the Sierra and let me know where she makes a new den."

"Thank you." Montgomery breathed out a sigh. "I worry about her."

"She is pack." Simon fiddled with the stack of requests. "But if her pups are going to survive, she needs a new pack now. One that doesn't include that Cyrus."

"I know."

Montgomery sounded sad, so Simon added, "I will tell you where she dens."

The human shook his head. "No. Jimmy will ask. If I know and tell him I don't, the lie will cause hard feelings between us—more than there are now. If I or my mother know how to find her, it's possible something will be said that will give away Sissy's new location. Maybe something Lizzy overhears and repeats without realizing the significance. And then Jimmy is on Sissy's doorstep again." He rubbed his forehead. "But she'll need to have the ration books forwarded to her new address, and that will leave a paper trail."

"Should I tell Air to stop following?" He was having trouble tracking this human logic. Montgomery wanted to know and didn't want to know. Well, he wouldn't ask the Elementals to stop following, because, no matter what Montgomery wanted, Meg needed to know what happened to the Sierra.

"No." Montgomery gave him a strained smile. "I would feel easier if someone I trust knows where she is."

It pleased him to know he was trusted with helping Montgomery look after the human's family.

"Well," Montgomery said. "I need to talk to my mama."

Simon nodded. "She was awake around the time the taxi left. She might already know about the Sierra."

"Look, bitch." Jimmy used the voice and attitude that cowed just about everyone—especially women he wasn't trying to charm into bed or out of some money. "I'm here to see my mama, so get your skanky ass out of my way."

The woman, wearing a black dress that looked like a costume out of a creepy movie, continued to block his ability to get more than a step inside the consulate. Then she smiled, revealing fangs, and the lower half of her body, dress and all, changed to smoke.

Fuck! One of those vampires.

"Mama!" Jimmy shouted. "Mama!"

His mother didn't come rushing to see what he wanted, but the fucking ITF agent, who had been sitting at a desk at the other end of the room, talking on the phone, suddenly hung up and came toward him while some middle-aged woman picked up the phone at another desk and punched in numbers, all the while keeping track of him.

"Something I can do for you, Mr. Montgomery?" the agent said.

He knew that tone when it came from a Government Man. "Not a damn fucking thing," he snapped.

"You don't have permission to be here," the vampire

said. Her smile widened. "Unless you'd like to stay for breakfast."

A chill went through Jimmy when the Government Man looked surprised but didn't object to the idea that she might sink those fangs into his throat and suck him dry.

Although . . . He'd heard stories about female vamps being able to give you a suck that blow jobs couldn't match.

He eyed the vamp and was about to say something, just to see how she would respond, when Twyla came down the stairs, followed by a man with thinning hair, amber eyes, and a suit that must have cost enough to buy a month's worth of mellow weed.

"You've got no business being in the consulate, Cyrus," Twyla said quietly but firmly. "This isn't one of the stores where you have permission to shop."

"We need to talk," Jimmy said. "Can we sit down for a minute?" He gestured to the desks. He might find all kinds of things of interest if he had a few minutes to look around. After all, information was a valuable commodity, and you could take it without anyone being the wiser.

"You can't come in. You can say what you want to say right here or we can step outside."

Stone bitch. Couldn't give in even a little bit.

Looking at the freaks and the Government Man, he realized they weren't going to step back and give even the illusion of privacy. "Outside, then."

The middle-aged bitch was still on the phone, still watching him, still reporting to somebody. CJ? That Wolf who gave orders?

Jimmy stepped outside, forgetting to play the caring son by holding the door for his mama.

"What's this about Sissy hightailing it out of here?" he demanded.

"She left on Earthday at first light," Twyla replied.

"Going where?"

"I don't know, Cyrus. She didn't talk to anyone, didn't leave a note. She just packed up her things and left with the girls."

"She must have said something." Shit. He'd counted on being able to tap Sissy for money or information or even getting her to make extra purchases of some of the soaps and things Sandee had said cost twice as much in high-end stores, which were the only places humans could purchase them.

Twyla shook her head. "She said nothing. She just left."

He didn't believe her words, but he believed the sadness in her eyes. Sissy had bolted with her brats. That meant his kids could tug the strings on Grandma's heart a little harder to get more treats.

But that wasn't going to fatten *his* wallet.

"Her choice," Jimmy said. Sissy had stopped being useful, so there was no point thinking about her unless things soured so much here that he really needed to find her. As he walked away, he added, "She was never family anyway."

Meg locked the Liaison's Office and strolled to the Market Square to spend her midday break with Sam. She wanted to hear about what he'd learned in school and about the new Wolf Team book. She wanted to think about something besides Sierra Montgomery and how everyone was stirred up over her departure.

The prophecy cards she'd selected that morning hadn't told her much—bus, east, and the third card, the result, was a picture of a village. And Simon didn't have anything to add when he came into the office minutes after she'd turned the cards. He just confirmed what she already knew. And neither of them had any thoughts about the village because the village card didn't indicate if the place was human, Intuit, or Other.

All the prickling and buzzing and reading of prophecy cards hadn't ended in a big dramatic moment or some significant event. Sierra had made her choice and left quietly—and yet that choice had negated the prophecies Meg had seen about Sierra and her children.

Sierra was free, and Meg could enjoy her time with Sam.

As she reached the archways that formed one side of the square, the Courtyard bus stopped. She recognized several of the Hawks and Crows who got off the bus. Some were reporting for work in the stores; others were there to do a bit of shopping in human form. The last ones off the bus were Jane Wolfgard, Sam . . . and Skippy.

Since Jane carried a mesh bag full of books, it was easy to guess she was heading for the library.

"We almost missed the bus," Sam said, rushing up to greet her.

"It would have been a long walk from the Wolfgard Complex if you had," Meg replied.

"It's a long walk for human legs," Sam agreed. He looked at her through his lashes. "But not so long for Wolf legs."

He was fishing for something, and she had a good idea what it was. "If you came to the Market Square in Wolf form, you wouldn't be able to shift and look human because you wouldn't have your clothes, and you can't shop in the stores if you're naked."

"You could carry the clothes for me."

She braced her hands on her thighs so they were eye to eye. "Do I look like a packhorse?" Seeing the spark of mischief in Sam's eyes, she added, "Before you answer, remember I'm the one who has money to buy a treat."

"*Roooooooooo.*" Skippy gave Sam a pleading look followed by a hard nudge, making it clear he understood the connection between Meg, money, and treat.

Sam returned Skippy's nudge and grinned at Meg.

"I have to pick up a couple of things at the general

store," she said, leading the way. "Then we can go to Meat-n-Greens for something to eat."

"I like looking in the general store." Sam slipped his hand into hers. "There's a lot of stuff in there that we can buy. But not as much stuff as the Crows have in Sparkles and Junk."

Thank goodness for that. For someone like her, the Crows' shop was a visual explosion. At least the shelves in the general store, which was run by Hawks and Owls, were organized and orderly. Even so, she'd learned to limit herself to one or two aisles during each visit to avoid being overwhelmed by all the different things that could be purchased.

Meg stopped at the door of the general store and looked back at Skippy. "Lots of stuff but no food."

The juvenile Wolf stared at her for a moment, then moved off to explore all the scents left by the Courtyard's other residents—and look for anything edible that someone might have dropped or left on a table unguarded.

"We're not allowed to pee in the square, remember?" Sam said when Skippy sniffed around a large flowerpot and started to lift a leg.

Skippy looked like he really wanted to leave a "Skippy was here" mark on the flowerpot, but he obeyed Sam and moved on.

Meg couldn't say why it pleased her so much that Sam was the leader of the puppy pack—which included Skippy as well as the human children—but it filled her with pride. Sam and Robert had had a couple of scraps in order to settle who was leader, but now they were friends who often went off to explore on their own—at least as far as they were permitted to go in the Courtyard—leaving the girls to play games that didn't include mud, dirt, climbing trees, or examining partially eaten remains of various kinds of prey.

Meg wished she'd been there when Simon and Pete

Denby had laid down the rule that *no one* who was in
human form could eat raw scraps of prey—and no puppy
of any kind could try to light a fire like humans did in
frontier stories in order to cook meat scraps that had
been out in the hot sun for who knew how many days
and were not fit to be eaten by human or Wolf.

Of course, the *terra indigene* had never interacted
with human children until now, so Robert's "interest
in the icky" and his somewhat faulty knowledge of frontier living were an education for everyone. Which was
why Ruth was researching frontier life as depicted in
nonfiction accounts rather than the admittedly more
fun fiction that was written about a time that was long
gone. Well, maybe not *that* long gone if you were among
the people who were resettling Bennett or the other
towns in the Midwest Region.

"I'll be over here," Meg said, releasing Sam's hand
as she headed for the aisle that carried the soap and
shampoo. None of the personal items sold in the Courtyard were scented—at least not enough for a human
nose to detect—but they were made with different ingredients. Now, in the heat of summer, she preferred
the yellow soap and shampoo because it felt more in-
vigorating and left the lightest scent of lemon on warm
skin. Or maybe she just imagined the scent because of
the association of lemon and yellow.

She had picked up what she needed and was walking
along the far end of the store, looking at a couple of
endcaps that displayed different items each week—an
exercise that allowed her to see other things the store
offered without seeing too much—when she spotted
two youngsters she didn't know. Must be Cyrus Montgomery's children. But what were they doing in the
Courtyard unsupervised?

The boy was touching things on the shelves. The girl
stood next to him, looking up and down the aisle. When
she saw Meg watching them, she whispered to the boy,
who slipped something into his pocket before they hur-

ried toward the door—and toward Sam, who had been standing at the other end of the aisle, also watching the strangers.

The boy looked older and bigger than Sam, but the leader of the puppy pack stepped in front of the door, blocking it in what was a clear challenge.

The pins-and-needles feeling filled Meg's lower lip. She hurried to the checkout counter near the front of the store and dumped the soap and shampoo. The Hawk behind the counter ignored her, his eyes fixed on the two boys squaring off at the door.

"You didn't pay for that," Sam said. "You can't take things from the store until you pay for them."

"Get outta my way, freak," the boy said.

Sam bared his teeth and growled. "Nobody steals from us."

"Boys," Meg began.

"Fucking freak!" The boy gave Sam a hard shove and bolted outside.

Sam went after him, grabbed the back of the boy's shirt.

The next thing Meg knew, they were rolling around outside, punching each other. She rushed to the door, but the girl was there, pushing at her, getting in the way while she tried to get outside and stop the fight.

"No!" she shouted, finally getting out the door. "Boys! Stop this!"

Adults were coming out of the shops around the square, but none of them seemed to be in a hurry to reach the fight. The Hawk from the general store had the girl by the arm, preventing her from running away or helping the boy.

Sam ducked quickly enough to avoid a fist in the face, but he took a hard blow to the side of his head.

"Enough!" Meg shouted. Couldn't anyone else see this wasn't a little scrap about dominance? That older boy really wanted to hurt Sam!

She saw a glint of metal on a couple of the boy's

fingers right before he hit Sam again, splitting the skin along Sam's cheek.

Oh gods, Meg thought, seeing the blood on Sam's face. *We need to find a doctor.*

She didn't think, didn't wait for help from the other adults. She just waded in, intending to grab an arm, a shirt, anything to pull the boys apart and stop this. As she reached for them, Sam grabbed the boy's wrist and bit the meaty part of his adversary's hand before jumping out of reach, ready to attack again.

Screaming, the boy stumbled away from Sam and flailed his arms.

Meg didn't feel the blow, didn't even know she'd been hit as she staggered back and sank to her knees. Then she tasted blood, felt the agony that was the prelude to prophecy. She didn't want to swallow the words, didn't want to swallow the pain.

"Our Meg! Our Meg!" Jenni Crowgard knelt in front of her.

Shouts. Snarls. Motion all around her now. But all she really saw was Jenni, who took her hand and said, "Starr has chalk. Speak. We will listen."

So she spoke, describing the visions. And as she spoke, she drifted on the euphoria that came from speaking prophecy, veiled from the visions she had seen . . . and the turmoil that surrounded her.

<Pups are fighting in the Market Square,> Blair growled.

Blessed Thaisia, Simon thought as he shelved stock. *Did they have to misbehave today?* <Who?> he asked, because it suddenly occurred to him that Robert was at home, being fed the midday meal.

<Sam and that Cyrus's pup.>

But Sam was with . . . "Meg." He hurried out the back door of Howling Good Reads, followed by Vlad, who had also heard the warning and flowed out the window of HGR's office.

By the time Simon reached the Market Square, adult *terra indigene* were converging on the youngsters and Meg was way too close to the fight—because even from a distance he could tell this was a real fight, not a scrap or rough play.

He ran toward the boys. So did Blair, in Wolf form, and Nathan, who was wearing swim trunks—probably the first piece of clothing he could grab when he shifted to human. Vlad veered off to intercept Skippy before the juvenile Wolf joined the fight.

They were Wolves, and they were fast. But not fast enough.

The human boy hit Sam and broke skin. Sam grabbed the boy's wrist and sank his teeth into the boy's hand— a punishing bite, even if delivered with human teeth.

Mostly human teeth, Simon amended, seeing Wolf fangs when Sam leaped away and snarled.

The boy screamed, flailed—and hit Meg in the mouth.

"Meg!" Sam howled as fur suddenly covered his face and limbs and his head began to change to accommodate a Wolf's jaws and teeth. He leaped on the boy, and Simon, feeling the same fury as he caught the scent of Meg's blood, knew what would happen if Sam managed to get his teeth into the boy's throat.

He grabbed Sam and hauled him away from the boy. "Enough, Sam. Enough!"

Sam snapped and clawed at Simon, trying to get away and reach his enemy. <He hit Meg!> Sam howled. <*He hit Meg!*>

Simon wrapped a hand around Sam's throat, a loose collar to prevent the pup from biting him. He snarled, "Stop. Now."

Then Blair was in Sam's face, snarling his own warning. The leader and the dominant enforcer had both given the order to stop. If the pup disobeyed now, he would be punished.

Sam sagged in Simon's arms, panting.

Simon released his hold on Sam's throat but kept his other arm around the pup. Nathan held on to the human boy, who was wailing as if he'd received more than a bite bruise and a bit of a tear in his skin.

Now that the combatants were secured, Simon looked for Meg, who was sitting on the pavement a few feet away. Blood dribbled from her split lip, staining her summer top. Her lips moved. He couldn't hear her, but he knew what was happening because Starr wrote on the pavement while Jenni held Meg's hand and stared at her face.

Emily Faire ran out of the medical office. Her eyes went from Sam, who was still in a between form, to Meg, to the boy. Then she looked at Simon, and he understood: who should she help first?

Seeing Jane Wolfgard running toward them, Simon tipped his head to indicate the boy. "Deal with him."

The girl broke away from the Hawk and tried to run. Blair leaped in pursuit, then stopped when the girl was suddenly buried under several feet of fluffy snow.

Simon stared at the white pony who was standing near the snow. Avalanche stared back and snorted.

Could have been worse, he thought. *The girls at the lake could have sent Quicksand to find out what was going on.* But he found it reassuring that the Elementals were keeping their promise to watch the Market Square while the Elders observed that Cyrus and the other humans.

<Blair, dig her out,> Simon said. <Let Skippy help. It will keep him from trying to lick Meg.> No telling what would have happened if the juvenile Wolf had thrown himself into the fight. Now he seemed intent on licking Meg's wound and snarling at Vlad, who kept dragging him away from where Meg now lay on the pavement.

Theral finally appeared in the office doorway. She, too, hesitated a moment before going over to help Emily Faire deal with the boy.

No need to call the humans, Simon thought as he watched that Cyrus run toward them, shouting. Montgomery and Kowalski were a step behind him, and Debany was doing his best to hold back the human females who were standing at the other end of the Market Square.

<Simon,> Henry said as he moved to intercept the human males.

He didn't need the warning. He felt the odd silence that suddenly filled the Market Square. And he saw the columns of smoke filling one of the archways—and would bet one of those columns was Erebus Sanguinati.

<Get Meg inside the medical office,> he told Jane Wolfgard.

She nodded and half carried Meg into the building with Jenni providing additional support.

<Nathan, get Sam inside. See if you can help him fully shift to one form or the other.>

Nathan released the human boy, who was making enough noise to attract the attention of every predator in the Courtyard, grabbed Sam, and took the pup into the office.

Blair, having uncovered the girl and provided a way out of the snow pile, stepped back, alert and wary but not sure which attack he might need to meet—human, Sanguinati, Elemental . . . or Elder.

Montgomery and Kowalski grabbed that Cyrus's arms as Simon turned to face the human.

"Look what that fucking freak did to my boy!" that Cyrus screamed at Montgomery. "You gotta shoot that fucker!"

"Jimmy," Montgomery said. "Stop. You're in the Courtyard."

"Who gives a fuck where I am? Did you see that thing? You gotta shoot it for what it did to my boy!"

"He received a bite," Simon growled. "He deserved it."

"The boy stole from the general store," the Hawk said. "He should forfeit a hand."

That silenced that Cyrus, but only for a moment. "What the fuck you talking about?"

"He stole from the store," the Hawk repeated. "If you steal from us, you lose a hand."

"Nailed him good," Emily Faire said loudly as she examined the teeth marks in the boy's hand. "Lost a little skin, and he's going to have a beaut of a bruise, but I don't see anything to worry about."

"Need to get my boy to the hospital," that Cyrus said.

Simon stared in disbelief. Hospital? It was a bite. From a puppy using mostly human teeth. You just licked it clean and let it heal.

Emily snorted. "I used to get harder bites from my little brother."

He wanted to object. Even in human form, a Wolf's jaw had more power than an ordinary human's, so Emily's brother *couldn't* bite harder than Sam. Then he realized that, as an Intuit, Emily was trying to defuse the anger in the Market Square. She might not be able to tell where all the anger was coming from, but she probably had a feeling that human emotions weren't that important right now compared to the rest of the beings who were involved in, or observing, this ruckus.

She looked at that Cyrus. "I can take him inside the office, wash his hand with soap and water, and put some healing ointment on the scraped skin, or you can go to the emergency room, wait your turn, and then pay lots of money to have a doctor do the same thing."

"You should pay for the hospital," that Cyrus said, glaring at Simon.

"Shut up," Simon snarled, "or we'll take the pup's hand as punishment for stealing and be done with it."

"Simon," Montgomery said, sounding courteous but weary.

But Montgomery didn't hear the odd silence, didn't realize the Elders were in the Market Square right now watching all of them—didn't know this was exactly the kind of clash that would get humans killed in other parts of Thaisia where the Elders were the only ones deciding who lived and who died.

Simon focused on that Cyrus. "Your pups are banned from the Courtyard. We will permit them to go into A Little Bite or Meat-n-Greens for food, but only with an adult. If we find them anywhere else or on their own, we'll take more than a hand."

That Cyrus stared at him. "You can't."

"Yes, they can," Montgomery said. "Come on, Jimmy. I have first-aid supplies at my place. We'll take care of Clarence's hand."

That Cyrus didn't move, and the boy looked like he wanted to start another fight when Kowalski tried to lead him away.

"Jimmy," Montgomery warned. "Let's go."

Simon studied the hatred in that Cyrus's eyes. Hatred, yes, but fear too. And no concern at all about the wailing female pup who had been buried under snow—and who had run to the female pack at the other end of the square instead of seeking comfort from her sire.

When the police and that Cyrus were gone, Simon turned to Emily Faire. "Your brother can't bite as hard as a Wolf."

She shrugged. "I'm going to take care of my other patients now."

Meg. He had taken a step toward the medical office when Vlad called him. He hesitated, but Jane knew about not licking Meg's blood and she knew how to care for Sam. And Theral and Jenni were inside to help as well. So Emily Faire didn't need anyone else crowding the office.

He walked over to where Vlad and Henry stood next to Starr Crowgard. Henry pointed to the words chalked on the pavement.

White car. Man. Pain face. Bullet. Numbers and letters that Simon realized must be a license plate.

Those images were the answer, but what had been the question?

"The police pack is dealing with that Cyrus and his pup," Henry said.

"Shall I call Captain Burke?" Vlad asked.

Simon nodded. "And we'll show this to Agent O'Sullivan as well."

Burke swore under his breath when he saw Agent O'Sullivan waiting for him outside the consulate. "I heard about the fight. A tempest in a teapot."

"If Cyrus Montgomery gets his hands on a weapon, it will become a lot more than that," O'Sullivan said, reaching for the door.

Burke shot out a hand, stopping the other man. "What do you know that I didn't hear?" Had Monty downplayed the severity of the collision between Sam Wolfgard and Clarence Montgomery? Or was Monty, caught between loyalties, unwilling to consider the worst about his brother?

"I think Cyrus is a bully who uses charm or belligerence to get what he wants, depending on the situation. I had the impression that he thinks shoplifting is an insignificant act when his children do it, and he becomes resentful when they're caught and held accountable. Seeing Sam Wolfgard in a form that wasn't completely human freaked him out, and he'll use 'he's not human' as a justification for any harm he does to the youngster—or anyone else in the Courtyard." O'Sullivan hesitated. "I didn't see anything, but there was something in the Market Square that seriously spooked Simon Wolfgard and the rest of the shifters."

Elders. Gods above and below. "Anything else?"

"I don't know if he understood the significance of her bleeding, but Cyrus did see Meg."

Not a cut with a razor, but that didn't make any difference for a blood prophet. If they were all lucky, Cyrus wouldn't have noticed the evenly spaced scars. But he didn't think they were going to be that lucky.

O'Sullivan opened the door. "None of which is what Simon wants to talk to us about."

When they walked into the consulate's meeting room, Simon didn't give him a chance to say anything about the altercation or inquire about Meg and Sam. He held out a piece of paper.

Burke looked at the words and sucked in a breath.

Simon touched the paper. "Meg said she saw Sam get hit and thought about needing a doctor. When she was hit and her lip split, she saw this."

"Dominic Lorenzo drives a white car," Burke said. "I don't remember the license plate, but that information is easy enough to find."

"The doctor was supposed to spend some time in our medical office every week, but he hasn't been here in a while," Simon said. "That's why we hired Emily Faire to be the human bodywalker in the Courtyard."

"Isn't Dr. Lorenzo part of the task force that was checking on the blood prophets?" O'Sullivan asked.

"He is," Burke replied. *And the last time I saw him, he'd expressed concern that members of the Humans First and Last movement might waylay him on a stretch of empty road and interrogate him for the hidden locations of the blood prophets. The Others put an end to the HFL movement, but greed could motivate men as much as a political agenda, and those girls could make some men very powerful and very rich.*

An uncomfortable beat of silence before O'Sullivan said, "I'll call the governor's office and make some inquiries, see if they've heard from Dr. Lorenzo recently."

"And I'll do what I can to locate him." Burke folded the paper and put it in his pocket. Since prophecy was about the future, maybe they could find Lorenzo in time to stop the pain and the bullet. Maybe Steve Ferryman could help with that, since most of the girls who had been freed from the compounds were hiding in Intuit communities. "Are your nephew and Ms. Corbyn all right?" he asked Simon.

"They will be." Simon pulled another piece of paper out of the back pocket of his jeans and handed it to Burke.

"Ravendell on Senneca Lake? What's this?" Senneca was one of the Finger Lakes, but he wasn't familiar with Ravendell.

"That's where the Sierra and her pups are now," Simon replied. "Ravendell is a human village within settled *terra indigene* land."

Not land leased and under human control, which meant there were no boundaries, no delineation between what was human and what was Other.

"Not on the rail line from Lakeside to Hubb NE," O'Sullivan commented. "Is it on a bus route?"

"Not on a route between human cities," Simon replied. "There is a bus that travels around the lake. It is considered local, the way the buses in Lakeside are local. Lieutenant Montgomery thought it safer for the Sierra if he and Miss Twyla didn't know where to find her, but I thought you should know this much."

"I will be officially relocating to Lakeside, but for now I still have a residence in Hubbney and try to get back there a couple of times each month," O'Sullivan said. "I could find an excuse to visit the Senneca Lake area if anyone wanted to send something to Ms. Montgomery."

"I'll keep it in mind," Burke said. With nothing left to communicate, O'Sullivan left, but Burke held back. "If Clarence was shoplifting, why didn't the shopkeeper stop him?"

"The Hawk would have let him get outside, so he couldn't claim he meant to pay." Simon shrugged. "Like all the *terra indigene*, the Hawkgard are larger than ordinary hawks. Not large enough to lift a human child that size, but the talons would have done a lot of damage. That's what would have happened, except Sam, and Meg, intervened."

"Clarence was wearing a couple of rings—a kid's version of brass knuckles. He could have caused some serious hurt on another child."

"Sam had one cut that bled." Simon smiled dryly. "A few months ago, I would have licked the cut clean and that would have been that. Today, Sam's cut cheek and Meg's split lip justify coming to the Market Square after dinner for ice cream, followed by a Wolf Team movie marathon."

"I'm surprised Sam and Meg didn't campaign to have ice cream for dinner as well as dessert," Burke said.

"They did. But Katherine Debany put on her mother hat and said ice cream wasn't enough for dinner and recommended scrambled eggs because they would be soft to eat. Everyone in the female pack is bringing an egg to A Little Bite for me to take home."

Sounded like Simon was still trying to figure out the pack status of Officer Debany's mother. Fortunately the Wolf didn't ask for a description of a mother hat. "Could be worse."

Simon nodded. "We could be eating yogurt."

Burke chuckled, but his amusement faded quickly. "How much longer is the tethered goat going to stay in Lakeside?"

"I don't know. If it were up to me, that Cyrus would have been gone the day he arrived."

"So they're still interested in Cyrus Montgomery?"

Simon looked thoughtful. "That Cyrus is not the kind of human who normally would go near the wild country."

WE LERNED FROM YU. The Elders had posted those signs, luring television and newspaper reporters to towns like Bennett to see for themselves what the primal forms of *terra indigene* in the Midwest and North-west regions had learned about what it meant to be human. Whole towns were slaughtered in retaliation for the slaughter of the Wolfgard in those areas.

That had been terrible enough and gave him sleep-less nights—something he would never admit to his men or his superiors—but with the Humans First and Last movement shattered, it wasn't likely that anyone would be able to rally humans to another all-out attack on the Others. At least, not for another generation or two. No, the next threat to humans could be more subtle and more terrible if it was a reflection of Cyrus Montgom-ery's more unsavory traits.

"He's not the kind of human anyone would want the Elders to imitate," Burke said.

"Well," Simon replied after a moment. "He's just the tethered goat. I don't think the Elders are that inter-ested in *him* anymore."

Jimmy sat at the bar in the Stag and Hare, nursing a drink. Sandee was boohooing about Clarence's hand and how dangerous it was to be around the Courtyard. And the kids were boohooing about every damn thing. A man couldn't get any peace.

Had to make some connections. Had to find some-thing he could turn into cash. He'd sold the extra package of lasagna easily enough, and the men he'd approached were interested in anything else he might have to sell. But with restrictions on how much of everything humans could buy at the Courtyard, and the freaks getting riled up about Clarence palming a couple of stupid things that weren't anything, he didn't think he'd be able to get enough food to sell—unless he sold half of what he could squeeze out of the Courtyard and told Sandee to pay for her food some other way.

Too bad the freaks didn't seem interested in hump-ing. Sandee might be worth her keep if they were.

The blond-haired man he'd seen before sat on the

stool next to his and gave him a smile that lacked sincerity and held a hint of mean. "Buy you a drink?"

Jimmy was inclined to like the man for the smile alone. The offer of a drink just added weight. "Appreciate it."

"You have some kind of hook into the Courtyard," the man said.

Feeling cautious, Jimmy sipped his drink. "I know people who have a hook."

"But you can get inside the Courtyard and walk around without raising any alarms."

"True, but humans are watched all the time."

The man downed his drink and ordered another round. "Not all the time. A distraction can have them focused on one part of the Courtyard, leaving another part . . . exposed." He turned his glass. Turned it and turned it. "They've got something that belongs to me. I haven't been able to reach it, but I know where it is. I need access to the Market Square for a few minutes. Just long enough to grab what's mine and get out again. And if I can't take it with me, I'm going to make sure it's of no use to anyone."

The man pulled some money out of his pocket and fanned the bills on the bar. Ten fifty-dollar bills.

"Just a distraction that would draw attention away from the Market Square," the man said. "Enough commotion and noise to let me get in and out. What do you think?"

Five hundred dollars to make some noise and cause some trouble for the freaks?

The man left one fifty on the bar and pocketed the rest. "Just for listening."

"If you need to move in a hurry, how am I going to get the rest?"

There was more than a hint of mean in the man's smile now—and in his blue eyes. "I'll make sure the money gets to you."

Jimmy licked his lips. Five hundred dollars would

set him up for a little while, especially if Sandee didn't know he had the money. "When?"

"Tomorrow." The man held out a hand. "Do we have a deal?"

Jimmy didn't hesitate. He clasped the man's hand. "I'm Jimmy."

The man squeezed Jimmy's hand just a little too hard. "I'm Jack."

To: Vladimir Sanguinati and Simon Wolfgard

Bennett's new residents arrived. The humans who will be working on the farms and ranches are staying in town for a couple of days to receive instructions from Tobias Walker, the foreman of Prairie Gold's ranch, and Stewart Dixon, a human rancher who was helpful to Joe Wolfgard and is making an effort to work with us in exchange for being able to visit Bennett to buy supplies and allow his people to attend social events like going to the movies or attending a concert or play. I'm not sure if there will be professional concerts or plays for a while, but the movie theater informed me that they have received several movies, so there will be some entertainment for the humans—and for us. I'll keep you informed.

—Tolya

Messis 14

Dear Jenni,

Arrived in Bennett. I'm staying at the hotel while I choose the furniture for my bedroom. I met Barb, my housemate, and Virgil, my new boss. I start work tomorrow.

—Jana

CHAPTER 13

As the Owlgard headed home and the rest of the gards still slept, their footsteps filled the Market Square with an odd, and frustrated, silence.

They couldn't find the scent of tasty Wolf cookies anywhere except the working den of the howling not-Wolf. There were interesting scents in the Harvester's working den, especially during the day when so many *terra indigene* and humans hurried and scurried in and out of the cluster of buildings. And then the scents, so fresh and strong, disappeared—the food consumed.

They were strong, and their claws could open doors so easily, but the Wolfgard and the Sanguinati were already unhappy about their insistence on keeping the insignificant human predator close by. If they broke into the working dens of the Harvester and the not-Wolf to look for the tasty or some other treat, the smaller shifters would be angry. So would the Harvester. And the not-Wolf? If she became frightened, she might abandon the working den—and enough smaller shifters, if willing to sacrifice many, could seriously wound an Elder. And the Harvester working with them would do the rest.

<The small human male took from the Hawk,> the male said.

<That was a bad human thing,> the female replied. <The small male was bitten by the Wolf pup, and the taking made all the adults angry.> And a small amount of the not-Wolf's blood had been spilled while the pups were fighting. That scent from Namid's terrible creation had carried through the air, dangerous and alluring.

They continued to prowl around the cluster of buildings, finally ending up at the back door of the not-Wolf's working den. How did the not-Wolf know when to supply the tasty for the Wolves? How did the not-Wolf know what to bring to the smaller shifters when she got into her box and did the baby-bunny scoot around the Courtyard?

<The Wolf receives little papers from *terra indigene* in wild country settlements,> the female said. <Little papers that say what they want.>

<We will tell the not-Wolf what we want.> The male studied his hands and the clawed digits that could do the writing thing.

<Yes,> the female agreed. <We will learn how to do this and tell the story to our kin in the wild country in case the learning is needed when they keep watch over humans.>

They went to the building across the access way from the not-Wolf's working den. The male yanked on the door, snapping the locks. While he went inside and selected paper and a writing stick, the female went hunting for something they could leave in exchange.

Exchange, after all, was different from taking. Taking was bad, but exchange was something humans did.

As he drove them to work, Simon kept glancing at Meg. She'd been broody last night, despite watching the Wolf Team movies with him and Sam, and it seemed that mood hadn't changed.

"Is your lip bothering you?" It looked sore, and he

wanted to take care of her by licking it—something he knew he shouldn't do.

"It hurts, but not too bad." She huffed. "You have to talk to Skippy. He can't keep pushing at people's feet to get them to corral his dish when he eats ice cream."

"He wasn't pushing at people; he was arranging *your* feet to hold his dish."

"Well, I'm a people!"

"But you're the one who taught him to do that."

She sputtered. "I didn't think he would remember. He forgets everything else."

"Not everything. Skippy remembers what's important to Skippy." He looked at her and laughed. "You're wearing your grumpy-pony face."

"Ha-ha. You are so funny."

He felt good. The cut on Sam's face would heal just fine. There was a question about whether Meg's lip would have a scar, but since it wasn't a likely place for her to deliberately make a cut, he didn't think it was a concern—unless it interfered with her ability to eat. In the wild country, an injury that prevented a Wolf from consuming food or water usually meant death.

But Meg had eaten scrambled eggs for dinner and had her ice cream in a bowl yesterday so that she wouldn't have to bite into the cone. She might not be able to eat everything she wanted, but she wouldn't grow weak while the wound healed. Simon pulled up behind the Liaison's Office, then watched while Meg unlocked the back door and went inside. He parked the BOW in the garage and connected it to the power hookup to charge. As he headed for Howling Good Reads, he passed Chris Fallacaro, who had a bag of tools slung over one shoulder.

"Have to replace the lock on the Three Ps' front door," Chris said. "Lorne already talked to Mr. Sanguinati about it."

The human smelled . . . odd. Not quite frightened but more than nervous.

Uneasy now, Simon hurried to the bookstore. But he glanced back at the Liaison's Office and wondered if he should tell Meg to lock the back door.

Vlad stood behind the checkout counter, setting up the cash drawer in the register. "There was sort of a break-in at the Three Ps last night or early this morning."

Simon scratched behind one ear. "Why? There's nothing but paper and office supplies in there. And how do you have 'sort of a break-in'?"

"Well, it's 'sort of' because someone entered by destroying the locks on the door and then took some paper and maybe a marker or pen. Lorne isn't sure how much is missing. He doesn't think it's much, and it was only the untidiness in a couple of places in the shop that helped him guess what was taken."

"If it was taken, it's theft," Simon growled.

"Not when a woodchuck is left on the counter as a kind of payment."

Simon looked at Vlad. Vlad looked at Simon.

"Oh," Simon said. "Why would *they* want pens and paper?"

"When you find out, let me know."

Meg opened the back door and scanned the surrounding area. Returning to the sorting room, she studied the scrap of paper that had been slipped under the door sometime before she'd arrived that morning.

want cukkies

"You may want cookies, but what you need are more spelling lessons," she muttered. And there was something about the thick pencil strokes that made her think it was a demand, not a request.

Well, she knew what to do with a demand.

"Arroo?" Nathan queried from the front room.

"Nothing," she replied as she crumpled the paper. Had Ruth met the teacher or teachers who taught in the Courtyard school? Maybe Henry knew who they were. She'd thought the *terra indigene* youngsters were learning some basic human lessons like reading and writing and arithmetic. Sam could spell better than this, and what puppy paying any kind of attention would misspell "cookies"?

She almost tossed the message into the recycling basket. Then she smoothed out the paper and looked at the message again. It *was* the first time anyone had left a request for cookies. Usually when a delivery arrived from Eamer's Bakery, the Wolves were happy with whatever they received.

Still, giving in to demands would be a mistake. Yes, it would.

Meg picked up the phone and dialed the number for Eamer's Bakery in Ferryman's Landing. Just because she wouldn't respond to a demand, that didn't mean she couldn't be ready to fulfill a request.

Jimmy sat out on the apartment's porch, ignoring Sandee's bitching and whining about the brats being stuck in the apartment without anything to do since the rest of the kids were in school and Clarence and Fanny couldn't even hang out in the Market Square.

Maybe Sissy had the right idea—light out without saying a word. With five hundred dollars in his pocket, he could catch a train back to Toland or go to Shikago. Maybe even go to a human-controlled city in the Southeast Region. Shake off the bitch and the brats and start fresh.

But first he had to take care of his part of the plan.

Jack, who had been watching the Courtyard for a while now, told him that late morning was the time when everyone was beavering away at their jobs and that's when there would be the fewest freaks in the Market

Square. He just needed to push CJ into returning to the apartment building at the right time.

Jimmy looked at his wristwatch—and waited.

Something thumped the back door of the Liaison's Office hard enough to startle a growl out of Nathan, who was in the front room, and had Pete Denby, in his office upstairs, hurrying toward the back of the building to check things out.

Meg opened the back door, then stepped on the scrap of paper that almost fluttered away. She picked it up.

want cukkies!

"Oh, you do, do you?"

Sure that whoever had left the paper was watching nearby, Meg stepped outside and shook her finger. "When someone makes a *request* for a treat, that person should say *please*. That's the polite thing to do."

She waited, sure that the puppies or juveniles who had left the paper would come slinking out of their hiding places with their heads down and their tails tucked. But there was nothing but an odd silence that made her feel strange.

Feeling uncertain but refusing to act like a scared bunny, she shook her finger again and shouted, "You are being bad puppies!"

"Meg?"

She looked up at Pete, who stood on the upstairs landing. "Just setting boundaries," she said, going back inside.

Nathan was in the back room waiting for her. As soon as she crossed the threshold, he sniffed her. When he sniffed the paper in her hand, he pushed her farther into the room, then hit the door with both front paws, slamming it shut.

"Nathan . . ."

He herded her into the sorting room and whacked that door shut before he shifted to human form.

The stunned look on his face stopped her from commenting about his being naked.

"Have you lost your mind?" He almost howled the words.

"Puppies need to learn manners," she replied, annoyed by his tone. "Just because they want cookies doesn't mean I'm going to run out and fetch a treat for them."

"Puppies." Nathan stared at her. "You think puppies left that note?"

"Well, who else . . . ?" She thought about the storm that had swept through Lakeside last month and how something had explored the Liaison's Office, poking around in all the cupboards while a thick fog had blanketed the city. And she suddenly remembered what other form of *terra indigene* liked fresh-baked Wolf cookies. "Oh."

Another thump shook the building.

"Stay here," Nathan said. He slipped into the back room.

It felt like she'd waited a week, but she was pretty sure it was only a minute before he returned and handed her another scrap of paper.

want cukkies pleeze

Meg sucked in air, only then realizing she'd been holding her breath while she waited for Nathan.

"Meg," Nathan whined, following her to the back room.

She opened the door and poked her head out. "The cookies will be here in a little while." She paused, then added, *"Arroo!"*

Closing the door, she sank to the floor. Nathan, back in Wolf form, licked her face before slumping next to her. She burrowed her fingers into his fur and felt the tremors going through him.

"Guess I shouldn't have scolded them, huh?" she said. Nathan looked at her. *"Roo."*

Meg pushed up from the floor when she heard someone calling her from the front room. "That's the mailman. I'd better get to work."

Vlad stared at Simon. "Meg told the Elders they were . . ."

"Bad puppies," Simon finished. "Yeah."

A minute passed before Vlad said, "Why?"

"They didn't say 'please' when they asked for cookies."

"I don't know what to say."

Simon scratched behind an ear that was now Wolf-shaped and furry. "That's okay. Meg said plenty for all of us."

"CJ? It's Jimmy. I need you back here. I got some things to say."

"I'm working, Jimmy."

"Yeah, that's right. You're always too busy for family."

"Jimmy . . ."

"No, you just ride around and look important, and I'll say what I have to say to Mama."

A pause. "I'll be there in half an hour."

Jimmy hung up and smiled. He could always count on CJ. He just had to push the right button.

Meg shuddered. The pins-and-needles feeling filled one side of her neck. She dipped her hand into the pocket of her capris and pressed her fingers against the silver folding razor.

No. Not a neck cut. Too dangerous. Too many things could go wrong.

Leaving the razor in her pocket, she removed the box of prophecy cards from the drawer, opened the box, and rested her hands on the cards. She didn't have a question, not even a vague subject. But her fingertips buzzed as she searched through the cards, selecting the three that created the strongest feeling.

She set them on the table in the order she'd picked them, then looked at the clock. She had a little time before the ponies arrived to deliver the mail around the Courtyard.

She turned the cards over. Then she called Howling Good Reads.

"Vlad? It's Meg. I need to see Merri Lee for a few minutes. I'm fine. Just . . . puzzled."

"What's up?" Merri Lee said a minute later.

Meg pointed at the cards. The explosion card. A person pointing in one direction, but she'd placed the card upside down. And the last card, the result, was the hooded figure holding a scythe.

"That's what I wanted you to see." Meg indicated the second card. "Upside down. That's never happened before."

"Never? But the cards are all jumbled up in the box. Maybe you've turned them right side up without thinking about it, and this time you were distracted?"

She shook her head. "The decks have different backs, and I recognize the nature deck from the cityscape deck, so I keep my eyes closed when I'm selecting the cards. I've never revealed an upside-down card until now."

"Then it means something." Merri Lee frowned. "The figure would have been pointing toward death, but turned that way, it's pointing to the explosion."

"Neither is a good thing."

"No, but . . ."

"Meg." Henry's face suddenly appeared at the sorting room's window. "There is trouble. You girls stay inside."

He turned toward his studio, so Meg and Merri Lee rushed to the front counter, where they could look out the office's big windows. Being a Grizzly, Henry didn't vault over the brick wall with a Wolf's grace, but the wall wasn't much of a barrier. He went up and over, then headed for Main Street, turning right when he reached the sidewalk.

Merri Lee pulled her mobile phone out of her pocket. "Eve is across the street. She'll be able to see what's going on."

Growling, Nathan took up a position in front of the glass door.

Meg retreated to the sorting room, followed by Merri Lee.

"Eve says there's an altercation between Lieutenant Montgomery and his brother. Some shoving and lots of shouting," Merri Lee reported. "Karl's there, but he's dealing with Sandee. Eve's not sure where Michael is. He could be at the station. Simon, Vlad, and Henry are heading across the street."

Meg stared at the cards and whispered, "They're going the wrong way." Hurrying to the Private doorway, she shouted at Nathan, "Tell Simon he's going the wrong way!"

The watch Wolf turned toward her, distracted. In that moment, Meg saw a blond-haired man run across the delivery area and head up the access way.

<Meg says you're going the wrong way!> Nathan shouted.

Simon leaped back to the sidewalk on the Courtyard side of Crowfield Avenue. He tried to grab Vlad's arm, but the Sanguinati had changed to smoke and started to rise in order to flow across the street above the traffic. The attempted grab was enough to make Vlad stop, and it made Henry hesitate.

"Meg says . . ."

A female screamed.

Simon cocked his head toward the Market Square. He moved toward the customer parking lot, ignoring Montgomery's fight with that Cyrus. He lengthened his stride to catch up to Henry, who was already turning into the parking lot.

The female screamed again, a sound full of hurt and fear.

Henry pushed open the wooden door leading to the employee parking lot, then stopped. The three of them stared at fog so thick they couldn't see Henry's hand when the Grizzly extended his arm.

Another scream, abruptly cut off. Male.

Then an odd and terrible silence filled the area around the Market Square.

Simon and Vlad backed away from the fog. Henry hesitated, then reached in and pulled the door closed before retreating.

<Nathan!> Simon called. <Keep Meg inside the Liaison's Office.>

<Merri Lee too,> Nathan said. <We can't see out the back window of the office, but there is no fog in the delivery area. Pete Denby is upstairs. I shouted at him to stay inside.>

That much settled, Simon turned to the next group. <Elliot!>

<We're all right,> Elliot replied. <Agent O'Sullivan is watching the door. I have shifted to Wolf. Katherine Debany and Miss Twyla are here. Lorne at Three Ps called and said he locked the door and will wait for the all clear.>

"Mr. Wolfgard?" Ruth stood just inside the glass door that provided street-side access to the efficiency apartments above the seamstress/tailor's shop.

"You and the pups stay inside," Simon said at the same time Kowalski, who was across the street, shouted, "Ruthie, get back inside!"

"Wait!" Simon said. He and Vlad, who was still in smoke form, eased past Ruthie and rushed up the stairs, leaving Henry to nudge the female inside and guard the door. As they hurried to the back stairs that gave them access to the area behind Howling Good Reads and A Little Bite, Chris Fallacaro opened the door of his apartment and blinked at them.

"What's going on?" Chris asked.

They didn't answer him, but at least another human was accounted for. Nadine was in A Little Bite with

Tess, and Eve Denby was across the street in her den. So that left . . .

Theral MacDonald alone in the medical office, since Emily Faire was visiting her family pack this morning and Elizabeth Bennefeld wasn't scheduled to do any massages.

<Let me,> Vlad said when Simon opened the door to peek outside. <I should be safe in my smoke form.>

<You don't know that.>

Vlad flowed partway out of the opening. <The fog is blowing apart and getting wispy. I think we're safe now.>

<The Theral is hurt!> Jenni called. <Her face is bleeding. Can we go out and help?>

Simon hesitated. <Do you see a male near Theral?>

<No, but the pavement is dark near her. Might be blood.>

If Jenni could see the pavement, the fog was dispersing in the Market Square too. Of course, that didn't mean it was safe to go out.

Then he heard the *clomp, clomp, clomp* of pony feet and watched the ponies trot over to the side door of the Liaison's Office and line up, waiting for Meg to fill their mail baskets.

Simon pulled off his clothes and shifted to Wolf. <Elliot, go over to the Liaison's Office and watch Meg. I need Nathan.>

<Done.>

Simon dashed down the stairs, with Vlad flowing beside him. In their pony form, the Elementals' steeds were as vulnerable to teeth and claws—and bullets—as any other creatures. He didn't think the ponies would have come for the mail and treats if the Elders were still in the Market Square.

Nathan met them at the archway into the square, and the three of them darted across the open space to the spot where Theral sat on the ground with Jenni crouched beside her.

"Jack," Theral gasped. "It was Jack. He hit me. He said he'd kill me if I didn't go with him. I still tried to get away. Then it got foggy and Jack screamed and was gone."

Vlad shifted to human form and helped Theral stand. "You are hurt. Let's go into the office. We'll have a bodywalker come to help you."

<Welby Owlgard is the closest bodywalker,> Simon said. <And flying will be safer than traveling overland.> At least he hoped the Elders wouldn't swat an Owl out of the air.

<Agreed,> Vlad said. <I'll ask Henry to relay information to Lieutenant Montgomery and Officer Kowalski. They can come here to talk to Theral or get her to a human doctor.>

After giving Theral a polite sniff for that Jack Fillmore's scent, Simon and Nathan turned toward the blood nearby. Some was Theral's; most belonged to another human. They followed the blood trail to within sight of the Green Complex's garden, where they met Blair, who was sniffing around . . .

Oh no, Simon thought. *Meg can't know about this.*

<The Elders,> Blair said. <I stayed at the Green Complex until they headed deeper into the Courtyard with whatever they didn't eat here.>

Simon approached the backbone stripped clean of meat, while Nathan pawed the torn clothes and found a wallet and keys. Blair sniffed a foot, still in its shoe, that had a few inches of leg attached to it.

They were shaped differently, but a grown human male would have as much meat as a deer. But that wasn't much of a meal for any of the Elders' forms when there were two of them consuming the meat.

The bones—what was left of them—were stripped clean. All the organs were gone, and the long bones of one leg had been cracked for the marrow. The only thing left intact was the foot in the shoe and the . . .

<What are you doing?> Simon yelped as Blair ate the flesh off the bit of leg still connected to the foot.

<I'm hungry,> Blair replied. <No point wasting the meat.> He started to pull the foot from the shoe, then sniffed the foot and stopped. <It's stinky.>

<You said you were hungry.>

<I'm not *that* hungry.>

<Found the other foot but not the other leg,> Nathan said. He trotted over to Simon, carrying the foot by the heel.

<Wc have to bury this.> Simon looked at some bushes several yards from the garden. Someone working in the garden wouldn't notice freshly dug earth behind the bushes. <Seeing a bunny backbone upset Meg. This . . . >

He closed his teeth over the backbone and headed for the bushes. Blair and Nathan followed with the feet, dumped them at the chosen spot, then went back to look for any other bits of bone and meat scraps.

<Some Hawks made off with a couple of bits,> Blair said. <But they won't leave anything where Meg would see it. I couldn't find the head. One of the Elders may have taken it to crack open the skull and eat the brains later.>

They gathered up everything they could find of the human. Nathan ran to the Green Complex to find a bag to carry the clothes and belongings while Simon and Blair began digging.

"Would the Wolfgard like some help?"

The Wolves looked at Earth, who sat astride a sand-colored steed.

<We need to hide this from Meg,> Simon said, backing away from the bones and scraps. <She'll be upset if she sees it.>

"Quicksand and I can do that."

The ground beneath the human remains turned into that deadly kind of sand. When the last bit of bone disappeared, the ground became solid, sandy earth.

<Thank you,> Simon said.

Quicksand pawed the ground, momentarily turning a patch of sandy earth back into quicksand.

Earth laughed. "Our Meg is handing out sugar lumps

as an extra-special treat. Quicksand wants to get her share." The Elemental turned her steed, and they galloped toward the Market Square—and the Liaison's Office.

<I found these,> Nathan said a minute later. He dropped a large paper bag and small blanket near the pile of torn clothes.

They put the jeans, shirt, underwear, and one shoe into the bag, along with a belt and the keys and wallet. That Jack might have carried other things in his pockets, but after a quick search of the area, they didn't find anything except the other shoe. They put the bag in the blanket and loosely tied the blanket ends to make it easier for the Wolves to hold. Then Simon and Nathan headed back to the Market Square while Blair returned to the Utilities Complex.

They came across several Crowgard, who flew off the moment they were spotted. Since there were a couple of dull coins in the road, Simon figured the Crowgard had made off with any shinies that might have fallen from that Jack's pockets.

When they passed the ponies carrying full mail baskets, Simon realized how little time had passed. That was good. Meg had been busy. Unfortunately, it also meant that Montgomery and Kowalski were still in the Market Square. The men watched as he and Nathan trotted past with the bag swinging in the blanket between them.

They hustled up the efficiency apartments' back stairs. Figuring he didn't have much time before Montgomery came looking for him, Simon shifted his front paws enough to have semi-human digits, then pulled the wallet out of the bag. He removed the money—lots of money—and dropped the wallet back in the bag.

If the police did the fingerprint thing on the wallet, they wouldn't find anything useful that would identify him.

Not that it would matter if they could identify him.

He set the money aside, shifted all the way to human,

and quickly dressed. Stuffing the money into his back pocket, he looked at Nathan. "I'll deal with Lieutenant Montgomery." He leaned down and sniffed Nathan's mouth. "You should eat some grass or something before you go back to the Liaison's Office. You have human-meat breath."

Which meant he probably did too. Good thing human noses weren't sensitive enough to make the distinction. Meg wouldn't be able to tell either, but with Meg, it didn't seem polite to breathe on her after munching on one of her species.

Simon grabbed the bag and opened the door. Nathan hurried down the stairs and past Montgomery. Simon came down more slowly and held out the bag.

"That's what we found."

Montgomery took the bag and opened it. "Nothing else?"

"There's nothing left, Lieutenant." Which didn't quite answer the question, but it was the truth.

Montgomery nodded. "Katherine Debany is driving Theral to the MacDonalds' family doctor. Welby Owlgard said he didn't know human bodies well enough to tell if Theral had a concussion and thought it best for her to see a human healer."

"That makes sense."

There were things to be said, questions to be asked. But neither of them wanted to say or ask.

"I'd best get this evidence to the station and fill out a DLU form," Montgomery said.

Simon nodded. He walked with Montgomery to the access way, then turned left toward the employee parking lot while Montgomery turned right toward Main Street.

He found Kowalski helping Theral into Katherine Debany's car. His amber eyes met Kowalski's dark, angry ones. Once Theral was settled, Katherine started her car. But when Kowalski rounded the car and moved toward him, Simon held up a hand, signaling Katherine to wait.

"If he'd gotten Theral out of the Courtyard, we wouldn't have found her alive," Kowalski said in a low voice. "It would have been hard on the MacDonald family to lose her at any time, but especially so soon after Lawrence being killed."

Simon watched the police officer until he was out of sight. Then he pulled the money from his back pocket, removed four fifties, and handed them to Katherine Debany. "For the doctor and whatever medicine Theral needs."

Katherine Debany studied his face and looked as if she wanted to ask where he'd gotten the money. Then she thanked him and took the bills.

Once she and Theral were gone, he went to the Liaison's Office to find out what Meg knew.

Meg heard the chorus of neighs at the sorting room's outside door. She looked at Merri Lee as she walked over to open it. "The ponies are here for the mail."

"Does that mean it's safe to go outside?" Merri Lee asked.

Meg thought about that, then shook her head. The ponies were a form of *terra indigene*, so their being outside didn't mean it was safe for humans. She opened the door a few inches. A black nose immediately pushed into the opening.

Thunder, who was always the first pony in line.

She opened the door all the way and tried to lean out to look down the access way, but all she saw were the last wisps of fog and the ponies.

As she turned toward the table to fetch the stacks of mail for Thunder's baskets, she realized what else should be on the table. Waving at Merri Lee to join her, she whispered, "I didn't prepare any treats. See what you can find in the back room."

While Merri Lee rummaged in the under-the-counter fridge and cupboards, Meg filled the baskets with mail going to the different complexes in the Courtyard. She was picking up the stack for the Wolfgard Complex when Merri Lee returned, holding something behind her back.

"All I could find was the box of sugar lumps," Merri Lee whispered.

"Well, I'll just make sure everyone knows this is an extra-special treat this week." "Everyone" would include Jester Coyotegard, just in case the ponies didn't want to believe her next week when she offered the regular treat of apples or carrots.

When Thunder was first in line again, Meg handed out the sugar lumps, to all the ponies' delight. Not all. Three of the ponies were missing. The rest of them trotted off to deliver the mail, looking quite pleased with themselves.

As soon as Meg locked the sorting room's door, she and Merri Lee hurried to the back room and looked out the window.

"Theral is in the Market Square," Merri Lee said. "Maybe she can see what's . . ."

"I saw a man running up the access way," Meg said, rubbing her throat. "Simon was going the wrong way, going to deal with the argument at the apartments."

The phone rang. They ran into the sorting room. Feeling breathless, Meg grabbed the receiver. "Hello? Vlad! What . . . ?" She braced a hand against the counter. "Is she . . . ? Okay. Yes. Okay." She hung up and looked at Merri Lee. "A man tried to abduct Theral. She's hurt, but she'll be all right. Mrs. Debany is taking her to the doctor's. Vlad says it's safe for you to go back to Howling Good Reads—Tess and Nadine are in A Little Bite, so they're nearby—but you can stay here a while longer if you want to."

"I want to stay," Merri Lee said.

Another chorus of neighs outside the sorting room door. Meg found Fog, Quicksand, and Whirlpool standing there, sans baskets. Obviously the other ponies had informed their friends about the special treat.

After handing out sugar lumps and washing her hands, she returned to the sorting room, where Merri Lee studied the cards that were still on the table.

"We still have a lot to learn about interpreting what is seen," Merri Lee said, "but I think you're getting better at using the cards to reveal prophecy."

"I saw death. But Theral will be okay."

"Did Vlad say anything about the man?"

Meg stared at her friend, but she was thinking about when she had hidden in the Pony Barn with Sam, Skippy, and Jester while Namid's teeth and claws roamed the city, hidden by the fog. She was thinking about the odd and terrible silence that had filled the Courtyard that day.

"No," Meg finally said. "No, he didn't."

Simon stared at the three cards on the sorting room table, especially the middle card, the upside-down figure of a person pointing. This explained why Meg had said he was going the wrong way.

Distraction. Diversion. The Humans First and Last movement had used the attacks in Thaisia as a diversion for the war in Cel-Romano. It hadn't changed the outcome of the war, but it had forced the *terra indigene* to ignore a distant threat in order to deal with the one right in front of them. Just like what happened in the Courtyard a little while ago.

Damned tethered goat.

A family dispute, no charges filed. As far as Simon was concerned, the fight was overdue. Unfortunately, the trouble in the Market Square stopped the fight between Montgomery and that Cyrus before Montgomery could settle the question of dominance once and for all. Equally unfortunate, Simon thought it likely that Montgomery would receive a thrashing from the leaders of the police pack for fighting where he was seen by all the humans driving by on Crowfield Avenue.

Well, that was Burke's job.

"You're all right?" he asked Meg and Merri Lee.

"We're fine," Meg replied. "I didn't see much."

"Captain Burke might want to talk to you. It's almost time for the midday break. Why don't you go over to A Little Bite and eat? Vlad is at HGR now, so I can watch the office here for a few minutes in case there are any last-minute deliveries."

Meg put the cards back in the box and put the box in the drawer.

"I'll wait outside," Merri Lee said.

"Simon?"

Don't ask, Meg. I won't lie to you, so don't ask.

"Tess told us a while ago that there is some mint growing in the Courtyard, so I wondered . . . Do Wolves usually chew on mint?"

"No. Why?" Before coming to see Meg, he'd gone into the bathroom at HGR to use some mouthwash. He'd also examined both sets of teeth to make sure there weren't any bits of human flesh stuck between them from carrying the backbone.

Did he smell minty from the mouthwash—or was the scent wafting in from the front room?

Meg confirmed that suspicion when she glanced at the Private doorway before leaning toward him and whispering, "When Nathan came back to the office, he smelled like he'd rolled in mint."

<You overdid it,> he told the watch Wolf.

<It's stronger than I expected. And I wasn't sure chewing on a leaf would be enough to hide that Jack's scent.>

Nathan had a point, especially since he was still in Wolf form.

"Theral won't have to be afraid anymore," he told Meg.

She nodded and left the office without asking for details. He didn't think anyone would ask for details about that Jack Fillmore.

Well, almost anyone.

＊　　＊　　＊

Burke gave Cyrus Montgomery his fierce-friendly smile and watched the man try not to squirm.

"You want to come in or something?" Cyrus asked grudgingly.

Burke shook his head and looked around. They were standing on the front lawn of the apartment building, within sight of neighbors and the traffic on Crowfield Avenue. "You didn't see anything wrong with having an argument with your brother where everyone could see, so I don't see any reason why you and I can't have a chat right here."

"That's family business."

"Do you know Jack Fillmore?" Burke asked.

Cyrus shook his head. "Don't know the name."

"Really? According to the bartender at the Stag and Hare, you and Jack were drinking together the other day and looked quite cozy. Some money changed hands."

"Don't know . . . Oh, *Jack*. Yeah. I know who you mean. He owed me some money and paid back a little yesterday."

"So you know him well."

"Wouldn't say that."

"But you know him well enough to loan him . . . how much?"

A hesitation. "Five hundred."

"That's a lot of money to lend an acquaintance when you keep telling your mother and brother that you're too broke to buy food for your family and expect them to help out."

Another hesitation. "Had some emergency cash stashed away. If my woman found out, she'd spend it all on stupid shit. You know how they are." Cyrus rocked his weight from one foot to the other. "Why are you asking about Jack?"

"He tried to abduct a young woman around the same time that you were having that public girlie fight with Lieutenant Montgomery. You know, lots of shouting and light slapping but no real hurt intended because, if you'd thrown a punch, you would have been arrested for assaulting a police officer. As his captain, I would have insisted that Monty file charges." Burke's smile turned fiercer. "This is what I find interesting. You call your brother, the police lieutenant, and insist on meeting him during his shift instead of waiting until he gets home. But the witnesses who overheard this shouting match didn't hear anything that justified your urgency to bring Monty back here right around the time of the abduction attempt."

"It was family business. I don't know about that other stuff."

"I hope that's true, Mr. Montgomery. We're going to be looking at Jack Fillmore very carefully and investigating everyone he's met in Lakeside to discover if he had anyone helping him with the abduction—either directly or by distracting the Courtyard security during the attempt. The young woman was injured when he tried to forcibly remove her from her place of work. He threatened to kill her. Everyone connected with him will be brought in for questioning, especially because the police will not be able to bring Jack Fillmore to justice."

"He got away?"

"In a manner of speaking."

No understanding in Cyrus Montgomery's eyes. He probably thought Fillmore somehow escaped and skipped town when the abduction was thwarted. He might even think Fillmore would be back for another try.

"Family discussions should be held after work from now on," Burke said. "Any discussions that are held during Lieutenant Montgomery's shift will be considered police business. Are we clear about that?"

"Clear enough."

Resentment. Slyness. How did a man grow up to be this, living in the same household as Monty, with a woman like Twyla for a mother?

Burke started to walk away, then stopped. "By the

way, I bought the Stag and Hare. In a few weeks, it won't be a good place to conduct any kind of business that can't withstand intense police scrutiny."

That was as much of a warning as he was willing to give the brother of Crispin James Montgomery.

Meg set the large plastic food container outside the back door of the Liaison's Office. She didn't see anything, but that didn't mean there wasn't a large someone keeping watch, waiting for the promised treat.

"Hello?" Her voice sounded wimpy. Being brave was easier when you didn't know how stupid you'd been, scolding a primal form of *terra indigene* that frightened everyone you knew. Well, maybe not the Elementals, but everyone else. "Hello? *Arroo?* Here are the cookies." She hesitated, because, really, would beings like the Elders care about little human concerns? "If you can, please return the container intact. Then it can be washed and used for another order of treats."

No movement. No sound. Henry had told her the Elders were seldom seen in any form, so she didn't really expect them to come rushing up like the Wolves would when cookies were delivered.

She started to retreat into the office, but she had one more thing to tell them—if any of them were listening. "Thank you for saving Theral today."

Back inside the office, she locked the door. Not that a lock kept out anyone but humans, but it made her feel a little better.

An hour later, when she closed the office for the day and stepped outside to wait for Simon, she noticed the container of cookies was gone.

Burke drove fast as he headed north toward a stretch of road near Lake Tahki. He glanced at Steve Ferryman, who had made the second phone call he'd taken just before he left the office. "Your counterpart is sure about this?"

"You asked me to put out feelers," Steve replied. "In response, I was asked to come to their village."

"Trap?"

"No."

They drove in silence for a few minutes. "I had to ask. Highway patrol called just before you did. They found Lorenzo's car—and they found bodies."

Steve looked at him. "They think they found Lorenzo."

"They didn't say that."

"You ever do highway patrol?" Steve asked when they reached the location and Burke pulled up behind the flashing patrol car.

"During my tours of duty in the wild country," Burke replied.

The officer in charge was young enough that Burke wondered why he'd been given this assignment. Then he caught the look the cop exchanged with Ferryman.

Intuit. They might have to hide what they were in order to stay safe among other kinds of humans, but their people still needed the same skills as any other community, and that included law enforcement.

"A car was torched just up the road," the officer said. "Two bodies inside. Another officer and I were walking the road to see if we could find anything else when we spotted the white sedan on the woodland track."

Not a paved highway. Not even a dirt road. But vehicles used that clear space between the trees often enough that there were visible tracks that another driver could follow to someplace rarely seen by humans.

"Got your BOLO about the same time as we found the cars," the officer continued. "And we found a couple of other things I think you'll want to see since I gathered you're more interested in the owner of the vehicle than the vehicle itself."

"That's correct," Burke said.

The officer led them to a body bag. "Male. Hands

don't look old, but I can't tell you much else. You can look if you want, but it's bad."

"He was shot?" Burke asked.

"Him? No, although there is some blood in the car, so whoever was driving it might have been shot." The officer blew out a breath. "No, something picked up this man and swung him like a club into that tree. Pulped his head."

"Hair color?"

"Light brown. Cut short."

Burke breathed out tension. "That's not the man I'm looking for."

"Might have been better for him if it was." The officer pointed toward the track in the woods. "This way."

The officer led them just far enough along the track that a curve hid the car from sight. Then he pointed. "The blood trail from the car ends here."

Steve Ferryman sucked in a breath. "Is that a paw print?"

The officer nodded. "Something picked up a body and carried it off up the track."

"Did you follow the prints?" Burke asked.

"No, sir. We're already beyond the right-of-way standing here. If you've seen enough, we should get back to the highway."

If Steve Ferryman hadn't been with him, he might have pushed to go a little farther up the track, regardless of the risk. But he knew that he wouldn't find Dominic Lorenzo around here.

The car would be towed to the nearest human settlement, but the officer handed over Lorenzo's medical bag and carryall. No reason not to since there was no one to arrest, and the highway patrol and crime investigation team didn't believe there was a body left to be found.

Back in the car, Burke followed Steve's directions as they continued north toward Lake Tahki until they reached a small village. No welcome sign with the village name. The houses looked a bit shabby—in need of paint—

but the yards were neatly kept and every house had flower beds or planters. The business district was the same mix of neat and shabby. An older place with not a lot of money to spare on extras, whether you were talking about the governing body or the individual families.

Burke pulled into the parking lot beside a clinic and drugstore. Saying nothing, he followed Steve inside the clinic—and found Dominic Lorenzo.

"I'm glad to see you," he said, studying the cuts and bruises on Lorenzo's face. Pained face. Meg Corbyn had been right about that. Judging by the bandages around the man's torso and the sling supporting one arm, it was a good bet some of the bullets that hit the car also hit the man but hadn't inflicted life-threatening wounds.

"I'm glad to be here," Lorenzo replied. "There were three men . . ."

"Not a worry anymore."

Lorenzo stared at him, then nodded in understanding.

"What do you want to do?" Burke asked.

Lorenzo gave him a tired smile. "I want to go home. I sent Governor Hannigan my final report and my resignation from the task force a couple of days ago. This was my last stop before heading back to Lakeside."

"You're going back to the hospital to work in the emergency room?"

"No. I know too much about the blood prophets and would be vulnerable in a city hospital. I was planning to sell my house, find a way to disappear—find someplace to work where unscrupulous men couldn't find me."

"We have an opening for a physician on Great Island," Steve said. "The work would include running the little clinic in the River Road Community, but that's safe ground too. Even if you're looking for something different, we'll find a place for you on the island until you recover from your injuries."

"I appreciate that."

When they were back on the road to Lakeside, Burke said, "Why resign?"

"Besides the risk of leading someone to the girls, or being run off the road by someone trying to capture me for information?" Lorenzo replied dryly. "We weren't doing those girls any good. I think the governor meant well when he set up the task force, but the girls didn't need someone coming in to ask questions and disrupt their routine. And sooner or later, someone watching the doctors would see a pattern, would figure out where the girls were located. Like they did with me."

"What was your recommendation?"

Lorenzo closed his eyes. "To leave them alone to find their own way to deal with the world and their cursed gift of prophecy. That would be the kindest thing we could do for them."

Messis 16

Dear Merri Lee,

The train ride from Lakeside to Bennett was equal parts exciting and frightening. Despite all of us arriving together, the conductor didn't want to let me take a seat in the earth native car. Technically, anyone can ride in either car, but that passenger car is reserved for terra indigene and Intuits, while the other passenger car is for regular humans. From what I can tell, and from the bits I picked up from chatting with other passengers when I went to the dining car, there is no difference between the railcars themselves—the earth native symbol is a decal that can be removed and put on any car that's available. And it's not like a regular human can't sit in the earth native car if the other car is full, but it's clear that if there is any trouble of any kind, the human will be blamed in order to protect the train and the rest of the passengers. So the train's personnel try to keep regular humans from spending much time with the Others in a confined space.

Fortunately, John Wolfgard spoke up for me, telling the conductor that we were traveling as a group to Bennett.

It was a long ride, but we swapped seats often to talk and get to know one another. We'd all seen the pictures of the dead Wolfgard piled into mounds after the attacks by the Humans First and Last movement. Even the Simple Life folk had seen a few of the pictures. And most of us had seen pictures of the mounds of humans who had been destroyed by the Others in retaliation. It would have

been easier for all of us if we could believe every-
one in Bennett had participated in killing the
Wolves. But the innocent had been killed too, and
what had killed them was out there, in the dark,
waiting for us to make a mistake.

I was told that if I can't accept that, I should ask
for a ticket back to Lakeside or some other human
community that's large enough to provide a buffer
from the truth—that no place on this world is free
from the Others who are called Namid's teeth and
claws. Their existence is just more obvious now in
a place like Bennett.

I met my boss, Sheriff Virgil Wolfgard. It's
one thing to mentally prepare yourself for harass-
ment and bullying by your coworkers because
your body doesn't have the same equipment as
theirs; it's quite another thing to have your boss
look at you like you're an item on the menu. I
guess he needed a deputy more than he needed a
meal. So I have a shiny new badge and a gun.
And I have a horse, which a couple of the Simple
Life men helped me choose—an easygoing bay
gelding with a high tolerance for human foolish-
ness, to say nothing of putting up with a novice
rider. Driving around town is discouraged, as a
way to save gasoline, so I am the horse patrol
within the town limits. No one has explained what
I'm supposed to do if I arrest someone and have
to take the person to jail. I guess I'll find out when
it happens.

On a lighter note, I'm glad I brought a couple
of the Crowgard cozies you recommended. They're
great fun and nothing I would have found in a
strictly human bookstore. I'm loaning them to
Jesse Walker after Barb Debany has a chance to
read them. I liked Barb the moment I met her, and
I think we'll be compatible housemates, especially

since she's okay with me adopting one of the young orphan dogs as long as the dog gets along with Buddy the parakeet.

I'll write again soon.

—Jana

CHAPTER 14

Thaisday, Messis 16

Standing on the apartment building's walk, Monty
watched Lizzy and Grr Bear go next door to wait
with Sarah and Robert until it was time for school. He
knew the routine. Before the school day began, his
mother would give the efficiency apartment/schoolroom
a quick dust and sweep before going to her job at the
consulate. Ruthie would pick up the food from A Little
Bite or the Market Square grocery store for the children's midmorning snack and get ready for the day's
lessons. Then the children would arrive. Just the three
of them again, now that Sierra and her girls were gone.

He thought Fanny wouldn't mind going to school as
a way to spend time with the other girls and have something to do. But she'd helped Clarence shoplift by acting as his lookout and she'd tried to stop Meg from
going to Sam's aid when the two boys were fighting.
Even if he could talk Simon into letting Fanny into the
Courtyard just for school, allowing the girl to go in when
Clarence was banned would only make things hard on
Fanny when she got home.

Lizzy smiled at him and waved. Grr Bear's wooden
paw was moved in a bye-bye motion.

Monty waved back. Then Lizzy bounded up the steps to the Denbys' porch, rang the bell, and went inside, not waiting for Eve or Pete to come to the door.

Watching his little girl cross that short distance was simply a father's caution. Not that he was the only one who watched Lizzy walk from one yard to the other. By now, one of the Hawkgard was perched on the porch rail of the apartment above his, another was riding the air currents and keeping an eye on the apartments and the Courtyard's business district, and a couple of Crows were on Kowalski and Ruthie's porch, enjoying the food that had been left for them. He didn't think Jenni and Starr ventured out of the Courtyard anymore, but from what Kowalski had said, Jake Crowgard stopped by for breakfast most mornings before taking up his position on the brick wall that separated Henry's yard from the delivery area—an ideal place to watch the humans coming and going, and keep an eye on Meg.

Now that Sissy was gone, the Sanguinati weren't guarding the apartment building during the day. At least, not where they would be seen. But he suspected they had quietly taken over the apartment above Jimmy's. After all, it did offer them a vantage point from which to hunt, and anyone who was out on the sidewalk or street after dark was considered fair game. In a weird way, the Sanguinati became a kind of neighborhood watch. Wrongdoers weren't arrested and their fines weren't paid in money, but the blood that was taken seemed in proportion to the wrongdoers' misbehavior.

Monty returned to his apartment to finish getting ready for work. Grandma Twyla had decreed that anyone dawdling in the morning and making other people miss work or school forfeited the cookie or muffin that would have been included with the midday serving of milk. Lizzy had tested that decree just once, since Eve supported Twyla and Ruthie was willing to enforce their decision. Now Lizzy and Grr Bear were waiting at the door before he could put the breakfast dishes in the sink so that any tardiness wouldn't be *their* fault.

He stepped out of his apartment a few minutes later. As he locked his door, the other downstairs door opened.

"Hey, CJ," Jimmy said. "You got a minute?"

Monty turned to face his brother, who had been conveniently absent yesterday, as if a day was enough time to erase everyone's suspicions about Jimmy's involvement in the attempted abduction of Theral MacDonald. "A minute."

Suspicions but not proof. Jimmy was still alive because there wasn't any proof.

Monty studied the "aw, shucks, I didn't mean nothing" expression and wondered what sort of flimflam Jimmy was going to try on him today.

"Been hearing about folks looking for a place to live," Jimmy said.

Monty nodded. "A lot of people have come to Lakeside recently, hoping to find work in a human-controlled city. Stands to reason that those who do find work also need a place to live."

He'd taken Pete Denby with him yesterday when he went to talk to his landlords about releasing him from the lease on the one-bedroom apartment near Market Street. The man had wanted him to continue paying the rent but also wanted to have use of the apartment to rent to another tenant. Monty had responded to that by indicating he would continue using the apartment— and would make sure he used the water that was included in the rent. The next ploy was complaining about the condition of the apartment—the lousy paint job, the nicks on the counters, the curling corner of linoleum in the kitchen. Monty asked if the man would like to see the photographs he'd taken of the apartment the day he moved in, which would prove the place looked exactly like it had then.

Finally the landlord's wife, who had rented the place to Monty, reminded her husband that *Lieutenant* Montgomery shouldn't be penalized for wanting to live closer to the police station where he worked.

So the papers Pete had already prepared were signed, releasing Monty from the rental agreement. He'd bet a week's pay that this morning's edition of the *Lakeside News* would have a listing for the apartment at twice what Monty had been paying.

"Thing is," Jimmy said, "there are two empty apartments in this building and another empty one in the other building. That's just a waste when someone could be living there."

"I don't think the *terra indigene* are planning to hire anyone else to work in the Courtyard. Not for a while anyway."

"Wouldn't have to work for those . . . for them. Folks could rent those places by the week or the month. I could take care of that, be a kind of overseer."

"Eve Denby is the property manager for these three buildings. That's her job."

"Then why isn't she doing anything about renting out those places? Not doing her job if she's letting apartments stay empty."

He heard the whiny belligerence in his brother's voice. Which meant Jimmy wasn't getting the answer he wanted—or needed? "Gods, did you already tell some people they could flop in one of the apartments?"

"What if I did? The places are empty. Where's the harm?"

"Anyone who comes here without the Others' permission is an intruder. They deal harshly with intruders. These apartments aren't on the open market for rent. They're only offered to Courtyard employees. And don't go thinking you can have overnight 'guests.' You *are* a guest, and the only reason they haven't tossed you out yet is that Simon, Vlad, and Tess like Mama. And if you think you can sneak someone in and pick the lock on one of the apartments upstairs so your pals can squat until they're caught, think again. They'll be caught before they can blink. They will disappear, and you will be standing at the curb with Sandee and the kids, and your choices will be getting out of Lakeside or going to jail." Or worse. "Jimmy, your free ride as a guest is pretty much done. If you're going to stay in Lakeside, you should find work and another place to live while you still have the choice."

"Fuck that." Anger in Jimmy's eyes now. "You don't work for the freaks. How come you're living here?"

"Because Elayne was murdered at the Toland train station, and the people responsible came after Lizzy, thinking she knew more than she did. Staying here was the only way to keep her safe."

A moment of shock and what Monty would have sworn looked like genuine sympathy.

"I didn't know," Jimmy said.

"Well, that's why I took the apartment here when it was offered." There were other reasons, personal and professional, but there was no point complicating things. Not with Jimmy.

"Look, CJ . . ."

The outer door opened. Kowalski stood on the threshold.

"Captain Burke is at the Courtyard. He wants to see you before we go to the station."

Monty headed out, then stopped and eyed Jimmy. "You'd better tell those people the apartments aren't for rent. If the Others link you to any more trouble in the Courtyard, Sandee and the kids will be relocating on their own."

"And where will I be?"

"You'll be in jail, if you're lucky. And, Jimmy? If that happens, there is nothing I can do to help you."

Vlad reviewed the booklists, then eyed his assistant manager. "Tell me again why I want to order four dozen of the same book?"

"Because we're going to act as a distribution hub for

a few other bookstores," Merri Lee replied with a smile that was meant to be disarming.

Vlad wasn't fooled. Just because the female pack weren't predators in the traditional sense didn't mean you could let your guard down. But, to be fair, there was a rational reason for what they did.

Usually. Mostly. Sometimes.

"I don't remember agreeing to be a hub."

"Yes, you did. Sort of. Well, maybe Simon was the one who agreed, but one of you did. Anyway, Toland publishers don't want to break cartons of books anymore, and we can't sell four dozen of the same book at Howling Good Reads. And we have the easiest access to the Intuit and *terra indigene* publishers in the eastern part of the High North because they can ship books to us across Lake Tahki. But books that will sell here will also sell at the bookstores in Ferryman's Landing, as well as the libraries on the island and mainland. Then we send more of the books to John Wolfgard in Bennett, as well as to Shelley Bookman and Jesse Walker in Prairie Gold. Meg wasn't sure if the Intuit village at Sweetwater had a library. We were going to draft a letter for you and Simon to review before sending it to Jackson Wolfgard to see if anyone there would like to participate. In turn, John Wolfgard will order books from publishers in the Midwest or on the West Coast if he can reach them, and send some copies on to us."

"The books still have to travel by truck from the port on Lake Tahki to us." Vlad frowned. "Are we making any money from this?"

"From being a hub? No, but we're not losing any either because the stores will pay for the books and the shipping costs to send them on. And we will make a profit on the books we sell here, just like we do now."

And it will keep the fluffballs busy, he thought. "I'll give the list a little more thought and have Simon take a look in case there is anything he would want to add." Because she looked disappointed, he felt compelled to add, "Your list is excellent, and quite extensive. But there may be one or two titles that we've heard of that wouldn't be available to you."

Merri Lee seemed sufficiently appeased. Vlad felt relieved until he looked out the store's front windows and saw Lieutenant Montgomery waiting for a break in traffic in order to dash across the street. That in itself was unusual. Crowfield Avenue had sufficient traffic in the morning to make going up to the light a prudent choice, and Montgomery made an effort to set a good example for the children.

"Find some work to do in the stock room," he said quietly. Captain Burke was in A Little Bite talking with Agent O'Sullivan, and Tess reported that both men looked grim. Montgomery moved as if his muscles were swollen with anger. "No." Vlad touched Merri Lee's arm, stopping her. "Go check on Meg."

Merri Lee hesitated. "Do you have a question I should ask?"

"Not yet."

He heard HGR's back door close moments before Montgomery walked in through the front door.

"Captain Burke is in A Little Bite," Vlad said.

"I have a question for you," Montgomery said, the usual courtesy in his voice sounding strained. "Are there Sanguinati living in one of the second-floor apartments in my building?"

"If there are?"

Montgomery's breath came out in a sigh. "That's good. It would be better if they were a little more obvious. Get a pizza and sit out on the porch, turn on the TV or radio."

"We thought humans would prefer us to be more discreet about our presence."

Montgomery looked uncomfortable. "My brother told some acquaintances that they could make use of the apartments."

The Sanguinati won't need to eat pizza.

"It's what Jimmy does," Montgomery continued. "He sets up situations to net himself a little cash, then blames someone else when the scheme is stopped. And he's always just far enough removed from the trouble not to get dirtied by whatever happens. I told him he should get a job and find another place to live, but as long as he gets that apartment rent free, he won't be going anywhere."

How much to say? "If your brother goes by his own choice, no one will stop him. But Simon can't force him to leave."

"Can't or won't?"

"Can't."

Montgomery looked uneasy. "Why would someone want Jimmy to stay around the Courtyard?"

Interesting that Montgomery didn't ask who wanted Jimmy to stay around, which meant the man had his suspicions about what was in the Courtyard keeping watch.

Vlad heard footsteps approaching the archway that connected HGR with A Little Bite. "You should talk to your captain. He's been waiting for you."

"Actually, I wanted to share this information with you as well," Burke said, walking up to the checkout counter. He looked at Montgomery, then at Vlad. "You know about highway patrol?"

"They're enforcers who watch the roads that connect towns," Vlad replied. "They have territories like the police packs within a city. Some are human, some are Intuit, depending on what kind of communities are connected by the roads. The *terra indigene* aren't considered part of the patrol, although they do keep watch over anything that goes through the wild country."

"Even places that are not under human control still have law enforcement."

"Did you do that kind of work?" Vlad asked, curious about the things Burke seemed to know that other humans didn't.

"In my younger days." Burke paused. "Two days ago, highway patrol found a white car that had bullet holes and blood. The license plate matched the numbers Ms. Corbyn saw in her vision—and the car is registered to Dr. Dominic Lorenzo."

"You found Dr. Lorenzo?" Montgomery asked.

"I found him. He was wounded, but he'll be all right." Another pause. "He's staying on Great Island for the time being."

"Emily Faire did tell Simon and me that she was needed here full-time because someone else would take care of the River Road Community," Vlad said.

"Did she?" Burke smiled, but the smile quickly faded. "Agent O'Sullivan talked to Governor Hannigan last night. Several of the doctors who were involved with the task force have gone missing."

"Maybe they've gone to ground in out-of-the-way villages," Montgomery suggested.

"Some of those men have wives and children who haven't heard from them in days. We'll hope to find them all and reunite them with their families, but I don't think all of them will be as lucky as Dr. Lorenzo." Burke took a breath and shook off the grimness. "O'Sullivan is waiting for me. We have a meeting with the mayor and police commissioner."

Vlad waited until Burke left before saying, "You have missed your bus, Lieutenant."

"Kowalski and I will grab a taxi."

"No." Vlad picked up the phone and called the Liaison's Office. "Meg? Is Harry still there? Tell him he's giving Lieutenant Montgomery and Officer Kowalski a ride to work before making his other stops. Yes, that will be fine." He hung up and smiled at Montgomery. "Harry will wait for you in the delivery area."

"You don't have to do this."

"Special circumstances."

Vlad waited until Montgomery left the bookstore before calling Eve Denby to tell her to be vigilant about anyone who might be trying to stay in the apartments without permission—and to let her know that a few

Sanguinati would be taking up residence in one of the apartments from now on.

That afternoon, Simon walked into the butcher shop, happily thinking about dinner. Bison burgers for him and Sam, and beef for Meg. Half the ground bison would be cooked and put on rolls to eat with a green salad. That was the human meal. The other half of the meat would be quietly consumed raw, as it was meant to be eaten. But he and Sam would wait until they were in Wolf form and Meg was working in the garden or reading a book before eating that part of their dinner.

He smiled at Eve Denby, who gave him a distracted look before studying the available meat in the display case.

<Problem?> he asked Boone Hawkgard, who looked pointedly at Eve and said, "Problem?"

"No," she replied. "It's just . . . we've been eating so much red meat. Which is very good meat, but every so often you get a taste for something different."

Why? Simon wondered.

"Do you ever have any poultry?" Eve asked. "Like chickens? Or maybe a turkey?"

Boone stared at her. "No chickens in the Courtyard. Our chicken eggs come from earth native farms. We do have ducks. And turkeys. And geese will be flying over soon. Many of them make use of the lakes here."

"Henry sometimes catches more fish than he wants to eat," Simon said.

"Do you want a duck tomorrow?" Boone asked. "The Hawkgard could catch one if there are ducks around."

"No, that's all right." Eve gave them a bracing smile. "Is there beef available? Then I'll have a pound and a half of ground beef. That will make a fine meatloaf."

Boone measured out the meat and wrapped it.

Hawk and Wolf watched Eve as she walked out of the shop.

"Humans are so fussy," Boone said. "We're happy eating whatever we can catch."

"But even we sometimes look for a particular kind of meat if we're not empty-belly hungry," Simon said. "And Eve and the rest of the female pack don't usually ask for anything not in the case."

"That's true." Boone sighed. "I could go hunting tomorrow and try for a duck. The geese aren't here yet."

"A duck might be too small to feed Eve, her mate, and her pups," Simon countered. "I'll talk to Blair. He and I can help you hunt poultry tomorrow. Nathan might like to come too."

That much settled, Simon took his packages of bison and beef and headed home to have dinner and playtime with Sam and Meg.

CHAPTER 15

Firesday, Messis 17

Boone, Marie, and Julia Hawkgard rode the thermals until they spotted some of the wild turkeys that lived in the Courtyard. Following the Hawks, Simon, Blair, and Nathan moved toward their prey.

<Which one?> Nathan asked when the turkeys were in sight.

<A big one, so we don't have to hunt a special order again anytime soon,> Blair growled. He studied the birds, which seemed more interested in what they were pecking at than in the Wolves stalking them. <They don't seem very frisky. Or they're not smart enough to realize they're edible.>

Nathan also studied the turkeys. <Do they look sick? I don't want to go through the trouble of catching one if it's sick and humans won't eat it.>

<We don't hunt in the Chambers, and that's where most of the turkeys live,> Simon said. Of course, the Sanguinati in smoke form made no noise in the dark, left no scent to disturb sleeping birds that didn't realize they were roosting among predators. Turkey blood was sipped when preferred prey wasn't available, and old birds that had been drained a little too much were

helped over the Chambers' black wrought-iron fences to be available meat for other Courtyard residents. Even then, the Wolves usually left the meat for the other gards instead of dealing with mouthfuls of feathers.

<Ready?> he asked Blair and Nathan.

<Ready,> they replied.

<Ready?> he asked the Hawks.

<Ready.>

The Wolves flushed their prey, sending the turkeys skyward. The Hawkgard struck three of the turkeys with enough force to drive the birds back to the ground, where the Wolves finished the kill.

Blair took the largest turkey—a black-feathered male—and trotted off to deliver the special order. Nathan and Simon took the other two turkeys to the Hawkgard Complex. One would provide food for the Hawks. Boone would dismember the other and take the pieces to the butcher shop to sell to other humans who might want some poultry—once he figured out what parts of the bird the humans would, and wouldn't, eat.

<Hunting turkeys is easier when the Hawks help us,> Nathan said.

<More fun too,> Simon said. This hunt reminded him of playing with the badminton shuttlecock—sending it into the air for the Hawks to catch. <But there's not enough meat to feed a pack.>

What about a pack with only three or four members? Something to think about, along with deciding which pack member would have to learn how to cook the meat. He'd wait and see if Meg wrinkled her nose at this kind of turkey the way she did when he brought home a hunk of bison.

Pleased with themselves, Simon and Nathan ran to the Market Square to start the humans' idea of a workday.

Meg sharpened pencils, lined up pens according to color, arranged the order of the CDs she was playing as that week's musical selections. She checked the back door, the sorting room's side door, and the office's front door.

She even looked under the Wolf bed in the front room, which she knew was ridiculous because there would be a Nathan-size lump under it if the Wolf was playing a trick and trying to hide from her.

Nathan wasn't there, and he was never late.

But Simon had left early to do some Wolfy thing with Blair this morning. Maybe Nathan had gone with them. Wouldn't he have called? If he was going to be late for work, he should have called so she wouldn't be worried about him.

She wasn't sure he received any pay for being the watch Wolf for the Liaison's Office, but there had to be some way to impress on him that not showing up wasn't acceptable. And then she knew exactly what to do. She would tell him that the next time he was late and didn't call, she would dock a couple of Wolf cookies from his quota of weekly treats. So there.

Then she saw Blair trotting across the delivery area, hauling a big black-feathered bird, and forgot all about Nathan. She pushed the door open and dashed to the sidewalk as the Wolf turned right, heading for Crowfield Avenue.

Turkey. Her brain kicked in to supply a training image of the bird as she trailed behind Blair, who ignored the people on the sidewalk and the cars that were in danger of becoming part of fender-bender gridlock because the drivers were staring at him instead of paying attention to traffic. With Blair's jaws clamped around the base of the turkey's neck, its head swung like a metronome and its toes bumped along on the sidewalk.

Blair reached the corner. He looked at a woman standing near the crosswalk, then pointed a front paw at the "walk" button on the pole and made a sound. Meg wasn't sure what the sound was supposed to mean, since Blair had a mouthful of turkey neck, but the woman pushed the crosswalk button and received a milder sound in response.

The light changed. The crossing sign lit up, and Blair and the turkey trotted across the street and turned down Crowfield Avenue.

Meg kept pace with him on her side of the street, then stopped when he trotted up the walk to the Denbys' residence. He hauled the turkey up the porch steps and pressed a paw against the doorbell, then stepped aside to avoid getting smacked in the nose when someone finally answered the door.

"Meg?" Merri Lee poked her head out the door of Howling Good Reads. "What's going . . . ? Oh goodness. Is that . . . ?"

Eve opened the screen door after Blair whacked the doorbell a couple more times. When she didn't say anything—probably couldn't with her mouth hanging open like that—Blair dumped the turkey on her porch before retracing his route back to the Courtyard.

Eve disappeared for a moment, then came outside, calling someone on her mobile phone.

"Come on," Merri Lee said. "She's not calling us, so we'll have to find out what's going on some other way. Besides . . ."

"Arrrroooo!" Nathan, howling from the currently empty Liaison's Office.

"Arrooooo!" Simon, upstairs in HGR's office, howling for the Wolfgard to hunt down one little human who might not be at her office as expected, but had not been late for work, thank you very much.

"Someone has noticed you're not at work," Merri Lee finished.

Meg followed Merri Lee inside HGR and yelled, "I'm here!"

"Arr—" Human found; hunt canceled.

"You could trade Wolf cookies for information," Merri Lee whispered as they hurried to the back door.

"I was going to dock Nathan a couple of cookies for being late."

"Do that next time."

"Meg!" Simon appeared at the foot of the stairs, wearing jeans that were zipped but not buttoned—and nothing else. In that moment, he looked more, and less, human in a way that made her heart beat a little bit faster. But her heart might have been beating faster because of the teeth, which were definitely Wolfy.

"Have to go." Meg gave him a wide smile as she opened the door. "Delivery just pulled in."

"I didn't hear—"

"You can tell me all about it after work."

"Tell you about what?"

She ran to the Liaison's Office and scooted inside in time for her imaginary delivery to become a real one.

Telling Katherine Debany she would be back in a few minutes, Twyla Montgomery hurried to Eve Denby's house. Usually unflappable, Eve sounded close to panic—or hysterical laughter.

As Twyla caught sight of the mound of feathers on the porch, she understood why Eve had called.

"Come inside," Eve said, opening the door as soon as Twyla stepped onto the porch. "There are cats in the neighborhood, so I don't want to leave . . . *that* . . . unguarded, but I don't want to be in public view right now."

Twyla stepped inside. "How did you end up with a dead turkey on your porch?"

"A Wolf brought it over a few minutes ago." Eve raked a hand through her short hair.

"Why?" She would have thought he'd want the meal for himself. Or herself.

"Boone only receives shipments of pork and beef twice a month, and we're all getting tired of venison and rabbit. We're even getting tired of beef. So I asked Boone if he had any poultry for sale. He said he'd try to get some."

"He did that," Twyla said, looking out the screen door.

"I was hoping to buy a chicken, not a turkey the size of a minivan."

An exaggeration, but it was a big bird—and looked bigger with the feet and feathers and everything else still attached.

Eve sagged against the doorframe. "What am I supposed to do with it?"

"Well, you can't tell them you don't want it—especially if they went out and caught it just for you."

"I know that!"

A neighborhood cat, a big tom from the look of it, must have caught the scent of meat. Twyla wasn't sure if the animal didn't see her through the screen door or didn't care. He sauntered toward the porch, too focused on the free meal to notice the Crows until they struck. Twyla wasn't sure which of the Crowgard she enjoyed more, the one who flew in and grabbed the cat's tail, giving it a yank before letting go and flying out of reach, or the one who flew over and dropped a rotten tomato on the cat's head. Either way, she didn't think that cat would be looking to scrounge a meal at Eve's house anytime soon.

Having successfully routed the thief, the Crows returned to their sentry post.

"You have a roasting pan big enough to hold it?" Twyla asked.

"No," Eve replied. "I don't have an oven big enough to hold it either."

Twyla nodded. "They have big pans at Meat-n-Greens, and big ovens too. So this is what we'll do. After work, we'll have one of the boys help us take the bird back to the Courtyard. There must be a place where they prepare some of the game they sell at the butcher shop. That would be the best place to deal with the turkey. And anything we would waste, the Others might be able to use. In the meantime, let's put some newspapers or cardboard under that bird so you don't have to do more than hose off your porch."

"That bird is going to be the family's meat quota for weeks," Eve said after they tugged the turkey onto a pad of newspapers.

"No, it's not. You're going to supply the meat for a residents' potluck. The rest of us who want to come will each bring a dish. You'll invite Mr. Simon and Miss Meg so they can have the experience of this kind of meal with friends. Better invite the Wolf who brought the bird too."

"Not sure who he is."

"Mr. Simon will know. I'd best get back to work."

"Twyla? I'm good with tools. I like working around the house. But I've never lived in a country hamlet or on a farm. I don't know the first thing about plucking that bird or doing anything else that's needed to get it ready to cook."

She smiled. "Good thing for all of us that I know a bit about that. Best have Ruth and Merri Lee join us for this. They should learn too."

Twyla hurried back to the consulate to help Katherine Debany with reorganizing the files. Throughout the morning, Elliot Wolfgard was uncharacteristically quiet about the amount of time she'd been gone on a personal errand. But just before her lunch break, he paused near the filing cabinets and said blandly, "At least, being human, you don't have to pluck the damn thing with your teeth."

CHAPTER 16

Watersday, Messis 18

Returning from Ferryman's Landing, Kowalski pulled his car into the Courtyard's customer parking lot and looked at Monty. "Did we just bend some rules or buy from the black market?"

"Neither," Monty replied. "Ferryman's Landing isn't under human control. Butchers and grocers may be limited when it comes to selling foods that are grown outside our area, but there are no purchase limits for anything grown or produced on Great Island or the land used by the Intuits who grow crops around the mainland part of the village."

Kowalski looked at the stuffed carry sacks in the backseat. "Even so."

Monty nodded. "Even so."

They'd gone to Ferryman's Landing to purchase dinner rolls from Eamer's Bakery since Nadine was busy making muffins and desserts as her contribution to the residents' potluck, as well as making the pastries, muffins, and other food for A Little Bite to sell since Meat-n-Greens was closed to everyone else in order to host their private party. Ruthie had asked them to check at the open market for potatoes because the female pack didn't have quite enough to make the mashed potatoes for the potluck and the potato salad Nadine wanted to make for the coffee shop.

After buying the rolls, they wandered around the open market, looking for the other items on the girls' list. Somehow, in the course of explaining that they were buying ingredients needed for the turkey and potluck dinner that some Lakeside Wolves and humans were putting together, Monty noticed that the quarter pound of butter he'd asked for turned into a full pound so that there would be enough for the corn on the cob that would be served, a dozen eggs became two dozen, a pound of sugar ended up weighing more than a pound, and a five-pound bag of flour from a shipment fresh from the Midwest was added to their purchases when they weren't looking. Vendors began calling out suggestions of dishes that would go well with turkey, even on a hot summer day.

Despite numerous assurances to everyone in the market that the Lakeside Courtyard did have fruit trees and the *terra indigene* and their human tenants had plenty of fresh fruit, Kowalski ended up lugging a large basket of assorted fruit to the car.

"Why do you think the vendors gave us so much extra food?" Kowalski asked.

"What we do in the Courtyard sets a precedent for Ferryman's Landing as well as human-Other interaction in Talulah Falls," Monty replied. "All those vendors at the market were Intuits. Maybe they had a feeling that what they were contributing to this meal would make a difference for everyone in the long run."

"That's a lot riding on one meal."

Monty looked at his partner, who was sitting in a rapidly heating car, staring straight ahead. Yes, there was a lot riding on this meal. "My brother and his family weren't invited," he said quietly. "Jimmy isn't an official resident."

"Is he pissed about that?"

"He is, but my mother and Eve were firm in their decision about whom to invite. Mama will make up a plate for Jimmy's family." *Not that he'll appreciate it,* Monty added silently.

Jimmy had had all kinds of things to say when he'd learned about the potluck—and learned he wasn't invited. Tess and Vlad had declined the invitation, saying they would take care of their respective businesses. Captain Burke had also declined. So had Greg O'Sullivan, who was on his way back to Hubbney for a couple of days to speak to Governor Hannigan privately about the task force doctors who were missing. But Simon, Nathan, and Henry would be there, and, gods, so would Blair, who'd surprised everyone by accepting Eve's invitation. Putting Jimmy, with his posturing and attitude, in the same room with the four of them was a recipe for slaughter.

And putting Jimmy in a room where he had time to study Meg Corbyn and realize what she was would hurt everyone eventually.

Monty got out of the car. "Come on. Let's get this food inside and let the girls figure out what needs to go where."

"Michael's on patrol," Kowalski said. "Since he's not here for the prep work, he said he'd help with the dishes."

"Did he see that turkey?"

Kowalski laughed. "Lieutenant, half of Lakeside saw that turkey."

"We're making a spinach salad?" Since he was in human form, Simon didn't sniff the colander of greens Meg was washing and patting dry the way he would have in Wolf form. He took one of the leaves and sniffed it before eating it. Then he looked at Meg. "Why?"

"Because that is what I was asked to make," she replied. "When I finish washing the spinach, I'll clean the mushrooms. Then you'll slice them."

"Why?"

"Because you whine whenever I use a knife to slice or chop things."

"I do not." He didn't feel easy when Meg held a knife for any reason, but he didn't *whine* about it.

"Let's call it a sound of concern," she said. "Ruth says she'll hard-boil some eggs to add to the salad, and Merri Lee is making a warm bacon dressing to pour over it."

If the girls put enough bacon and grease on the leaves, the spinach might be tasty enough for a Wolf to eat.

He studied Meg, who seemed to be concentrating awfully hard just to wash a few leaves. "What's wrong? Don't you want to go to this potluck thing?"

"I do. Ruth, Merri, and I have talked about it, about what to expect. They're excited. So am I. So is Sam." She shut off the water and stood with her hands over the sink, drops of water falling from the tips of her fingers.

Simon waited.

"Skippy spends a lot of time with me and Sam. And he eats a few meals with the three of us every week."

"He can't join us for this meal," he said quietly. "We're all going to be in human form, and this is different. None of us have shared food with humans in this way before."

"I know. But he isn't going to understand why he's being left out."

She sounded sad, but she shook her head and went back to drying the spinach leaves.

They worked together to prepare the salad, saying little, not really needing words. And if Meg also noticed the odd silence that passed by the Green Complex, neither of them mentioned it.

Grr Bear sat in a chair that had been turned to look out at Crowfield Avenue, which made Monty wonder if the stuffed bear had been put in a time-out for some reason.

Taking the other chair on the porch, he wasn't surprised when Lizzy came over and leaned against him. Pulling her into his lap, he put his arms around her.

"Did Grr Bear do something I should know about?" He'd returned home to find Lizzy, Fanny, and Sarah on his porch playing jacks, watched by three Crows and a female Sanguinati he didn't recognize. Well, the Sanguinati was watching the girls; the Crows were watching the game—or waiting for an opportunity to "borrow" some of the shiny jacks.

Lizzy shook her head and said very quietly, "But he wanted me to ask you if Frances can come live with us."

"You call her Frances instead of Fanny?" Only his mama called Jimmy's daughter by her proper name.

"She doesn't like being called that word, Daddy. Especially . . ." Lizzy looked at Grr Bear as if for courage.

Monty felt a chill, despite the summer heat. "What is it, Lizzy girl?"

"Clarence is mean. He shakes his bum and slaps it and says things like 'Fanny kisses fanny' and makes a smacking sound like big kisses. When they lived in Toland, he told her he'd give her a quarter if she kissed his friends' bums. And one time, a boy said he'd give Clarence a dollar if Frances kissed his boy stuff." Lizzy wrinkled her nose to show her opinion of doing such a thing. "Frances doesn't want to be bad, Daddy. She told me and Grr Bear that she doesn't want to help Clarence when he does bad things. But if she doesn't, he pinches her really hard until she cries, and then Uncle Jimmy calls her a crybaby and says mean things."

Monty felt sick, dizzy, shaken. Clarence was a boy who might be growing up too fast and in the wrong way, but he was still a child. Was he really trying to pimp his younger sister? Had he learned that behavior from his father? Had Jimmy, who always preferred to use someone else in order to make money, tried to pressure Sissy into providing sexual favors to his friends or to acquaintances who had something he wanted?

Maybe Jimmy had tried, the same way Clarence was now trying to pressure Fanny, but he hadn't succeeded. Mama and Daddy would have known if something was *that* wrong. Maybe they hadn't realized how much hurt Jimmy was inflicting with his talk when they weren't around to stop him, but if it had become physical in any way, they wouldn't have cared that he was their flesh-and-blood son and Sissy was their adopted daughter. They would have called the police and reported Jimmy. They would have done right by Sissy.

"Daddy?"

Monty studied his daughter, wanted to ask if Clarence had tried to show her . . . Well, she'd seen Sam Wolfgard's boy stuff, but Sam had shifted from Wolf to naked boy after rescuing most of Boo Bear, Lizzy's previous bestest stuffed friend. And Sam had been in a room full of adults, many of whom saw no difference between seeing a human penis and seeing a male Wolf lift a leg to water a tree.

"Lizzy, has Clarence tried to hurt you?" Her hesitation made his chest tighten until it was hard to breathe.

"He called me names one day—used the bad words—because I said I wouldn't play with him, just the two of us, and I felt really sad. But Sarah and I promised Grr Bear that we wouldn't play outside alone and we would go to Sarah's house if Clarence came outside. And we promised to include Frances whenever she was allowed to play with us."

"Those are good promises." Monty studied the stuffed bear sitting in the other chair. Not a time-out. Grr Bear was keeping watch for a young two-legged predator.

The Others might not understand the harm that could be done with words, but they would recognize—and respond to—any physical threat directed toward anyone who was considered part of the Courtyard.

"Daddy? Can Frances stay with us?"

"It's complicated, Lizzy," he said. For humans anyway. "But Fan—Frances can play here with you as much as she wants. And I'll speak with Miss Eve about letting her play at the Denbys' house too."

"But not Clarence." Not a question. It sounded more like a plea.

"No, not Clarence." He set her down. "Can you and Grr Bear stay here for a little bit? Out here on the porch?" He'd ask Kowalski to keep an eye on things for a few minutes.

"Alone?" She looked at him with those big brown eyes. "Couldn't Miss Leetha stay with us?"

"Leetha? Who is that?" He had a feeling he already knew.

"She used to live in Toland. Now she lives upstairs."

Monty studied Lizzy as if he'd never seen her before. A few months ago, she'd lived in an apartment building where the adults would have panicked at the sight of one of the *terra indigene*. Now, having Sanguinati for upstairs neighbors wasn't worth a second thought—was, in fact, an odd kind of comfort.

"I'll ask. I won't be long, and I'll lock the door. Don't you or Grr Bear answer it. Promise?"

"We promise."

He went inside and called Pete Denby. "Pete? It's Monty. I need to talk for a few minutes."

"Sure. You want to pop over?"

"No. I'd like to meet at your office. This talk is more . . . official."

Silence. Then, "I'll see you there in a few minutes."

"Someone is coming over to watch Lizzy." Meaning, Robert and Sarah were welcome to come over if Pete needed someone to watch them.

"That's covered."

Wondering which of the Others was currently at the Denbys', Monty hung up, left his apartment, and locked his door. He went up the stairs quietly, not wanting to see Jimmy right now. He knocked on the upstairs apartment door just as quietly.

The female who opened the door was the same Sanguinati who had been on his porch a little while ago. If she had been human, he would have put her in her early forties. He had no idea how old she really was, but something about the look in those dark eyes told him she had seen, and done, a lot in her life.

Unlike Nyx Sanguinati, this vampire didn't wear old-fashioned clothes or move as a blend of smoke and human form, making it obvious what she was. In fact, this female would be noticed for her mature beauty and grace, and no man who admired her as she walked by would see a predator dressed in black trousers and a T-shirt, both made from some silky, rich-looking material.

"Miss Leetha?" Hard not to add an *l* to the end of her name.

"Lieutenant?"

"Would you mind staying with Lizzy for a few minutes? I need to take care of some business."

"I can keep watch."

"Thank you." He turned to go.

"Lieutenant? If your business gets too complicated, we can simplify it for you."

He didn't look back, didn't dare make even a noncommittal sound that she might interpret as tacit permission to kill his brother.

He arrived at the Liaison's Office just as Pete reached the upstairs landing and had his key in the outer door.

"How official are we?" Pete asked when they were inside his office. He opened the small fridge and held up two bottles of beer.

"Not official enough that I would refuse one of those," Monty replied.

Pete opened the bottles, handed one to Monty, then sat in one of the chairs in his waiting area.

Monty settled in the other chair, took a long pull of his beer, then told Pete everything Lizzy had told him.

"So far it's just verbal abuse," Monty began, then remembered the pinching. Hard to say where that would fall on a scale between sibling squabbles and abuse. "Mostly."

"Just verbal abuse?" Pete made air quotes as he repeated the words. "You know better than that."

He rubbed his forehead with the cold bottle. "Yes, I know better. Words can do as much damage as fists." He drank more of the beer. "The motto in my parents' house was 'no unkind words, no unkind deeds.' And if you were unkind, even unintentionally, you were expected to at least try to make things right."

"Your brother doesn't seem to have embraced your family's motto."

"No. But he learned how to avoid being caught too often for misbehavior, and when he was caught, he always tried to shift the blame to someone else—or persuade the other person to deny there was any wrongdoing." Monty put the bottle on a coaster Pete provided. "He certainly trained Sissy to be collusive in what he took from her when we were children—and nothing I said to either of them seemed to make a difference."

Monty hesitated, then wondered why, since he had asked for this meeting. Pete had already formed opinions about members of his family. He doubted anything he said now would alter those opinions—or shock an attorney. "The man Sissy was involved with, the girls' father. He was a nice guy, steady. And he really loved her. I only met him a few times, but I liked him. He was happy when she became pregnant with Carrie, and he and Sissy talked about getting married. Then something happened, and he wasn't talking about marriage anymore. But they stayed together, and despite him backing away a bit, things seemed to settle down."

"You didn't marry Lizzy's mother," Pete said gently.

"I wanted to get married. Elayne didn't. Or, more to the point, her mother didn't want her to marry a social and financial inferior."

"What happened with Sierra?"

"We never knew. He walked out on her and the girls

about a year after Bonnie was born. The one time I confronted him after he left, he said he didn't mind working long hours to support his own children, but he'd be damned if he'd break his back for a moocher. I didn't understand at the time. Now, having seen Jimmy and Sissy together here, I think about how her partner paid some of the bills directly, or bought clothes and toys for the girls, or brought over a bag of groceries when he came to visit his children. But he wouldn't give Sissy any money."

"Jimmy was taking a share of the house money, and Sierra's partner figured out why they were having trouble paying bills." Pete sighed. "She probably promised to stop giving her brother money, and things would settle down for a while."

Monty nodded. "Then Jimmy would show up again and wear her down. And when she broke one promise too many, her partner left."

"Do you know where to find him?"

He shook his head. "Mama might know. Doesn't matter now. Sissy is out of Jimmy's reach. But Frances . . ."

"You can't take a child away from her parents because you were told about something that happened in another city," Pete said. "There is no proof that Clarence coerced Frances to do anything, and it would be his word against hers."

"Human courts couldn't, and wouldn't, take Frances away from her parents on hearsay, but human law doesn't apply in the Courtyard," Monty said. "I wouldn't need to convince a judge that Frances was endangered."

Pete leaned forward. "There was enough of an age gap between you and Sierra to provide some distance, but brothers and sisters close to the same age don't always get along. If you have any doubts about that, I'll let you spend an afternoon with Sarah and Robert when they're being the bane of each other's existence. Monty, if this is a tempest in a teapot, if Frances has embellished a sibling quarrel and added a dramatic flourish for sympathy, and you convince Simon Wolfgard to act on it, there is no going back. You have more experience with the Others than I do, but having observed how the adults let the kids scrap to settle things among themselves and only step in when it looks like one of them will get hurt, they'll take your word that the threat is serious enough to remove the child. But what happens if Simon or Vlad or Henry decides Frances should be relocated? You won't be able to withdraw your request, won't be able to soft-pedal what you told them in order to keep her in Lakeside."

"I know." It could be nothing more than Frances being unhappy and lonely. She'd been uprooted from her home in Toland and had limited contact here with the children she could play with. Even now, the apartment was a temporary home, one her family could lose at any time. This could be nothing more than a somewhat introverted child wanting to feel settled. Or she could be in real danger of being pimped by her own brother.

Monty picked up the beer and drained the bottle.

"What are you going to do?" Pete asked. "What would you do if we were talking about Lizzy?"

"Talk to Eve and Ruth so they're aware of a potential danger. Talk to Karl and Michael in an unofficial capacity." Monty released his breath slowly. "And talk to Simon and Vlad about when human behavior requires intervention regardless of the age of the humans."

"Before or after the potluck dinner?"

"After. No point getting everyone stirred up just before they're supposed to sit down together for a meal." But he'd ask Leetha Sanguinati to let him know if Jimmy, or Clarence, had any visitors.

Skippy arrived at the Market Square before Simon, Meg, and Sam. So had Nathan and Blair, but they were outside Meat-n-Greens, blocking the door to keep the juvenile Wolf from dashing inside and making a grab for some of the food.

"Pup, did you tell him about this meal?" Simon asked Sam.

"No. Maybe. A little. But that was before Meg told me everyone had to look *human*."

Spotting them, Skippy headed straight for Meg, who was carrying the large bowl of spinach salad.

Blair growled a warning and Simon stepped in front of Meg, giving Skippy two reasons to veer away instead of leaping on, and possibly scratching, Meg to find out what was in the bowl. Nathan joined them, surrounding her until she reached Meat-n-Greens and went inside.

"We'll stay out here until everyone else is inside," Blair said.

"The female pack and the rest of the food are here," Nathan said. "The males are just arriving. Is that normal? I thought males helped with food."

"I did," Simon replied.

Blair gave him a look. "You brought leaves and fungus."

Simon bared his teeth. Then he sighed because it was true. "Come on, Sam."

But Sam was staring at Skippy, whose amber eyes held a puzzled earnestness.

"You can't come in," Sam said with quiet authority. "You have to be able to shift to human form to eat here today."

The adult Wolves didn't move, didn't intrude. The moment stretched. Then Skippy slunk away, crying in a way that made Simon's heart ache.

"We'll make sure he gets some of the food," Simon whispered to Sam as he opened the door. He and the leader of the puppy pack went inside.

The tables had been moved together to form one long table down the center of the room. Other tables had been grouped to hold bowls and platters of a variety of foods.

"There is so much," Meg said, taking slow steps toward the food tables.

Were there more choices than usual, or was seeing it displayed in a different way confusing her?

"We may have gone a bit overboard with the number of dishes we prepared," Merri Lee said, putting a dish of green beans on the table. "But we wanted enough variety for everyone, and everything here can be eaten as leftovers. Meg, give me the spinach salad and I'll add the warm bacon dressing and the hard-boiled eggs. Oh, and we have steamed corn on the cob, so make sure you take a piece to try it. Lieutenant Montgomery and Pete have gone to fetch the children. Eve is mashing the potatoes, Miss Twyla is about done with the corn, and Michael and Karl are carving the turkey."

Simon would have liked to see this carving, but he didn't ask. He didn't care about getting in the males' way, but this seemed like a good time to steer clear of Miss Twyla and Eve.

Montgomery, Pete, and the three human pups arrived, followed by Nathan, Blair, and Henry. Nadine and Chris Fallacaro came out of the kitchen area carrying baskets of muffins and rolls, and a plate with some kind of dense bread.

Nadine pointed to the foods. "Peach muffins, dinner rolls, and zucchini bread. I'm making use of what's in season."

Fruit in the muffins sounded good, but vegetables in bread?

Simon looked at Blair and Nathan. They looked at him.

<You distract her, and I'll give the bread thing a sniff,> Blair said.

<Too late,> Simon said as Michael Debany carried out a large platter piled with meat, including the turkey's legs, which were the only intact—and recognizable—parts of the bird.

Kowalski came out of the kitchen area carrying two sacks filled with containers of food. "Miss Twyla is sending over some food to Cyrus and his family to keep the peace. I'll be back in a few minutes."

Montgomery came over to them. "Do you want help, Karl?"

"Better if I do it alone, sir."

Montgomery nodded.

"I'll walk out with you and make sure Skippy doesn't ambush you," Nathan said.

Eve Denby set a big bowl of cooked bread cubes next to the turkey and clapped her hands. "All right, everyone. Grab a plate and help yourself. Anyone shorter than Meg will be helped by an adult."

Meg and Merri Lee looked at Eve and said, "Hey!"

The rest of the humans laughed. Simon had no idea why.

Merri Lee rolled her eyes. "If that's the standard you're using, Meg and everyone exactly her height get to be first in line."

That brought more laughter. He still didn't know why this was amusing, but Meg and Merri Lee, with Sam between them, were first to choose food, so he didn't snarl at anyone. Nathan returned, gave him a nod to indicate that Kowalski—and the food—had escaped Skippy's notice, and joined the line.

Green bean casserole, broccoli-and-cheese casserole, potato salad, macaroni salad, and spinach salad; muffins, rolls, and zucchini bread; mashed potatoes, stuffing, turkey, and gravy; corn on the cob and melted butter. He gave up trying to identify the rest of the food the female pack had made for this meal.

Meg didn't take more than a spoonful of anything, but neither did the rest of the females. They still had full plates of food. The pups weren't given as many different foods, but the quantity was still sufficient, even for Sam. As they took their seats at the table, Kowalski returned, and something about the pity in the man's dark eyes made fur spring up on Simon's shoulders and back.

"You need to come outside," Kowalski said quietly when he reached Simon.

Montgomery set his plate on the table. "Is there a problem?"

Kowalski nodded, but he kept his eyes on Simon. "You need to come outside."

<Simon?> Blair set aside his food. So did Nathan and Henry.

<Wait,> Simon said. <Guard Meg.>

He heard the whimpering before he reached the door. Wolf but not Wolf. When he stepped outside, he understood the pity in Kowalski's eyes, knew why Montgomery sucked in a breath.

Not human. Not Wolf. Not even that terrible but harmonious blend most of them took when they were stressed or needed aspects of both forms. This was the worst kind of between.

He didn't want to be left out.

Before he could decide what to do with Skippy, Miss Twyla stepped outside and looked at the whimpering juvenile.

"I'm not having a naked boy sitting at the table, so you'd best get him some clothes," she said.

"Miss Twyla . . . ," Simon began at the same time Montgomery said, "Mama."

She ignored them and pointed at Kowalski. "You run over to the store and get this boy a T-shirt and a pair of those elastic-waist exercise pants you all wear when you're lifting weights and doing whatever else you do to make those muscles. Should be easy enough to take out a few stitches in the back seam to make room for his tail. Don't bother with shoes right now."

Shoes? They didn't have anything that could accommodate Skippy's feet. One looked mostly human but furred. The other was a Wolf's paw with human toes.

"Shirt and pants will be enough," Miss Twyla continued. "Run along, now. The food is getting cold."

"Yes, ma'am." Kowalski ran to the clothing store in the Market Square.

"Crispin, you go on in and make sure everyone gets started."

Montgomery's hesitation lasted only a moment. "Yes, Mama."

"Miss Twyla . . . ,"Simon tried again.

"No."

The word was said quietly and courteously—and made it clear that there would be no arguing and no discussing.

Miss Twyla gave Simon a long look. "You think I don't understand what happened here, and why? Trying takes courage. How many of you got it right the first time?"

Most of the *terra indigene* who tried the form never managed to shift all the way, so they couldn't pass for human. But they also didn't try to sit at a table with humans and eat.

"Anyone who has a problem with this is welcome to fix a plate and eat elsewhere," Miss Twyla said. "And that includes you."

Stung, he snarled at her—and felt vaguely ashamed for doing it when she folded her skinny arms and just looked at him.

Kowalski returned. "I guessed at sizes. Figured the T-shirt would be okay if it was a little big. It's hot and the rest of the kids are wearing shorts, so I brought these."

He'd seen Kowalski and Debany wear shorts like those when they worked out at Run & Thump, the Courtyard's fitness place.

"Those will work fine," Miss Twyla said. "Now I need—"

Eve and Nadine poked their heads out the door.

"Twyla, what's going . . . ?" Eve began.

Simon saw the shock and horror on the two females' faces. Then those feelings disappeared, in the way a

Wolf would disappear behind the mask of looking human. The feelings weren't gone, just hidden.

Had they hidden feelings that way the first time they'd seen Meg's scars?

"Need a seam ripper or a small pair of scissors," Miss Twyla said.

"I have scissors in the mini sewing kit I keep in my purse," Eve said. "I'll get them."

"You boys help him stand up and get dressed."

He wasn't sure who the boys were until Kowalski moved to stand on one side of Skippy and gave Simon an expectant look. After they hauled Skippy upright, the juvenile needed a minute to find his balance—not an easy thing when standing on two differently shaped feet. Nadine helped them get the T-shirt on while Miss Twyla held the shorts to Skippy's waist and decided where to rip the seam to provide an opening for the tail.

When Eve returned with her sewing kit, she not only opened the seam but also added a couple of stitches to keep the seam from opening further.

Then they took Skippy inside.

Blair, Nathan, and Henry had guessed what had happened. The humans . . .

<Eve told them so they would be prepared,> Henry said.

"Skippy, you sit next to me," Miss Twyla said. "Ruth, you fix a plate for him. Start simple."

"Yes, ma'am." Ruth hurried to the tables with the food and began filling another plate while Merri Lee poured milk into a plastic cup.

Simon and Kowalski settled Skippy in the chair. The juvenile panted, stressed from the physical change and a body that must have felt like disjointed pieces.

Robert stared, a forkful of mashed potatoes suspended over his plate. "Is that Skippy?"

"So what?" Sam challenged.

"How did he do that?" Robert looked at Sam. "Can you do that?"

"We'll discuss this later," Pete interrupted. "Eat your dinner."

Ruth brought a plate that held mashed potatoes, stuffing, turkey, and a spoonful of the broccoli and cheese casserole. "Wasn't sure if he could handle corn on the cob."

Miss Twyla nodded. "This will do for now."

Skippy lunged for the food on the plate and got a smack on the nose.

"You wait until I cut it up for you." Miss Twyla cut up the turkey, then put the plate in front of Skippy. She picked up a fork and tapped her finger on the end of the tines. "This is pointy and will hurt if you poke your tongue or the inside of your mouth. I expect you'll stab yourself a time or two—all children do—but you try to be careful." She put the fork in his hand and guided it until he'd speared a piece of turkey, then released him. "There you go."

"How come you cut up Skippy's food?" Sam asked.

Funny thing for the pup to ask since he'd pushed his plate over to Meg to have her cut up the turkey for him.

"I did that for all my children and grandchildren when they were little," Miss Twyla replied.

"Grandma Twyla used to cut up my food, but she doesn't have to anymore," Lizzy piped up.

<That's because Pete Denby cut up her food when he cut up Sarah's,> Henry said, sounding amused.

Sam cocked his head and studied Miss Twyla. "If you're cutting up his food, does that mean you're Skippy's grandma?"

Montgomery choked but didn't look surprised when Miss Twyla said, "Does he have a grandma? No? Then I guess I am."

No one spoke for several minutes. The Wolves and Henry kept an eye on Skippy to make sure he didn't try for the food on anyone else's plate. The humans kept their attention focused mostly on their own plates.

"So," Miss Twyla finally said, "what have you children been up to lately?"

Silence. Then Montgomery looked at Simon before turning to his mother. "Which children are you referring to, Mama?"

She looked at everyone around the table, including Blair and Henry. "All of you."

"We caught a turkey the other day," Blair said.

"And it's a fine bird. Isn't it, Eve?"

Eve Denby swallowed. "A very fine bird. And big enough to share."

Merri Lee mentioned the new Crowgard cozy she was reading. Kowalski asked if Alan Wolfgard had a new book coming out. Michael Debany wondered if the Wolves had ever played a pickup game of basketball.

Bit by bit they all relaxed, talking about books and games that involved balls of one sort or another, talking about the foods that were a new experience for Meg as well as the *terra indigene*.

"Corn on the cob is *wonderful*," Meg said. "We'll have to get Jenni, Starr, and Jake to try it this way."

Merri Lee laughed. "Yeah. I don't think melted butter on raw corn would have the same taste appeal."

They talked and laughed and asked Henry about his sculptures. Nathan growled a protest when Meg said she would dock him cookies the next time he was late for work, and that made the female pack laugh, especially when Meg confessed to looking *under* the Wolf bed to see if Nathan was hiding from her.

Through it all, Skippy sat among them, welcome and accepted.

Padding to the kitchen as quietly as possible, Jimmy scratched his bare belly, then reached under his boxers to scratch his ass. He opened the refrigerator and swore silently when jars stored in the door's shelves rattled. When he'd left the bedroom, Sandee had been doing her pig snuffle—a disgusting sound, unlike an honest snore—so she wasn't likely to hear him, but the damn kids had been trying to sneak food all evening and might wake up and want to join him. Hadn't he let them have their portion of the food that had been sent over with that damned cop? That should have been enough.

He should have been invited to that big blowout dinner they'd had at Meat-n-Greens. He was living in one of these apartments, wasn't he? Mama could have insisted that he, at least, be included. But it was that bitch, Eve, who'd had the stones to ask the freaks to bring her a big-ass turkey, so she was the one who had handed out the invites.

Something he wasn't going to forget. Just like he wasn't going to forget that she was supposed to take care of things around the buildings and usually worked alone. Backed-up toilet? She'd have to deal with it, and he wouldn't need more than a couple of minutes alone with her to teach her why she should be nicer to him— and to persuade her to keep her fucking mouth shut.

Jimmy pulled out the plate of turkey, the three remaining rolls, and the jar of mayonnaise. He would have preferred heating up stuffing and mashed potatoes along with the turkey, but the *ding* of the wave-cooker might wake the brats, so he settled for sandwiches.

He cut the rolls, slathered them with mayonnaise, then stuffed as much turkey as he could into each one. Sitting at the small table, he bit into one sandwich, tasting resentment along with the meat.

His stash of money was getting low, and Sandee wasn't bringing in enough to buy food every day, let alone anything else. Wasn't their turf, and the Stag and Hare, the only tavern within easy reach without spending money on taxis or bus fare, had cops and vampires hanging around who would recognize her—and the cops at least would know why she kept leaving with different men. Even if CJ could be persuaded not to arrest her for prostitution, that bastard Burke wouldn't hesitate. He didn't seem the type who would look the other way for freebies.

There were bars closer to the bus station that had the sort of customers he was used to rubbing elbows with. Like everything else these days, drugs trickled into the city in small quantities, and the price of a little mellow weed was almost triple what he'd paid in Toland. A middleman could sample the product and still make a hefty profit. But he was a newcomer, and the middlemen already in Lakeside had staked out their territories and weren't interested in making room for a competitor.

Which meant he had to be able to sell something else, something those other men didn't have.

Jimmy stared at the turkey sandwich for a long moment before taking another big bite.

Even in the grimiest bars, the talk was the same: you usually could buy some kind of food at the stores where your ration books were registered, but butcher shops still ran out of meat before the next shipment arrived from the slaughterhouses. You couldn't always buy a loaf of bread, and even when you could, how much you could buy was strictly enforced. Canned goods? Foods in jars? The canning factories and food-processing companies were operating again, if not in the same capacity because some of those places had a shortage of workers. Grocery stores stocked those foods whenever possible, but just as often there were empty shelves in those stores too. Women who had a fruit tree on their property and knew how to preserve fruits and make jams and jellies were selling whatever extra their family wouldn't need during the coming year, but it was more like a neighborhood market day, and unfamiliar faces were watched by everyone—and police officers on horseback or on foot tended to patrol those streets during the market hours to discourage misbehavior or outright attempts to steal food.

The patsies made do with what was available, but the real men wanted something better. How were they supposed to do business eating nothing but fucking greens and a few measly ounces of meat each day?

The freaking Others ate rats and mice and all kinds of shit not fit for humans, and *their* butcher shop always had plenty of pork and beef. The good dogs even went out and brought back a fucking turkey for that bitch Eve just because she wanted one. If the meat in the butcher shop disappeared one night, they could just hunt up some more. At least then they would be good for something.

He couldn't take the meat himself. He'd overheard one of the freaks telling the brats that everyone had a different smell, and the Others could tell where each human had been in the Courtyard. So he couldn't be obviously connected to the disappearance of the meat.

But he'd met some men who could do the job and would be smart enough to give him his share of the haul.

His commission. Yeah. Businessmen received a commission for their part of a job.

Smiling, Jimmy ate the last sandwich and put the remaining turkey and mayonnaise in the refrigerator. Enough left for one person. Sandee would gobble up the turkey for breakfast before the brats could shovel it into their greedy faces. They could eat that broccoli shit or go hungry.

He needed to shake himself free of Sandee and the brats and get out of Lakeside. Nothing for him here. Unlike Toland, it was too small a city for him and his preferred kind of business to escape notice. He had to figure that CJ or, more likely, that bastard Burke had already told the police in other precincts who he was. With things the way they were right now, he didn't think anyone could be persuaded to look the other way—especially if a theft involved food or some other essential goods.

So he needed a big score, something that would give

him the means to get out of Lakeside and set up else-where. Had to think about where that would be.

He'd find his ticket out of here. Yes, he would. But he would have to wait until Moonsday. Then he'd approach a few men and make a business deal.

CHAPTER 17

Having finished his lunch at Meat-n-Greens, Simon put the plate, silverware, and glass in their respective bins. No food except an apple core to dump into the food-recycling container.

His hand paused over the container. How many apples were left in their little apple house? How many would they need to set aside for the treats Meg gave the ponies? Henry would know. He knew apples ripened at different times, but he hadn't paid much attention. Ripe apples were picked and eaten. But according to the female pack, some kinds of apples were better for eating while others were better for cooking and baking.

Who knew human females could be so fussy? A Wolf would munch on a ripe apple and be happy. Of course, making distinctions between apples was just one of many things that were different this year.

A Little Bite and Meat-n-Greens had gone through some changes over the past few weeks, especially now, when most of the humans who were allowed access to the Market Square ate at least one meal per day at one place or the other. That made sense for the humans employed in the stores or working at the consulate. And to be fair, the humans who had a share of the Green Complex's garden made food that they passed around as a side dish, and they always gave some of the prepared food to Meg and showed her how to make the dishes she really liked.

All in all, considering the number of humans who were allowed to eat or purchase foods that came from the Courtyard's land or from the *terra indigene* farms that supplied the things that weren't grown, gathered, or caught right here, no one felt a real lack. Sure, some foods weren't always available, depending on the success of a hunt or when the supply of flour reached Lakeside, but there was always something to eat.

That was part of the change at Meat-n-Greens and A Little Bite. Nadine's Bakery & Café made foods for breakfast and lunch, and Tess would sell those foods in the coffee shop until she ran out. Then it was just coffee and other drinks. Meat-n-Greens had changed to providing food for lunch and throughout the afternoon, but patrons were expected to pick up their order when it was ready and clean up after themselves. In the evening, the place still acted more like a human restaurant with servers. In that way, *terra indigene* guests had a chance to experience several ways of eating in a human establishment.

All good things, when thinking of the Lakeside Courtyard as a place for advanced training in human interactions. But every day, humans still did things that were just peculiar. Like today. Having heard that there were no more turkey leftovers, he went into the kitchen area and offered to dump the turkey carcass where critters would find it so that it wouldn't go to waste. Eve and Nadine had told him they were making turkey soup and he should keep his paws off the carcass until they were done with it.

He should have reminded them that he was their employer and they shouldn't speak to him that way, but he'd been hungry and outnumbered and there had been too many sharp knives and pointy utensils within their reach.

He would talk to them later—or send a memo.

Making his way to the door, Simon noticed Lieutenant Montgomery, who had also stopped in for lunch. Something must have caught the human's attention, because he took a step back from the door in order to remain unseen. Simon hurried to join him.

"You do not want to go out there right now," Montgomery said. He held out an arm to block the door.

"Why? What's going on?" Simon scanned the open area of the Market Square but saw nothing alarming. In fact, when Simon considered voice rather than actions, Montgomery seemed amused.

"Negotiations." Montgomery pointed a finger at Miss Twyla, who was sitting on a bench eating an ice-cream cone, and Skippy, who was chasing a bowl of ice cream until he finally pushed the bowl against one of Miss Twyla's feet. Since her legs were crossed at the knee, the other foot dangled.

"*Roo-roo.*" Skippy planted a paw on Miss Twyla's dangling foot and tried to pull it down so he could wedge the bowl between her feet instead of chasing it.

"No," Miss Twyla said mildly.

"*Roo-roo!*" Skippy batted at her foot, more insistent.

"You can 'Grandma' me all you want. Doesn't change the fact that you can hold that bowl by yourself. Miss Meg showed you how."

"*Roo?*" Skippy looked around.

"She's not here." Miss Twyla licked her ice cream. "You just sit yourself down and put your own paws around the bowl."

"Oh," Montgomery breathed. "He's going to try the 'I'm too helpless to do this' routine."

Skippy did look pathetic, pushing at the bowl with one paw while the ice cream rapidly melted.

"We could go out and help him," Simon said.

"You could do that. Of course, you'll have to get around Mama now that she's decided Skippy can do it himself."

"But when we all had dinner the other night, she cut up his food, helped him eat."

"The other night he needed help. This he can do by himself." Montgomery studied him, openly curious. "Do you continue to feed your young once they're old enough to do for themselves?"

"Of course not. They have to learn to hunt, as well as learn to protect their share of the food." Simon considered what Montgomery was asking. "Doesn't mean juveniles won't act like puppies sometimes and try to coax an adult into giving them an easy meal."

"Not much different from humans that age. How often do your adults give in?"

When Simon didn't answer, Montgomery grinned. "That's what I thought. I guess Wolves and my mama have some things in common when it comes to raising children."

Put that way, it explained why the Wolves treated Miss Twyla more like one of their own than like a human.

They watched Skippy flop down and put his front paws around the bowl. He gave the remaining ice cream a lick, then looked at Miss Twyla.

Montgomery laughed softly. "Oh, there are the big sad eyes. Lizzy tries that look on me every so often. Hard for me to say no to that look, even when I know giving in would be bad for both of us, but Mama is made of sterner stuff. Every grandkid has tried that look, and every grandkid has failed."

They stood in the doorway, watching, until Miss Twyla turned her head and looked right at them.

"Are you two going to keep gawking, or are you going to get some work done?"

"That's our cue," Montgomery said under his breath

before he raised his voice enough to be heard. "We were just leaving, Mama."

Simon strode out of the Market Square with Montgomery but said nothing until they were out of sight. "I am the leader of the Courtyard. I'm the one who makes decisions."

"Yes, you are." Montgomery waited a beat. "You going to tell her that?"

He growled. "Maybe I'll send a memo to her too."

Montgomery just laughed.

Late that evening, when the Market Square stores had all closed, Vlad walked to the back of Erebus Sanguinati's mausoleum, where Grandfather and Leetha waited for him.

"Simon will be here in a few minutes," he told them. The Wolf had been a little confused, to say nothing of wary, about being asked to have this discussion in the Chambers. After all, it was only the second time since Simon took over the Lakeside Courtyard years ago that he'd been invited inside the black wrought-iron fences that marked the boundaries of the Sanguinati's part of the Courtyard.

"Why does he need to be involved?" Leetha asked.

Vlad studied the female who had relocated here when the *terra indigene* abandoned the Toland Courtyard. She was an intelligent, beautiful hunter. Not in Stavros's league as a predator, or his, or even Nyx's, but deadly nonetheless.

"Simon Wolfgard is the leader of this Courtyard," Vlad replied.

"And why is that with Grandfather residing here?" she challenged. "The Sanguinati always rule the Courtyards in prominent human cities. While this city isn't as significant as some of the cities we rule on the East Coast, it's still a major port on the Great Lakes."

"The Sanguinati support the Wolfgard here." Vlad felt his temper sharpen.

"Enough." Erebus's snarled command was directed at both of the younger Sanguinati, but he had turned toward Leetha to make it clear that she was the provocation. "It was decided many years ago that shifter forms were better suited to lead Courtyards in certain areas of Thaisia, just as we were better suited to rule the large urban cities and coastal towns."

"Then why . . . ," Leetha began.

"Perhaps the Sanguinati ruled in Toland so long they began to think of other *terra indigene* as subordinates rather than strong predators whose ancestors chose a different shape that better fit the other predators and prey where they lived. Your attitude displeases me, Leetha."

She looked stunned. "I—I'm sorry, Grandfather. I didn't mean to give offense."

"Then learn. Simon and Vladimir are friends. They work together, live as neighbors, have fought well together. There is true cooperation in this Courtyard, not just an agreement to work together to defend against the human infestation as is the case in so many Courtyards. And that cooperation has opened up opportunities for all the *terra indigene*. Tolya now rules a Midwest town, a rustic place compared to Toland, but the Sanguinati have a foothold in a part of Thaisia as never before—because Tolya was willing to work with the Wolfgard and other shifters in the area."

"So isolated," she whispered.

Vlad studied Leetha. Was there a hint of fear in her voice? Tolya, and the Sanguinati he had selected to join him in running Bennett and some of the town's important businesses, seemed to be thriving. But unlike the Wolves, who usually hunted four-legged animals and liked living in the wild country, the Sanguinati were better suited as urban predators, with humans being the preferred prey. That wasn't as easy to do when you knew everyone in a small town—and they knew you. That was one reason the Sanguinati preferred using larger human cities as their hunting grounds.

The other reason was that, in larger human cities, his kind didn't often deal directly with *terra indigene* like the Elders.

"If you cannot accept Simon as leader, perhaps you would rather be living in Talulah Falls," Erebus continued. "It is under Stavros's rule now."

"No." Leetha's tone made it clear that she didn't want to answer to Stavros.

Interesting. Vlad knew Stavros had agreed to rule Talulah Falls so that he would be close enough to present himself as a potential mate the next time Nyx came into season. Had he turned away from Leetha's invitation the last time she was in season, unwilling to become the mate of a female who wasn't his first choice? Or perhaps Stavros, who could poke fun at his own kind, had sensed on some level that he and Leetha would not suit each other once the physical mating concluded.

And, in truth, Talulah Falls was even smaller than Lakeside and in far more turmoil, as *terra indigene* and even some Intuits moved into the town to join the remaining humans in keeping the power plant and other necessary businesses running.

It suddenly occurred to him that both Stavros and Tolya had seen the possibility of working in a mixed community because of their visits here.

<Vlad?> Simon called. <I'm at the fence. If I need to be in human form for this meeting, I'll have to find some clothes.>

<Not necessary.> Vlad smiled, almost feeling that amber stare despite being out of sight. <Being in human form, I mean. Should I open the gate?>

<Not necessary.>

He looked at Grandfather Erebus. "Simon is here."

"Open the gate for him, Vladimir."

"Not necessary."

The fence that defined the Chambers wasn't tall, wasn't trying to keep anyone out. Anyone who entered uninvited didn't leave. But maybe leaping over the fence to join them was Simon's way of telling Leetha, and any other Sanguinati who might be in doubt, that he was, in fact, the leader of the Courtyard and he respected their boundaries by choice.

<Grandfather Erebus,> Simon said politely once he joined them.

"Wolfgard." Erebus tipped his head in the slightest bow.

<Meg wanted me to tell you she received a catalog today that lists a lot of movies for sale. She'll bring it tomorrow when she makes her deliveries.>

Erebus smiled. "The sweet blood knows how much I enjoy watching my old movies."

Leetha looked at Grandfather, then at Simon.

Yes, Vlad thought. *The sweet blood is the link between our kind and Simon's. We would not have come this far this fast if she hadn't stumbled into the Courtyard. Some of us would not have survived the recent conflicts with humans. Even with her warnings, some of us didn't survive.*

"Tell the Wolfgard what you heard," Erebus said, waving a hand toward Leetha.

"A couple of us followed Cyrus Montgomery earlier this evening," Leetha said. "The bus station and downtown bus stops are good hunting grounds, especially after dark. And businesses that stay open later than the police recommend are also prime hunting grounds. Lights are lowered and the door is locked, but the patrons who come in before the official closing aren't asked to leave." She smiled, showing a hint of fang. "The owners tend to live above the business and don't really care what happens to the customers when they make their way home."

<Why did you follow him?> Simon asked.

"I don't like him."

<You followed him to one of these locked businesses?>

"Yes. He met with four men. He's going to case the Market Square tomorrow to confirm the earth native trucks are making a meat delivery. When the stores close for the evening, he'll call the men. They'll slip into the Courtyard, break into the butcher shop, and steal all the meat. You Wolves will howl about the loss, but all you'll do is hunt a couple extra deer to make up for it."

<Is that what they think of us or what you think of us?> Simon asked.

Challenge, plain and simple. A Wolf couldn't win a fight with a Sanguinati who was in smoke form, but Simon must have heard something in Leetha's voice that he wouldn't allow to go unchallenged.

"Leetha?" Grandfather Erebus's voice was quiet—and more threatening because of that. "The Wolfgard asked you a question."

A hesitation, but they all knew her answer would determine if she was allowed to remain in Lakeside.

"Cyrus Montgomery said those words," she finally replied. "The words were said sneeringly, as if you deserved no respect."

Simon didn't move, didn't reply.

"Simon?" Vlad said. "What do you want to do? How do you want to stop them?"

Simon stared at him as if Henry had given him a brain-rattling swat and that's why he would ask such a silly question. <We're not going to stop them. We're going to give them more incentive to steal from us tomorrow night.>

Vlad suddenly realized why Leetha was having trouble accepting a Wolf as the Courtyard's leader. She'd observed Simon dealing with the female and police packs. She'd seen him with Meg, who brought out his playful side. But she didn't take into account that there was a reason he was dominant over strong Wolves like

Blair and Nathan, didn't take into account what it meant to have a Harvester like Tess living among them. She hadn't really seen Simon yet.

"What reason?" he asked.

<We're going to make sure that Cyrus hears about a delivery of special meat.>

CHAPTER 18

Sunday, Messis 21

Jimmy waited until the lunch crowd thinned out before he meandered over to the Market Square. Wouldn't do to run into Mama or CJ. Wouldn't do to run into any of the bitches who spied on other people for the freaks. But three of them were sitting at one of those umbrella tables, eating salads like that crap was real food. He recognized the two women living in the apartments with the cops—Ruth and Merri-something—but he didn't recognize the third one, a black-haired girl who was wearing a big gauzy shirt despite the heat.

She looked vaguely familiar, like he'd seen her in passing. Didn't matter. Couldn't be much of anything interesting about her if she was hanging around with the other two.

He wanted to take a look at what had arrived at the butcher shop that morning, needed to tell his crew what they could expect. He resented having to buy fresh meat. Sandee would cook it to the point of being inedible—the bitch could mess up spreading peanut butter and jelly on bread—but he needed a reason to be there instead of buying prepared food at Meat-n-Greens or A Little Bite.

Going into the butcher shop, he confirmed there was no bell on the door to be making noise that might carry late at night. Nothing fancy about the lock either. Shit, even Clarence could pick that lock inside a minute.

He waited near the door, but the shopkeeper seemed intent on talking to one of the male bloodsuckers who were squatting in the apartment above his.

"Delivery of special meat will be arriving tonight," the shopkeeper said. "Rarely get it anymore. That's why I'm not posting a sign, just passing the word."

"How much is being delivered?" the vampire asked.

"Not sure. That's why I can't guarantee you'll get a particular cut, but I'm making a list of anyone who is interested in receiving a bit."

The vampire glanced at Jimmy, then turned away but didn't lower his voice quite enough. "You going to let the humans reserve some of the special meat?"

The shopkeeper laughed quietly. "Nah. I'm not going to mention it to any of *them*. If there is any left over after I fill *our* orders, I'll sell it to the humans, but it isn't likely there will be anything left."

The vampire nodded. "Put us down for a piece. Don't want to miss out on a delicacy."

Jimmy barely contained his excitement as the vampire walked out, leaving him alone with the shopkeeper. Special meat. Delicacy. Hot damn, they'd picked the perfect night to empty the butcher shop.

"Afternoon." He gave the shopkeeper a big smile. "I was hoping to buy some meat for the family's dinner."

The shopkeeper waved at the glass counter. "What I've got is here. If you want a quick meal, I've got slices of cooked meatloaf with gravy today. Was made fresh this morning. By a human."

On any other day, he would have tried to buy a whole meatloaf, figuring to sell or trade half of it. But he didn't want the freaks looking at him too hard today—and he didn't want them whining to CJ or that bastard Burke about him taking more than could be eaten at one meal.

"I'll take three slices," he said. When the shopkeeper raised eyebrows that had more brown feathers than hair, he added, "The kids won't be able to eat more than half a slice each, not when they'll be having their vegetables too."

Three slices went into one of those containers customers were expected to wash and bring back. Jimmy made the purchase and walked out. He kept his pace leisurely, even waved to the three bitches who were finishing up their meals.

Sandee was out when he got back to the apartment, and the brats were out too, so he heated one slice of meatloaf, then another half for his own meal. Having put the rest in the refrigerator, he spent the afternoon sitting on the porch waiting for nightfall.

Meg hung up her gauzy shirt in the back room of the Liaison's Office, then went into the bathroom to splash some water on her face, brush her teeth, and pee. Euphemisms, she had learned, were wasted on Wolves. As soon as Nathan returned from his own midday break, he would sniff around the back room and be able to report exactly what she'd done, so what was the point of saying anything else? She'd tried the whole "I'm going to powder my nose" thing once, but every Wolf she knew had come around trying to sniff her face to be able to identify the scent of this powder.

Even with Merri Lee's and Ruth's help, she couldn't convince the Wolves there was no powder until Simon confirmed that, in some stories, "powder the nose" meant peeing. Then Katherine Debany ruined it later that afternoon by taking out a compact and actually powdering her nose within Elliot's sight. Naturally, Elliot informed Blair and Nathan—and Simon—and the whole "let me smell your face" routine started all over again.

She found Nathan in the front room, already stretched out on the Wolf bed. He yawned at her, showing off all his teeth. She wasn't fooled. He only looked lazy and half-asleep. Any deliveryman who believed the ruse and acted inappropriately discovered how fast a Wolf could move—and just how much damage those teeth could do.

"Merri Lee, Ruth, and I had an excellent lunch," she told him. "It was a salad made from fresh greens and garden vegetables with the last chunks of leftover turkey and hard-boiled egg, along with a variety of mini muffins we bought from Nadine. What about you? Did you have a good lunch?"

Nathan made a hopping motion with one paw.

"Fresh bunny," she translated. "Yum." Then remembering that he might misinterpret that as a request, she added, "Yum for you."

Returning to the sorting room, she considered what to do with her afternoon until it was time to make her deliveries. The mail was already sorted and out with the ponies; her packages were organized on a cart so that she could load—and unload—the BOW efficiently as she made her rounds. She already had the library books she was delivering to the girls at the lake.

Meg blew out a breath. She could write a note to Jean or Hope or Barb Debany, or even to Jesse Walker in Prairie Gold. She could read one of the books she'd taken out of the library. Normally the thought of doing those things gave her pleasure, but now she felt restless, uneasy. Not prickling, not the pins-and-needles feeling that warned of something about to happen. It was more subtle than that, but it made her a little queasy.

Taking her box of prophecy cards out of the drawer, she opened it and rested her fingertips lightly on the cards. But she didn't have a question, didn't even have a clue what to ask. She'd told Nathan about her lunch, he told her about his, and . . .

Sharp prickles filled her fingertips. She closed her eyes and chose the cards that produced the sharpest prickles. With her eyes still closed, she turned the cards over in the order she chose them.

She opened her eyes, studied the cards . . . and called Merri Lee.

"Can you duck out for a couple of minutes? It's important."

"I have a customer," Merri Lee replied. "Let me finish with him, and then I'll run over."

A few minutes later, they were both staring at the three cards on the sorting table.

"So, what was the question?" Merri Lee finally asked.

"I'm not sure. When I choose three cards, it's subject, action, and result."

"All three of these are food cards. Okay, one shows a table full of breads, dairy products, and bowls of fruit; one shows a feast with cooked meats and vegetables; and one shows animals that are considered food." Merri Lee frowned. "Are you still feeling the prickles?"

Meg shook her head. "But something is going to happen that concerns food."

"Doesn't look like it's about a lack of food."

Frustrated, Meg blew out a breath.

"Do you have PMS cravings? Maybe that's why you're fixated on food. I tend to want chocolate, pizza, and salty snacks. Of course, then I drink a lot of water—and retain a lot of water—and get bloated, which makes me crabby." Merri Lee gave her an expectant look.

She considered that and shook her head. "I guess it's nothing important, but I'll tell Simon about it anyway. It might make sense to him."

She told Simon about it when they got home from work, and she could see that it made sense to him. What worried her was the look in his amber eyes—and the fact that he wouldn't tell her what it meant. And for the first time, he snarled at her when she pushed for an explanation. Told her it wasn't any of her business.

That worried her too.

What worried her the most was waking up sometime in the night and realizing Simon was gone.

*   *   *

Everything went like clockwork. The four men parked in the lot adjacent to the Stag and Hare, then crossed Main Street to the delivery entrance of the Courtyard. From there, they went up the access way and into the Market Square, keeping close to the shops instead of dashing across the big open area in the middle.

They slipped inside the butcher shop, found the walk-in refrigerator, and stared for a moment, transfixed by the quantity of meat—trays of prime cuts of beef, as well as roasts and steaks. Other trays held chops, hams, sausages, bacon, and slabs of ribs.

They'd each brought a big rectangular backpack lined with straw around thick plastic. The late-night heat wasn't much better than the daytime temperature; it wouldn't do to have the meat start going bad before they had a chance to get it into their own freezers or sell most of the best cuts for profit.

Jimmy Montgomery was a blustering, arrogant prick who thought he was hot shit just because he'd lived in Toland, as if picking a lock there required more skill than it did here in Lakeside. He'd walked into the bar, bought himself a drink, and sat down at their table, as if he'd been invited. Started talking about needing a crew for an easy job—one he guaranteed would put food on the table. Illegal? Of course not. Human law didn't apply in the Courtyard, so how could anything done there be illegal?

No guards, no sentries around the business district after the shops closed. Yeah, being out at night might be tricky, but if you picked the right time, even the cops wouldn't be doing much patrolling, preferring to stick close to their stations unless they were called out.

He'd scoped out the shops, knew exactly where the butcher shop was located, had told them about the lock and lack of a bell on the door. Had confirmed the delivery of meat from one of the earth native farms. Even his reason for not going in with them made sense. Of course, his "commission" would reflect the chances he wasn't taking tonight. Not that they'd encountered any problems.

They filled their packs with the best cuts of meat, leaving the sausages and bacon, along with the roasts and hams they couldn't fit in their packs. They hadn't found the special meat Jimmy had said would be there, but that didn't matter. They had everything they'd come for and more.

Yes, everything had gone just like clockwork. Right up until the moment when they left the butcher shop and found the vampires and Wolves waiting for them.

Heart pounding, Monty scrambled out of bed, yanked open the drawer in the bedside table, and removed his recently acquired backup weapon, holster and all. Then he quietly moved to the screen door that opened onto the porch and stopped to listen.

He'd heard something that his training had responded to before he was fully awake. A brief scream, high-pitched and terrified. Now . . . nothing.

He unlocked the screen door and stepped onto the porch.

So quiet. Most people were following the police recommendation about being home before midnight, so there were no cars on the roads at this time of night—except official vehicles. But it wasn't a siren he'd heard.

In that quiet, Monty heard another door open. Bracing his free hand on the railing, he leaned forward and looked up at the second-story porch of the house next door.

Kowalski, dressed in nothing but pajama bottoms. Something about the way he stood told Monty his partner had also grabbed a weapon in response to . . . what?

Another door opening, farther down. He couldn't see, but Monty knew it was Debany. So. They'd all heard something.

Monty whistled, a soft sound, but it was enough to have Kowalski turn in his direction. Then the younger man disappeared. A minute later, he reappeared, ghosting across the front yards until he reached Monty's porch.

"Yeah," Kowalski said quietly into the mobile phone. "Yeah. I'll let you know."

"You heard it?" Monty kept his voice low to avoid waking Lizzy, whose open bedroom window was at the other end of the porch.

Kowalski nodded. "So did Michael." He looked around. "No lights coming on in any of the houses down the street, and nothing stirring across the street. Whatever it was didn't alarm the Courtyard's sentries."

Going to the end of the porch, Monty saw two Owls perched on rooftops that gave them a good view of the Courtyard's businesses.

"Could have been a rabbit," Kowalski said. "They do scream when they're killed."

Rabbits weren't the only things that screamed.

"Michael and I could go over and take a look around."

"No. None of us should go poking around the Courtyard at this time of night." Monty's heart still pounded. It was tempting to go across the hall and bang on the door until Jimmy answered, surly at being woken so abruptly.

If Jimmy answered.

"No," he said again. "We weren't called to assist. Just keep your eyes open tomorrow."

"Yes, sir. Good night."

Kowalski didn't go inside his own home. He went over to the apartment building on the other side of the double to talk to Debany. A couple of minutes later, he went home.

Doors closed. Everything was so quiet.

Monty went inside and tucked his backup piece in

the drawer, where it would remain, close at hand, until he got up and locked it in the gun safe with his service weapon. He stretched out on his bed, but he didn't sleep. Didn't mean to anyway. But at some point he slipped into an uneasy doze, dreading what he'd have to face in the morning.

CHAPTER 19

Windsday, Messis 22

Meg walked down the stairs from her apartment and turned toward the side of the Green Complex that held the mail, laundry, and social rooms, as well as the archway that led to the garages. Then she turned in the opposite direction and took the few steps to the front door of Simon's apartment.

He hadn't come back last night. Well, he had. He'd left a note on her kitchen table, saying he had to go in to work early, so she should drive herself to the Liaison's Office. But she woke up alone this morning. If he'd returned last night to get some sleep, he hadn't returned to her.

Had she done something to upset him? Could she ask? Would he tell her? Was this what it felt like to break up with someone you . . . what? Cared for? Loved? How could she tell what she felt for Simon? She'd never had these feelings before. Right now, she felt lost and lonely and scared.

The way things were between her and Simon wasn't the same as the way things were between Merri Lee and Michael, for example. Their relationship wasn't anything like the ones she'd read about in what Simon and

Vlad called the kissy books. It wasn't uncomplicated, but it wasn't fraught with misunderstandings—which, according to Merri Lee and Ruth, were a lot more fun to read about than to experience. Not all relationships worked. And sometimes people were confused and unsure of what they felt and what they wanted to have from, and give to, someone else.

Maybe this was normal. Maybe Simon just needed a night to go out and do Wolfy things with other Wolves. Which wasn't something she could do.

"You're looking at something, but I'm pretty sure it isn't me."

Meg let out a breathy sound that might have been a yip, could have been a scream, but wasn't much of anything since there was barely any sound.

"Don't sneak up on me!" she scolded Jester.

The Coyote stared at her. "There wasn't any sneaking. I walked up to you. I thought you saw me. It's not my fault you were looking at something that wasn't here." He studied Simon's closed front door, then considered her. "What *were* you looking at?"

She felt her face heat with embarrassment. "Nothing."

"Huh. Must be a human thing. When *we're* that focused, we're looking at *something*."

"I have to get to work, but I'm going to A Little Bite to get breakfast first." Maybe Tess would know why Simon had to go in to work so early.

"I've already had breakfast, but I'd like a mug of long-grass tea."

Something about the look in Jester's eyes, something about the way he licked his lips when he said he'd already had breakfast, made Meg uneasy. "Did you eat a bunny?" *Or a rat?* She knew that, for most of the Courtyard's residents, bunnies and rats were interchangeable meat, and what was consumed depended on what you could catch. But she was human, and while she'd eaten the meat of one critter, she had no desire to taste the meat of the other.

"No, not a bunny."

That look in the Coyote's eyes—a sharp reminder that he was as much a predator as the rest of the *terra indigene* who lived in the Courtyard.

"Are you driving to work?" he asked, sounding—and looking—more like the Jester she knew.

Since he had a hand under her elbow and was herding her toward the archway and the garages, he didn't seem to need an answer from her. In fact, neither of them said anything until they drove past the Market Square and she saw Closed signs tacked to sawhorses that blocked all the archways that provided access to the businesses.

"Did something happen last night?" She spotted Nathan, Blair, and Vlad—and Simon—walking out of the butcher shop.

"Oh, somebody made a bit of a mess," Jester replied. "I guess the Business Association decided to close the whole market for a couple of hours to do a thorough cleaning."

"What kind of mess?"

"I can't say—and since I don't want to get into trouble over this, please don't ask me again."

Jester didn't want to get into trouble? Who could intimidate the Coyote who looked after the Elementals' steeds?

She could think of a few individuals besides the Elementals themselves. Simon, for one. But there were also Henry, Vlad, and Tess. Even Mr. Erebus. Because Jester was a friend, she didn't ask again.

When they reached the garages behind the Liaison's Office, Jester hopped out of the BOW and opened the garage door for her. Then he hurried into A Little Bite, not waiting for her.

Appetite gone—not that she'd wanted any food since she'd seen Simon's note on the kitchen table—Meg got her purse and carry sack out of the BOW and headed for the back door of the Liaison's Office. She'd just opened the door when Kowalski walked up the access way, dressed for work.

"Hey, Meg." Kowalski smiled, but he seemed distracted by the sawhorse and sign that blocked the third archway leading into the Market Square. Then he looked at the second story of her building. "Do you know if Agent O'Sullivan is here? Or if he has company?"

"I think he's still in Hubb NE," Meg replied. Then she blinked. "Company? Like, romantic company?" Greg O'Sullivan seemed too intense to have a girlfriend, and if he did have one, she probably lived in Hubbney. Besides, O'Sullivan knew the rules about bringing anyone into the Courtyard without telling Simon or Vlad. She couldn't imagine him doing something that might get his friend killed.

"Being an ITF agent doesn't eliminate canoodling."

"Canoodling?" What an odd-sounding word.

He grinned. "Something you and Simon might like to try sometime."

She couldn't say one way or the other until she figured out what the word meant.

The humor faded from Kowalski's face. "I asked because I noticed a van in the Stag and Hare's lot. Could be someone parking there to make an early delivery to one of the other buildings on that side of the street. But if it belonged to someone's friend who had stayed overnight without permission . . ."

"You would encourage them to cease canoodling and go out for breakfast before anyone else noticed?"

"Something like that."

His answer provided no clue, so she mentally flipped through the training images of games, since that's what the word brought to mind. Maybe it was something like bingo? But she couldn't picture anyone risking Simon's wrath—or Blair's teeth—to stay up all night playing bingo.

Kowalski tipped his head toward the Market Square. "Know anything about that?"

"Jester said someone made a mess."

He tensed for a moment before trying to give the impression of being curious but not overly concerned. "A mess? Stores were vandalized?"

"Don't know. When I drove by, it looked like they were working on the open area, not the shops. You'd have to ask Simon or Vlad. I didn't know about it until I drove by a few minutes ago." Meg studied him. "Karl? Is something wrong?" Suddenly the banter about canoodling seemed off, made her uneasy—just like the look in Jester's eyes had made her uneasy.

"Probably not. But as Captain Burke likes to say, we try to keep things smooth." He smiled. "It's my turn to get the coffee, so I'd better get going."

She had a feeling Kowalski stopped smiling the moment he headed for A Little Bite's back door and she could no longer see his face. She had a feeling Kowalski, like Jester, knew more than he was saying.

And she had a very bad feeling that she should know what had happened in the Market Square last night.

Simon walked out of the butcher shop and saw Meg drive past in the BOW. For a moment, he felt happy, excited to see her. Then he felt uncomfortable. Queasy. Guilty.

"Boone is washing the display case, making it human clean," Henry said, coming to stand beside him. "When he's done, he'll put out the remaining meat."

"No. That meat will go to Meat-n-Greens for the meals served there."

"Then Boone won't have anything to sell until the next shipment of meat comes in from the farms," Henry said. He waited a beat. "Nothing wrong with the meat that was taken. It wasn't out of the refrigerator long enough to start spoiling."

"The meat is fine for us, but not for the humans."

"Meat is outside longer than that when humans buy it from a butcher shop and carry it home."

Simon hesitated. Henry was right. The meat hadn't

spoiled in the short time it had been out of the butcher shop, and there was no reason to tell the humans it had been outside. Then he pictured himself bringing home one of those roasts for Meg to cook and eat, and he shook his head, frustrated that he couldn't explain his feelings, even to himself. The pork and beef might not be spoiled in a way that made it inedible for humans, but the theft had spoiled it nonetheless. "It won't be cow or pig, but Boone will have something to sell to anyone who wants to purchase meat."

Everyone in the Green Complex, and every freezer in the other complexes, had some packages of frozen bison meat from the yearling they had killed a few weeks ago. The *terra indigene* wouldn't understand why the cow and pig meat that had been taken out of the butcher shop couldn't be rinsed off and put back in the butcher shop for Boone to sell, but most would come to the conclusion that this meat, for some reason, would upset Meg and the female pack, and they would give Boone a package of bison meat to sell at the butcher shop in exchange for fresh cow or pig.

But Meg didn't like bison meat. Maybe, when he wasn't so full, he could catch a bunny just for her. Or he could call Steve Ferryman and see about purchasing a little beef, or even a chicken, from one of the shops in Ferryman's Landing.

Thinking of Meg and the reason he was so full made him snarl. "They were invaders. Thieves. Bad humans. It wasn't like we ate one of her friends."

"They were invaders and thieves," Henry agreed. "And that made them enemies. And meat."

Simon felt the weight of Henry's stare. The Courtyard's spirit guide would either speak or whack him with a Grizzly paw.

"You're not human, Simon," Henry said in a quiet rumble. "You will never be human. And those who are human will always be meat."

"Not all of them. Not anymore." Then again, the way

he, with the agreement of Vlad, Henry, and Tess, had chosen to punish the remaining thief was going to cause all kinds of upset among the humans.

He felt something shift inside him, a flutter of change there and gone.

He wasn't human. Would never be human. But was he still, truly, a *terra indigene* Wolf?

Once Lizzy entered the Denby home to have breakfast with Sarah and Robert, Monty and Pete Denby joined Kowalski and Debany where the double's walkway and the public sidewalk met.

"Something happened last night, and I don't think it's over," Kowalski said, holding out the drinks holder so that everyone could take a coffee. "Meg doesn't know, but Tess does. Her hair is red and green, and it's coiling in that way that makes it look alive. The way she looked at me . . ." He shuddered. "Like she's waiting for something."

"What should we do?" Pete asked.

Monty considered the question and considered his men. Kowalski was in uniform, ready to go to work. Debany was in a T-shirt and denim cutoffs, since his official shift started later in the morning.

"Karl, I want you to stick close to the Courtyard for a while and keep an eye on things." Monty looked at his own apartment building, then waited for the nod that indicated Kowalski knew exactly who needed watching. "Michael, you go on duty at your usual time, but keep your mobile phone handy until then in case Karl needs backup for any reason." He looked at Pete. "The rest of you should go about your business as usual."

"You think it's safe for the children to go to the schoolroom?" Pete asked.

"I think, today, it's the safest place for them to be," Monty replied.

He pulled out his mobile phone and called the Chestnut Street station, requesting a car and driver to pick him up. He also talked to Captain Burke, reporting what he knew.

They lingered on the sidewalk, drinking coffee and talking quietly so they wouldn't be overheard.

"If a patrol car keeps checking the cairn, the Hawks or Crows will notice and report it," Kowalski said. "Maybe Captain Burke can talk to the captain of the mounted patrol and have them check the cairn. They patrol Lakeside Park, so it wouldn't look strange for an officer to ride past the spot."

Pete looked at the three officers. "There's a mounted patrol? Men on horses?"

"There was a mounted patrol in Toland," Monty said. "Officers walking a beat too."

"Here the officers on horseback mainly patrol around the park and the university, and the beat cops are mostly in the downtown area," Kowalski said.

"With the emphasis on conserving fuel, the mayor and police commissioner may want to expand those ways of policing." Monty thought of Jana Paniccia, the young woman who went to Bennett to become a deputy because she couldn't get a job as a police officer in a human-controlled town. She was now patrolling with a horse and a six-gun. He wondered how she was getting along with the sheriff, who was a Wolf.

Officer Daniel Hilborn pulled into one of the on-street parking spaces near the double.

"That's my ride," Monty said. "I'll check the cairn. If I don't find anything, I'll talk to Captain Burke about getting assistance to monitor the site." He got into the patrol car and instructed Hilborn to drive to the cairn. It was a place in Lakeside Park, across from the Courtyard, where identification and other personal items were left when humans entered the Courtyard uninvited. When that happened, there wouldn't be a body to find, so the ID left at the cairn was the only means the police had to fill out a DLU form that a family needed in order to get a death certificate.

But there was nothing at the spot where hunters had stood the night they killed Daphne Wolfgard and tried to shoot Sam. Nothing tucked among the stones. No wallet, no keys, no ration card or driver's license. Nothing.

Returning to the patrol car, Monty called Kowalski.

"I called in the license plate," Kowalski said after telling Monty about the van parked in the Stag and Hare's lot. "We checked the glove box. No insurance card or registration. But the passenger side door was unlocked."

"If the owner doesn't show up in a few minutes, have the vehicle towed to the station."

"Yes, sir."

Monty ended the call. After a minute, he realized Officer Hilborn was watching him.

"Where to, sir?" Hilborn asked.

If you leave a vehicle, why not lock all the doors? And why would the driver exit from the passenger side? But there were ways into a vehicle that would leave no trace—a window open a crack to let in fresh air, the air vents, probably other ways he couldn't name. Any opening that smoke could flow through would provide access. Easy enough then to remove any material that had a person's name or address. Easy enough to unlock the passenger door and leave with the material.

It also would have been easy enough to relock the passenger door. Oversight or deliberate?

"Back to the station," Monty said. "But I'd like you to remain available as a driver today."

"Yes, sir."

The humans connected to the Courtyard needed to maintain the illusion of business as usual—right up until the moment that it wasn't.

Meg closed the Private door almost all the way. The front door was still locked. It wasn't time to open the office yet, so Nathan wasn't there to keep an eye on things—including her. Especially her.

Returning to the sorting room table, she picked up the silver folding razor. One side of the handle had pretty leaves and flowers. The other side was plain and had *cs759* engraved on it. It had been her designation; the closest thing she had to a name for twenty-four years.

No one wanted to tell her what was going on, but the razor would tell her. Except she didn't feel any prickles that would guide her to the right part of her body to make the cut.

Frustrated, Meg shoved the razor into her pocket, opened a drawer, and pulled out the box of prophecy cards. She spread all the cards over the table, including the new ones that were actually a children's game that had simple illustrations. She ran her fingers over all of them, moving back and forth.

Needed a question.

One good thing about using the cards was she could ask as many questions as she wanted. If she didn't get it right the first time, she could try again. But she still needed a starting point and didn't know how to distill the question.

Something had happened in the Market Square last night. Was it done, or would something happen because of it?

Her fingertips tingled, then began to burn as she brushed the cards.

One, two, three. Subject, action, result.

She turned the cards faceup. The hooded figure with the scythe. A police car with the lights flashing driving down a city street. A fierce-faced cartoon man gripping the bars of a jail cell.

Meg picked up the card of the man in jail and frowned. The cartoon face made her think the card was from the children's game, not from the cityscape deck of fortune-telling cards. She turned the card over to look at the back. She was working with several decks in order to create a new deck of prophecy cards that could be used by *cassandra sangue*, but she could tell which deck a card came from by the design on the back.

The card fluttered out of her hand. When she picked it up and turned it over, she realized she'd picked up two cards.

The new card was a sign that read DANGER!

"That's not much help," she muttered. "What kind of danger? Who is in danger?"

The tip of her tongue prickled at the same time a harsh buzz filled her fingertips. Then her mind went blank for just a moment. No, not blank. Her mind became . . . veiled.

Meg blinked. Braced her hands on the table.

That was odd. There had been no feeling of the euphoria that usually veiled a blood prophet's mind from the images she saw, but Meg had definitely experienced the protective veil.

She examined her hands for paper cuts or punctures that might have bled, then pressed her tongue against the roof of her mouth. No cuts, no feeling of pain.

But there were three more cards turned faceup on the table.

The first card was a dappled forest, as if a person was walking between the trees toward a sunlit meadow. The second card was a tombstone. The third card was a mirror.

She swallowed hard and wished she hadn't asked any questions.

Somehow, whatever had happened in the Market Square would lead to a grave in the woods. As for who was in danger . . . Well, who did a person see when she looked in a mirror?

Meg put the cards back in the wooden box, put the box in the drawer, and slammed the drawer shut. Prophecy wasn't absolute, even with the razor. And she still didn't know enough about using the cards to be sure of her interpretation. Besides, if she kept asking questions and turning over cards for answers, how could she know if any of them were the question that *needed* to be asked?

And there was that disturbing experience of her mind being veiled without the euphoria that followed being cut.

Maybe she should check with Theral and find out if Emily Faire, the nurse practitioner, had office hours today. And she should write down the details of this episode for Dr. Lorenzo, since he was working with a task force to check on the well-being of the *cassandra sangue*. This was exactly the kind of thing he should know about.

Stress or anxiety could cause the body to react oddly. She'd read an article about that recently. So maybe her mind hadn't veiled the way it did when she used the razor and that's why she hadn't felt the euphoria. Maybe she'd blanked out because of stress or anxiety. Did that happen to people?

She pulled out the notebook she used to record anything revealed by using the cards, dated a clean page, and wrote:

hooded figure with scythe + police car + man in jail

↓

Danger sign

↓

woods + tombstone + mirror

How did a sequence of events begin with death and end with her? Assuming her interpretation was remotely accurate.

"Arroo!"

Nathan, reporting for work.

Nothing more she could do right now. Even if her brain was just being wonky and the cards didn't mean

anything, she should show someone. Henry or Vlad or
Merri Lee.

She wanted to show Simon, but what if he wanted
an excuse to stay away, to back away from being friends?
The Wolves didn't turn away from pack members who
had wonky brains. Skippy was proof of that. But she
wasn't a Wolf, wasn't really pack.

If she told Henry or Vlad, they would tell Simon.
Merri Lee, then. She would show Merri Lee during their
midday break.

"Arroo!" More insistent. If Nathan had to wait much
longer, he'd *really* start howling.

Meg put the notebook in the drawer with the other
notebooks and hurried to open the office door for the
watch Wolf.

Simon flipped the lock on Howling Good Reads' front
door and poked his head out as Kowalski drew abreast
of the store for the second time.

"You looking for something?" he asked.

Kowalski smiled and shook his head. "I'm doing a
foot patrol while Lieutenant Montgomery is taking care
of some things at the station."

Marie Hawkgard had watched Kowalski watch other
police tow away the vehicle that had been left in the
Stag and Hare's parking lot. Crows had watched him
check the Courtyard's customer parking lot and test
the wooden door in the wall that divided the customer
lot from the employee parking lot. The police officer
seemed pleased to find the door locked and had continued walking along the perimeter of the Courtyard's
fence, crossing the street during a break in traffic in
order to head back toward Main Street. He looked at
all the cars parked on the street, then walked the Denby
children, Lizzy, and Ruthie up to the corner when it
was time for them to go to the schoolroom for their
morning lessons.

He wasn't peeing on tires or giving anything a good
sniff, but in his own way, Kowalski was marking territory. To the *terra indigene*'s way of thinking, there was
nothing odd about that—except he'd never done it before, and this morning seemed a strange time to start.

"Anyone see anything going on at the Stag and Hare
after hours?" Kowalski asked.

"Why?"

"Abandoned vehicle in the lot. Could have broken
down and someone left it there, or it could have been
abandoned by someone causing mischief and being scared
off. Since Captain Burke bought the business and the
building, I took a good look around, checking for broken
windows or other signs that someone might have tried to
break in. Stolen bottles of liquor are easy to sell out of
the back of a van."

He hadn't known that liquor was valued enough to
steal. Then again, the closest the *terra indigene* came
to consuming liquor was eating fruit that had started
to ferment. Or in the case of the Sanguinati, drinking
the blood of someone who had consumed alcohol.

With Burke being the owner, the Stag and Hare would
become part of the police pack's personal territory. Now
it made sense that Kowalski was sniffing around.

"I'll let you get back to work," Kowalski said.

Simon watched as the police officer walked up to
the corner of Main Street. But Kowalski didn't cross the
street to the Stag and Hare. He turned left toward the
Courtyard's Main Street entrance—and the Liaison's
Office.

"Fucking assholes." Getting voice mail—again—Jimmy
ended the call and tried another number. "You think
you can cheat me out of my share?"

No ruckus last night. No cop cars wailing to indicate
his crew had been caught liberating meat from that
shop. Everything had gone as slick as spit.

But no one had called to tell him what time to meet them to pick up his share of the meat. And no one was answering his calls.

Maybe they had lost their nerve and hadn't done the job at all. Maybe that's why they didn't want to talk to him. Easy enough to find out.

"Where are you going?" Sandee demanded when he headed for the door.

"Out. I got business."

"What kind of business?" She hurried after him, wearing those stupid high-heeled slippers. What kind of woman wore shit like that?

Before he married her, he used to think stuff like that made her look sexy. But that was when just looking at her body made him hot. And what looked sexy for a couple of hours looked pretty damn stupid when you had to live with it.

"Jimmy, the kids are hungry, and there's nothing to eat," Sandee whined as she grabbed at his arm.

He shook her off and left, glancing at the apartments as he walked up to Main Street. CJ was already gone. Couldn't tell about Denby or his bitch wife. One of the cops was on the porch, drinking from one of those mugs everyone was supposed to purchase from the coffee shop instead of paying extra for a disposable cup. Not dressed for work yet.

Jimmy raised a hand in greeting. The bastard just stared.

"Here." Merri Lee held out one of the travel mugs from A Little Bite. "Nadine was showing Tess how to make an iced mocha, and I volunteered to take a quick break and bring one over for you to try."

"Who's minding the bookstore?" Meg asked, taking the mug.

"Vlad is there now." Merri Lee hesitated. "There's something odd about them closing the Market Square. Normally Vlad would grumble a bit about me taking a break earlier than usual—although I think he does it because he thinks a human employer would—but when I told him I was popping over to see you, he gave me this strange look, like he was trying to decide if I knew something. Which makes me think there is something to know."

"Karl is patrolling on foot," Meg said. She took a sip of iced mocha. "Oh, this is good."

Merri Lee nodded. "Cold and caffeinated. Definitely a winner in this heat."

"Karl has never patrolled that way before. And he keeps checking out the Market Square, but human law doesn't apply in the Courtyard."

"Michael is on call. We're supposed to go about our business like we usually do, but I think Lieutenant Montgomery is waiting for something to happen."

Meg set the mug down and pulled out the prophecy card notebook. "Maybe this?"

Merri Lee studied the page with the newest notes. "What you predicted is disturbing, but I think you're really tuning in to the cards. This looks more like the images you relayed previously to reveal a prophecy."

"It does?" Meg looked at her notes in surprise.

"Sure. You've even grouped them. If I was going to do one of our story cards based on these images, there was a death and police were called, which ended with someone going to jail."

"Which is good."

"Yes," Merri Lee agreed. "But something about the person going to jail is going to create danger. And because of the danger, you—because you would see yourself in a mirror—are going to be in a woods for some reason and find a grave." She frowned at the notes. "What are you going to tell Simon or Henry?"

"There's nothing to tell."

Merri Lee tapped the word "danger" with her finger.

"That doesn't apply until the first set of images happens," Meg argued. But she looked at Merri Lee and knew her friend was also thinking about the closed Market Square and Kowalski patrolling the area around the Courtyard's business district.

She put the notebook back in the drawer. "If something happens and Vlad or Henry—or anyone else—needs to know, then one of us will tell him."

Merri Lee looked like she wanted to argue, but she nodded and said, "I'd better get back. If I happen to hear anything, I'll let you know."

Meg nodded. "I'll do the same."

After Merri Lee went back to work, Meg spent the next hour waiting for deliveries, waiting for mail, waiting for something to do to keep from fretting while she waited for whatever was going to happen.

He was done waiting for those shitheads to call and tell him where to meet them for his share of the haul.

Jimmy sat in A Little Bite, drinking coffee and stewing about the lack of quality help to be found in Lakeside. If he'd still been in Toland and put together a job like this, his crew wouldn't have tried to jerk him around. After all, he'd put together the deal—and if they believed his cop brother was a little bent and sufficiently under his control that they might have an accident the next time they were in jail, so much the better. But he hadn't been around Lakeside long enough to have a rep, and CJ wasn't working much of anything that didn't involve the freaks, so he wasn't known to the city's more enterprising citizens.

Jimmy sat and stewed, unwilling to go back to the apartment and listen to Sandee bitch and whine, along with the brats whining that there was nothing to do. Shit, Fanny was so bored she wanted to go with Lizzy to that room everyone was pretending was a real school. But if Fanny was allowed to go, then Clarence would want to go because he wouldn't want to be excluded, and Clarence more than Fanny had been banned from the Courtyard. As if those freaks had any right to ban a real human from anything. But you couldn't say shit like that, not since the Humans First and Last movement fell.

He sat and stewed until the sawhorses were removed from the archways and the Market Square was once again open for business. Then he sauntered to the butcher shop.

The glass case was so clean, even his mother wouldn't find fault. It was also completely empty.

"Morning," Jimmy said when the brown-feathered freak walked out of the big refrigerator. "I was hoping to get a couple more slices of that meatloaf. The kids really liked it."

"Got nothing," the male replied. "We got cleaned out last night."

So those bastards had managed to do the job.

Jimmy put on his down-on-his-luck expression. "That's too bad. But, really, you got nothing? I wouldn't be asking but . . . the little ones."

The male shook his head.

Furious but knowing better than to show it, Jimmy headed for the door. As he reached for the handle, the male said, "Wait."

He went back to the glass case. The male didn't look happy and kept glancing at the door, as if he needed to make sure no one would see him.

"After this happened, a delivery of special meat came in. We don't usually sell it to humans, but you need to bring something back for your mate and young, right? I've got one piece left—part of a foreleg. It should be enough to feed the four of you."

"How much?" Jimmy asked.

"Ten dollars."

He thought about trying to bargain for a better price but realized that was pointless. If this was the only piece of meat available, the male could sell it for twice that price to the next person who walked into the shop. Which meant Jimmy could sell it for at least that much outside the Courtyard. "Sold."

"Being the last piece, it's already wrapped," the male said. "I'll get it for you." He was back in less than a minute with what looked like a long roast wrapped in heavy butcher's paper and tied with string.

Jimmy eyed the package. "You sure there's enough meat on that?"

"Plenty. Lean meat too. Hardly any fat."

Jimmy paid for the roast and left the shop, feeling triumphant that nobody else would have meat tonight. Not that bitch Eve Denby or the bitches who were sleeping with the cops. Maybe he'd be a generous son and invite Mama over for dinner. Maybe he could talk her into doing the cooking so the meat wouldn't end up overcooked or too tough to chew.

Seeing Kowalski walking toward him, he held up the roast in triumph. "You're too late. I bought the last piece of special meat."

He had just enough time to register the weird-ass crazy look in Kowalski's eyes. Then he was on the ground, struggling as Kowalski hauled his arms behind his back and handcuffed him. Then Kowalski stepped back, not trying to restrain him any further.

"You fucker!" Jimmy screamed as he rolled to his side. "This is harassment! This is— I'll have your badge for this! I'll have your ass for this!"

A girl with dark eyes and long black hair rushed out of a nearby shop, wearing nothing but a white slip.

"Officer Karl!" she said when she reached Kowalski. "What's happening? Do you need help? Should I peck its eyes out?"

Jimmy stopped thrashing as if he were helpless and sat up. Peck its eyes out? What kind of shit talk was that?

"No, thanks, Jenni," Kowalski replied, sounding way too calm when his eyes still had that weird-ass crazy look. "I've got it under control. But could you ask Officer Michael to bring me a large evidence bag and then call a patrol car? Tell him we need both ASAP."

She pulled the slip over her head and let it fall. Nice

body, Jimmy thought, momentarily distracted from the crazy-ass cop. Nice and naked and . . . Seeing downy feathers covering her pussy instead of normal hair creeped him out. Seeing her change into a large Crow and fly off creeped him out even more.

He didn't know how long he sat on the ground. Felt like forever but couldn't have been more than a minute or two before Debany came running and said a patrol car was on the way, before Kowalski and Debany hauled him to his feet and carefully put the roast in an evidence bag.

Evidence his ass. This was a shakedown. That's what it was. They would haul him in; CJ would spring him because he hadn't done anything wrong; and those two bastard cops would "lose" the evidence until they cooked it for dinner.

Full of righteous anger that he would blast at Captain Bastard Burke and CJ, he didn't resist when Kowalski put him in the patrol car that pulled into the delivery area, then got in the front with some officer named Hilborn. No, he didn't resist because he'd take this all the way up to the mayor's office if he had to—and he'd do it before any of the scrapes and bruises caused by Kowalski slamming him to the ground had begun to fade. Yes, he would take this to the top, and when he was done, he wouldn't have to pay for a single mouthful of food for the rest of his stay in Lakeside.

Meg watched the patrol car pull out onto Main Street with Lieutenant Montgomery's brother in the back. Being taken in to the station wasn't the same as being arrested. But given a limited number of images that could be used to convey a vision, would the prophecy cards make such a distinction? Or was it enough that someone was going to jail, even if the stay was temporary?

If that was the case, if this was the first part of what the cards had revealed, there had also been a death. Whose death?

She looked at Nathan, who watched her with an intensity that made her feel small and tasty—and made her glad being a blood prophet made her inedible.

That thought made her uneasy—and a little bit queasy.

"Do you know what's going on?" she asked Nathan.

He didn't answer, didn't even try. But he seemed pleased about Cyrus Montgomery being taken away in handcuffs, and Meg wondered if whatever pleased Nathan was the reason Simon had avoided her since last night.

CHAPTER 20

Windsday, Messis 22

Monty walked into the interrogation room sick with fear. When he'd first caught sight of Kowalski as his partner hauled Jimmy into the station, he'd thought Karl had been hopped up on some kind of drug. And there was Jimmy with scrapes on his face and bruises already blooming, screaming that Kowalski was off-his-head crazy—and judging by the scared expression on Officer Hilborn's face, Jimmy's assessment of Kowalski might not be wrong.

Then Monty unwrapped the "roast" Jimmy had bought at the Market Square butcher shop and understood Kowalski's behavior. He understood a lot of things as he slammed into a stall in the men's restroom and threw up. Now he needed to convince Jimmy to give him the information he would never get from Simon Wolfgard—because Wolfgard had already sent a clear message that Jimmy was involved up to his neck in whatever had happened in the Courtyard last night.

Setting a closed folder on the table, Monty took a seat opposite his brother.

"Look what that bastard Kowalski did to me," Jimmy shouted, waving a hand at his own face. "You better fry his ass for this, CJ, or I'll raise a stink that will smell right up to the mayor's office in this fucking city."

"Have you made out a will?" Monty asked quietly.

"What? Are you listening to me? Kowalski—"

"Have you made any provision for your wife and children? Is there any legal document I should know about?"

Jimmy stared at him. "What are you talking about?"

"Whatever you did this time, you might not survive it."

"I didn't—"

Captain Burke walked into the room. He closed the door, walked up to the table, and pressed his hands flat against the surface, all his attention on Jimmy.

"Your brother shouldn't do this interview," Burke said. "But I figured you would lie and stall and wheedle and waste everyone's time if I had anyone else asking the questions. I'm not willing to waste anyone's time, especially mine. So this is what is going to happen. Lieutenant Montgomery is going to have ten minutes to get information from you about an incident that occurred last night. I'm going to be standing on the other side of that glass, listening. If I'm convinced that you've provided accurate information, you'll be free to leave. If I'm not convinced, you'll be charged with mishandling human remains, accessory to murder, and cannibalism. And you will be relocated to a secure, undisclosed location by nightfall—the kind of place people like you never leave. I can, and will, make that happen." He straightened and stepped away from the table, finally looking at Monty. "Your ten minutes starts now."

As soon as Burke left the room, Jimmy started in again. "What is this shit? I didn't kill anybody. I was home last night."

Monty took the first photograph out of the folder and laid it between them. It showed a tattoo on a man's forearm. "Do you recognize this tattoo? Do you know this man?"

Jimmy looked at it—and hesitated a moment too long. "Never seen it."

Monty removed another photograph from the folder, which showed the whole forearm—and showed the ragged edges where something had bitten through elbow and wrist. "You sure? You were carrying this man's forearm when Officer Kowalski arrested you. Which is why you could be charged with mishandling human remains as well as cannibalism."

Jimmy shook his head so violently Monty wondered if he would tear a muscle. "No way. No. That bastard is lying, trying to set me up. I bought a piece of special meat from the butcher shop and that Kowalski—"

"Gods, Jimmy! Humans *are* the special meat. *All* the *terra indigene* in the Courtyard consider humans a prey animal, same as rabbits and deer. Anyone who enters the Courtyard without the Others' permission is *meat*."

Jimmy stared at Monty, his eyes blank with shock.

"I've been informed that a person or persons unknown broke into the Market Square butcher shop last night and stole all the meat. Since there was a delivery made yesterday, that equals a lot of beef and pork. Gone. So are the people who tried to steal it."

Jimmy blinked, seemed to come back to himself. "What do you mean, tried to steal it?"

"They didn't get away, didn't leave the Courtyard. And the Others know you were involved in the theft."

"I was home last night."

"Yeah." Monty smiled bitterly. "You're always the one with the alibi if things go wrong. You're as dirty as the men who do the job, but you're always distant enough that you can't be charged."

"So you can't hold me for something I didn't do."

Jimmy sounded like he always did—sure that he was going to walk away unscathed to start thinking up his next scheme. But not this time.

Monty tapped the photograph of the full forearm. "The Others know you were involved, Jimmy. It doesn't matter if you were at the butcher shop last night or home in bed. *They know.* And this was their way of telling you, and the police, that they know. But what they aren't telling us is how many men entered the Courtyard last night. They haven't left any identification for us to find, which they sometimes do. Whoever was in the Courtyard last night is dead. We know that."

"Then why aren't you asking the freaks?" Jimmy demanded.

"Human law doesn't apply in the Courtyard. I told you: if humans aren't invited in, we are meat. Right now, these men have disappeared. Maybe they were killed by other men and their bodies haven't been found. Maybe they took the first bus out of town and walked away from their families. It happens. But if those men have families, have wives and children, those wives will never be able to get a death certificate, will never be able to get on with their lives or receive any assets their husbands had tucked away. Those women will spend the rest of their lives not knowing if they're widows or abandoned. Would you want that for Sandee and your kids?"

Jimmy wouldn't think twice about something like that. Monty saw it in his eyes, in his face. He would leave Sandee wondering and wouldn't care.

"You knew him, Jimmy."

"I told you I didn't."

"You're lying. I know the signs." Yes, he knew the signs. Jimmy was sly; he was cunning; he never told the truth if a lie would work. And he enjoyed beating people down with words and intimidating them with a large body and a big voice. As Jimmy had done to Sierra. As he was doing to young Frances, giving his son a nod of approval for doing the same.

"Fine." Monty put the photographs back in the folder. "You've been implicated in an attempted burglary that resulted in the deaths of six men, so you'll be charged with accessory to—"

"What are you saying?" Jimmy was sweating now and looking sick.

"I'm saying Captain Burke was right. This is a waste of time, so you'll be charged."

Now, for the first time, Cyrus James Montgomery truly looked afraid. "You giving up on me? What's Mama going to say about that?"

"I don't think she'll say anything when I tell her you had a chance to cooperate, but you refused to meet the conditions of your release and were sent to the place where dangerous criminals are held while they await trial."

"When I tell her my side of it—"

"You'll be gone. She won't hear your side of it." Monty leaned across the table. "And with you out of the picture, not filling her head with crap, Mama will believe whatever I tell her."

Oh yes. Jimmy was sweating now.

Monty wondered if his brother remembered saying those exact words to him a couple of years after Monty left home and Jimmy hadn't moved out of his parents' home yet.

"Bastard." Jimmy looked like he wanted to spit in Monty's face. Might have done it if someone hadn't rapped on the glass at that moment, signaling that their time was up.

Monty stood and reached for the folder.

"There weren't six of them," Jimmy said suddenly.

Monty sat.

"Don't think there were six," Jimmy amended. "And maybe it was a little bit my fault, but not like you think."

He waited. Monty said nothing.

"Saw the meat being delivered yesterday." Jimmy shifted in his seat, as if he was uncomfortable all of a sudden. Monty could believe that. Jimmy did better when he had time to make up a story. "Seems a waste, bringing good meat like that to the freaks when they could be catching rats and squirrels and shit."

"I didn't hear you complaining about the meat deliveries when you were eating at Meat-n-Greens or A Little Bite. Where did you think that food came from?" Monty asked.

"Yeah, well, it seemed like a waste. And I was having a drink at a bar near the bus station and heard these men complaining that there wasn't any meat in the shops and their women were bringing home tripe and shit like that instead of real food, and maybe I was a bit too full of drink and said how the Courtyard always had good meat, said I'd seen a delivery of steaks and pork chops and roasts and all kinds of food that was fit for a man to eat. And the four of them—there were four of them, not six—started buying me drinks and we were just talking about how hard it was now to take care of a family and they were asking about the butcher shop and maybe I told them more than I meant to—more than I remember saying, that's for sure. Then I went home and I slept all night."

In the end, Monty had the name of the bar and the names the four men were known by in places like that. Hopefully it would be enough that the police could fill out DLU forms to give to the next of kin.

"Can I go now?" Jimmy asked when Monty stood again.

"I'll find out." He took a step away from the table, then stopped. "Jimmy, you should think hard about getting out of Lakeside and starting fresh somewhere else. You haven't done anything to give the *terra indigene* here a reason to think well of you, and now they definitely have reason to think you're an enemy."

"You think I give a shit?"

Didn't take long for Jimmy to fall back into his entitlement mind-set.

"You should," Monty said quietly, "because there are beings in the Courtyard who are so powerful and dangerous that they can turn your brains to soup with just a look. Just a look, Jimmy. And now, because of this bit of stupidity, *all* the Others are going to be watching everything you do from now on."

Monty walked out of the interrogation room and leaned against the wall, exhausted.

Four men had gone into the Courtyard last night. Only one had had time to let out a high-pitched, terrified scream.

The door of the observation room opened and Commander Louis Gresh stepped out.

"Captain Burke said I should drive your brother back to the apartment building," Louis said.

When no one else came out of the observation room, Monty asked, "Where is the captain?"

"He's kept Kowalski isolated in his office since your brother was brought in. He knew you'd get the truth out of Cyrus, or enough of it, and he figured watching Kowalski right now was more important." Louis blew out a breath. "This shook up your boy something fierce."

"It shook all of us." Monty looked at the ceiling. "The *terra indigene* aren't human, but they have studied us, and, gods, they know how to send a message."

"Do you think your brother got that message?"

"No. He'll go on believing he can work this just like he worked his schemes in Toland. Despite the evidence right in front of him, he'll be like a lot of other people who still want to pretend, maybe *need* to pretend, that there aren't lethal repercussions when they mess with the Others."

Louis sighed. "It could have been worse."

"How?"

"The Others could have waylaid Kowalski, made sure he wouldn't cross paths with Cyrus. Then Cyrus would have brought the package home and opened it there. How much more shocking would it have been to cut the string, unwrap that package, and recognize the tattoo?"

And Jimmy would have bragged about it, made a big

deal about snagging the last piece of special meat, just like he'd done when he saw Kowalski. But it would have been Sandee and the kids looking at a man's forearm, unprepared for the harsh reality of what the *terra indigene* saw when they looked at humans. Most humans. He had to keep believing that Simon and Vlad and the rest of the Others no longer saw all humans as prey.

But the Others had known the theft was going to happen and hadn't asked the police for help, so he had to wonder if Jimmy had created a wedge between himself and Simon Wolfgard, had cracked the trust that had been building.

And he had to wonder what that meant for the mixed communities that were being created and the people who were now living among the world's dominant predators without even the pretense of a barrier between them.

Burke studied Kowalski, who sat in his office looking pale and still a bit shaky. But the officer's dark eyes didn't have the wild look anymore, so now it was time to talk.

"What happened?" Burke asked.

Kowalski shook his head. "I saw Cyrus waving that package and bragging about scoring a piece of special meat, and I lost it. I don't remember taking him down. Things snapped into focus again when Jenni Crowgard asked if I needed help, if I wanted her to peck its eyes out. *Its* eyes, not *his* eyes. I knew I needed an excuse to get her away from him and I needed to get him out of the Courtyard, get him back on land where human laws did apply. I needed to arrest him and get him out of there because he was drawing attention to himself, to all of us, and . . ." He stopped, seemed to choke.

"It's one thing to pick up a wallet that was dropped for you to find and know the person who owned it crossed some line and was killed and eaten because of it. It's quite another thing to see the proof of it."

"Whenever word got out that the Wolves had bitten

off the hand of a shoplifter, Howling Good Reads would be packed with customers for days after," Kowalski said.

Burke smiled. "The perversity of human nature. But a severed hand isn't the same as a corpse. The *terra indigene* in the Courtyard are true to their nature, Karl, and that makes them very dangerous. But they're still the only chance of survival that we have because no matter how dangerous Simon and Vlad and the rest of them are, they are nowhere near as much of a threat to us as the Others who live in the wild country."

Kowalski sat back. "I know." He sighed. "I know. What happens now?"

"I don't want you out on the street, so you ride a desk for the rest of the day, give yourself time to settle. If the lieutenant needs a driver, Debany or Hilborn can handle it."

Burke clasped and unclasped his fingers a couple of times, debating the wisdom of saying anything, even now. "When you're a cop serving in a small human village within the wild country, sometimes you make hard choices that you wouldn't—couldn't—make in a human-controlled city. And you look the truth in the face when its fangs are bared and its fur is smeared with the blood of the prey you had gone out to talk to that morning. But you'd taken a walk beyond the village lights the night before, and you were mulling things over out loud about how to handle a difficult situation, about the nice woman who had a broken arm again, how her mate beat her but she was too frightened to say anything against him so there was nothing you could do, and that was a shame because she really was a nice woman who had shown a couple of *terra indigene* females how to mend clothes, which is what started the argument that ended with her arm being broken, along with a couple of fingers to keep her from doing any mending for a while. And when you go to talk to the man the next morning and discover he isn't home, you follow the game trail behind his house and you come upon a savaged, partially eaten body and you look the truth in the face—not the truth that has fangs and fur but the hard truth about yourself, that you're just as dangerous as the beings the rest of the people fear but you can't afford to be as honest about it. You can't tell those people that you'll make deals with what they fear in order to keep them safe from the monsters who look just like them."

Kowalski said nothing for a long minute. "You think I should have stepped aside?"

"No," Burke said gently. "You interfered because you've been around the Others long enough to understand that it's one thing to know something intellectually and quite another to look the truth in the face. The police? We've seen plenty of evidence of how the *terra indigene* respond when they're angry with humans. But civilians like Ruthie and Merri Lee who are living so close to the Courtyard and working among the Others? They don't need that much truth."

"Protect the women?" Kowalski gave him a dry smile. "They might take exception to that."

"Of course they would—and should—but I'll deny I ever said it."

The smile faded. "You're giving me a lot of credit for a few seconds I don't remember."

"I recognized the look in your eyes when you got to the station. I saw it in a mirror once or twice when I was around your age."

Burke's phone rang. He glanced at it, then focused on Kowalski. "You steady enough?"

"Yes, sir."

"Then get to work." He picked up the receiver as Kowalski walked out of his office. "Burke."

"It's O'Sullivan."

Trying to remember if the ITF agent was back in Lakeside and had heard about the debacle in the Courtyard, Burke merely said, "What can I do for you?"

"Do you have any news about Dr. Lorenzo?"

He'd tell O'Sullivan everything once they could talk face-to-face, but he didn't want to say anything about Lorenzo over the phone. "I heard he resigned from the task force. And his car was found. Had some bullet holes."

A hesitation. "Are you checking hospitals and the morgue for any John Does?"

"Not necessary."

"Did you fill out a DLU?"

"Not required." Did O'Sullivan understand the message, that Lorenzo was alive and his whereabouts were known?

"Could you check the hospitals and morgue anyway?"

Burke sat up straighter. "Problem?"

"Half the doctors who were gathering information about the *cassandra sangue* resigned from the task force after being threatened by members of the Humans First and Last movement. During my talk with the governor, I confirmed that several other doctors besides Lorenzo have disappeared."

He wrote down the names O'Sullivan gave him. "I'll see what I can find out."

"Appreciate it," O'Sullivan said. "I'm on my way to catch a train back to Lakeside. Should be arriving late this afternoon."

"Give me your ETA when you know it, and I'll have someone pick you up."

"Thanks."

Burke hung up and sat back. There were still plenty of blood prophets living in the compounds where they'd been held all their lives, unwilling, or unable, to conceive of any kind of independent life. But there were also plenty of those girls who were now trying to shape a life for themselves, struggling with their addiction to cut, pushed into that self-destructive act by visions that wouldn't be denied. Even the least talented among those girls could give a handler a very nice living, and the best among them . . .

He'd done a little digging, a little research, called a

couple of places posing as a possible client before all the dirty secrets about benevolent ownership and what was done to the girls in those places came crashing down on the prophecy industry. One question, one cut on a girl with low-end talent and basic training, cost a couple of hundred dollars. Someone like Meg Corbyn, who was intelligent and absorbed information perhaps too well, who saw strings of images and was frighteningly accurate? A cut on someone with Meg's skill would cost thousands.

Plenty of motivation to abduct and interrogate men who would know where to find girls who might not be as well protected as the Others believed—mainly because they would never consider that a human would be rash enough and greedy enough to try to get past them and snatch a girl.

Burke pushed away from his desk. He wanted to go to the Courtyard and assess the situation. But first he would get Kowalski started on locating the missing doctors, or at least getting some idea of where and when they were last seen. And then he needed to apprise the mayor and police commissioner of the potential trouble this attempted theft of meat might cause the city.

"What?" Simon snapped when Vlad, who was behind HGR's checkout counter doing nothing useful, continued to stare at him.

"I noticed that all the books you're putting on the display table are thrillers by *terra indigene* authors and are the type that could be described as 'rip and tear.'"

"So?"

"Don't you think the message is a little too blunt?"

Snarling, he turned toward the counter—and noticed Miss Twyla standing quietly between the shelves that separated the front area from the rest of the store.

"Is there something we can do for you, Miss Twyla?" Vlad asked.

"I understand that all the meat that was delivered yesterday was stolen."

"Currently there is nothing in the butcher shop for sale."

"I see."

Simon couldn't stand having her think there was no meat, that the female pack would have nothing to eat but greens. "The meat the thieves didn't take we gave to Meat-n-Greens to use. And we can thaw a couple of packages of bison meat."

Miss Twyla nodded. "That's a good plan. And humans don't need as much meat as you folks do, so a little can go a long way."

He wanted to believe her. Wasn't sure he did.

"The girls tell me you have creeks running through the Courtyard. Any of you catch fish in those creeks?" Miss Twyla asked.

"Henry does."

"Fish is another kind of meat."

Did Meg like fish?

When Simon didn't say anything, Vlad smiled at Miss Twyla. "Thank you for the suggestion." When she didn't go away, he added, "Is there something else?"

Miss Twyla looked at Simon in a way that made him want to back up a step—or show her his better set of teeth as a warning.

"My James was a good man, and I loved him for all the years we were married. Still do, even though he's been gone some years now. But he enjoyed eating a cheese that smelled up a house worse than a bad case of farts."

Simon blinked. Scratched behind one ear. He didn't know how to respond to Miss Twyla saying "farts." "Did you like the cheese?"

"I did not. But once or twice a year he would get a craving for it and buy enough of that cheese to make a sandwich, and it was the best treat he could think to buy. He ate those cheese sandwiches before we were married and every year we spent together."

"But it was stinky."

"It was. But it was part of who he was. He didn't ask me to eat it, and I didn't ask him to give up eating it. That's how it works when two people are partners."

She took a step forward. Simon held his ground as long as he could before taking a step back.

"You have more courage than you're showing right now, and avoiding that girl doesn't do either of you any favors. You talk it out, set it right, decide what each of you can live with."

"I ate a human," he snapped, feeling cornered.

"All by yourself? You must have been hungry."

"No, not by myself! We—" Simon glanced at Vlad, who shrugged.

"You think there's anyone here except the children who hasn't figured out what happened to the thieves? Miss Merri Lee says you used to put a sign on the butcher shop door when you'd caught some of what you call special meat, although the only thing I can see about it being special is you didn't catch it all that often and certainly didn't go looking for it off your own land." She looked pointedly at Vlad. "Not the meat anyway." She turned back to Simon. "Am I right in thinking you don't mix that meat with other kinds?"

"We never sold it at the butcher shop," Simon growled. Before Meg, they might have stored a bit in the big refrigerator because meat was meat, but they learned the difference between clean and human clean, and as they got to know the human female pack, it began to matter that they not do things that could make the girls sick. "And we haven't kept any of that meat in the shop for a long time now." Not since the day Meg called Boone and asked for some special meat for Sam, not knowing that there *was* a special kind of meat.

"You had one package in the shop," Miss Twyla said.

"In a separate cooler. And the cooler wasn't in the shop for very long."

"Just long enough for Cyrus to take the bait?" She nodded again, as if something had been confirmed. "If he deserved being given that package, then he did, and while I can't say it surprises me, it makes my heart heavy to know he was involved with those thieves. But I'm grateful Officer Kowalski stepped in and didn't let Cyrus bring that package home for the children to see."

"We weren't going to let him leave the Courtyard with the package," Vlad said quietly. "We wouldn't have let his mate and young see the meat. Selling it to him was punishment and warning for that Cyrus. Kowalski had no authority here to arrest that Cyrus and take him, and the package, to the police station. But we let him do it."

"Just shows you're all learning to pull as a team." Miss Twyla gave Simon a hard look—the same kind of look a nanny would give an erring pup. But a nanny might add a paw-whack or a nip to the look. "You talk it out with Miss Meg and set things right."

She walked to the back of the store. A moment later they heard the door open and close.

Still feeling cornered, Simon glared at Vlad. "You didn't help."

"You weren't being scolded for eating a human; you were being scolded for upsetting Meg, which I haven't done."

"It's not the same for you," Simon muttered.

Vlad stared at him. "You weren't bothered by this when we killed those intruders and the Wolves were tearing into the flesh. You weren't bothered by it when you bit through the hand and elbow and gave the inked meat to Boone to wrap up for that Cyrus. You were fine with all of it until you went home and saw Meg sleeping—and weren't sure you would be welcome." Vlad looked away. "Miss Twyla is right. You need to find out if this changes things between you and Meg."

Seeing the truth in Vlad's words, Simon nodded and went back to working on the display in order to avoid finding out for just a little while longer.

Meg stood at one end of the Green Complex's kitchen garden and stared at the woven baskets filled with zucchini. "Is this normal?"

"Even for zucchini, this is a bumper crop." Ruth wiped sweat off her forehead with one hand and pressed the other hand to her lower back as she straightened up.

"Nadine said she'll take some to make zucchini bread for A Little Bite," Merri Lee said. She held out two modest-size zucchini. "You should take these, Meg."

Meg sighed but she took them. Eating foods that were in season was all well and good, but she now understood about having too much of a good thing.

"You don't have to eat them tonight," Merri Lee said. "They'll keep for a day or two."

Goody. A no-zucchini meal. Of course, she wasn't sure what they *would* eat—or if she'd be eating alone.

Then she saw the Wolf moving toward her. Simon, with his dark coat shot with lighter gray hairs. It had been a while since she'd had that odd sense of not being able to see him clearly when he moved, as if she were seeing an overlapping image of something even larger poking through a Wolf suit, making the outline indistinct. Maybe a little of his true form, whatever it was, showed through when he was stressed, like when he was in human form and things shifted involuntarily because he was angry or upset.

Did anyone else experience this when they looked at the Others? Or did seeing the visions of prophecy skew the way she saw the mundane world? If you could call any of the *terra indigene* mundane.

Ruth and Merri Lee looked around and spotted Simon.

"We should go," Ruth said.

"You don't have to," Meg said quickly.

Merri Lee picked up one of the baskets. "Yes, we do. You're not always going to agree or get along, but you're going to be unhappy until you talk it out."

"I could just conk him on the head with a big zucchini."

Laughing, Ruth picked up the other basket. "Something every woman has imagined doing to a man at one time or another."

She watched her friends put the woven baskets into the wire baskets on the front of their bicycles. She watched them ride away. Then she looked at Simon, who had edged closer to the garden as Merri Lee and Ruth moved farther away.

"We need to talk," she told him.

She didn't hurry back to the Green Complex. Simon walked beside her, not stopping to sniff anything to find out who had been nearby today. That was so unusual it made her wonder if he was unhappy too.

Unlocking his front door, she let him into his apartment, then went up to her own place to put the zucchini in the fridge and pour two glasses of cold water. A minute later, he opened the kitchen door and sat down at the table.

What to say? How to start?

"They were bad humans." Simon's voice was rough, but his amber eyes didn't have the flickers of red that indicated anger.

Meg took a sip of water. "It was wrong of them to steal the meat from our butcher shop, same as if they had stolen from a human shop."

"Yes."

Of course, it would have been smarter for those men to steal from a human shop. The police would have arrested them instead of eating them. "How many were there?"

"Four."

She didn't know all the Wolves personally, but between the ones who looked after the puppies and the Wolfgard Complex and the ones who, like Simon and

Nathan, worked in more visible parts of the Courtyard, she had a fairly good idea of how many Wolves lived in Lakeside.

"Were they scrawny men?" she asked.

Simon narrowed his eyes and cocked his head. "Not what I would call scrawny. They weren't fat, but they were bulkier than Kowalski or Debany and just as tall."

"And the pack ate *four* of them?"

He sat back, looking a bit put out. "No. The two Elders who are in the Courtyard each ate one, and the rest of the *terra indigene* ate the other two."

That explained Jester's comment about breakfast. "Did Sam . . . ?"

Simon shook his head. "We didn't give any of the special meat to the puppies or Skippy. They're playing with human pups now, and we didn't want to confuse them."

Meg sighed out a breath. She couldn't say why the thought of Sam and Skippy chomping on a hunk of human bothered her more than Simon tearing into a person, but it did. And it made her wonder about something.

She ran her fingers up and down her glass, wiping away the condensation and avoiding a direct look at the Wolf sitting across from her. Should she ask? Could she ask? "What does human taste like?"

Simon scratched behind one ear. "Doesn't taste as good as deer but better than chicken." He thought for a moment. "Lots better than chicken."

She tried to visualize the illustrations on a prophecy card that would rank the tastiness of meat. On a scale of one to ten, deer would be a ten and chicken a one? Would cows and pigs be a seven or eight and humans be a four or five?

"Meg? What are you thinking?"

She told him.

He stared at her before saying slowly, "You don't need a prophecy card like that."

No, she didn't. But . . . "How accurate would it be if the card was illustrated that way?"

"Close enough."

"So special meat isn't special because it tastes so much better than other meat; it's special because you don't get to eat it that often."

He seemed relieved when his mobile phone started yelping. He hauled it out of one of the cargo pockets in his shorts and said, "What?" He listened a moment and looked at Meg. "Kowalski is making a pizza run. You want one?"

"Yes." She'd even cut up and sauté one of the zucchini for the vegetable side dish.

"Thanks," Simon said, then hung up.

Meg started to rise but realized she had one more question. "If those men had tried to steal anything but food, would you have killed them?"

"Last summer? Yes, we would have. Now?" He met her eyes. "We would have torn into them as a warning to other humans, but we probably would have howled for Montgomery and let the police pack deal with the intruders."

After Simon drove the BOW to the Market Square to pick up their pizza, Meg got everything ready to cook one of the zucchini.

Death, police, jail. Those things had happened today and would result in danger, which would result in her being connected somehow to a woods and a grave.

She should tell Simon. She *would* tell Simon. But not tonight. Saying anything now would stir up the Others, and she didn't want to get everyone riled just because her tongue was prickling again.

Meg braced her hands on the kitchen counter. She didn't want to make a cut on her tongue. Too easy to make mistakes and do permanent damage. And a *cassandra sangue* who couldn't speak clearly wasn't any use to the people who had traveled to the compounds to buy a look at their future. But sometime soon her tongue was going to bleed and she would see the prophecy waiting to be revealed.

* * *

The more time he spent around humans, the more confusing they became. Every other predator the *terra indigene* had absorbed had a social structure that made sense. But humans!

Simon pulled into the employee parking lot, got out of the BOW, and opened the wooden door that provided access between the employee and customer parking lots.

No sign of Kowalski yet.

They might not eat each other, but humans killed humans all the time. He'd seen that for himself when Lawrence MacDonald had been shot and killed at the stall market when men from the HFL movement attacked their group. While the human pack had grieved, their behavior didn't change toward the *terra indigene*. In fact, the deaths of MacDonald and Crystal Crowgard made the bond between the human pack and the Others even stronger.

Were they that accepting of the *terra indigene* seeing humans as meat because they realized that those who lived in the Courtyard didn't see them that way anymore? Or were they accepting because they understood that they, too, would be seen as meat by the *terra indigene* living beyond Lakeside and the connected places of Great Island, Talulah Falls, and the River Road Community?

Simon watched Kowalski and Pete Denby pull into the customer parking lot. He saw Montgomery leave the apartment building and walk as far as the public sidewalk. The lieutenant seemed to be listening for something, but Simon didn't detect any unusual sounds.

Kowalski opened the back door, pulled out a party-size pizza, and said, "I wasn't sure if Sam and Skippy were joining you tonight, so I wanted to make sure you'd have plenty. Half is pepperoni and sausage; the other half has veggies."

Simon took the pizza box. "That's good. I owe you money."

"It's our treat tonight."

Trying to make up for something other humans did. Trying to help take care of the pack.

Kowalski closed the back door, then hesitated. "Do you have any meat at home? Something frozen?"

"Hunks of bison."

"Ruthie made a pot roast the other day. Beef. She froze part of it in a couple of containers. A container probably wouldn't be enough for big appetites like ours, but for the girls, for Meg . . ."

"I'll ask her. Thank you for the pizza." Simon went back to the BOW, pausing long enough to close and lock the wooden door between the two parking lots. He wasn't surprised to hear someone rattle the door—Kowalski, checking to be sure it was locked.

On the way back to the Green Complex, he thought about what was said. Appetites like ours. A Wolf could eat pounds of meat at one time, far more than a human stomach could hold. But Kowalski had made it sound like the difference was between what males and females could consume, not humans and Wolves.

He wasn't sure what it meant, but he thought it was interesting.

Jimmy sat on the porch, brooding. He'd been on the porch since that cop drove him back here. If Sandee had been out when he returned, he would have packed one carryall, taken his stash of money and the couple of pieces of jewelry she kept hidden, and slipped away and caught a bus to anywhere, free of that bitch and her brats. But she'd been home, whining about food and money until he showed her his fist. He didn't need to use it—not often, anyway—to make her shut up quick and leave him alone to think.

Nothing wrong with his plan. It should have worked. His crew should have gotten in and out instead of being dead and . . .

He swallowed hard to keep his gorge from rising.

What was wrong with the people in this town, acting

like it was *normal* for those fucking freaks to *eat* people?
That had never happened in Toland! In Toland, regular
folks didn't have to see those Others, didn't have to
worry about being clawed or bitten or worse. This
wouldn't have happened in a big human city, a *proper*
human city. But here the cops were all bent, bought off
by the freaks. Even that bastard Burke must be working
for the Others. Why else would he be going after a man
just looking to take care of his family instead of shooting those freaks? Why else would that Wolf lover Kowalski go after a man who had been tricked into buying . . .

Jimmy pushed that thought away.

Those freaks had known his crew was coming. They'd
known before he'd made the final plans. How was that
possible?

He became aware of the commotion inside—crybaby
Fanny squealing for Mommy, and Clarence . . .

Jimmy flung himself out of the chair and went inside
to stop whatever shit the brats were doing, but he halted
in the bedroom doorway.

Clarence held a butter knife and was chasing Fanny
around the living room, laughing as he jabbed at her face.

"Gonna cut you, bitch," Clarence said. "Gonna turn
you into a scar girl. Then you'll tell fortunes and make
us a pile of money."

"Mommy!" Fanny screamed.

He'd heard something about scars and girls, but how
was he supposed to remember with Fanny screaming
like that? And if she kept on like that, how long before
one of the fucking cops started pounding on the door?

"Stop it!" he roared. "What is this shit?"

The glee on Clarence's face that he might "accidentally" cut his sister changed to wariness when Jimmy
stepped into the living room. "We're just playing, Daddy."

"What's this about scar girls?" He ignored Fanny,
who ran out of the room crying for Sandee, and focused
on the boy. "Well?"

"The girls with all the scars. You remember, Daddy. We saw them on TV. The girls who can see the future."

"Sure, I remember. Why are you teasing Fanny about them?"

"They got one of those girls in the Courtyard. Her name is Meg. She has really short black hair and pals around with the cop bitches."

A vague memory of being warned away from someone named Meg. Then he remembered more. He'd seen her when that Wolf brat attacked Clarence. His boy had been wounded, had needed a trip to the hospital, but everyone had been looking after some bitch who didn't have more than a bloody lip.

That was Meg?

A hard rap on the apartment door. Sandee eased out of the kitchen, glanced at him, then hustled to answer it.

Jimmy saw CJ at the door holding a big pizza box. Did CJ think buying a pizza would set things right after the way he'd let the other cops treat his own brother? After the way *he'd* treated his own brother, showing him those sick pictures of a severed arm, trying to scare him into confessing to something he didn't do?

No. Not CJ. Burke. Yeah. Burke had it in for him, was trying to set him up. Bastard could have killed his crew and taken all the meat from the butcher shop, could have cut off that arm himself and paid the freak to make sure it ended up in the hands of a man just trying to feed his family. Yeah. Burke had set him up—and CJ was helping to put him away.

Sandee took the pizza box, closed the door, and hurried to the kitchen. Jimmy hurried after her, grabbed both kids by the arms, and hauled them away from the table. He came first. Sometimes they forgot that.

The dishes were still in the sink, so Sandee pulled a wad of paper towels off the roll to use instead. When she opened the box, Jimmy felt anger burn his stomach.

"What's this?" he demanded.

"CJ bought a big pizza to split with us," Sandee said, looking a little frightened by his tone.

"He tosses you what he doesn't want, and you're ready to drop to your knees and give him a big kiss."

"Jimmy!" She looked appalled as she glanced at the brats. Then her face got that hard look it always did when she stopped trying to please him. "If you don't want your brother's leftovers, don't eat any. But there's nothing else in the house."

He looked at Fanny, whom CJ had taken an interest in lately. Was she another example of his brother's leftovers? No wonder he'd never warmed to the little bitch.

Sandee reached for the pizza. He shoved her away from the table. Taking a stack of pieces and the last beer in the refrigerator, he retreated to the porch to eat in peace, letting the three of them squabble over the remains.

He bit into the pizza. Chewed. Swallowed. Thought and thought of how nothing had gone the way it should have since he arrived in Lakeside.

He needed to get out of this fucking city. It was too small, too constricting for an enterprising man like him. He needed something that would bring in money, that would give him clout, that would let him live large the way he was supposed to.

He chewed. Swallowed. Thought.

He needed a way to stay ahead of the freaks and the cops. He needed one of those prophet girls—and wasn't it fucking fate that one of them was right here, ripe for the picking? Just cut her skin and make a fortune. He could offer a prophecy to a skilled forger in return for a new identity. Then he would become someone else in one of the big human cities. He could get around the travel restrictions and go all the way to Sparkletown on the West Coast and get into the movie business. Using the scar girl, he'd have the means of telling the wheelers and dealers if a movie would be a hit even before they hired the first actor. And he'd have his pick of beautiful women who would do anything he wanted for just a peek at their future.

Yeah. That was the way he should live. He just needed to shake off all this petty shit—and he needed to get the scar girl away from the Courtyard and get them both out of this fucking city. But this time, he'd do it alone. He wasn't going to trust *this* plan to screwups like the ones who couldn't take a bit of meat from a bunch of animals.

So he chewed and swallowed and thought. By the time the sun had set and the streetlights came on, Cyrus James Montgomery had a plan.

CHAPTER 21

Thaisday, Messis 23

Meg dreamed about the prophecy the cards had revealed.

The cards had grown tall, like trees, and surrounded her. Penned her in.

So thirsty. How long since she'd had a drink of water? So thirsty.

Hooded figure with a scythe. Police car. Man in jail. Danger!

More cards appeared, repeating and repeating until they formed a prison. Woods. Tombstone. Mirror. Woods. Tombstone. Mirror. They closed in slowly, relentlessly.

Hoping to find a way out, Meg turned, took a step, and tripped. Fell. A pile of leaves in front of her. Her hands reaching out to break her fall. Her hands disappearing into the leaves, slipping on something underneath.

She touched a cold hand.

Something touched her arm.

She screamed, thrashed, tried to hit whoever held her. She had a moment to realize she was free before something soft hit her back, her shoulders, her butt.

"Meg!"

He found me. Relief made her dizzy. *He found me!*

"Simon!" She threw herself toward the sound of his voice. Her hands closed on something soft, something not Simon. "Simon!"

Hands grabbed her again and hauled her toward something unknown, but what she grabbed in turn were thickly furred human shoulders.

A light came on, blinding her, and Vlad said, "Blessed Thaisia! What is going on?"

"I don't know," Simon growled. "Meg? Meg! Look at me. Are you awake?"

"I—" Was she awake? "It was cold. The hand was so cold."

"My hands are *not* cold. Look at me, Meg."

She looked at his face, not sure what had happened or why he was angry.

Was she really awake, or was this part of the dream?

"I am not naked," Simon said.

She didn't know why that was important, but she said, "Okay," which seemed to satisfy him.

Something thumped the front door. Hard.

Meg leaped, wrapped her arms around Simon's neck and her legs around his waist. His arms came around her, supporting her, protecting her.

"Meg, it's all right. It's just Henry," Simon said.

"And Jester," Vlad added. "And Tess." After a moment, he added, "You can let go of Simon now."

She tightened her legs and was glad when Simon said, "She doesn't have to."

"I'll let Henry in before he knocks down the door," Vlad said. "Then we all need to discuss what happened."

Once Vlad left the bedroom, Simon sighed, his breath warm against her neck. "Bad dream?" he asked.

Dreamlike certainly, but was it a dream? "I don't know. I saw . . . felt . . . things."

His arms tightened around her. "Then you'd better tell us what you remember."

*   *   *

Simon took the pitcher of water out of the refrigerator and filled a glass. He drank half the water, refilled the glass, and put the pitcher away before going into Meg's living room.

Meg sat on the sofa next to Henry, her knees drawn up and her arms around her legs—a scared little ball of human. Tess sat on the coffee table, Vlad leaned over the back of the sofa, and Jester crouched to one side of the table, where he could see and hear everything without being in the way. The Green Complex's feathered residents were perched on the porch, where they could hear everything through the open window.

"Here." Simon held out the glass to Meg, who just stared at it. "You woke me up because you were thirsty, so I got up to get you some water. That's how this all started."

She didn't take the water, so he sat on the other side of her and put the glass on the floor. Her brain wasn't working right, and that worried him. It was like she was stuck between seeing the images of prophecy and seeing the physical world and she couldn't shake herself free.

Then Tess said, "Speak, prophet, and we will listen."

Responding to the promise and command in the words, Meg kept her eyes on Tess and told her listeners everything she could remember. She told them about the cards she'd drawn yesterday and what came after the events the first three cards had revealed. She told them the details of the dream—details that provided substance, context.

Had Meg always seen this much detail but had been trained to compress what she saw into a series of images that someone else would interpret? Or was this like Jackson's prophet pup, Hope, who could draw a few lines that could be recognized as a howling Wolf but could also make a detailed drawing that would reveal a specific Wolf? Maybe these kinds of dreams were the only way Meg's brain could tell her more when she wasn't cutting.

Vlad's voice. Soothing, almost seductive, asking about details. Any rings on the hand? Color of skin? Could she see the color of the clothes in the moonlight?

She answered his questions. She didn't smell lusty like she did when she cut herself and then spoke prophecy, but her voice had the same dreamlike quality it had during those times.

Meg closed her eyes and sagged against Henry. Then she opened her eyes, blinked at all of them, and said, "Is there any water? I'm thirsty."

Simon handed her the glass of water. She drank it all.

"Still thirsty." She unfolded her body and stood up.

Before Simon could stop her, Jester hopped up and said, "I'll help you find the water." He made it sound like they needed to find a stream in the dark rather than turn on a faucet—and Meg didn't say a thing to indicate she saw anything odd about that.

Simon waited until he heard Meg and Jester talking in the kitchen. Then he looked at the others in the room. "Do you think she's sick?"

Vlad came around to the front side of the sofa. "No, not sick exactly."

"Humans walk in their sleep," Tess said. "They talk to people, do things around the house, even leave their homes and have no memory of it in the morning."

"She hasn't done that before," Simon said.

"She's had upsetting dreams before, but this was different, and it's something Emily Faire needs to know about," Vlad said. "It may be an indication of something wrong—or something right. The Intuits don't hurt themselves in order to have the feelings that tell them if something is wrong. Maybe the *cassandra sangue* didn't cut themselves in the beginning. Maybe they had dreamed about the future and discovered by accident that the cutting gave them control of the time and place to see the visions."

"Control of time and place and the euphoria that clouded their minds and prevented them from seeing things that might terrify a young mind to the breaking point," Tess said.

Simon nodded. "She needs to see the human body-walker."

"Maybe our Meg should spend a few days on Great Island," Henry said. "Merri Lee could go with her. Steve Ferryman and Ming Beargard would watch over them."

Tess had managed to control her emotions while Meg had looked into her eyes, but now her hair had broad streaks of red and was starting to coil as she focused on the Grizzly. "Why? That would be upsetting."

"Yes," Henry agreed. "But she would be out of reach of potential enemies."

Hearing Henry's words made Simon feel cold, but he understood. "Meg's vision at night is no better than any other human's," he told Tess. "She was outside and it was dark, but she could still see well enough to describe what was around her."

"You're applying waking logic to a dream, which had prophecy cards the size of trees," Tess argued. "What does her being able to see in a dream have to do with sending her to Great Island?"

"Vlad kept asking her what she'd seen in the moonlight. She didn't correct him, didn't say she had a flashlight or there was a campfire that allowed her to see in the woods at night."

Threads of black mingled with the red streaks in Tess's hair. "Meg would need sufficient moonlight to see in the dark, and next week is the full moon."

Meg stared at the glass in her hand. She stared at the clock. She stared at the Coyote.

"Jester? Why are you in my kitchen at this time of night?"

"You should ask me why I'm here at this time of the morning since we're close enough to dawn." He studied her. "Are you awake now?"

Why did everyone keep asking her that? Then she remembered.

Dream. Vision. Something in between. This had happened a couple of times since she arrived in the Courtyard. The first time, she thought she was driving the BOW at night and Sam wouldn't stop howling. But she and Sam had been out making deliveries in daylight—and he hadn't been howling yet. Then there was the dream of making a cut and seeing prophecy. She recognized the trigger when it came in the real world, and her actions had saved Simon and the rest of the Wolves in the Courtyard.

This was another personal vision, warning her of something approaching in her own life.

Which didn't explain the Coyote being in her kitchen at that hour.

"Why are we in the kitchen?" she asked.

"You were thirsty and wanted water. I came with you to help you find it," Jester replied.

Meg looked at the sink. "I think I can find the faucet by myself."

"If you're looking for a faucet instead of a stream, you must be awake now."

Why would she look for a stream? That didn't make any sense—and that wasn't the only thing that didn't make sense. "Did Simon hit me with a goose?"

Jester laughed. "He whacked you with a pillow. But some of the pillows are stuffed with down, so I can see how you might confuse the two."

Meg heard a rumbling voice coming from the living room. She knew that voice, but she asked, "Who else is here?"

"Henry, Tess, and Vlad."

She sighed. "I guess it was a loud dream."

"That's the most entertaining kind, even if we'll all need a nap because of it."

He sounded cheerful. She should worry about that.

Instead she drank the water and set the glass beside the sink. "I'm going back to bed until it's daylight."

"You should pee first. You drank a lot of water, even if you don't remember doing it."

Since her bladder suddenly agreed with him, she followed Jester's advice. And she admitted to herself that it was a wee bit cowardly to sneak back to her bedroom and not say anything to the friends who were still talking in her living room.

Jester stepped into the living room and gave everyone a gleeful smile. "Now that *we're* all awake, Meg has gone back to bed."

Simon looked out the window. "Why? It's almost time to get up anyway."

Jester shrugged. "Human time makes less sense than ours."

"Nothing we can do right now," Vlad said. "We've been warned that danger is coming, and we know the result when it strikes."

"But not the danger itself," Henry rumbled before looking at Simon. "You'll talk to Meg about spending a few days on Great Island?"

"There are woods on the island," Simon said.

"But there wouldn't be a body hidden under leaves," Tess said. "The Intuits would have a feeling about something like that, and the *terra indigene* would have found it by now."

Simon rubbed his forehead. "It might not happen during next week's full moon. It could happen a month from now."

"Not likely," Henry said. "These days, our Meg's visions are more often about the immediate future."

"Talk to her, Simon," Vlad said. "Talk to Blair and Nathan so they'll be on the lookout for trouble in the evenings. I'll talk to Grandfather Erebus and Nyx."

Jester slipped out of Meg's apartment and stopped at his own place just long enough to remove the jeans he'd pulled on when the commotion started. Then he shifted to his Coyote form and ran to make his own report to the girls at the lake.

Jimmy left the apartment and walked to the nearest bus stop on Main Street to catch one of the early-morning buses. There were things he needed to find, calls he needed to make, and he couldn't do that from the apartment. For one thing, there was no phone in the place. You would think the freaks could put in a phone, even if it was a pay phone in the small, piece-of-shit entryway. But no. Either you used a mobile phone, which you paid for, or you had a landline connected at your own expense.

He'd bet his shoes that Sissy and Mama hadn't paid to have a phone in their places.

Didn't matter. Despite what he'd told Sandee, he did have a mobile phone, which he would ditch as soon as his plans were made.

More annoying today was the lack of a phone book in the apartment. The last tenants must have taken the thing. Which meant he needed to find a coffee shop or diner that had a phone book he could look at while he had breakfast.

The bus pulled up to the stop, and the people going to work downtown piled in. Some smiled at people already on the bus and sat next to them. Coworkers maybe. Others found an empty pair of seats and claimed both, daring other passengers to ask them to move their daypack or carry sack. Jimmy was big enough and looked rough enough that he didn't need a daypack to claim extra room. He just looked at a person eyeing the seat. That was usually enough to convince them that standing was good exercise.

The bus pulled away from the stop, and Jimmy began to relax.

He'd spent most of the night thinking it through, considering the plan step by step. Easier to reestablish himself in Toland or Hubbney, but those would be the first places CJ and the other cops would check. So it had to be somewhere new, someplace large enough for him to disappear. Shikago. Yeah, he'd start his new life in Shikago, give himself time to learn how to use his new asset and acquire enough money to grease the necessary palms to travel anywhere he wanted in Thaisia. Then he would set himself up on the West Coast and become a behind-the-scenes big shot.

Asset. Yeah, he liked that word. Made him sound like a businessman. He should invest in a suit and a couple of dress shirts. That would attract better customers than the lowlifes he used to deal with. His asset would help him find the right people, the ones who could pay his fees.

She could, and would, help him with a lot of things once she understood who was in charge.

CHAPTER 22

Thaisday, Messis 23

Jimmy spent the morning selecting the things he would need, always aware that the best chance he had of succeeding was today at the start of the midday break. The cops and the Others wouldn't expect him to make a move so soon after those men screwed up the theft of a few pounds of meat. They wouldn't be ready for anyone to do something *bold*.

There were places around the bus depot and train station where a person could rent a car for a few days, but even the places that rented junkers wanted things like an address and payment made through a bank card or a cash deposit that covered the full cost of the time the car would be used. A nice car would be better—less chance of breaking down considering how far he was driving—but a junker wouldn't be reported stolen if it was an hour late being returned.

Not finding the right balance of reliable and nondescript, Jimmy took a taxi up to the university area, not wanting to waste time waiting for the next bus. The bookstore near the campus had maps of all the regions. He bought maps for the Northeast, High Northeast, and Southeast—the three regions within reach if you were flexible about where you crossed a regional border. There were bound to be operators of small boats plying their various trades along the coastline, hauling in fish and dropping off a passenger or two on the other side of an arbitrary line.

A backup plan in case he decided heading for Shikago wasn't his best move.

The salesperson mentioned a couple of times that the maps weren't totally accurate anymore—some places that were listed didn't exist now or were no longer under human control. Could be hard to find gas if you left the toll road with its rest stops that were kept supplied with fuel. And you needed to figure out where to stop once the daylight began to fade. Couldn't risk driving on any road after dark, especially the ones running through the wild country, and hotels and motels that were built conveniently close to the toll road tended to fill up fast.

Jimmy smiled at the girl and thanked her for her help, doing what CJ would have done. He explained that the maps were a hobby—he just liked studying places—but he did have business on Great Island and didn't want to hire a taxi for a day. Did she have any suggestions?

He expected her to haul out a phone book and direct him to the rental places he already knew about. Instead, she pointed to the store's large vestibule, where a bulletin board was conveniently located next to the pay phone. University students sometimes rented out their cars for a day to help with the costs of owning a car. Usually they rented to other students, but he seemed like a nice guy and a day trip to Great Island at this time of year wouldn't put wear and tear on a car. He could check out the cars that were available today.

He thanked her again and went out to look at the notices tacked to the bulletin board. He found a few cars that sounded like they would be suitable—new enough that he wouldn't need to worry about breaking down in the wild country but not so new that they would attract the attention of cops.

The first two numbers he called didn't pan out. The cars were already rented for the day. But the third car was still available and the guy who owned it lived a few blocks from the bookstore.

Jimmy walked to the address he'd been given, and within minutes he'd handed a hundred dollars to a scruffy-looking young man, had confirmed that the registration and insurance card were in the glove box, and promised to replace whatever fuel he used before returning the car that evening.

He drove carefully, partly to reassure the fool who had just handed over a vehicle to a complete stranger and partly to avoid being pulled over for something stupid. Spotting a coffee shop, he parked and went in to study the maps.

He wanted to stay in the Northeast Region for the first stage of this new venture, so he needed to head south or east. Only one road out of Lakeside headed south besides the toll road, but that one road branched out like fingers spreading from a hand. The "thumb" continued south, following Lake Etu until it angled west toward Shikago. The "fingers" branched out, some heading toward the Southeast Region while the rest headed east toward the Finger Lakes. He could make it look like he was heading to Shikago—a destination CJ would expect him to choose—then take one of those branches heading toward the Finger Lakes, changing direction whenever two routes intersected in some town, always heading east, toward the coast. He would put enough distance between himself and Lakeside that CJ wouldn't have a clue where to start looking. And since he wasn't using a car from a rental place, the cops couldn't track him that way.

Jimmy folded up the maps, finished his coffee, and left the coffee shop smiling. Once he had the asset away from Lakeside, he would know which roads to use to elude the cops and the freaks.

He drove back to the neighborhood around the

Courtyard. Time to put the last part of his plan into motion.

"Playdate?"

Setting aside the book order he was trying to fill for one of the *terra indigene* settlements, Simon glanced at Vlad, who shrugged. Then he focused on Eve Denby, who had combined ordinary words in a way that made no sense. "Humans designate a time for puppies to play?"

No wonder humans were all a bit peculiar. Puppies played. A lot. That's how they learned much of what they needed to know about the world. They played with puppies their own age. They played with juveniles. They played with adults. They played with sticks and pine-cones and just about anything they could pick up that interested them.

"Robert and Sam want to play a board game," Eve said. "A game played on a board." Using two fingers, she traced a square on the counter.

"We know about board games," Simon grumbled. Okay, so the *terra indigene* might not play the game according to the rules printed on the box or in a way humans would understand, but they had some of those games shelved in their various social rooms.

"Well, this game has small pieces that could be lost if the boys play it in the Courtyard," Eve said. "I don't want some youngster spotting a game piece in the grass, thinking it was edible, and choking on it. The boys will be playing on the porch, have already been told there will be dire penalties if they take so much as a step off the porch without supervision." She placed her hands on the counter and leaned toward Simon. "And if they don't stop pestering me about this so that I don't have an hour's peace to get some work done, I am going to get cranky and bite somebody."

Her eyes held a feral quality that made him think it wasn't the puppies who would get bitten.

Simon breathed in her scent and thought she might

be in season. That would explain the snappishness, especially if she was one of those females who gave the "come here, come here, come here" signals one moment, then wanted to bite off her mate's face the next.

Should he warn Pete Denby? Then again, the man had been mated to Eve enough years to recognize the warning signs.

"Sam . . ." He stopped. Let Sam go out among the humans alone? "Sam has never been out of the Courtyard. My sister was pregnant when she arrived in Lakeside. He's never . . ."

Sympathy in Eve's eyes now and in her smile. "It's hard, isn't it, letting them take those first steps away from you? It's been just as hard for me letting Robert cross the street and play inside the Courtyard with Sam and the other young Wolves."

Considering the results of mixing human and Wolf curiosity, innocence, and boy boldness, he couldn't say the *terra indigene* adults had kept Robert and Sam out of trouble; they'd just put a stop to things before trouble became dangerous.

Of course, after dealing with a boy who had learned why you don't tease a skunk—a smelly but useful lesson—Eve might not share a Wolf's scale of "okay to dangerous" when it came to learning experiences.

"I'll escort them across the street," Eve said. "You can watch from the window right here. If they disobey and I don't get to them first, feel free to come over and bite them. Better yet, send Nathan. I'm not sure Robert believes you'll bite him, but he *is* sure that Nathan will."

"I can bite as well as Nathan."

"The logic is that a friend's uncle can scold you—and be ignored—but a cop can arrest you?" Vlad asked, looking amused.

"Exactly," Eve replied. "You don't mess with the Wolf police."

Laughing, Vlad went into the back to pull more stock for the out-of-town orders.

"Wait," Simon said. "How can Robert pester you? He's in school in the mornings."

"Ruth needed a mental health day, so the kids don't have school."

"Ruthie is sick?"

Eve patted his hand. "When a woman takes a mental health day, she needs alone time, and a wise man lets her have it."

Okay. Not sick. Calm unless riled, then watch the teeth. He understood that. But it made him wonder about something else. "Does a human female get as testy when a male asks about a mental health day as she does when he asks if it's that time of the month?"

Eve showed her teeth. Might be a smile. Probably not.

"Okay," Simon said. "They can play on the porch at your house."

Eve patted his hand again. "I'll feed them lunch if they haven't lost interest in the game by then and returned to the Courtyard to play."

Simon stood at the door of Howling Good Reads and watched while Eve walked Robert and Sam down the sidewalk on the other side of Crowfield Avenue. He watched Sam stop and wave to him before Eve and the pups went up the walkway to the Denbys' porch.

"Worried?" Vlad asked, coming out of the back of the store.

"Meg saw danger." She didn't see anything that indicated any of the pups were in danger, but that was no reason to be careless.

"I know," Vlad said. "That's why I asked Leetha to keep an eye on the children. You could ask Jake Crowgard to go over."

"He'd steal pieces of the game."

"Probably."

Leetha wasn't Vlad or Nyx, but she did answer to Grandfather Erebus. If there was any trouble at the apartments across the street, she would sound the alarm.

* * *

Meg wrinkled her nose at the picture of bison on the front of the postcard, then smiled when she turned it over. It wasn't addressed to her, but she figured every individual who had handled the card on its journey here had read the message that Jana Paniccia had sent to Jenni Crowgard.

She left the postcard on the sorting table next to her purse, along with a letter from Jana addressed to Merri Lee, which she put on the stack of mail going to HGR. She'd deliver the card to Jenni at Sparkles and Junk when she went out for lunch. Which would be a choice of bison burgers, bison meat loaf, or roast bison sandwiches.

She sighed. She'd been an idiot to turn down Simon's offer to drive up to Ferryman's Landing and buy some meat for her. But she hadn't wanted special treatment— and regretted that decision when Merri Lee and Ruth told her they wouldn't have turned down the offer; that because he was a Wolf, bringing her choice cuts of her preferred meat was probably Simon's equivalent of giving her flowers and chocolate. Put that way, it sounded like she was turning down a suitor instead of passing up a pot roast.

Which left her with a choice of bison, bison, or bison for lunch. Yum.

She walked up to the counter in the front room, drew back the slide bolt on top of the go-through, and headed for the door, saying, "Time to close up for the midday break."

She spotted Greg O'Sullivan walking across the delivery area at the same moment he spotted her. Changing course, he opened the door of the Liaison's Office and stepped inside.

Skippy leaped to his feet and growled menacingly. Nathan looked at the ceiling, as if pretending to take no notice of the juvenile Wolf's behavior. O'Sullivan froze by the door.

There was no reason to threaten the ITF agent. He rented a room above the office. He'd been given work space in the consulate. But he'd been gone for a few days, so it was possible that Skippy didn't remember him.

"That's an impressive-sounding growl," Meg said. "Very watch Wolf. Agent O'Sullivan, don't you think that's an impressive-sounding growl?"

"I certainly do," O'Sullivan replied.

Nathan looked at the two humans and grunted.

Okay, they were slathering praise with strokes so broad most juveniles would feel insulted at being treated like puppies, but Skippy was Skippy.

"But we know Agent O'Sullivan, and we don't growl at people we know," Meg said.

Nathan stared at Meg and growled.

"Unless they are doing something bad," she amended.

"A growl is just a warning," O'Sullivan said. "No harm in warning someone that there are consequences to doing something bad."

O'Sullivan and Nathan looked at each other and moved their heads in tiny nods of agreement. Meg rolled her eyes at this display of law enforcement solidarity.

Skippy flopped down on his Wolf bed, clearly pleased to have performed his watch Wolf duties.

"I'm working alone at the consulate right now, so I was heading over to the Stag and Hare to pick up a sandwich. Would you like me to pick up one for you?"

"I don't know what kind of food they have there." But it was a safe bet that they wouldn't be serving bison.

"It's basic pub grub," O'Sullivan said. "The food at Meat-n-Greens is better, if somewhat more creative, but the Stag and Hare gets its supplies from human sources. With the loss of the meat in the butcher shop, it didn't seem fair to buy a sandwich here when I can go across the street."

"Okay, thanks. I'll get some money."

"We can settle up after. Any kind of meat you don't like?"

Nathan snorted. Meg ignored him. O'Sullivan smiled.

"I'm fine with any of the ordinary meats people eat," Meg said.

"I'll choose a couple of things and you can take your pick."

"Thank you." Meg scowled at Nathan. "Why don't you and Skippy go out for your break now?"

O'Sullivan had pushed the door open. Now he stopped and looked at her. "Like I said, there is no one at the consulate right now. If your friends are going out, you should lock the door until I get back."

"Arroo," Nathan agreed as he stepped off the Wolf bed and stretched.

Skippy made no move to leave. He just watched Meg with bright-eyed eagerness.

She looked at O'Sullivan, then nodded when he held up three fingers to show he understood he would be buying a sandwich for Skippy. The ITF agent went out the front door, holding it for Nathan. The Wolf looked toward Main Street, then turned sharply and trotted up the access way. She watched O'Sullivan look toward the intersection of Main Street and Crowfield Avenue. She watched him gauge the traffic and dash across the street to the Stag and Hare instead of going up to the crosswalk.

"Roo?"

Meg blinked. Focused on Skippy.

She looked at her right arm. Her left hand hid the evenly spaced scars on her upper arm. Her hand clenched around the arm so hard the muscles hurt.

And the spot on her tongue began to prickle.

She turned the simple lock on the front door. She would get her keys and lock it properly when Agent O'Sullivan returned. Maybe she would ask him to escort her to Howling Good Reads or the Market Square.

Then again, maybe he was the reason she was starting to feel prophecy prickle and burn under her skin. Maybe something was going to happen to him.

She pressed her hand against the pocket of her jeans and felt the shape of the folding razor. Something was going to happen, was happening now. She had the uneasy feeling that even if she made a cut, it was already too late to give a warning.

"Simon! Vlad!" Merri Lee shouted. "Something is going on across the street."

Dumping a handful of books back on the cart, Simon rushed to the front of HGR with Vlad right behind him. Merri Lee stood on the sidewalk, mobile phone pressed to one ear, shouting, "You kids! Clarence! Knock it off!"

Simon wasn't sure what he was seeing. Four human pups were on the grass between the Denbys' den and the apartment building. That Clarence seemed to be taunting the Frances while Lizzy and Sarah stood nearby, looking like young prey who didn't know if they should run or huddle together to defend themselves against a predator. Was this a different kind of play the Others hadn't seen before?

Sam and Robert were still on the porch, obeying Eve's orders, but they were on their feet, watching that Clarence and the girls. Leetha moved toward the girls but seemed uncertain about whether to act.

"Leetha says this is typical play between that Clarence and the Frances," Vlad said.

"That isn't play," Merri Lee snapped, rounding on Vlad. "That is *wrong*. Damn it, Eve, pick up."

Not play. Wrong.

The light was green, so traffic moved in both directions on Crowfield Avenue, cars bunched together and going too fast for him to safely dash between them. It would be like leaping into a bison stampede, with much the same result for anything that wasn't just as big. He'd wait until the light turned red and the cars stopped moving before going over and showing his teeth. Besides, there was no real urgency to cross the street since Leetha was already there and that Clarence wasn't doing anything except yelling things that upset the female puppies.

Except something about this reminded him of the mock battle Montgomery and that Cyrus had last week.

<Nathan?> Simon called, feeling uneasy.

<Here.> Nathan stepped onto the sidewalk in front of the customer parking lot.

<Where is Meg?>

<In the office with Skippy. She locked the door until O'Sullivan returns with food.>

Still watching the ruckus across the street, Simon started moving toward the intersection. It was daylight, not the time Meg saw in the prophecy dream, but he still wanted to stand at the corner where he could see the entrance to the delivery area—and see anyone heading for the Liaison's Office.

"Girls!" Leetha shouted. "Over here."

Perhaps because she was more familiar with the Sanguinati who lived in her building, Lizzy was the first to obey, dragging Grr Bear by one arm. The Frances, dodging a swipe of the Clarence's hand, raced after Lizzy. But Sarah had been standing closest to the sidewalk and was now farthest away from protection—and was the most innocent fawn among the three girls. In her effort to escape, she ran too close to the predator, and that Clarence grabbed her. He locked one arm around her, bending her at the waist, and pulled her shorts and underpants down, shouting, "Show 'em your bald pussy, bitch!"

In that moment, annoying behavior turned into a real threat.

Vlad turned to smoke and raced over the cars, startling some drivers into hitting the brakes.

Robert screamed, "Sarah!" and leaped off the porch to defend his sister, with Sam right there with him.

Changing direction, Simon grabbed Merri Lee to keep her from leaping between a car that had stopped and the one behind it that didn't stop in time, adding the crunch of metal to the shouts and snarls of a fight—

and the sound of horns honking and tires squealing on Main Street. Despite Merri Lee's swearing at him and digging her short nails into his arms as he hauled her away from the curb, he noticed how Sam and Robert moved as a team to harass the somewhat larger predator. That Clarence flung Sarah to the ground and turned his attention to the other young males.

"Gonna stick you, Wolf," that Clarence shouted, pulling a small knife from his pocket. "Gonna stick you good."

Sam didn't respond. The puppy pack had been learning this lesson as play: harry a larger predator away from weaker members of the pack while avoiding teeth or claws that could injure or kill. Snap and retreat, snap and retreat. Work as a pack to push, push, push the predator away from the den.

Vlad shifted to human as soon as he reached the other side of the street. He scooped up Sarah and rushed to the spot where the other girls stood. Then he and Leetha turned toward the boys to break up the fight. Realizing the Sanguinati would deal with the trouble, Merri Lee stopped fighting Simon.

Then the Sandee came out of the apartment building. She screamed as she ran toward the boys and raised something thin and pointed as if she intended to drive it into Sam's back.

Leetha grabbed the Sandee and scraped her fangs over the skin between neck and shoulder. Then Leetha stumbled away, screaming in pain. Distracted, Robert didn't react fast enough when that Clarence jabbed at him. He went down, leaving Sam facing that Clarence.

Releasing Merri Lee, Simon ran to the space in front of the crunched cars and prepared to leap into the other lane of traffic. The damn light hadn't changed yet and the drivers on that side had sped up, trying to flee. Then two ponies galloped out of the customer parking lot and a small tornado made of snow slammed into some of the cars, knocking them sideways and turning them into a barricade that stopped all hope of fleeing. Within moments, the tornado expanded, burying several car lengths of the street under a furious snowfall.

With all the traffic stopped, Nathan bolted across the street and headed straight for the Sandee. He didn't try to bite. Leetha was still on the ground, wounded somehow, and Vlad was guarding the girls and calling to Sam. No, Nathan hit the Sandee from behind. She flipped over his back and landed on her belly. Nathan spun and jumped on her back, his nails digging into her bare skin as she screamed and bucked.

Simon leaped into the whiteout to reach the other side of the street, bumping into trapped cars and pushing through snow already up to his thighs. He heard Merri Lee shouting, "There's a snow tornado blocking Crowfield Avenue. You'll have to come another way."

Sirens. Smart human. Blocked from getting across herself, she had called the police pack.

<Sam!> he shouted as soon as he stumbled into the sunshine and heat of a morning in late Messis.

Sam leaped out of reach of that Clarence's knife. Simon would have dealt with the enemy, but that was the moment Eve Denby rounded the back of the house and came running to protect her young. Not sure what she intended to do with the big wrench in her hand, Simon rushed to block her before she crushed someone's head. As he wrestled with Eve, Marie Hawkgard dove and hit that Clarence in the back, driving the boy to his hands and knees. Her talons left deep furrows in his shoulders as she launched herself toward the porch railing of the apartment above Lieutenant Montgomery's.

Then it was over. Panting, Simon released Eve Denby and looked around. All this in the time it had taken for a traffic light to change. He didn't see any police cars, but Debany, Kowalski, and Hilborn were suddenly there, cuffing the Sandee and assessing who else needed to be arrested while Lieutenant Montgomery called for ambulances for Robert, that Clarence, and any wounded

humans who were in the crunched cars. Tornado and
Avalanche trotted back to the Pony Barn, leaving cars
half buried in snow and a traffic mess that would take
hours for the police to sort out.

Vlad carried Leetha up to the Sanguinati's apartment and summoned their bodywalker. Merri Lee and
Miss Twyla hurried across the street and took the girls
and Eve into the Denbys' home. Montgomery followed
them but returned a minute later.

Sam stayed near Simon. The pup looked a little stunned,
but he wasn't hurt.

More sirens. Probably the ambulances.

Montgomery approached, looking closely at Sam.
"Are you all right?"

Sam nodded. "Robert's hurt."

"They'll take him to Lakeside Hospital. Looks like
he'll need some stitches, but I think he'll be fine. I called
Pete Denby. He was doing some work downtown today."
Montgomery looked sad. "Simon, I—"

Three gunshots in quick succession.

No, Simon thought as he and the police turned toward the sound. Then he ran to the delivery area in
front of the Liaison's Office.

Monty pointed at Debany and Hilborn, who was now
a probationary member of the team. Hilborn hesitated,
but Debany nodded and turned back to deal with the
trouble at the Denbys' residence while Monty and Kowalski ran after Simon.

Nathan overtook them, turning into the delivery area
just ahead of Simon.

Greg O'Sullivan knelt on the ground next to Skippy,
who was whimpering and trying to get up.

"He's hurt," O'Sullivan said. "Leg might be broken.
Maybe some ribs. Looks like he also took a hard blow
to the head."

"Nathan, check on Meg," Simon growled as he knelt
and put a hand on Skippy to stop the juvenile Wolf's

struggles. "She's not out here with Skippy, so she might be hurt."

"She might be in the Market Square," Monty said, hoping for a benign reason for Meg's absence. He shuddered when Nathan made one of those disturbing partial shifts, looking neither human nor Wolf, in order to open the office door. The moment he was inside he shifted back to Wolf, leaped over the counter, and went into the sorting room.

O'Sullivan stared at the door, frowning. "That door should be locked. When I spoke to Meg a couple of minutes ago, I told her to lock the door while I picked up sandwiches at the Stag and Hare."

"We heard shots," Monty said.

"That was me." O'Sullivan stared at the door while he wagged a thumb in the direction of the blue mailbox positioned outside the consulate. "I'll arrest myself later for shooting government property, but I wanted to get your attention and I didn't know who might get hit if I shot in the air."

Blair arrived in a BOW, driving down the access way too fast to stop if someone had been heading up.

Inside the Liaison's Office, Nathan leaped back over the counter, sniffed around the front of the office—and howled.

Monty didn't need Simon's and Blair's reactions to know it was a battle cry.

"She's gone, isn't she?" O'Sullivan said flatly, getting to his feet and stepping back from the injured Wolf.

Simon rushed into the Liaison's Office, vaulted over the counter, and disappeared. He returned in less than a minute, his amber eyes turned red with rage.

Blair stayed outside guarding Skippy and watching all the humans as if they had just transformed into enemies.

"Maybe this was a crime of opportunity, but I don't think so." O'Sullivan scanned the area. "I do not think so." He focused on Monty. "Where is Cyrus Montgomery at this moment?"

No. Jimmy couldn't be that selfish, that stupid. What O'Sullivan was implying . . . Gods above and below. Would the city be torn apart because of Jimmy?

A crime of opportunity? He thought about the ruckus at the apartment and felt sick that they might have fallen for a distraction a second time. "Let's be sure," he began as Simon slammed out of the office.

"We're sure," Simon snarled. "That Cyrus's scent is in the office—and Meg is gone."

CHAPTER 23

Thaisday, Messis 23

Vlad looked around the table in the consulate's meeting room. He'd expected Captain Burke to arrive as soon as he'd heard the news, but he hadn't expected Mayor Walter Chen and Police Commissioner Raymond Alvarez to be part of this meeting.

He also hadn't expected to be outnumbered. Besides Chen, Alvarez, and Burke, Montgomery and Kowalski were also in the room. He and Elliot Wolfgard, who was the Courtyard's consul, were the only *terra indigene* at this meeting.

"Mr. Simon Wolfgard will not be joining us?" Chen asked Elliot.

Elliot hesitated. "He's too upset to be around humans right now."

Chen nodded as if that was the expected response. He looked at Alvarez, then at Burke. "What are we doing to find this young woman and return her to her family?"

Interesting choice of words, Vlad thought. But he detected no hypocrisy in Chen's voice.

"We're doing everything we would do for any abduction," Burke replied. He looked Vlad in the eyes. "With some help, we can do more."

"What kind of help?" Vlad asked. "I've contacted Stavros Sanguinati. If that Cyrus goes to Talulah Falls, Stavros will find him—and Meg."

Burke nodded. "I called Roger Czerneda. He'll patrol River Road between Ferryman's Landing and the Lakeside city line. It's not likely that Cyrus will go there either—too easy to get boxed in—but that route away from Lakeside is covered."

"I have contacted the station chief of every precinct in Lakeside," Alvarez said. "All the stations are being mobilized, and roadblocks are being set up as we speak." He hesitated. "But we still need a starting point, especially if this man is already beyond the city limits."

"Starting point?" Vlad asked quietly. He could think of two places to start. Wouldn't need to break too much of that Clarence for the pup to wail everything he knew. He'd prefer breaking the Sandee, who had been so hopped up on something that just contact with her skin had injured Leetha. The Sanguinati bodywalker was optimistic that the wounds in and around Leetha's mouth would heal without permanent damage. Vlad hoped that was true.

And he wondered: was the Sandee's life force as contaminated as her skin or could she be a meal for a Harvester?

"Jimmy . . ." Lieutenant Montgomery stopped. He looked ill and angry. "Cyrus couldn't take a struggling woman on public transportation. We've checked with the taxicab companies. None of them sent a taxi to pick up a fare near the Courtyard's Main Street entrance. Right now we have people at the Chestnut Street station making calls to all the car rental places in the city."

"He might have stolen a vehicle," Burke said, looking at Vlad. "That's what Commissioner Alvarez means by a starting point. Cyrus Montgomery can't have used any kind of public transportation—not taxi, bus, or train. Which means he's in some kind of private vehicle. You need papers to cross borders these days, so Cyrus can't travel to another region. And Agent O'Sullivan already spoke with Governor Hannigan about the situation. All the official border crossings are on alert, and I just don't see Cyrus having the skills needed to try to go off road through the wild country to reach another region."

"He could drive north to a town and take a boat across Lake Tahki," Alvarez said.

"Possible," Burke agreed, "but all the villages along the Northeast side of Lake Tahki are Intuit, *terra indigene*, or human settlements controlled by the Others. I talked to Steve Ferryman, who is the mayor of Ferryman's Landing. He's sending out an e-mail alert to every Intuit village he can reach, informing them that Meg Corbyn was abducted."

Burke leaned toward Vlad. He wagged a finger to indicate the humans at the table. "First we need to identify the car. Then we need to know what help you can give us. It's possible that Cyrus has found a hidey-hole in the city and is lying low, thinking the search won't stay hot that long."

"It will stay hot forever," Vlad whispered. "Or, when Winter hears of this, it will stay very, very cold for a long time."

Burke paled—the only sign that he understood exactly what the threat meant. "Cyrus won't want to stay in a city where he can't exploit Ms. Corbyn's abilities. Assuming he's already beyond the city limits, he's in the wild country. We'll figure out how he got Meg out of the city, what kind of vehicle he's driving. What information is most useful to the *terra indigene* in the wild country? A shape? A color? I'm assuming make and model of car means nothing. I'm also assuming not everyone understands human letters and numbers."

"Colors and shapes," Elliot said. "Most of the *terra indigene* who would watch the land around the right-of-ways would know a big truck from a pickup from a car."

"And the Crowgard are very good at recognizing faces," Vlad added.

"We have a recent photo of Cyrus," Montgomery said, sounding like he was swallowing tiny shards of bone. "From when he was brought in for questioning about the theft of meat in the Market Square. But Ms. Corbyn . . ."

"Ah . . ." Kowalski raised a couple of fingers. "I took a few pictures recently of Meg, Merri Lee, and Ruthie. I also have a shot of Meg and Sam. Before coming to this meeting, I gave my digital camera to Lorne at the Three Ps. He's over there now, cropping one of the photos and running off some copies."

"Well done," Burke said. Then to Vlad, "With your permission, we'll e-mail the shot of Ms. Corbyn to every police station in the Northeast."

Vlad hesitated. Most of the *cassandra sangue* were well hidden from the humans who would abuse them. At least, the ones who had wanted to get away from the compounds were well hidden. Meg's picture had been on a wanted poster a few months ago when her owner was trying to find her. He wasn't sure it was smart or safe to remind too many humans that she was out there. After all, what she was learning about herself and how to cope in the outside world was the reason so many other blood prophets were managing to survive without benevolent ownership.

"No," Elliot said. "Simon would never agree to telling humans that Meg was vulnerable. Someone else might kill Cyrus in order to take her. Then we would never find her."

"We understand." Mayor Chen looked at the other men around the table. "Perhaps the photo of Cyrus Montgomery and a description of Ms. Corbyn would be enough?"

Vlad nodded.

Kowalski's mobile phone rang. He excused himself and walked away from the table. He rejoined them a minute later. "Ms. Lee remembered that students sometimes rent their cars to other students for a day or two.

Some stores near the university have bulletin boards where notices are posted. Might be places like that around the tech college too. While it's unlikely that a student would rent his or her car to a stranger who clearly was not a fellow student, it would be another place to look if the rental car companies don't pan out."

Burke pushed away from the table. "If there's nothing else, we'll get to it."

"There's nothing else," Vlad said. He waited until the humans left the building before turning to Elliot. "The meeting with the mayor, the reason you weren't in the consulate, where you might have seen or heard a struggle."

"It wasn't an excuse or part of a plot, if that's what you're asking." Elliot gave him a long look. "Katherine Debany had a dentist appointment—routine checkup. She made the appointment months ago and told me about it last week. Even wrote it in the day planner in my office in case I forgot she wouldn't be in. And I gave Miss Twyla the morning off because the women had caught up on all the work."

Ruthie's mental health day didn't matter. School in the summer ended at lunchtime. The children would have been outside playing regardless.

"We fell for the distraction when that Cyrus started a fight with Montgomery to give that Jack Fillmore an opportunity to find Theral."

"And that gave us an opportunity to end that threat." Elliot sat back. "Would so many of you have been focused on this fight if it hadn't involved the children?"

Vlad thought about that and shook his head. The *terra indigene* protected their young. "It all happened in the time it took a stoplight to change. Simon believed Meg was safe in the daylight. We all did. And so many things could have gone wrong with that Cyrus's plan—Nathan could have stayed until O'Sullivan returned with the food; cars could have jammed up, blocking that Cyrus's escape from the delivery area or even delaying the time when he was able to pull into the delivery area; Meg could have insisted that Skippy wait to pee until O'Sullivan returned. If she had, the door would have been locked and she would have had time to call for help." That was the only bit of information they had gotten out of Skippy—that Meg had opened the door and he had gone out just before the car leaped at him and bit his leg.

If Simon had run to the Liaison's Office instead of preventing Merri Lee from getting crunched between two cars, he would have reached Meg in time to stop that Cyrus from taking her. But he'd protected the pack member who was in immediate danger—a truth that might make it difficult for him to be around Merri Lee in the future, depending on the outcome of this hunt.

Elliot looked uneasy. "I'm his sire, but I think you know Simon better, understand him better. If we don't find Meg, do you think he'll survive?"

"No." The certainty of his answer made Vlad feel cold. "If we lose her, we'll lose him too."

In human form, Henry Beargard was a large man. As a Grizzly, he was massive. But when he walked in his true earth native form as spirit bear, he was much larger than the Grizzly—and still smaller than the two Elders who were visiting the Courtyard. That didn't matter, because he was swelled with rage.

He found them in the part of the Courtyard that bordered Crowfield Avenue. Human eyes couldn't see them, any more than those eyes could see the spirit bear, but some primal instinct sometimes told small predators and prey that *something* was there. Henry knew that by the way a few of the humans who were still trapped in the snow and traffic pileup kept looking toward the fence, searching for the cause of their alarm.

<This is your fault.> Henry rose on his hind legs, ready for battle.

The Elders turned toward him in surprise. <No. The steeds made the snow and trapped the little predators.>

<Your fault,> Henry repeated. <Simon told you that Cyrus was a bad kind of human, not one we wanted around the Courtyard, because he would cause trouble.>

<Small trouble for other humans,> they replied dismissively. <Not big trouble that threatens the world. And the trouble over there was nothing but a puppy fight.>

Almost blind with rage, Henry took a step toward them. <That Cyrus stole Meg!>

<It took a human female from the Courtyard?> No longer dismissive since they had promised to help protect the female pack.

<It took the sweet blood, the howling not-Wolf, the one who will be the Wolfgard's mate!>

An odd, and terrible, silence.

Humans couldn't see the Elders, but Henry could. He watched them stare at the buildings across the street, where that human pup had conveniently caused trouble. He watched their hackles rise. He saw their lips curl away from teeth that could tear apart something his size, let alone a human.

<Distraction,> Henry said. <Humans killed Wolfgard in Thaisia as a distraction for their war against the *terra indigene* living near Cel-Romano. That Cyrus used his pup as a distraction so that he could steal the not-Wolf away from us.>

Namid's teeth and claws turned away from the street and the puny humans and fixed their eyes on him. They had seen how a big distraction worked and, in turn, had used it themselves when Elders and Elementals had struck humans here in Thaisia to cause confusion before they crushed the enemy in Cel-Romano. They had seen big distractions but hadn't understood that a small one could be just as dangerous.

Finally they said, <We made a mistake keeping the small trouble here.>

<Yes, you did,> Henry agreed.

They didn't like that. They didn't like that at all.

<That Cyrus doesn't know how to take care of a not-Wolf,> Henry said. <He could hurt her, even kill her.>

They snarled at him, angered by his words. But they didn't attack. Instead they moved past him, one on either side, leaving his back exposed no matter which one he turned to face.

He felt them heading toward the center of the Courtyard, where they had staked out a small area as their own.

The Elders had been intrigued enough by Meg and Simon to return to the Courtyard and observe. But they were so used to being the ones who knew what the world needed that they hadn't listened to Simon because that Cyrus was no threat to them.

Henry dropped to all fours and returned to his apartment in the Green Complex. But none of the other residents were there, and a sadness seemed to cling to the building. A piece was missing and might never be found.

He knew Simon was at the Wolfgard Complex, looking after Sam and helping Jane deal with Skippy while she tried to fix as much of the damage to the juvenile's leg and ribs as she could. No one knew yet if it would be enough.

He should go to the Market Square and help Vlad deal with the humans, but he couldn't. Right now, he didn't want to deal with the humans; he wanted to kill them. Better to stay away so that he didn't lash out and gut one of the female pack.

He shifted from spirit bear to his Grizzly form. Then he left the Green Complex and its scent of sadness.

They had made a mistake. They had wanted to watch an insignificant two-legged predator that caused trouble for its own kind, had wanted to understand what that kind of creature might do that could pose a danger to the earth natives who guarded the edges of the wild country and came in contact with small human settlements—what kind of danger it might pose to the smaller shifters who were living in settlements with humans and might absorb too much human badness and become a small enemy to their own kind.

They had thought the male was a troublesome predator but not a particularly dangerous one. But the male had shown cunning and a disregard for his own young. Having observed the other humans who entered the Courtyard and had young, they had not considered that he would do such a thing.

And the not-Wolf was the Wolfgard's chosen mate? When they told the Wolf to consider how much human the *terra indigene* would keep, they had not considered *this* because this was not how new forms of earth natives came into being. Earth natives did not mate with the form they were absorbing. They mated with others of their own kind who had successfully absorbed the form.

But the Wolf and the not-Wolf had changed things. Had changed each other. Could they make something this new? Would the world want what might come from such a mating?

The not-Wolf amused them, even when she sounded like a scoldy squirrel. Maybe then most of all. And the stories of what she and the earth natives did here traveled into the wild country. But if she disappeared, there would be one last, sad story—because they, the Elders, had not understood that the troublesome male was truly dangerous.

They had needed to learn too much too quickly, and they had made a mistake.

Now they would fix it.

CHAPTER 24

Thaisday, Messis 23

Jimmy turned off the car's radio and kept driving. The news was still talking about the weird snowfall that snarled up traffic on Crowfield Avenue in Lakeside. But he'd heard nothing that he needed to be concerned about.

His plan had worked perfectly, as he'd known it would. And he'd been lucky. He'd been a couple of cars back from the delivery entrance when that ITF agent walked out of the delivery area and dashed across the street. By the time he pulled up to the Liaison's Office, the agent was inside the Stag and Hare.

His luck had held when he pulled in fast and clipped that Wolf, and the scar girl ran outside to help the freak. She didn't even look at *him* until he grabbed her arm. Then she tried to fight, so he pulled out a blackjack and gave her a tap on the head. He opened the trunk and dumped her inside, taking a moment to feel her pockets and remove the folding razor. When his back was turned for those few seconds, the Wolf managed to get up on three legs and tried to bite him.

He hit the Wolf over the head with the blackjack, putting everything he had into the blow. Once the Wolf was down, he jumped into the car and pulled out onto Main Street, tires squealing as other drivers hit their brakes and their horns.

He was gone in a couple of minutes, with no one the wiser.

He'd been tempted to take the toll road once he left the city limits, either heading east toward Hubbney or following the shoreline of Lake Etu south and west. But toll roads meant people manning the booths. While there was no reason for anyone to be looking for him—not yet anyway—and no reason to think there was anything suspicious about a dark-skinned man driving an older-model car, the little cha-ching in the trunk might realize why they weren't moving for that minute and start hollering and drawing attention to herself. Couldn't have that, so he'd taken one of the roads that had a route sign and was going in the general direction he wanted to go.

He'd been on the road less than an hour when he spotted a rest area and a sign that indicated the next village was another thirty miles away. The rest area looked rustic. The crappers were probably nothing more than seats positioned over holes in the ground, but if there was no one else there, the place would serve just fine.

He pulled into the rest area, then backed up as close as he could to the side of the small building that was designated for women. No other cars around, but he still checked the men's side as well as the women's before he opened the trunk.

"You evil human! You hurt Skippy!"

The cha-ching tried to sit up without permission. Jimmy slapped her hard enough to split her lip. The slap wouldn't have fazed Sandee, not to the point of looking like she'd taken a hard blow to the head. He hauled his prize out of the trunk and hustled into the women's side of the building. He pushed her down on the dirty floor and pulled the folding razor out of his pocket. He'd heard enough about the scar girls to know you cut them and asked a question. Then they gave you an answer.

But where to cut? He figured he could get a hundred—maybe even two hundred—dollars for a cut, but customers would want fresh skin. He studied the cross-hatching of scars on the top part of her left arm, then looked at the evenly spaced scars on her right arm.

She still seemed dazed from the slap, but when she saw him bring the razor close to her right arm, she started to struggle.

"No, don't," she said.

His hand tightened on her arm, a bruising grip. "You do what I tell you from now on." He made a cut across several of the existing scars. Blood flowed from the wound, running down and pooling where his hand held her arm.

"We're going to a city on the coast," he said. "Tell me what roads to take to avoid being found by the fucking cops. Speak!"

Her gray eyes went blank, and her expression as she began to speak . . . He knew what it meant when a woman had that look. The little bitch needed a man, and she needed one bad.

First he had to concentrate on what she was saying. He didn't need to write this shit down; he'd remember it just fine, but . . .

When she finished speaking, she sighed and stretched out on the floor.

Jimmy dropped the razor and shoved a hand down her pants. Gods! She was hot and wet and just begging for a quick fuck. He reached for his zipper, then froze when he heard car doors slam.

Shit!

He grabbed the razor and almost closed it and put it in his pocket. But he'd dropped it on the floor and he could see bits of dirt on the blade. If he cut her with a dirty razor she could get an infection and be worthless. Did he have time?

Male voices, going into the other side of the building.

He turned on the water in the sink, rinsed off the razor, then dried it with a couple of paper towels before closing it and shoving it into his pocket. He wet a couple more paper towels and wiped the blood off her arm. The cut was still bleeding. Was that normal? He didn't have bandages or any of that first-aid shit. Maybe he'd look for some when he stopped for gas.

Pressing the wet paper towels against the cut, he hauled her to her feet and walked her to the door. He opened it enough to make sure no one was hanging around outside. Then he pulled her outside and dumped her into the trunk. He slammed the lid down and swore fiercely when the latch didn't catch. Fucking piece-of-shit car. Yeah, the car's owner had told him the latch wouldn't catch sometimes if you slammed the lid down hard, which just proved the owner was a pussy.

He slammed the lid again. This time it caught. He got in the car and was pulling out of the rest area when two young men came out of the other side of the building, laughing and talking. Traveling somewhere. They looked in his direction.

Jimmy pulled out of the rest area too fast and bumped onto the road, heading south and east. He didn't notice the trunk lid bounce up a couple of inches before something held it down.

Jolted out of a haze of colliding images, Meg saw a strip of daylight and grabbed the trunk lid before it might be noticed. She couldn't remember anything she'd told Cyrus when he cut her arm, but she had swallowed the blood and the pain and the words when he slapped her and split her lip.

She'd seen only a couple of the images when he cut across the scars of old prophecies and asked his question, but combined with what she'd seen after he slapped her, those images were a start. She had been asking questions of her own ever since her head cleared from

the blow Cyrus gave her when he took her from the
Liaison's Office: How could she escape from this man?
Where could she hide until Simon found her?

She'd seen an image of a trunk lid partially open and
she'd seen . . . Or was it a memory?

Carefully shifting position, Meg took hold of the
trunk lid's catch with her right hand and tucked her left
leg toward her belly until she was able to undo the lacing
on her sneaker. She used the lacing to secure the trunk
lid, leaving just enough space to provide some fresh air
and light. Then she lay back, aware that her arm was
still leaking blood. Not good. Cyrus must have made
the cut a little too deep. But it would clot—eventually.
She hoped.

She had to stay awake and aware. If Cyrus stopped
the car, she needed to untie the lid and hide the shoe-
lace. No guarantee that the lid wouldn't latch on its own
if the car hit a bump or that Cyrus would be so careless
the next time he stopped. But . . .

Yes. She remembered this. A trunk safety release.
After Karl Kowalski had read the new Wolf Team story
where one of the Wolf Team had been trapped in a car
trunk, he told her that all cars made by humans had a
safety release, had even shown her the release on his
car. So she could get out of this trunk even if the lid was
closed. But not while the car was moving. That would
be dangerous for anyone, and the cuts and scrapes on
skin for someone like her would be devastating, leaving
her helpless to the prophecies released with every cut
and scrape.

And then there were the other images she'd seen when
Cyrus split her lip. Images like snapshots of places she'd
never seen. And road signs. STOP! GO BACK! WRONG WAY!

Was she seeing opportunities to escape, along with
warnings that those places weren't the right place?

When she escaped from the Controller, she had followed the visions. There had been other stops, other
towns where she could have left the train. But she had

remained free because she had kept going until she reached Lakeside and the Lakeside Courtyard—a place that had put her out of the Controller's reach. Now, like then, she had to make the whole journey, follow all the visions. If she didn't, she might escape Cyrus but never get back home.

So she would wait. For now she had light and air and the knowledge that, when the time was right, she would escape. There would be more images to mark the trail. Cyrus had taken her razor, but there were other ways to cut skin. She would find them, use them if she had to.

She would escape when the real world matched the vision that *didn't* have a warning sign. Then she would run until she reached the place in the woods that held a grave. That was an image Simon would remember from her prophecy dream—and that was the place where Simon would go to find her.

CHAPTER 25

Thaisday, Messis 23

The police set up roadblocks at every road leading out of Lakeside, but everyone already knew it was too late. With the chaos and blocked traffic on Crowfield Avenue, there had been time for Cyrus Montgomery to get Meg Corbyn out of the city. Officers from each precinct had been assigned to the manhunt, and patrol captains were sending in their findings to Captain Burke as well as Police Commissioner Alvarez.

Nobody had expected any luck at the bus and train stations, but the police checked them anyway, talked to the ticket sellers, showed Cyrus's photo around.

They tried hard to find Meg Corbyn, but the minutes ticked by into an hour—and then two.

While waiting for any news from the police, Vlad, Blair, Nathan, and Officer Debany went through Cyrus Montgomery's apartment, first looking for any clue that would tell them where he might be heading and then looking for whatever drugs Sandee might have ingested before her clash with Leetha. They found her stash of pills hidden beneath the tampons in what looked like an unopened box. They found some money in the fridge's freezer box, hidden in a small, hollowed-out loaf of something labeled cranberry-artichoke bread— an unappealing combination that explained why no one had been hungry enough to thaw out the loaf and discover the money.

After checking the apartment a second time, Debany said, "I think we've found everything there is to find."

"Then it's time to pack up their possessions," Vlad said. "Miss Twyla offered to help with that."

Debany frowned. "Pack? But I had understood that you weren't pressing charges against Sandee."

"We're not. But we are evicting her for breaking our no-drugs rule." Vlad smiled, showing a hint of fang. "If she ever comes within sight of the Courtyard again, the Sanguinati won't bother to bite. We'll just snap her bones, one by one, until we get to her neck."

Debany went white.

"But that is unlikely to happen because either you will arrest her for the drugs you just found and she will go to jail, or she will be on the first train out of Lakeside tomorrow morning."

Debany swallowed hard. "Alone?"

"Alone. As for that Clarence, you may hold him accountable according to your laws for his part in Meg's abduction, or we will hold him accountable according to ours. Either way, he isn't coming back here."

"What about Frances?" Debany asked.

"For now, Eve Denby is looking after Frances and Lizzy since we all feel that it is easier to protect the children if they're all in one place."

Debany gathered the evidence bags. "If any of you or Miss Twyla notice anything else that doesn't look right, give me a call."

"I don't think it will take long for Miss Twyla to pack the carryalls. You should wait a few minutes and take what belongs to that Sandee and that Clarence."

"All right. I'll be nearby." Debany walked out with the evidence bags.

Vlad knew the patrol car was parked in the Courtyard's employee parking lot. The other officer, Hilborn, was still helping to free the motorists who had been buried under several feet of snow—snow that was getting harder to move by the minute as the Messis sun beat down, compacting it and making it heavy with water.

This time no Wolves came to help dig out the cars. This time it was humans with shovels.

Vlad took out his mobile phone and called Twyla Montgomery to let her know she could come over and pack up the things that had belonged to the humans who had stayed here. Then he called Chris Fallacaro to come over and change the locks.

He hadn't seen Henry since they all realized Meg had been taken by that Cyrus. He hadn't seen Tess.

Some of the *terra indigene* in the Courtyard had gotten too close to the humans, had become too involved—had developed feelings that, in the future, might be the very reason they chose to shun contact with humans. If they failed to find Meg, Simon wouldn't remain in Lakeside where he would listen for a voice that would never be heard and search for a scent that would fade day by day. No, Simon would head into the wild country, alone, and simply disappear.

But Vlad would remain in Lakeside with Grandfather Erebus. He wasn't sure Henry would stay. Maybe the Grizzly would relocate to the River Road Community or Great Island, where he would be able to continue working on his sculptures and totems. Maybe he would go farther west. Maybe all the way to Bennett. Elliot would take Sam far from here to a place that had limited contact with humans. As for Tess . . . Vlad wasn't going to think about what would happen to the humans who crossed Tess's path while she looked for some other place.

A pebble dropped in a pond created so many ripples, disturbed the surface of the water, revealed possibilities.

When Meg first came among them, they had seen her as a puzzle, a confusion. But she had become so much more.

It was still possible to find her. There was still time to save her—and Simon.

Jenni, Starr, and Jake Crowgard walked into the Three Ps.

"Hey," the Lorne said. "Any news?"

"You gave the police pack pictures of that Cyrus," Jenni said.

The Lorne nodded. "They're distributing them to the police in the city."

"Those are big pictures. Can you make smaller ones that would fit into this?" Jenni held up a mesh bag no larger than a human hand, with woven handles that a Crow's foot could grasp and carry over a distance.

"I could print some out small enough for that. When do you need them?"

Jenni stared at him. "Now."

The Lorne went behind the wall that hid the computers and the printers. He returned quickly with a piece of paper that held one picture of that Cyrus.

"We need many," she said, wondering for a moment if this human had helped that Cyrus steal their Meg.

"I wanted to be sure it was the right size before I started printing multiples," the Lorne said. "You want them on the photo paper like the ones I did for the police?"

"Yes."

While they waited, Jenni looked at the postcards in the spin rack. The police had found one in the sorting room addressed to her. From the Jana. She hoped their Meg had read it and smiled before . . .

Lorne returned to the counter with a stack of photos that would fit in the mesh bags. The Crows took them and hurried back to the Crowgard Complex. Every Crow had acquired a small bag to carry little treasures. Now the bags would carry something else.

Once all the photos were distributed and put into the bags, all the Crowgard in the Lakeside Courtyard shifted to their Crow form, picked up the bags, and flew away. They flew hard, in all directions. While waiting for Jenni, Crows who knew about the telephone called Crowgard in *terra indigene* settlements, telling them about the theft of their Meg, telling them to meet up with the Lakeside Crowgard.

Crows who lived and worked at one of the *terra indigene* farms met up with Jenni, who pulled one of the photos of the enemy out of the mesh bag so that all the Crowgard could study the face. This enemy would stay on human roads, so that was where the Crows should search.

Crows flew off in small groups. One Crow took Jenni's mesh bag with the photo and flew hard to meet the Crowgard farther down the road, who would study the face of the enemy and tell more Crows, who would tell more Crows, who would tell more Crows.

Simon ran back to Howling Good Reads. Having let himself in by the back door, he bounded up the stairs to the office, where he had a spare set of clothes. After shifting to human and getting dressed, he went to the Liaison's Office.

There was nothing to track, no scent to follow to find Meg. Unable to stand being around humans, he had gone to the Green Complex and lain on her bed for a while, breathing in her scent. As it always did, her scent soothed him so that he started to think past the anger and fear.

Meg had dreamed about being thirsty. She had dreamed about finding a body—or at least a cold hand. Details of something she had seen in the prophecy cards? Maybe, before she was taken, she had asked another question, had selected more cards. Skippy had been wounded and needed help, so Simon hadn't looked for cards once the Wolves confirmed that Meg was gone.

She had seen where her journey ended. He just

needed to figure out how to find that specific place. When he did, he would also find her.

He walked into the sorting room and stopped, not sure what to think when he saw Merri Lee, Ruthie, Theral, and Agent O'Sullivan already standing around a map of the Northeast Region that was spread out on the big wooden table. Next to the map was the notebook Meg used to write down the images on the prophecy cards.

"We could use your input if you feel up to it," O'Sullivan said.

Simon reluctantly approached the table. He'd wanted to look at the notes Meg had made about the last vision; he hadn't wanted to deal with any humans. But here was part of the human pack sniffing around for clues.

Merri Lee tapped the notebook. "Tombstone means a grave, but it's not Meg's. It isn't. It's something she'll see in a woods somewhere."

"Which made me wonder if there were any failed settlements that might be near any of the current roads," Ruthie said, waving a hand over the map. "Someplace small from a few decades ago, someplace that could have had a graveyard. By now, the buildings might be gone and the land might be wooded, and the gravestones could be weathered to the point of looking like ordinary stones."

"Would the *terra indigene* have any records of places reclaimed by the wild country where humans might have been?" O'Sullivan asked.

Simon shook his head. "If a place was reclaimed, it either disappeared or the *terra indigene* turned the buildings into a settlement and gave the area a different name. But Meg didn't see a tombstone or grave in the prophecy dream; she saw a body hidden under some leaves."

It sounded like a tree full of squirrels had suddenly landed in the room. So much chatter out of so few bodies.

He snarled at the female pack. They ignored him and kept chattering, so he snarled louder. They kept asking him questions and questions and questions, but they wouldn't stop talking long enough for him to answer.

"Mr. Wolfgard has more information," O'Sullivan boomed.

The chattering human squirrels shut up and stared at him. That annoyed him enough that he wanted to nip someone, but he decided to take advantage of the momentary quiet and told them about Meg's dream.

"A white hand," O'Sullivan murmured. "Not Cyrus Montgomery, then. As a member of the governor's Investigative Task Force, I can mobilize the police in every city in the Northeast."

"Hasn't the governor already done that?" Ruthie asked.

"Yes, but my being part of ITF means they'll give any requests coming from me or the other agents top priority." O'Sullivan looked at Simon. "Any sense from Meg if the body was adult? Male or female?"

Simon tried to think. Couldn't remember.

"Well, I'll do what I can," O'Sullivan said.

Simon understood what wasn't said: there were a lot of humans missing these days. Some had disappeared by choice, while others hadn't survived the Elders' wrath. A lot of those bodies would never be found.

O'Sullivan hurried back to the consulate to make his phone calls, leaving Simon with the female pack.

"We'll find her," Ruthie said.

"She didn't see anyone else in the dream?" Merri Lee asked. "Then she got away from that man."

Alone and thirsty and scared. Was that better? "When?" he countered. "A day from now? A month? A year?"

"Why not an hour ago?" Merri Lee demanded. "Meg is smart."

Simon retreated to HGR. Yes, Meg was smart and had escaped a bad human once before. But he also knew better than the female pack how many "smart" blood prophets had died in the past few weeks when they could no longer cope with the outside world.

The Elders' anger rippled beneath the skin of the world, making big trees shiver, scaring flocks of birds into flight. The Elementals' fury was a scent in the air, a taste in all the creeks and streams that flowed in the Northeast.

That anger, that fury, became a message to all the *terra indigene*.

The sweet blood. The howling not-Wolf. Broomstick Girl. Taken away from the *terra indigene* by a human.

Find the human.

But more important, find the not-Wolf.

Jimmy backed into what looked like a farm road—dirt with no road sign or marker at all. Taking a bottle of water, he walked to the back of the car and opened the trunk.

"You want some water, cha-ching?"

"My name is Meg!"

"Now it's cha-ching. You know why? Because that's the sound of money." He opened the bottle of water and tipped it so the water began to pour onto the ground.

"Stop!" Meg said.

"Ask nice." He saw the defiance in her eyes. Well, he could fix that. He dropped the water bottle, shoved her back in the trunk when she tried to scramble out, and pulled the razor out of his pocket. He pinned her down with one hand, flicked the razor open, and held it over her face. "You sass me, I'll cut your face. I'll cut you so much you won't look human anymore and people will run from you, screaming. You want that? Do you? Answer me!"

"N-no."

"Then do what you're told." Remembering the way she became a hot pussy after speaking prophecy, he added, "And maybe I'll give you something nice."

Yeah, he could haul her out of the trunk and put her on the backseat for a few minutes. Maybe even let her stay there for a while as a reward.

He grabbed her right arm, moved it into position, and made another cut across the old scars. "Where do I go to keep ahead of the cops? Speak!"

"Crows watching roads. Photo of Cyrus Montgomery. Crows looking at cars. Calling police."

"Where?" Jimmy shouted. Fuck! They had a photo of him? "Where?"

She sighed, her visions revealed.

He pulled her up and made another cut. "How do I avoid the fucking birds?"

He listened hard, too scared to be distracted by lust as she spoke route numbers and a name. He listened, looked at his wristwatch. "Shit." Had to get moving right now if he was going to stay ahead of the search.

He closed the trunk, got back in the car, and drove off as fast as he dared. He had to find that roadside diner where he could blend in. If the cops put up a roadblock before he reached it, he didn't know the names of any places where humans were living around here—if there were any places. But as sure as shit, the cops would know. No reason to think they knew about the car yet, so he just needed to find a place to catch his breath. Needed to get ahead of the freaking birds and the freaking cops.

Jimmy drove, glancing in the rearview mirror, looking to either side, as sweat beaded his face and made his hands slick on the wheel.

Maybe the cops weren't the worst things looking for him.

The visions from old prophecies collided with the images from the new cuts, producing things that looked so bizarre they made her queasy. Clocks melted, dripping over the edges of tables like ice cream on a summer day, and Skippy ate all the numbers that ran off the clockfaces. Stumps of trees tore roots out of the ground to become twisted legs that scampered through the woods while the stumps themselves sprouted black feathers on the tops and grew huge mouths with teeth made of saws. Just before her mind shut down, Meg saw a series of images that revealed the next stage of the journey. Then rocks rolled together to form the shape of a wolf—and they howled.

"I don't need supervision, Crispin," Twyla said as she folded another small top and set it on the bed. "I've packed a carryall before."

"Procedure, Mama," Monty replied holding a pen and small notebook. "We need to inventory everything we're removing so that no one can claim later that someone took his or her possessions."

Twyla turned to him. "You think Frances is going to make a fuss over a shirt after what happened today? And if something is missing, one of the Wolves can come over here with her and help her find it."

"She's not the one who will make a fuss."

"I don't think Cyrus is going to call and ask any of us to forward his clothes, do you?" Twyla checked the closet and chest of drawers. She went down on her knees and one hand, lifted the sheet and lightweight blanket, and checked under the bed. "This place needs a good cleaning. The only thing that woman ever tried to keep clean was herself, and even that . . ."

Monty helped his mother to her feet. "Right now this apartment is part of the investigation. After . . . Well, I think Eve will appreciate some help cleaning it up."

She placed her hand over his. "Why are you here, Crispin? One of the young officers could be doing this. You should be out there, helping Mr. Simon find that girl."

"My brother abducted Meg. My nephew created the diversion that helped him do it. If my involvement provides a loophole . . ."

She gave his hand a light slap. "You're feeling guilty.

So am I. Cyrus was here because we are here. We're not responsible for what he chose to do. But either of us using Cyrus as an excuse for not doing what we can now?" She shook her head. "When you needed help with Lizzy, Mr. Simon stood by you, helped you protect your own. Now you do the same for him, as a police officer and as a man."

Monty put his arms around her and held on for a long moment. "You're right, Mama. You're right." He released her and stepped back. "Two of these carryalls need to go to the station, so I'll wait until you get everything packed. Then I'll go to the station and see what I can do about locating Jimmy."

Clarence's clothes were mostly in a pile on the floor. Twyla picked up a piece, sniffed it, and made a face. "I'll wash these first. See if you can find anything clean for him right now."

Monty found a T-shirt that looked like it had been run over by a lawn mower, but it smelled clean enough. "Is tattered the new fashion in Toland?"

"Boys," Twyla said with a shrug.

Not sure how to interpret that, despite having been a boy himself, Monty went into the living room to call Captain Burke while Twyla went into the other bedroom to deal with Sandee's clothes and personal items.

"Any news?" Monty asked when Burke answered the phone.

"Nothing yet, but we've eliminated all the car rental places, so the vehicle Cyrus is driving was either stolen or rented from a private citizen."

"Needle in a haystack."

"Officers are going to places around the university that might have bulletin boards for such things."

"Anything I can do?"

"Crispin?" Twyla called.

"Supply whatever assistance you can to the Courtyard," Burke said.

"Crispin!"

"Captain, I have to go." Monty ended the call and hurried into the bedroom where Twyla had been packing up Sandee's things. "Mama?"

Twyla held out a plain glass jar with some kind of white cream inside. "Careful. It looks like skin cream but it has a sharp smell, like something I would use for cleaning. Could this be the stuff that hurt Miss Leetha?"

Monty opened the jar and took a cautious sniff. Then he closed the jar. Had someone developed something that wouldn't harm a human but was toxic to the Sanguinati? Or had the substance been aimed at anyone living in the apartments—especially the women, who would be more likely to use a moisturizer—and Leetha had been injured by accident?

"I have to take this in and get it tested," he said. He eyed the makeup and powders and lotions. "I'll take all of this into evidence. Don't touch any more of it, okay, Mama?"

Twyla nodded. "I'll pack up the clothes."

He noticed she didn't offer to wash anything for Sandee—or for Jimmy.

Pulling out his mobile phone again, Monty called Vlad and told him his suspicion about the skin cream and suggested that the Sanguinati healer talk to a doctor at Lakeside Hospital if the healer didn't have any experience with treating someone who had ingested a toxic human-made substance. Then he called Burke in case the substance *was* intended to harm any human who put it on her skin. Finally he called Debany, since Kowalski was escorting Clarence from the hospital to the station. The boy had stitches on his back and shoulders from the Hawk's talons, but she hadn't raked him as deeply as she could have—as she would have if she had known about Meg being abducted.

"Officer Debany, I need evidence bags brought to the apartment."

"But we checked everything," Debany protested.

"We missed something."

*   *   *

Jimmy sat at the end of the counter, chomping on a hamburger and fries. He'd found the diner with the name the cha-ching had given him. So far he was ahead of the cops and the freaks, and he intended to stay that way.

Two cars pulled in. A deeply tanned young man and woman got out of one car and three teenage boys got out of the other. As they walked into the diner, they were all talking.

"Weirdest thing I ever saw," one of the teenage boys said. "Keeping pace with the cars."

"It was creepy the way they kept trying to look into the car," the woman said.

"I slowed down and took off my sunglasses," her companion said. "They seemed okay with us driving on after that."

"They're looking for somebody," another teenage boy said. "Did you see the roadblock? We saw a couple of cars the cops had pulled over and were searching. I think if you didn't slow down enough for the Crows to look at you, they signaled to the cops somehow to block the road. Like if you didn't slow down, you had something to hide."

Jimmy dropped the hamburger on the plate. It wasn't sitting so well anymore.

"We heard on the radio that roadblocks were being set up at all the towns in the Northeast," the woman said. Then she shuddered. "A manhunt like this? Somebody must have done something really bad."

The two groups split up as the waitress showed them to their booths. But other men eating at the counter turned to ask them about the roadblocks and the Crows who were pacing cars.

The men at the counter shook their heads and agreed that this was a bad place to be if the Others were looking for you. Crows and Hawks were often seen around the rest stops or small places like this. The men who drove delivery trucks and made regular runs along this route swore the Others knew their trucks and their faces. Didn't bother them any. In fact, it was advantageous when some of their deliveries were made to little towns that looked human but weren't.

Stomach burning and appetite gone, Jimmy paid for his meal and accepted the offer of a to-go container because leaving the food would give the waitress a reason to remember him. He bought a small bottle of water and went to the car.

As soon as he opened the trunk a few inches the bitch tried to push the lid up a little more.

"Get your fucking fingers back inside or I'll slam the lid on them."

Her fingers retreated.

He tossed the water bottle into the trunk. "If you mess yourself before I let you out, you'll be breathing in the stink."

He closed the trunk, got behind the wheel, and dropped the to-go container on the passenger seat. Then he headed south. He'd passed unmarked dirt roads that intersected with the paved roads. He'd take one of those as soon as he could.

Meg struggled to open the water bottle. After she got it open and managed a couple of sips, she felt the rough edge of the plastic screw top. Nothing a normal person would think about, but it might just be sharp enough to cut her kind of skin.

But not yet.

She screwed the top back on the bottle. She'd probably dump the water when she made the cut. She didn't want to lose it, so she would wait. She needed to wait. She'd seen enough when Cyrus opened the trunk to know this wasn't the right place to escape even though she'd heard voices and thought there were other people around.

Then the car made an odd turn and bumped hard. Because she was unprepared, her teeth snapped shut, catching the edge of her tongue—the spot that had prickled and burned a couple of times over the past few days.

Meg swallowed the blood, swallowed the agony, swallowed the words. She heard the warning blast of a truck horn and saw the moment when she would run away from Cyrus Montgomery.

Douglas Burke walked into the interrogation room, dropped a folder on the table, and sat down opposite Sandee Montgomery. They had taken her to Lakeside Hospital for treatment as soon as Monty called about the substance in the jar. Judging by the way her chest and shoulders looked, he thought the lab that tested for poisons and toxic substances would find a stew of caustic chemicals mixed into that skin cream. She hadn't even noticed that something was wrong until she started to come down from whatever she'd taken, and he wondered what would have happened to her if she hadn't gone outside when the kids were fighting, if Leetha Sanguinati hadn't been injured from contact with her skin.

He had some thoughts about why she might have been targeted, but discussing that with the station chief would have to wait.

"Where's CJ?" Sandee demanded.

"Not available," Burke replied, giving her his fierce-friendly smile.

"I want a lawyer."

"You can certainly call one, although you're not being charged with anything."

"Then why am I here?"

Burke sat back. "Where can you go?"

"Back to the apartment."

He shook his head. "You broke the *terra indigene*'s

no-drug rule and have been evicted, effective immediately. Your belongings are being held here at the station until you decide which train you're taking tomorrow morning. Not a lot of choices first thing in the morning, but if you're still in Lakeside when that first train pulls out, the Sanguinati will gather in force and hunt you down." He opened the folder and put a handwritten list on the table, turning it for her to read. "These are the towns where you're allowed to resettle. They're still in the Northeast, but they're all small. No Toland, no Hubb NE, no Shikago for you. Small, isolated towns where everyone will know your business before you have time to unpack. I imagine some of those towns would have need of a prostitute. That is how you earn a living, isn't it?"

Her eyes flashed with anger, and she looked like she might try to rake him with her long nails. "You got no right to talk to me like that. You got no right to try to run me out of town. What about my husband, my kids?"

"I'm not the one running you out of town. In fact, the Others would like you to stay, if only for the excuse of killing you slowly. As for your children, Frances has been removed from your home for her own safety. Or weren't you aware that your son was making the first moves to pimp his little sister?"

She knew. He saw it in her eyes before she looked down at the table.

"Clarence is an accessory to the abduction of a young woman, and he will go to prison."

"What?" Fear, and a hefty dose of shock, filled her face.

"Cyrus Montgomery abducted a young woman around noon today. He managed to get out of the city with her. Every police department in every city in the Northeast is now involved in the manhunt. We will find him. The only question will be if Cyrus and Clarence are charged with kidnapping or with murder if the woman doesn't survive."

Sandee swayed. "What?" The word was barely a sound. "Clarence is a boy. He's just a boy."

"His crime is not a youthful mistake, Sandee. His actions, like yours, were an attack on the *terra indigene*. Going to prison is the only chance he has of surviving. The Others don't often kill children, but I can tell you with no doubt at all that Clarence won't last a day if we release him."

He'd gutted her, finally got past her self-involvement for her to understand how bad things were.

"I want to talk to CJ," Sandee said.

"No."

"Twyla then. I want to talk to Twyla."

"No." Burke pulled out a photograph of the unlabeled jar of skin cream and set it on the table. "Want to tell me where you got this?"

"Piss off."

He shrugged. "We're testing it—along with all your other lotions—but I'm pretty sure this is what injured the Sanguinati who bit you. So you should know that, no matter where you resettle, the Sanguinati are going to be watching you from now on. They'll know everyone you talk to, everyone you sleep with, every purchase you make, legal or otherwise. And sooner or later, they will kill you."

"You've got to protect me!"

"No one is going to start a pissing contest with the *terra indigene* to protect you, not when it could end with the whole city being destroyed."

"I'll never be safe," she whispered.

Burke leaned forward and tapped the photograph. "Tell me about this. Tell me where you got it, what you know about who's making it—because this is a death sentence for the people of this city, maybe for people in every city. We'll have corpses stacked floor to ceiling in the morgue just like we did after that storm last month. You tell me where you got this, and I'll arrest you for possession of drugs and you can go to jail for a little while. Long enough for the Sanguinati to forget about you. You wouldn't be free, but you'd have a place to sleep and three meals a day because the prisons have their own farms and grow most of their own food—and you'll stay alive. That's a better deal than you'll get outside."

In the end, she told him what he wanted to know and he arrested her for the drugs and had her taken away to be processed.

Already tired and knowing they had a long way to go before any of them could breathe easy—if they could ever again—Burke walked out of the interrogation room and found Commander Louis Gresh waiting for him.

"You heard?" Burke asked, tipping his head to indicate the observation room.

"Sometimes you're a bastard," Gresh said quietly.

"I got the information we needed, and I made the deal that would give Sandee and Clarence a chance to live."

"Deal with who?"

Burke shook his head. The phone call hadn't come from Vladimir Sanguinati; it had come from Stavros, who had been the Toland Courtyard's problem solver—the one who made all kinds of problems disappear. And Stavros had made it very clear how the Sanguinati would respond if Burke didn't uncover information about the new weapon the humans had developed to smear on their skin.

Thank the gods it hadn't been meant as a weapon against the Sanguinati. It was petty and personal and cruel, but he was confident the investigation would confirm that Sandee Montgomery had been the intended target.

"I have work to do." Burke pushed past Gresh and almost ran into Monty.

"Steve Ferryman and Roger Czerneda are here," Monty said. "They have information—something we need but can't show to the *terra indigene*. They're waiting in your office."

The three men hurried to the office, Burke in the lead.

Oh gods, Burke thought when he saw their faces.

Roger Czerneda pulled a piece of paper out of his shirt pocket. "License plate number. I've already sent it to the authorities in the Intuit communities that might be anywhere along the route."

"Where did you get this?" Monty asked.

Louis Gresh took the paper. "I'll call the motor vehicle department and start looking for the vehicle's owner."

The moment Gresh was out the door, Burke turned to Ferryman. "What else?"

Ferryman hesitated. Then he opened a manila envelope and pulled out a piece of paper but didn't turn it around for them to see. "The Intuits have communications cabins near the tip of Lake Superior, one in the Midwest Region and the other in the Northeast. They're located close enough to deliver messages from one region to the other via citizens band radios. An urgent message came in from Tolya Sanguinati, who had received it from Jackson Wolfgard."

Burke felt his blood go cold. An urgent message from Jackson Wolfgard meant one thing: the young blood prophet living in Sweetwater had seen something.

"So Hope saw the license plate?" Burke asked.

"And this." Ferryman turned the paper around, revealing the drawing.

Monty sagged against Burke's desk.

Hope's vision drawing was a partial map showing the roads leading out of Lakeside. Only the roads running south and east, and one road was drawn heavier than the others—the road Cyrus Montgomery must have taken.

The drawing also showed the back of a brown car, with the license plate clearly rendered. The trunk was partially open. Meg Corbyn looked out of that dark space, her arms and clothes smeared with blood.

But it was her eyes that chilled Burke, because he couldn't tell if those blank eyes meant she was seeing visions or if they meant she was dead.

CHAPTER 26

Thaisday, Messis 23

Needing gas, Jimmy found his way back to a paved road and drove until he came to a cluster of businesses, including a gas station and a place called Miller's Trading Post. He pulled up to a pump at the gas station and filled up the tank. There was a small diner, but the trading post might have food and drinks too, and the cha-ching should be properly grateful for some food by now. Then he saw the way the old guy at the cash register looked at him and looked at the car when he came in to pay for the gas.

Fuck! Did the cops know about the car already? How'd they find out? The kid who owned it had rented it to him for the day and wouldn't be calling the cops about it yet, so how did they know what he was driving?

He stared at the old guy, daring him to pretend he had balls enough to take on a man years younger and heavy with muscle, not a beer belly.

Having sufficiently cowed the old guy, Jimmy walked out of the gas station, not looking at the other businesses. But he was pissed that he couldn't go into that trading post and pick up a few things for the road, pissed that he couldn't sit down in the little diner for a while.

He hadn't gotten as far from Lakeside as he needed to go. He'd thought he'd have at least a day with CJ sending out inquiries and shit to places like Shikago and Hubbney. But he was still in the middle of the Finger Lakes, which was fucking nowhere, and he had to find a place where he and the cha-ching could go to ground near a bus depot or train station so that he could ditch the car. If an old fart at a nowhere gas station had heard something that made him look at the car, then the cops were going to be all over anyone driving any of the roads heading away from Lakeside. He'd thought that talk about a region-wide manhunt was just a reporter's way of hyping a story. But if all the cops really were hunting for him . . .

Had to get some distance from this place before the old fart decided he had balls enough to call the cops. Had to find an empty piece of road. Then he had a few questions for the bitch in the trunk.

Meg drifted among the visions that folded into one another—the result of tangled prophecies. Unable to anticipate the jolts and bumps, she knocked her arm against something in the trunk, and one of the new cuts reopened, leaked blood. Showed her . . . things.

Human bodies mounded on cracked, baked soil, rotting in the sun.

Bloated bodies washed up onshore, a feast for crabs.

The land burning, the sky a cloud of black smoke. New things? Old things?

Cities drowning while blood dripped from water faucets.

Sitting in the back of a car, hugging Simon.

Nail. Tire. Balloon leaking air.

Sam bringing down his prey—a human—while another human hit Skippy with a club that had a metal hook at one end.

Old things? New things? Had she told the Cyrus

Controller about those images? Had he asked? Didn't have to tell if he didn't ask. *Wouldn't* tell if he didn't ask.

A tombstone made from a mound of old leaves.

Was that past or future?

She was property again, a thing again. Weak. Helpless.

No. She *wasn't* weak or helpless. She lived with Wolves, and she could run fast and far. There was a place where she could hide from the Cyrus Controller. She would follow the images and escape. Like she did the last time.

Then the car slowed down. Stopped. And Meg had one clear thought as Cyrus Montgomery opened the trunk and hauled her out: *It's time.*

Radio stations throughout the Northeast continued to interrupt programming with special bulletins about the region-wide hunt for Cyrus Montgomery, a man accused of abducting a young woman from the city of Lakeside. The police had issued a description of the man and the car, including the license plate number. They also gave a description of the young woman—short black hair, gray eyes, fair skin. A scar on the right side of her jaw.

Even radio stations in towns too far away to be within the target zone were running the story, keeping their citizens apprised of the dangerous situation—not because they thought this man would reach their town before he was caught. No, they were keeping the citizens apprised because they had seen the Hawks and Eagles soaring over the roads, watching; they had seen the Crows flying low, attempting to inspect any car coming into town.

They didn't know why this particular woman was important enough for this kind of attention, but they knew if the *terra indigene* were this involved in the hunt, there were good reasons for humans to be afraid.

* * *

Meg didn't struggle when Cyrus hauled her out of the trunk. Her legs were too stiff and she felt a little dizzy. Lack of food, loss of blood. She couldn't think about those things now. She had to focus on the moment when she would escape.

"You left out a few things, bitch," Cyrus said, looking and sounding menacing.

Meg kept one hand on the car. Her legs and feet tingled and burned, but she thought that was circulation and not prophecy. "When the *cassandra sangue* speak prophecy, we don't remember the images. It's up to the listener to remember."

His hand closed into a fist. "You didn't say it right."

"Maybe you should have been listening instead of playing with yourself." The words fell out of her mouth as if she'd rehearsed them—or read them somewhere.

Cyrus gave her a nasty smile. "Don't need to be playing with myself when you're so wet and horny after you're cut."

Had he . . . ?

Her courage started to crack as suppressed memories threatened to rise and overwhelm her, but she didn't have time for old hurts. Cyrus didn't know much about blood prophets, and that lack of knowledge was a weapon. "If you used me for sex, then it's *your fault* that you're not getting accurate prophecies."

"What're you talking about?"

"They don't use us for sex," Meg lied. "Ever. It dilutes the accuracy of the prophecies. Being used that way can drop the accuracy of the prophecy by fifty percent for several days."

"If you're not seeing things right, it's not because of me." Cyrus stared at her. "You been doing the nasty with that Wolf?" He stepped closer. "Is that why you've been telling me stuff that's wrong?"

"I don't remember most of what I see, but I remember one thing, Cyrus Montgomery. The Crows are going to eat your eyes."

Images collided for a moment, and she felt a blow before his hand connected with her face so that she was already turning and falling against the car.

She looked up and saw the freight truck. About half the size of a tractor-trailer, it could handle the roads that wound through the wild country to small human communities that needed supplies. It wasn't a huge truck, but it was big enough.

The sharp look on the driver's face. The warning blast of the horn.

Meg bolted in front of the truck and avoided being struck by a finger's length. She ran across the road, ran across the grass verge, and disappeared into the trees, following the game trail she had seen in the visions. She ran hard—not play-prey pursued by friends who would gently bump her and lick her and laugh a little at the panting human. This time the predator was real.

She heard Cyrus shouting, swearing, searching. But she was short and wasn't wearing bright clothes, and the game trail forked. She took the right-hand trail and kept running.

"You come back here, bitch! You come back right now or I will beat you black!"

After searching for several fruitless minutes, Cyrus scrambled back to the verge and crossed the road to the car. He didn't have time for this shit. The truck hadn't stopped after the bitch dashed across the road, but he'd had the impression that the driver was reaching for a radio or mobile phone, was going to tell someone about the car and the girl.

Had to move, had to get away from here. Just because the truck hadn't stopped, that didn't mean it wouldn't pull in to the first place on the road where there were other people.

He'd backtrack; that's what he'd do. That way he

wouldn't end up behind the truck and the man who had seen the bitch. Yeah, he'd backtrack, maybe stop at one of those little towns in the Finger Lakes long enough to pick up bleach or some other shit that would erase the blood in the trunk. Then even if the cops found him, what could they prove? He'd rented a car, all legal and aboveboard, and gone for a drive. He was heading back to Lakeside to return the car. What was all the fuss? They couldn't prove the bitch had been with him. If she took off, what was that to him?

Jimmy turned the car around and headed back the way he'd come—and didn't notice that the right rear tire was rapidly going soft.

"Simon!"

Turning at the sound of Greg O'Sullivan's voice, Simon dropped the books he'd been moving off the display table in order to have something to do.

O'Sullivan burst into the front area of Howling Good Reads. "The car's been spotted."

Simon glanced at Vlad, who had been working behind the checkout counter, then focused on the ITF agent. "Meg?"

The ITF agent shook his head. "Not—" He pulled out his mobile phone and looked at the caller's number. "It's Burke. Yes, Captain? They were? Where?"

Simon moved closer to O'Sullivan, trying to hear.

"I'll be ready." O'Sullivan hung up. "A truck driver reported seeing a man and woman arguing by the side of the road. The woman's general description matches Meg's, and it was on the same road as the first report of the car. Police from the communities nearest to those locations are on the roads right now, searching for the car. Burke is picking me up. Lieutenant Montgomery and Officer Kowalski will be following in a second car. We're heading for the last known location." He hesitated. "The truck driver thought the woman ran into the woods. We can arrange for a couple of officers with search-and-rescue dogs to meet us there if you'd rather wait . . ."

"The Wolfgard can find Meg better than some dog," Simon snarled.

O'Sullivan looked relieved, which made Simon feel more forgiving about his suggesting dogs in the first place.

"I'll be ready when Burke gets here." He rushed upstairs to the office, stripped, stuffed his clothes into a carry sack, then shifted. He dragged the carry sack to the stairs, then gave it a push so that it rolled to the landing. Another push landed the carry sack on the floor of the stock room.

O'Sullivan arrived at HGR's back door carrying a daypack. "Water and food. The police already have first-aid kits in their vehicles." He opened the back door just as Burke's black sedan drove up the access way.

By the time they crossed the area behind the stores and reached the back of the Liaison's Office, Burke had turned the car around. He stepped out of the car, opened the back door and the trunk, then held up one finger to indicate he would be a moment. He walked up the access way.

Simon eased into the back of the car, careful not to leap and smack his head on the doorframe. He dropped the carry sack with his clothes on the floor behind Burke's seat, then stretched out on the backseat.

<Simon?> Blair called. <Nathan and I are going with you to find Meg. We'll ride with Montgomery and Kowalski.>

<I'll ride with Burke,> he replied. <There will be enough room in the back for me and Meg.>

His heart pounded. His body quivered with anxiety and anticipation.

The humans had found the car. The Wolfgard would find his Meg.

"So," Burke said dryly, "instead of one Wolf to help us track, we have three?"

Monty nodded. "Blair and Nathan were scratching on the back doors as soon as Kowalski pulled into the delivery area. Don't know what they know, except that the police found something and they're coming with us."

"They can track as well as the dogs," O'Sullivan said. "And if we have to leave the road and the right-of-way area for any reason, the Wolves can smooth the way, right?"

"How much did you tell Simon?" Burke asked.

"That the car was spotted, giving us a starting point for the search," O'Sullivan replied. "And the woman ran into the woods."

Monty's stomach churned. "You didn't tell him about the blood the truck driver saw on her clothes?" Jimmy had cut Meg. Of course he had. He wouldn't resist the chance to hear predictions about his future or how to acquire easy money. Wasn't that the reason he'd taken her in the first place? He'd force her to help him avoid capture. So why had someone spotted the car this quickly? Was it a diversion?

"No reason to mention it yet," Burke said, "or to tell any of the Wolves about Hope Wolfsong's vision drawing."

"Simon may think we're being dishonest," Monty said quietly.

"When Meg Corbyn was last seen, she was alive and well enough to run away from Cyrus," Burke countered. "For now we stick with that. Besides, you've got two large Wolves filling up the backseat of that patrol car. Do you really want them more upset than they already are?"

Monty shook his head.

Burke waited a beat. "Lieutenant, I can assign someone else for this."

"No, sir. I'm the leader of the team that deals with the Courtyard. So I'll deal with this."

Monty returned to the patrol car. As Kowalski pulled over to let Burke take the lead, Monty prayed to all the gods he could name that Jimmy hadn't done any serious damage to Meg Corbyn. And if Jimmy had, he prayed that his brother would have sense enough to surrender so that he wouldn't have to be the one to put a bullet between Jimmy's eyes.

Meg ran and ran, following paths that blurred or became too sharply focused. Cyrus had cut her across the scars of old prophecies, and he'd made the new cuts too close together. The prophecies weren't distinct because of that. The images bled into one another. Worse, she kept seeing superimposed images, and she couldn't tell what was real and what was part of a vision. She could walk off a cliff because she thought she was walking on a road.

But she had to run no matter what she thought she saw, had to find the right place.

Finally slowing to a walk, she wiped her left hand on her shirt to remove the stickiness. When it felt sticky again a moment later, she finally looked at the blood welling up from a cut.

How had that happened? When had that happened?

She kept walking. She needed water. She needed to figure out which of the visions she'd been seeing for the past little while were the ones that would help her.

Preoccupied with her thoughts and a path that was or wasn't real, she took a step and overbalanced when her foot hovered in air before she rushed headlong down a slope into a small bowl of land.

Her foot caught on something beneath the leaves, propelling her forward. Reaching in front of her, her hands hit something and slid along its length as she fell.

Meg looked at the jacket sleeve. She felt the cold white hand—and screamed.

Jimmy swore and kicked the car. Fucking piece of shit. What was he supposed to do way the fuck out here with a flat tire?

That bitch knew. She *knew*. He should have softened her up, taught her who was boss. If he'd done that, he could have stopped at that trading post and picked up some food and water. He wouldn't be standing out here with *nothing* if she hadn't been such a bitch.

Suddenly he stopped swearing, stopped making noise, and listened to an odd silence he could almost feel against his skin.

The blow knocked him off his feet, lifted him so high he flew through the air and watched a strange rope uncoil from his belt before he hit the ground in the grass verge. When he tried to sit up, he saw the slices in his torso that had been made by big claws sharp enough to cut glass.

As he lay there, unable to move, the air shimmered around him and turned into shapes so old they were remembered only in nightmares.

Something wrong with her ankle—wrong enough that she couldn't walk, couldn't even support her weight enough to stand.

Meg scooted a little farther away from the cold white hand. Then she looked around.

This was it. This was the end of the prophecy. She had found the grave in the woods, the tombstone made of old leaves.

It was cool and dark beneath the trees, but she wasn't cold. It would be night before the temperature dropped enough for her to feel cold. But she was hungry and tired and so very thirsty.

And alone.

But she was part of the Wolfgard pack at Lakeside. Just because she was alone, she wouldn't turn into some blubbering human. She would . . .

"Arroo! Arroo!" *I am here. I am here, Simon. Come find me.* "Ar-r-rooo!" *Please find me.*

Then she turned into a blubbering human after all.

A strange sound. Familiar but not. And nothing made by one of them.

Their kin near Lake Etu had sent out a call to all who could hear them: find the sweet blood howling not-Wolf, the little female called Broomstick Girl.

Could this sound be coming from what they sought?

As they moved toward the sound, their footsteps filled the land with an odd silence.

O'Sullivan took the call, spoke quietly for a minute, then hung up. "The local police found the car."

"Are we on the right road?" Burke asked, his voice neutral.

O'Sullivan nodded. After a minute of brittle silence, he added softly, "They think they found Cyrus Montgomery."

Burke didn't ask what that meant. He already knew.

CHAPTER 27

Thaisday, Messis 23

Snapping out of a light sleep, Meg tried to rub the crusties out of the corners of her eyes without rubbing dirt into her eyes. Had she really heard sirens? The sound carried, but it still meant that, maybe, she wasn't that far from a road that was patrolled.

Of course, not being able to walk meant "not that far" was still too far.

She looked around again. Maybe there was a fallen branch that she could use like a crutch. Or something within reach that she could wrap around the injured ankle.

She looked everywhere—except at the body lying a couple of feet away from her.

Burke pulled onto the left-hand shoulder a few yards in front of the brown car and the police car parked behind it. The officer leaning against the side of the patrol car wore captain's bars and had a look Burke recognized—tough, experienced, and with enough knowledge of what was, no doubt, watching them from the woods to appreciate the danger they were all in at this moment.

"Mr. Wolfgard . . ." Burke didn't bother to say more, because Simon was already scrambling to get out of the car, shifting his front paws enough to have fingers that could pull at the door handle and snarling in frustration when the door wouldn't open.

Burke released the door locks. The moment Simon was outside and no longer interested in them, Burke said quietly to O'Sullivan, "Do what you can to keep Monty up here on the road." Then he pushed out of the car, glancing back at the Lakeside patrol car.

Kowalski didn't bother to pull over to the shoulder of the road. With two Wolves going nuts in the backseat, he just stopped the car, jumped out, and opened a door for them.

Nathan and Blair rushed to join Simon, who was busily sniffing around the brown car. While the local police captain watched, not daring to move closer or move back, they got the doors opened and their large bodies stretched across the seats. They sniffed everything, trying to find the scent they were looking for.

Simon clawed at the trunk, leaving scratches in the paint until Kowalski hurried over and opened the trunk. Suddenly all three Wolves were pushing their heads and shoulders into the trunk, sniffing and sniffing before they left the car and spread out across the road.

And not one of them even looked toward what lay in the center of a square made of yellow crime scene tape and tall garden stakes.

Burke raised a hand and strode toward the other captain. As he came past the brown car, he saw another police officer searching the grass between the tape and the trees.

"Captain Miller?"

The officer nodded. "Are you Burke?"

Burke nodded in turn, then looked at the two objects that had been placed on a pile of shredded clothing.

"Jimmy?" Montgomery's voice.

"Lieutenant!" Kowalski shouted.

Burke didn't hesitate. He body blocked Monty, pushing him back while Kowalski and O'Sullivan grabbed Monty's arms.

"Jimmy!"

Hearing the anguish in Monty's voice, Burke felt pity for the man. Monty must have considered the possibility that they wouldn't find Cyrus alive, but nothing could have prepared him to see this.

"Monty, I'll handle this," Burke said. "Wait by the car. Do you hear me, Lieutenant?"

A blank-eyed moment. Then Monty took a deep breath and said, "Yes, sir."

Burke glanced at O'Sullivan, who nodded and said, "Come on, Monty."

He watched Kowalski, who was watching the Wolves and frowning. Then he turned to Captain Miller.

"Your lieutenant knew this man?" Miller asked.

"His brother."

Miller paled. "Gods above and below. I'm sorry he had to see this."

"So am I." He walked into the grass until he stood beside the crime scene tape and could get a good look at what the unseen residents of the wild country had left behind.

He'd seen this a couple of times before when he'd been posted to human villages in the wild country, but in those cases, enough of the bodies had been left behind for the medical examiner to do an autopsy and run some tests. When the results came in, he remembered seeing tough, experienced cops vomit when they learned one particular detail about the Others' form of justice.

And he remembered what human action had triggered this degree of savagery.

"What's your procedure when this happens?" he asked Miller.

"We don't have one," Miller replied. "Out here, we either find the person alive or we don't find them at all.

Unless the person was killed by another human. We've had body dumps along this road over the years. Domestic disputes that turned fatal most of the time. When that happened, we usually found the woman—and the car. We rarely found the man. Not even this much."

"This wasn't domestic," Burke said, confirming whatever Miller had heard about the manhunt. "This was a kidnapping." As he pointed to one object lying on the shredded clothes, he choked on the rising fear that they might be too late. "The silver folding razor belonged to the young woman."

"Is she one of those girls?"

He nodded.

Miller looked toward the road and the Wolves who had returned to the brown car, sniffing and searching before they headed down the road in the opposite direction.

"Friend of theirs?" Miller asked.

Burke nodded again.

"We didn't find anything to indicate there was another person out here." Too much knowledge in Miller's eyes. "This is a few miles west of where the truck driver called in the position where he'd seen a young woman and this car. She may have been lucky enough to get away from her kidnapper, but it takes more than luck to get away from *them*."

He knew that. Meg Corbyn had a better chance of surviving in the wild country than anyone he'd ever met—if she wasn't having a psychotic episode because of the cuts Cyrus Montgomery made.

"Did anyone search the area where the truck driver saw her?" Burke asked.

"Don't know. That's just beyond my jurisdiction. I called the captain who handles that part of the road. He could have searchers out there now . . ."

"Or he could still be waiting for permission to send men into the wild country." Not always an easy thing to receive—and never a guarantee of safety for the humans going in. He understood a leader's caution. He also knew he would have gone in without permission, taking with him whatever help was offered.

He spotted Kowalski slowly walking toward them and turned to Miller. "Can you get me the exact position?"

The truck driver who called it in had included the number on the closest milepost. He would be able to start his own search close enough to Meg's last known position for the Wolves to pick up her scent.

"Didn't you . . . ?" Miller noticed Kowalski and nodded understanding. "Will do." He walked away.

Kowalski came up beside Burke and stared at the second object that had been placed on the shredded clothes: Cyrus Montgomery's lower jaw.

"The Wolves can't find Meg's scent," Kowalski said. "Wherever she is, she didn't leave the car anywhere around here. Nobody is shifting to human form to talk to me, but my impression is they didn't find her scent in the car; just in the trunk." He hesitated. "Captain, there's blood in the trunk. I don't think it's enough to be life-threatening, at least for any of us, but it struck me as being more than usual for one of Meg's cuts."

That was disturbing but not surprising. Very few people would know how to properly cut a *cassandra sangue* to avoid her suffering physical or mental problems, and Cyrus Montgomery wasn't one of them. Even if he had known, Burke doubted Cyrus would have cared.

"The Wolves may not realize that we're miles from the spot where Meg escaped from Cyrus. Go up and tell them so they understand why they can't pick up her scent. As soon as Captain Miller confirms the location, you and the lieutenant pack up the Wolves and get over there to start the search."

"Yes, sir." Kowalski didn't move, just stared at the jaw.

"Don't ask the question if you don't want the answer," Burke said quietly.

Monty had an ingrained courtesy and courage that

had opened a door, allowing some humans to communicate with the *terra indigene*. Karl Kowalski had the grit to see the truth about what was on the other side of that door and still walk through it.

But did he have enough grit?

"Was he dead when they ripped off his jaw?" Kowalski asked.

Burke took a deep breath and blew it out. "No."

So thirsty. And scared that Simon wouldn't find her. The *terra indigene* weren't the only wild things out here. And unlike the *terra indigene* who knew she wasn't prey, other wild things might decide she looked, and smelled, pretty tasty.

She couldn't run. Even if both legs worked, she'd never outrun predators who were used to chasing their dinners.

She didn't have much strength or courage left, but she had enough for one more bit of defiance.

"Arroo!" Meg howled. *"Arroo!"*

I am here. I am here!

Then she noticed the odd silence.

They circled the small bowl of land, trying to decide what they were seeing.

Looked human but didn't smell human. Didn't smell like prey. Smelled . . . intriguing.

"Arroo!" it howled. *"Arroo!"*

Tiny voice. Puppy howl. All puffed up and challenging. And hurt. Hind leg didn't work right.

"Arroo!" it howled again. *"Arroo!"*

Tiny voice. Puppy howl. But brave to challenge them, to warn them off.

Was this the howling not-Wolf?

They circled the small bowl of land and considered the messages that had rippled under the skin of the world, that had been a scent in the air and a taste in the water.

It was not a Wolf, it was not prey, and it was howling.

Crows had told them there were Wolves in their territory, searching along the road. Was the not-Wolf howling for its mate? Tiny howl. Wouldn't be heard.

One of them stayed to watch the not-Wolf. The others moved silently along the game trails, traveling far enough to ensure that they would be heard.

Then one of them howled.

Simon staggered into the middle of the road and stopped moving.

Meg was gone? Really gone?

He was supposed to find her. There was supposed to be a trail for him to follow.

But Meg's scent wasn't on the road or the grass, wasn't anywhere except in the trunk of the car. Without her scent, he didn't know where that Cyrus had left her.

Had no way to find her.

Lifting his muzzle, Simon howled the Song of Sorrow, joined by Blair and Nathan.

Then he stopped howling as a thought occurred to him. Nothing Meg had seen had indicated that he would lose her forever. She had escaped from that Cyrus and run into the wild country where a human couldn't follow her. She would run until she found the place in the woods that had the grave and the cold hand—the place she had seen in the prophecy dream. She would get there and wait for him. So his Meg wasn't *gone*; she was just lost until he found her.

If the humans couldn't help him find Meg, the *terra indigene* who lived around here could—and would.

When he howled again, it was a Song of Battle. And it was answered.

Monty leaned against the patrol car, blinking away tears as he listened to Simon's heartbroken howl.

Jimmy had done this to Simon, to all of them. Just another scheme that might have consequences for everyone but Jimmy. Except this time he had miscalculated and had paid dearly. Would his wife and children grieve, or would they secretly be relieved that he wasn't coming back?

Gods, what a thing to wonder about a brother.

Monty wiped away the tears. This wasn't the time for him to grieve or wonder. Meg Corbyn was still out there, somewhere.

He pushed away from the car and noticed how O'Sullivan immediately turned toward him. The ITF agent didn't need to worry; he wasn't going to try to see what had been left inside the crime scene tape. Not again.

Kowalski hurried over to join him.

"What's our status?" he asked, taking in the Wolves' body language as Nathan and Blair stood with Simon, howling: defeat.

"Captain Miller gave me the exact location where Meg escaped from Cyrus," Kowalski said. "Sounds like a few men started at that point and searched along the edge of the woods for a couple of miles in both directions. So far, there's been no sign of her."

"How far could she travel?"

Kowalski snorted. "You've never played chase with the Wolves. Uninjured, I think Meg could cover some distance."

And if that distance took her deeper into the wild country, they had no chance of finding her because there was no mercy in the wild country, no safety in the dark—even when the dark was the shade and shadows of the woods. The men who patrolled these roads knew that, and while a commander might risk his men if they had a solid location and were going in to rescue someone, no one would send in men to search for a body.

Simon howled again, but it sounded different now.

"Lieutenant, I have to tell the Wolves . . ."

"ARROOOOO!"

The Wolves froze. Burke and the local police officers scrambled onto the road.

"ARROOOOO!"

Based on the deep voice, whatever was out there was huge.

"Arroo!" Simon replied. *"Arrrrrooooo!"* He turned east, running past them as he headed down the road in the direction of the howl. Blair followed him.

"Nathan, wait!" Monty said when the other enforcer started to follow Simon. "What is it?"

The Wolf bristled with impatience, but Nathan shifted to a mostly human form. "The Elders found something."

"Meg?"

"They're not sure. It might be the not-Wolf." He shifted back to Wolf.

"Wait." Monty held up a hand. "Let us go with you as far as we can."

Nathan growled. Not a welcoming sound.

"We have water," Kowalski said. "And food. And a first-aid kit. When you find Meg, she'll need all those things. It will be easier to carry them in the car."

Nathan stopped growling. Monty decided that was as much agreement as they would get. Apparently Kowalski thought the same thing because he was behind the wheel of the patrol car in seconds.

Monty pulled open the passenger door, then stopped and looked at Burke.

"Go," Burke said. "O'Sullivan and I will handle things here. Good luck, Lieutenant."

Monty dove into the passenger seat. Kowalski had the car rolling before Monty closed the door.

The Wolves ran, and the patrol car stayed close enough to see them but far enough back to maneuver around anything unexpected.

Then Simon caught a scent—fresh enough and so familiar.

He stopped, explored the shoulder of the road. Followed the scent across the road and into the trees on the other side.

The patrol car pulled up. "Wait!" Montgomery shouted.

He hesitated, but the need to find his Meg was stronger.

<I'll help them follow the trail,> Nathan told Simon and Blair.

That much decided, Simon waited just long enough for Blair to join him. Then they headed into the woods, following Meg's scent on the game trail.

<This way,> Simon said when they reached the fork. He lifted a leg and marked a tree for Nathan to find.

<Why would she go east?> Blair said, also marking the tree.

<Meg would follow the trail in her visions.>

They followed the game trail, followed the scent, moving at a steady pace that wouldn't leave Nathan and the police pack too far behind.

<Blood,> Blair growled, sniffing some leaves.

<More here.> Just drops from a small wound, but for Meg, there was no such thing as a small wound.

They kept moving, following the game trail and the blood trail.

Then Simon stopped, his ears pricked. Was it . . . ?
"Arroo!"

They were barely in range of that howl, but it filled him with joy. *"Arroo!"*

"Arroo! Arroo!"

Found you. He ran toward the sound.

The odd silence wasn't quite so silent anymore, and Meg felt very grumpy about that—but not quite grumpy enough to tell an Elder that it wasn't polite to laugh at someone else's howl just because it wasn't . . . whatever.

"Arroo!" Practice makes perfect. Miss Twyla had said that. She hadn't said it about howling, but she had said it. In fact, she'd said a few other things about howling when Lizzy and the other children had been trying to see who could howl the loudest, but they didn't apply to Meg.

She looked out of the corner of her eye. She couldn't

see the Elder, but she sensed that something large had settled just above one end of the small bowl of land. It hadn't tried to communicate with her, but maybe its presence would attract some of the Crowgard and she could ask one of them to take a message to Lakeside.

Meanwhile, she was still tired and thirsty, and her ankle hurt. But that presence, while not benign, didn't feel threatening either. At least she wasn't alone.

She closed her eyes, took a deep breath . . . and howled. *"Arroo!"*

Moments later she heard *"Arroo!"*

"Simon," she whispered. *"Arroo! Arroo!"*

She waited, hardly daring to breathe. She didn't wait long before a big Wolf came over the lip and leaped into the small bowl of land.

"Simon!" She threw her arms around him and held on, shaking. Then she felt skin instead of fur, and strong arms wrapped around her as Simon pressed his face against hers.

"Meg." His voice shook. His body trembled. "Meg."

"I knew you'd find me." She squealed when something licked her ankle. Something that wasn't Simon.

"Blair says you're hurt."

Meg pulled back enough to see Simon's face. "He can tell that by licking my ankle?"

A deep growl near her hip discouraged her from saying anything sassy. She thought of telling Blair that there was an Elder nearby, but she figured he already knew that—and would nip her anyway.

"I tripped and hurt my ankle—and found . . ." She turned her head just enough to indicate a direction without actually looking at the body.

Blair moved away to inspect the body. Simon just hugged her.

"There's an Elder here," she whispered in his ear.

"I know," he whispered back.

"It laughed at me when I howled to tell you I was here." She could feel his smile.

Then Nathan was there, practically stepping on her as he sniffed and licked.

"Okay for us to come down?" Monty asked.

Meg looked up and saw Monty and Kowalski.

"Come down," Simon said.

They moved more carefully than the Wolves, their shoes slipping on old leaves as they made their way down to her.

Kowalski knelt in front of her, opened the daypack he carried, and produced a bottle of water. He opened it and held it out. "I have some food too, but we'll start with the water. Drink slow. Small sips. Okay?"

So thirsty, but she obeyed.

"Her ankle is hurt." Simon helped her move her leg to a position where Kowalski could look at it.

Apparently look didn't mean touch, because Simon snarled and his canines lengthened to Wolf size.

"Have to touch to tell what's wrong," Kowalski said, looking at Simon.

The snarling quieted but didn't stop—and got quite a bit nastier and louder when Karl's prodding made her yip.

Kowalski opened the first-aid kit. "I'm pretty sure it's sprained, not broken. Got an elastic bandage in here. We can wrap the ankle to give it some support until we can get Meg home for a proper checkup." He pulled out other things and handed them to Simon. "You can clean the cuts on her arm, then put some of the antibiotic ointment on them and wrap them. We'll need to watch them for infection since I don't think the cuts were made under the most sanitary conditions."

Not wanting Simon to think about why that had happened, Meg held out her left hand. "A bush attacked me when I was running."

Since she couldn't say when the cut was made, she couldn't point out the bush for him to bite—although she didn't doubt that, if he really wanted to, Simon could find the exact bush by sniffing out the tiny chunk of skin she'd left behind.

The bush bite calmed him a little, probably because it sounded ridiculous. Simon cleaned the cuts, grumbled about the stinky medicine, and used an unreasonable amount of gauze to wrap her arm and hand while Kowalski wrapped an elastic bandage around her ankle.

"Meg?" Lieutenant Montgomery crouched beside her.

It wasn't your fault, she thought.

He gave her bandaged arm an odd look as he held up a slim brown wallet. "While you were running through the woods, did you wonder about finding a doctor for your arm?"

"I wasn't always running through the woods. I *was,* but . . . Visions become strange when the cuts are too close," she said. "I couldn't tell what I was thinking from what I was seeing. Why?"

Monty studied her. "Some of the doctors on the governor's task force were reported as missing. I think you found one of them."

CHAPTER 28

Thaisday, Messis 23

After Meg told them she had heard sirens, Nathan retraced their steps and led Kowalski back to the patrol car while Blair searched the area for a more direct trail to the road. Simon would have preferred shifting back to Wolf, especially after sensing the presence of more Elders, but if he did that, he couldn't talk to Meg. On the other hand, he couldn't express himself properly in this human form.

And he couldn't sniff what he wanted to sniff to find out if that Cyrus had hurt his Meg in other ways.

"I'll have to give a statement?" Meg asked Montgomery.

"Yes, but not today." Montgomery smiled. "We'll take you home. Emily Faire can give you a checkup, make sure there aren't any cuts we missed."

Simon thought Montgomery wanted to ask about something else, then thought better of it.

"Arroo!" <Found the road,> Blair said. <I told Nathan. He said he and Kowalski will be there once the Crowgard give the patrol car back.>

<What did the Crows do with the car?>

<Nothing. But Kowalski left the car unlocked. The

Crowgard went inside to look around and decided they wanted a ride to the spot where Broomstick Girl not-Wolf had gone to ground. And Kowalski says he won't drive with a Crow perched on the steering wheel because that isn't safe.>

"Problem?" Montgomery asked.

"Only if the Crows around here learn how to turn on your police cars—and drive."

Montgomery looked alarmed.

"He's teasing you," Meg said, patting Montgomery's arm. "Aren't you, Simon? Simon?"

He looked at her.

"Oh dear."

Eventually Kowalski and Nathan arrived with a carful of Crows, who obligingly hopped out and then perched on any part of the car where they didn't slide off. Burke and O'Sullivan arrived a few minutes later with Captain Miller and his officer following in their own car.

After a brief discussion, it was decided that Burke and Montgomery would take Simon and Meg home, while Kowalski and O'Sullivan, along with Blair and Nathan, would help Captain Miller and the humans from the medical office retrieve the body in the woods. With the Elders so close, it wasn't safe for the humans to go in without the Wolfgard going with them.

While Simon carried Meg to Burke's black sedan, she didn't say anything about his not wearing clothes. But as soon as they were settled in the backseat, she glanced at him and blushed. "Simon, could you . . . ?"

Another human had hurt her, and right now she didn't trust this form. He shifted to Wolf and did his best to find a comfortable position after she hauled him halfway into her lap and held on.

It took longer to return to Lakeside than it had to drive to the spot where the car and Cyrus Montgomery had been located.

Burke hadn't said anything about a patrol car full of Crows, but every time the Crowgard flew toward the road, he slowed down to let them keep pace with the sedan for a minute or two—to let them see the sweet blood in the backseat, sleeping with her cheek on the head of a large dozing Wolf.

Then the Crowgard flew off to spread the word: Broomstick Girl and her Wolf were going home.

CHAPTER 29

Messis

The Crow took the small mesh bag and flew west. He had not been the first courier; he wouldn't be the last. When he was ready to return home, there would be another Crow waiting and ready to take the mesh bag on the next stage of its journey.

It took a few days, but eventually the mesh bag was delivered to Jenni Crowgard, as promised. She took it and flew off to a private spot in the Lakeside Courtyard, then invited Starr and Jake to join her.

With deft moves, she opened the bag with her beak and plucked out the prize. It wasn't as fresh as when the Feather Lakes Crowgard had taken it for her—with the Elders' permission—but that didn't matter.

The three of them tore at the soft tissue and, with a vengeful glee, ate one of Cyrus Montgomery's eyes.

CHAPTER 30

Firesday, Messis 24

Douglas Burke followed Greg O'Sullivan into the mayor's office and took a seat at the round table. Mayor Chen and Police Commissioner Alvarez occupied the other two chairs.

"Shouldn't the Chestnut Street station chief be here?" Burke asked. He'd gone over the head of his own chief as well as those of the rest of the station chiefs in Lakeside enough times over the past month—or more—that he was a little surprised he still had a job.

"I'll have a meeting with all the station chiefs later today to discuss how we proceed going forward," Alvarez replied. "To do that, I need an accurate assessment of whether or not Lakeside has a future, or if the incident with Cyrus Montgomery was, in effect, a death sentence for all of us."

Silence. Then O'Sullivan said, "Kick a pebble, start a landslide."

Burke nodded and addressed the explanation to Chen and Alvarez. "For the *terra indigene*, the attacks by the Humans First and Last movement were somewhat understandable—two opposing packs fighting for territory, winner take all, and everything that lives within that territory has to adjust to the rules laid down by the victors. But the disruptions and conflicts within a human pack that could be created by someone like Cyrus Montgomery weren't something that had been seen by the Others in the wild country—especially the Elders. Maybe there was concern that that kind of behavior could be absorbed by shifters who had too much contact with us. Sort of a psychological kind of rabies. Or maybe the Elders needed to study the effect one disruptive personality could have on a small community of humans before they allowed us to resettle places under their control. I doubt we'll ever know for sure."

"Captain Burke and I talked with Henry Beargard earlier this morning," O'Sullivan said. "We had the impression that the Elders took some responsibility for what happened because they didn't heed Simon Wolfgard's warnings about Cyrus being a danger to the Courtyard's residents. We also had the impression that seeing the police and Wolves working together to find Ms. Corbyn had shown the *terra indigene* who had little interaction with us that humans could fit in with other creatures." He paused. "Governor Hannigan received a message last night. He doesn't know how it was delivered or who, specifically, it was from, but the gist of the message was that police, firemen, and medical personnel can do their jobs after dark without fear of attack by the *terra indigene*, and that those who clearly belong to those professions won't be harmed if they enter the wild country to search for a missing human."

"That's a big concession," Alvarez said.

"With some luck and more work on our part to continue to build trust, some phone lines between regions may be restored as well," Burke said.

"The mayor's office will do what it can to help build that trust," Chen said.

Alvarez shifted in his chair. "What about the blood prophets? Is the governor going to replace the doctors who were killed by people trying to find those girls?"

O'Sullivan shook his head. "The task force has been disbanded. There are less obvious ways for caretakers to share information about the girls, and letting those girls remain hidden is safer for all of us."

Chen looked at Alvarez, then at Burke. "What is being done about Sandee Montgomery and young Clarence Montgomery? Were their crimes against the Courtyard premeditated?"

Burke shook his head. "Cyrus had given Clarence twenty dollars to cause trouble and draw attention away from the Liaison's Office at the time he had planned to abduct Meg Corbyn. The boy did it as much for the pleasure of causing trouble as for the money, but he didn't know what his father intended—or that Cyrus had no intention of coming back for him."

"The boy can't be charged as an adult," Alvarez said. "And given the nature of his crimes and the fact that they took place on property belonging to the Courtyard, human law is rather flexible. There is a 'tough love' school tucked away in the Addirondak Mountains. It's connected to a village that discourages visitors and is, in fact, so deep in the wild country, there aren't many people outside of law enforcement who even know it exists."

Burke wondered if the village was an Intuit community. Something to ask Steve Ferryman the next time they talked.

"I'm going to recommend that Clarence be sent there," Alvarez continued.

"It's a good solution," Burke said. "He'll receive care and a chance at an education, and maybe he'll turn away from the path his father had encouraged. One thing is certain: he won't survive if he stays in Lakeside."

"What about Sandee Montgomery?" Chen asked. "She was arrested for drugs, but she was on property that we've already established is not bound by our laws."

"Prison is a rough place, but it's about the only place right now where she would have enough time to make some choices," Burke replied. "She was told the skin cream would repel the Sanguinati, which it does since it was laced with heavy-duty household cleaners. But Sandee was the actual target, not the Sanguinati. She'd gotten in a dispute with a couple of other prostitutes who were freelancing in the downtown area. The women's male friends came up with the idea of the cream as a way to disfigure Sandee enough that she would no longer be competition."

"And the men who made this skin cream?" Chen asked after a moment.

Burke wondered if Chen and Alvarez appreciated the danger of even asking the question.

"Before we could bring them in for questioning, the three men died under suspicious circumstances," Alvarez said. "Two of them contracted the strange plague that has struck our city a few times and is still a mystery to the doctors. The third man drank the mixture of household cleaners, possibly thinking it was a more merciful death."

It probably was, Burke thought. But when Chen and Alvarez looked at him, as if inviting him to confirm what they suspected, he said nothing—for all their sakes.

CHAPTER 31

They gathered in the wild country between Tala and Etu, and their footsteps filled the land with a terrible silence.

While the rest of the Elders listened, the two who had returned from Lakeside told the story of the sly predator that wasn't a danger to the world or to Namid's teeth and claws but was still dangerous because of the harm it could cause within a human pack—a harm that touched the smaller shifters. They told their kin about the sweet blood howling not-Wolf and the Wolf who wanted to be her mate. They spoke of job-fair migrations and the proper way to ask for tasty Wolf cookie treats. And they spoke of their mistakes in ignoring the animosity the smaller shifters felt toward the Cyrus human and how the not-Wolf had been lost and could have died because they had not heeded the Wolf's warnings about that particular kind of human.

The two who had been in Lakeside told their story. And when the Elders made the journeys back to their own territories, they took the story—and its lessons— with them.

CHAPTER 32

Moonsday, Messis 27

Vlad filled the checkout counter with the book requests from *terra indigene* settlements. A few of the requests mentioned a specific book or author—human, Intuit, or Other. Most were requests for a kind of story that sounded similar to the hunt for Cyrus Montgomery and the rescue of Meg Corbyn: police and *terra indigene* working together; resourceful but wounded girl; plenty of blood and gore as the hunters tore through the bad human's accomplices to find the girl before she received a fatal wound.

The requests themselves held a hefty dose of fiction—although he suspected variations of the story would be written in the next few months—but he still needed to find something among the published books that might come close to the story requested. And he'd ask the police to recommend a nonfiction book about police cars that would satisfy the request from the Crowgard living around the Feather Lakes.

Tess walked through the archway and stopped at the counter. He hadn't seen her since Meg's abduction. Her hair was brown and wavy with a few narrow streaks of green, a sign she was almost relaxed.

"There are strange humans in my coffee shop," Tess said. "Nadine said you would explain."

Vlad walked over to the archway and looked into A Little Bite before returning to the checkout counter. "Officer Daniel Hilborn is Officer Debany's new partner. He comes here a couple of hours before his shift starts and observes. He's learning who is who and who works where."

"He called me ma'am. I think he's afraid of me."

He has good reason to be, Vlad thought. "Sally Esposito is a psychologist from Ferryman's Landing who has volunteered to come to the Courtyard a couple of days a week to provide counseling for anyone who needs some help."

"Meg?" Tess's voice was quiet, but Vlad wasn't fooled—not when black threads suddenly appeared and her hair began to coil.

"She's having bad dreams. And she's had a few episodes of seeing things that aren't there. The doctors at Lakeside Hospital are fairly confident that her brain wasn't damaged by . . ." He stopped. How much did Tess know about the way that Cyrus had cut Meg? Better not to bring it up since he didn't want to deal with her if her mood turned deadly. "Anyway, Ms. Esposito came here with Steve Ferryman to talk to the Business Association about providing some counseling—not just for Meg but also for Lizzy, Frances, and Sarah Denby."

"Getting inside the brain of a blood prophet must be a professional coup."

"You weren't here to voice an opinion when we had to decide," Vlad said coldly. "Then again, you weren't exactly absent, were you?"

"I didn't ask Nyx to come with me on that hunt," Tess replied just as coldly. She looked away. After a brief silence, she said, "How is Leetha?"

"She'll heal, although she may have some scarring around her mouth when she's in her human form." Thinking of that, Vlad relented. "The newspaper said the men drank household cleaners in some kind of lethal, winner-take-all game."

"One of them drank what they had added to the skin cream." Tess didn't look at him. "Harvesters are usually lone predators. Do you understand how rare it is for one of us to have friends? What happened to Leetha . . . She barely touched that . . . *human*, wasn't trying to feed. But it could have been Nyx—or you. It could have been a Wolf biting an enemy." She used one finger to shuffle a book request back and forth on the counter. "When we found those men, one of them smeared the cream on his arm and told Nyx they would give her two hundred dollars and all the blood she could drink if she could bite his arm."

"Fucking monkeys," Vlad muttered.

Tess nodded. "We made a counteroffer. Or I did."

Seeing a companion die because of one look at Tess would be a game changer.

"After they saw the first one's brains leaking out of his ears, they swore they were just getting their own back at that Sandee for cutting into their girls' profits, swore they didn't know the cream would really hurt the Sanguinati. We knew he was lying because of what that Sandee had told Captain Burke."

Either Burke hadn't noticed smoke hiding in the shadows when he interrogated that Sandee or he'd pretended not to notice. Either way, it explained how Nyx and Tess had reached the men first.

"When it started to rain inside the second one's skull, the third one grabbed the liquid and chugged it down." Tess shrugged. "Maybe he really believed he would survive drinking the stuff. He already knew he wouldn't survive me." She turned toward the archway but didn't step away from the counter. "Sandee made a bargain with the police to avoid the *terra indigene*'s wrath. Jail in exchange for information. Is that acceptable to Simon?"

"As long as she never returns to Lakeside, it's acceptable."

"Well," Tess said. "I'll let you get back to work."

Vlad watched her go into A Little Bite, but he didn't go back to work. Contact, familiarity. Those things cut both ways, exposed the Others' vulnerabilities as much as it exposed the petty ways humans hurt one another. That pettiness could lead to actions as deadly as a flat-out war, could wipe out Courtyards or towns. One human like Cyrus Montgomery coming into a mixed community could sour everything, shatter trust.

Perhaps the Elders had been right and studying that Cyrus and his family pack had been a useful lesson that they would share with the rest of Namid's teeth and claws. But Vlad wondered if Simon and Meg, and even Lieutenant Montgomery, felt that way.

To: Jackson Wolfgard

We found Meg. She sprained her ankle and has to use crutches for a while. Her brain is a little strange right now, but she'll get better. Tell Hope her vision drawing helped the police pack find the bad human's car, so Meg wasn't lost very long.

—Simon

Dear Meg,

Steve Ferryman and a woman named Sally Esposito came to see me at the Gardners' farm yesterday. They told me you had been abducted, but you were missing for a few hours at the most, and you're safely back at the Lakeside Courtyard now. They told me the man had cut you across old scars and had made the new cuts too close and too deep so they reopened while you were captive. They said you've been having "episodes."

I have "episodes." I guess that's why they wanted to talk to me. When I told them what I could remember about the times when old and new prophecies collided—and continue to collide even now, even when I haven't made a new cut—Sally Esposito said it sounded like whenever something provided a trigger that unlocked some of the memories of old prophecies, my mind spewed out the images in a dreamlike jumble—a visual hairball I cough up to feel better. (She didn't say "spew" or "hairball"; she used nicer words, but it amounted to the same thing.)

But there is something I didn't tell them. Something you need to know. Those episodes show me terrible and terrifying things. Bizarre things, like a huge chicken with a cow's legs and a goat's head. Images that got stuck together because, while the parts belong to animals, the whole doesn't make sense. A jumble, like Sally Esposito said. But since I came to live at the farm with the Gardners, whenever I have one of those episodes, there is always one image that appears every time, whole and unchanging. For me it's the image of someone handing me a jar of honey. I saw that image when I was still in the compound, and it was something Lorna Gardner did the first day I came to stay with them.

I think you have a constant thing too, something you can trust when you're not sure what is real and what is a vision. You know what it is. You recognize the symbol for it. Hold on to your talisman until you heal. You're strong, Meg. You won't have these episodes forever. And, hopefully, neither will I.

Your friend,
Jean

CHAPTER 33

Windsday, Messis 29

Walking out of the Market Square Library, Monty spotted Simon standing in a bit of shade watching the medical office on the other side of the square. Then he looked at an office on the second level. There wasn't a sign on the door—not yet anyway—but Monty was already familiar with Sally Esposito's office.

Get some counseling, Monty, Burke had said. *And take some personal time.*

Sound advice, especially when he closed his eyes at night and saw Meg's silver razor and Jimmy's lower jaw positioned on the shredded clothes.

There was no mercy in the wild country.

But there was a kind of rough compassion. The doctor who had been found in the woods had been tortured by people who wanted to locate the *cassandra sangue* who were hidden in settlements throughout the wild country. But something else had piled leaves over his body, had prevented small scavengers from eating what was left of the man.

"Simon." Monty joined the Wolf.

"Lieutenant Montgomery."

"My friends call me Monty."

Simon studied him, then nodded. "Monty."

An acknowledgment of more than a name; a choice that wasn't made lightly, not by a Wolf. "Is Meg having a session with Sally Esposito?"

Simon nodded. "She sleeps a lot, but she's always tired. The dreams chase her at night, and during the day she sees things that aren't there—and doesn't always see things that are. She's afraid." He hesitated. "So am I."

"I would be more concerned about her if she wasn't afraid, at least for a while." He studied the Wolf. "Are the cuts healing okay?"

A shrug. "There was some worry about infection, but Emily Faire gave Meg medicine to take for a few days, and I sniff the arm and her hand a couple of times a day to make sure there is no whiff of badness in the wounds."

The smile that had begun when Monty thought about Meg's reaction to being sniffed faded when he heard the word "wounds."

"She's not supposed to walk on the sprained ankle, and she's not happy about that or about needing to use the crutches or the wheelchair or about being carried upstairs. She growls at everyone—except Miss Twyla."

Now he did smile. "Nobody growls at Mama."

The Courtyard's minivan pulled up near an archway leading into the Market Square. Blair opened the side door. Sam leaped out, ran a few steps, and then waited until Blair picked up Skippy and set the juvenile on the ground.

The blow to the head hadn't made Skippy's brain any more skippy, although he yelped if anyone touched that part of his head. The broken foreleg would have been a death sentence in the wild country, unless the Wolf pack had a bodywalker who knew how to set bones. Even then, a Wolf with a broken leg couldn't help with the hunting.

"Emily Faire convinced Jane Wolfgard to take Skippy

to a vet in Ferryman's Landing," Simon said. "There wasn't anything the vet could do that Jane hadn't done already, but it was . . . friendly . . . of the Intuits to offer the help."

"Yes, it was." Monty hesitated. "Simon? What are you going to do about Meg?"

Simon stared at him, a warning flicker of red in the amber eyes. "Do about Meg?"

"You love her, and she loves you. You're in love, Simon. Maybe that's not how you would describe what you feel, but it's obvious to the humans who know both of you."

The medical office's door opened and Meg hobbled out, supported by Sally Esposito and Theral MacDonald, who helped settle her in the wheelchair.

"Meg!" Sam ran to her. Skippy, with one leg in a cast, hobbled after the boy.

Simon watched them, then said in a rough voice, "I'm not human. I will never be human."

"Is that so important?" Monty asked quietly.

Surprised, the Wolf looked at him.

Monty subtly pointed at Meg, Sam, and Skippy. "Do you know what I see when I see you and Meg and Sam together?"

"Two Wolves and a human?"

"No. I see a family." Monty sighed. "I envy you, Simon Wolfgard. You and Meg aren't the same species and you have an unconventional relationship, but you also have a better working partnership than I ever had with Elayne. She and I were both human, but we couldn't find a way to make the differences in our backgrounds work for us."

"What if Meg wants puppies? I'm not sure humans and *terra indigene* can do that."

"Roo-roo!" Skippy hobbled toward Twyla Montgomery as she came out of Chocolates and Cream with a tray and four bowls of ice cream.

Setting the tray on one of the outdoor tables, she

waved for Meg and Sam to join them and said sternly, "Sam, Miss Meg isn't a toy. Don't be racing with her in that chair—or taking shortcuts down the steps."

"But the ice cream will melt if we go slow!" Sam protested.

"Samuel Wolfgard."

"Yes, ma'am."

Monty shook his head. Could a boy move any slower?

He turned his attention back to Simon. "Maybe it's different for Wolves, but plenty of humans who are mates don't have children for one reason or another."

Watching his mother sitting with Meg and the two young Wolves, Monty thought about his sister, the adopted child. In a day or two, he would make a few discreet inquiries and see if he could locate her. Knowing Jimmy was no longer a threat, hopefully Sissy would get in touch with Mama. It would be good for all of them if that much could be mended.

Thinking of Sissy, Monty said, "Even if you can't have children of your own, you have Sam."

"Yes," Simon replied quietly. "We have Sam."

Mated pairs didn't always stay together. Sometimes the bond between them broke. But sometimes it was the surviving mate who broke if the other died. Was that what humans called love? The joy of being together and the killing sense of loss when one of them ceased?

If he hadn't found Meg, he wouldn't have returned to Lakeside. He would have left Sam in Elliot's care, and he would have . . . What? Disappeared? Died? Looked for a pack deep in the wild country who had minimum contact with human things and no contact with actual humans?

Was that love?

Or was he trying to think too much like a human? Their brains were so full of confusion it was a wonder they managed to do anything at all, let alone establish a proper social order within a pack.

Simon walked into the back room of the Liaison's Office and stopped when he heard the muffled sound.

<Nathan?> he called to the watch Wolf, who had become extra vigilant when humans came into the office—even humans he knew. After all, none of the Wolves had liked that Cyrus, but they hadn't thought he would steal Meg.

<She's crying,> Nathan said. <I don't know why.>

Simon stepped into the sorting room. "Meg?"

"I can't find it!" she wailed. "I've looked and looked, and it's not here!"

"What isn't here?" Noticing the prophecy cards spread out on the table, he walked over to see what had upset her. All the cards were faceup.

"The card! I can't find the card!"

Is it a real card? Couldn't ask her that. "Real" was a slippery word right now. "You've held the card?"

"Yes, I've held the card."

"You're sure it's not under these cards?"

Meg sniffled and nodded. "I've looked through them three times. It isn't there."

"Then it's hiding, and we'll have to find it." Simon turned toward the back room.

"How?" Meg was back to wailing.

"You held it, so it smells like you."

He hurried into the back room, stripped off his clothes, and shifted. In Wolf form, he returned and began sniffing his way around the sorting room. The screen was inserted in the side door to help cool the room. The air brought in the ponies' scent and . . . cow? He followed that scent to a cargo pocket in Meg's shorts and found additional scents—hay and feathers.

He placed a paw on the pocket. *"Arroo?"*

Meg put her hand over his paw. "The card isn't in there. I received a letter from Jean."

Ah. Farm. That explained the smells. As for the other, far more interesting smell, well, she was standing and his nose was *right there*, but he didn't want to startle her into putting weight on her bad leg, so he went back to looking for the card.

He picked up a whiff of mouse in one corner. He'd talk to the Owlgard about hunting around the Market Square and the Liaison's Office more often.

He caught Meg's scent under the cupboards and spotted the smallest piece of something that wasn't wood or floor. He whined at it and growled at it and scratched at it until he finally pulled it out.

"That's it!" Meg said. She bent over and put her hands on the floor. She picked up the card, bracing herself on the side of one hand.

Simon waited, wondering if this three-limbed position was something she had learned in Quiet Mind class.

"I'm stuck," she growled.

Oh.

He crawled between her hands and her working leg. Then he stood up, lifting her torso until she could grab the table and lift herself the rest of the way. Having seen her sit down on the tall stool they had provided for her, he hurried into the back room, shifted, and pulled on his jeans and shirt before returning to get a look at this card that had to be found.

A man and woman, standing close together in a garden under a full moon.

"Why is the moon shaped like that?" he asked.

"It's a heart," Meg replied. "Haven't you seen this symbol before?"

"Sure. But it's not the thumpy-thump good-eating kind of heart."

"It's a romantic heart." She looked up and narrowed her eyes. "Is that why you shelved the kissy books with the cookbooks? Because a heart is a heart?"

"Vlad did that," he said too quickly. Did it really matter that a Sanguinati wouldn't have any interest in eating either kind of heart?

She looked doubtful, but her attention was drawn back to the card.

"Why is this card so important to you?"

"It's a constant thing," she replied softly. "I see this card every time I have one of those episodes where the images from prophecies bleed together until nothing makes sense. But this card doesn't change."

"So romance is your constant thing?"

She shook her head. "Love. That's more than romance."

You love her, and she loves you. You're in love, Simon. Was Monty right?

"Meg? Are we mates?"

"I—I don't know."

"I'm not human. I will never be human. But maybe I can be human enough to be your mate."

Meg looked at him. "I'm not a Wolf. I can never be a Wolf. I can't even *look* like a Wolf. So how could *I* be *your* mate?"

Meg didn't need to shift to be pack, to be his mate. Was that love?

"You're Wolf enough for me," he said.

"And you're human enough for me. But I don't know about . . ." She waved a hand at her torso.

"Sex?" Judging by her blush, he'd guessed correctly. This form was harder to control because it responded even when a female wasn't in season, but he shrugged. "Wolves mate once a year."

"Once a year?" She blinked. "Just once?"

Did she sound disappointed? "Since human females come into season more often, we could try something closer to the human way." He didn't need to tell her that he would be able to smell when she was receptive, did he?

She looked scared, confused—and maybe a little hopeful? How could he encourage the hopeful? If he was in Wolf form, he could lick her nose and make her laugh. He wasn't sure what to do in this form that wouldn't cause confusion and scare her away.

Meg swallowed. "What will happen if we do become

mates officially, like Karl and Ruth or Merri Lee and Michael?"

"Ask." Simon waved a hand over the prophecy cards and noticed a little fur on his knuckles. Nerves. He wondered what his ears looked like. His teeth . . . Hmm. Well, she'd seen them before.

He helped her stand, kept his arm around her waist for balance while she turned all the cards facedown.

"What will happen if Simon and I become mates?" Meg closed her eyes and moved her hands over the prophecy cards. She picked a card and turned it over without opening her eyes.

Simon looked at the card and laughed softly.

"That bad?" Meg opened her eyes, alarmed. Then she looked at the card. "Oh."

She had chosen the romance card, the symbol for her constant thing. The symbol for love.

"Before we tell anyone about our decision, I think we should kiss," Meg said suddenly. "To see if we like it."

Why wouldn't they like it? Kissing was similar to licking, and he always liked licking Meg. In fact, the times when he had given her a human kiss, he'd liked that too.

He put his arms around her and brushed his lips against hers once, twice. Then his mouth settled over hers and lingered. As he eased back, she leaned forward and pressed her lips against his.

"I think we like it," Meg breathed.

"I think we should try it again. Just to be sure."

They tried it several more times, just to be sure, and eventually decided that they did like kissing. They liked it a lot.

Read on for an exciting excerpt from
a novel in Anne Bishop's
World of the Others,

Lake Silence

Available now from Ace

CHAPTER 1

VICKI

Moonsday, Juin 12

I wouldn't have known about the dead man if I hadn't walked into the kitchen at the exact moment my one and only lodger was about to warm up an eyeball in the wave-cooker.

Until that moment, I hadn't known I had a scream that could crack glass; I hadn't wondered if an eyeball would puff up and explode in a wave-cooker like those animal-shaped marshmallows; and I hadn't realized my lodger—Agatha "call me Aggie" Crowe—was *that* kind of Crow.

She seemed so normal, if you overlooked her timely payment of the rent each week and the fact that she had taken up residence in The Jumble three weeks ago and seemed to be enjoying herself.

"You can't eat that!" I tried to sound firm, like a responsible human and business owner should. In truth, I sounded a wee bit hysterical, and I wished with all sincerity that I had walked into the kitchen five minutes later.

Then again, since the kitchen was one of the common rooms in the main building, I could have walked in when

Aggie was halfway through her lunch, which I'm sure would have been more distressing for at least one of us.

"Why can't I eat it?" She looked at the eyeball rolling around in the small bowl that was now sitting on the counter. "Nobody else wants it. It's starting to get squooshy. And the dead man doesn't need it."

The words got me past the physical evidence. "What dead man?"

"The one who doesn't need the eyeball." Little black feathers suddenly sprouted at her hairline, confirming the nature of my lodger. I was going to have to rework the rental agreement so that there was a space for unimportant bits of information like . . . oh, say . . . species.

"Where did you find the dead man?"

"On the farm track that runs alongside Crabby Man's place."

I should have pointed out that Mr. Milford wasn't usually crabby, but he did get exercised when someone took one bite out of all the ripe strawberries or pinched fruit from his trees, since he and his wife needed the income they made from selling fresh fruit and homemade preserves. But there were other priorities.

"Show me." I held up a hand. "Wait. And don't nibble."

"But . . ."

"You can't eat it. It could be evidence."

Her dark eyes filled with reproach. "If I hadn't wanted to warm it up because it was squooshy, you wouldn't have known about the dead man and I could have had eyeball for lunch."

I couldn't refute that statement, so I backed up until I reached the wall phone in the kitchen, and then I dialed the emergency number for the Bristol Police Station. Bristol was a human town located at the southern end of Crystal Lake. Sproing, the only human village near Lake Silence, was currently without its own police force, so Bristol had drawn the short straw and had to respond to any of our calls for help.

"Bristol Police Station. What is your emergency?"

"This is Victoria DeVine at The Jumble in Sproing. One of my lodgers found a dead man." Okay, Aggie was my only lodger, but there was no reason to advertise *that*. Right?

I started counting and reached seven before the dispatcher said, "Did you see the body?"

"No, but my lodger did."

"How do you know the body is dead?"

"I'm looking at an eyeball that used to be attached to the body."

This time I counted to eight.

"We'll send someone." The words were slow in coming, but at least they were said and would be officially noted somewhere.

I didn't blame the dispatcher for hesitating to send someone to Sproing—after all, the police officer we'd had before last year's Great Predation had been eaten, and a couple of officers who had answered calls since then had provoked something in the wild country and never made it back to their station—but I resented that I could feel her blaming me for whatever the police were going to find. On the other hand, I did withhold one tiny bit of information.

Just wait until the responding officer realized he had to interview one of the *terra indigene*.

A bit of useful information. My name is Victoria "call me Vicki" DeVine. I used to be Mrs. Yorick Dane, but giving up my married name was one of the conditions of my receiving valuable property—aka The Jumble— as part of the divorce settlement. Apparently the second official Mrs. Dane didn't like the idea that someone else had had the name first. Fortunately, she didn't seem as possessive about Yorick's Vigorous Appendage. I could have told her that a couple dozen other women had had it before she took possession. But it wasn't likely that she would keep solo possession of the appendage for long, so let her figure things out the hard way like I did. Of course, if she had been one of those indulgences, then she already knew the signs and might be able to nip them in the bud. Maybe that's why, before I had moved away from Hubb NE, I had seen her in the garden center buying long-handled loppers—the kind used to prune branches—when I'd heard her loudly proclaiming the previous week that gardening was a hobby for women who couldn't do anything else and so not of interest to *her*.

Anyway, I was married to Yorick Dane, an entrepreneur—aka wheeler-dealer—although I never understood what sort of deals were wheeled. He said I didn't have a head for business. I finally said I didn't have a head for cheating of any kind. Suddenly, after a decade of marriage, he said I wasn't living up to the promises that were implied by my name, meaning I wasn't hot or in any way sexy. The fact that it took him a decade to realize I was five foot four and plump instead of a five-foot-ten pole dancer with big tits was confusing. But once he made that discovery, he decided that he needed someone who would stand by him, and that would not be me.

So that's how I came to be the owner of The Jumble. According to the story that was muttered by Yorick's family once they'd had a little too much to drink, The Jumble was conceived and built by Yorick's great-great-aunt, Honoria Dane, a woman who was equal parts visionary and eccentric. She and her brothers were given equal shares in their father's fortune, the shares being dispersed upon the child's twenty-fifth birthday. Great-great (I never heard anyone refer to her by her given name) had sunk her part of the fortune into building The Jumble. It was supposed to be a self-sufficient and self-supporting community. It began its genteel decline almost from the moment Great-great finished building it.

The Jumble consisted of the sprawling two-story main house, which had a small but fully equipped apartment for the owner as well as two suites with private bathrooms for guests. It also had a big communal kitchen, a dining room, a library, a social room, an office for the owner, several empty rooms whose use I couldn't identify, and a large shower area off the kitchen that could accommodate up to four people at a time as long as they weren't shy. Besides the main house, there were four sets of cabins—three connected cabins to a set—within easy walking distance from the main building. Each cabin was similar to an efficiency apartment with an open floor plan—no walls or doors for anything but the bathroom. Well, the three lakeside cabins that were closest to the main building had en suite bathrooms. The other nine cabins were a bit more primitive and an ongoing project.

There were acres of land that could be used by the . . . beings . . . in residence—plenty of room for growing food or raising a goat or two for whatever reason one keeps goats. There was even a chicken coop, sans chickens. It was probably sans a few other things, but if the chickens couldn't pay rent, I couldn't afford to update their lodgings. But The Jumble had one thing the village of Sproing did not—it included easy access to Lake Silence, which was an afterthought body of water compared to the other Finger Lakes. There *was* a public beach at the southern end of the lake, but I thought The Jumble's private beach and dock were a lot nicer.

Whoever negotiated the original lease agreement for the use of the land knew every devious loophole a person might try to use to rezone/repurpose/re-something the land. But the terms were brutally simple: it was The Jumble, with its set number of buildings of a particular size and so many acres of cultivated land (being a modest percentage of the overall acreage), or nothing. The Dane inheritance was actually the buildings and their contents. The land could be used only within the terms of the lease.

Last bit of information. Sproing is a human village with a population of less than three hundred. Like most, if not all, of the villages in the Finger Lakes area, it is not human controlled. Sure, we have an elected mayor and village council, and we pay taxes for garbage pick-up and road maintenance and things like that. The main difference is this: on the continent of Thaisia, a human-controlled town is a defined piece of land with boundaries, and humans can do anything they want within those boundaries. But villages like Sproing don't have a boundary, don't have that distance from the *terra indigene*. The earth natives. The Others. The dominant predators that control most of the land throughout the world and all of the water.

When a place has no boundaries, you never really know what's out there watching you.

The surprising thing is there hadn't been a reported interaction with one of the Others in decades. At least around Sproing. Maybe the Others have been coming in and buying COME SPROING WITH ME or I ♥ SPROINGERS T-shirts without anyone realizing it, but even though the village lost about a quarter of its residents because of last summer's Great Predation, everyone still wanted to believe that the Others were Out There and didn't find us interesting enough—or bothersome enough—to hunt down and have as snacks.

Which made me wonder if the Others came into town seasonally, like tourists. And that made me wonder if everyone had missed the obvious when stores ran out of condiments like ketchup and hot sauce some weekends—and whether a run on ketchup and hot sauce coincided with people disappearing.

Something to ask Aggie once we got past the whole eyeball thing.

CHAPTER 2

GRIMSHAW

Moonsday, Juin 12

Officer Wayne Grimshaw drove toward the village of Sproing, the cruiser's flashing lights a warning to anyone else on the road that he was responding to a call and was all business. But the siren remained silent because that sound would have drawn the attention of everything for miles around—and when a man was in the wild country, even on a paved road that was a vaguely acknowledged right-of-way, it was better not to alert the earth natives to his presence.

Dead body reported at The Jumble near Sproing.

Sproing. By all the laughing gods, what kind of name was that for a village? It sounded like some kind of initiation or razzing—have the new guy respond to a call and then have to keep asking for directions to Sproing. Plenty of off-color jokes could be made about that.

Except he knew the name wasn't a joke. He had seen it on the map at the Bristol station and had been told calls from citizens living around Lake Silence were part of Bristol's jurisdiction. Added to that, the emergency dispatcher, who was a no-nonsense woman, had sounded reluctant to send him—and he'd been advised a couple of times by other officers at the station that if he had to answer a call around Lake Silence, he should get in and out as quickly as possible because things around that particular lake were a wee bit . . . hinky.

The village had a small police station but no longer had its own police force—not a single cop patrolling its streets. The people there were dependent on the highway patrol that worked out of the Bristol station, and even then . . .

Over the past few months, two officers who had answered calls around Sproing hadn't returned. One officer was found in his patrol car, which had been crushed by something powerful enough to flatten a car with its fists or paws or some freaking appendage. The other man . . . Most of that officer had been found, but no one knew what had set off the attack or why it had been so vicious. Both deaths were harsh reminders that the highway patrol traveled through the wild country as part of the job, and a man never knew what was watching him when he stepped out of his vehicle.

Grimshaw had been patrolling the secondary roads south of Bristol—a loop that would have taken him close to Lake Silence anyway—so when he spotted a sign for the lake, he turned onto the dirt road, hoping it would take him to The Jumble, which he'd been told was some kind of resort right on the lake. Instead he found himself in the parking area for the lake's public beach.

From what he had gathered from his captain's orientation speech, the land on the western side of Lake Silence was privately owned—or at least privately controlled—as was most of the eastern side. There was no vehicle access to the northern end of the lake, which left only the southern end for anyone who wanted to take a cool dip on a hot day or take a boat out for fishing or recreation.

Grimshaw frowned at the two signs attached to the low stone wall that separated the parking area from the beach.

The first sign read:

PACK OUT YOUR TRASH OR ELSE

The second sign read:

**YOU MAY SWIM, FISH, SAIL, ROW, CANOE,
OR FLOAT ON RAFTS AT YOUR OWN RISK.
IF YOU PUT A MOTOR IN THE WATER,
YOU WILL DIE.**

Nothing ambiguous about either message.

Grimshaw turned the cruiser around and got back on the main road, heading north. The next turnoff had a weathered sign for The Jumble. He made the turn and followed the gravel access road up to the main building. As he shut off the car, he pressed two fingers against his chest and felt the round gold medal for Mikhos, the guardian spirit of police officers, firemen, and medical personnel—a talisman he had worn under his uniform every day since he graduated from the police academy a decade ago.

"Mikhos, keep me safe." It was the prayer he whispered every time he answered a call.

A woman stepped into view, looking agitated. Curly brown hair, a pleasant enough face, and a build he would describe as stocky if she had been a man. He couldn't tell more than that from this distance, so Officer Wayne Grimshaw got out of the cruiser and went to see Ms. Victoria DeVine about a body.

CHAPTER 3

VICKI

Moonsday, Juin 12

"**B**ut I can't!" Aggie wailed, sprouting more feathers when I told her she would have to talk to the police.

The additional black feathers in her hair were less distressing than the ones that suddenly appeared on her face and forearms.

"You have to," I replied, striving to remain calm. I placed a saucer over the bowl with the eyeball. "You're the only one who knows where to find the body. You'll need to show the police when they get here."

"But I'll get in *trouble*!"

My breath caught and my heart thudded. Aggie was petite and had a small-boned physique—and my purse probably weighed more than she did. But being one of *those* Crows, she could be a lot stronger than she looked.

"Aggie, you didn't . . . ?" What would I do if she admitted that she had killed a man in order to eat his eyeball? I imagined myself being strong and brave and performing some kick-ass self-defense moves despite not actually knowing how to do them. Then I imagined myself smiling weakly right before I ran away.

I liked the idea of running away. Much more sensible.

"I didn't kill him!" Aggie sounded insulted. "He was already dead when I found him and only had the one eyeball."

"What happened to the other one?"

"Dunno. Probably got eaten."

Since I liked Aggie, I really didn't want to ask more questions. I grabbed the bowl with the eyeball and went outside to wait for the police. Aggie followed me out the front door but started edging toward the trees.

"Aggie . . ." Hearing tires on gravel, I turned to watch the police car as it drove up within sight of the house and stopped at a spot that blocked the access road. When I turned back, a pile of clothes lay under a tree and Aggie was gone. So I stood there, alone, holding the bowl while I waited for the police officer to get out of the car.

You know those cartoon heroes with the strong lower jaws, sparkly teeth, *broad* shoulders, and tiny waists? The man who stepped out of the police car could have been the model for the caricature, but he was correctly proportioned and looked really official with all the doo-dads on his belt. He was wearing sunglasses, so I couldn't see his eyes, couldn't tell if the expression in them was a warm "Can I help you, ma'am?" or a cold "You're being a pain in my ass, so talk fast."

If he had stopped to help when I was stranded on a dark, lonely road, I would have been happy to see him. But that presence was less reassuring when I wasn't sure I wouldn't be labeled the villain.

"Are you the lady who called about a suspicious death?" he asked, approaching warily.

He was a big man and had a big voice. Not that he was yelling at me or anything, but it was the kind of voice that could hammer a person—the kind of voice that, when used with a threatening tone, could trigger a panic attack.

He stopped and studied the claw marks on a tree—

marks that were high enough that I hadn't noticed them because they weren't in my usual line of sight.

Something to think about on a hot summer night when I'm trying to convince myself that it's safe to leave the windows open to get some air. Safe from thieves maybe, since I have nothing to steal. Safe from the mysterious Clawman?

I'd read somewhere that an ordinary bear could hook its claws in a car door and rip the door off the hinges in order to get to the snacks someone foolishly left inside. Odds were good that whatever prowled around in The Jumble's woods didn't qualify as ordinary, although, to be fair, Aggie was the only *terra indigene* I had seen— "seen" being the qualifying word. If one of the crows hanging around The Jumble was Crowgard, how many others were more than they seemed?

"My lodger found a body near the farm track that is the boundary between my property and the Milfords' orchards," I replied, trying for matter-of-fact helpful. I held out the bowl. "Here. This is evidence."

He took the bowl, lifted the saucer, and stared at the eyeball. At least, I assumed he stared at the eyeball. Since he was wearing those mirrored sunglasses, he could have been staring at me—and it suddenly occurred to me that if he asked to look in my refrigerator, I had no idea what he might find.

"Wait there." He walked back to his car and opened the trunk. He returned in a minute without the eyeball. It didn't look like he was going to return my bowl and saucer either. "I'll need to speak to your lodger."

"She's a little shy about talking to the police."

He removed the sunglasses. The look in his blue-gray eyes said my lodger better get un-shy in a hurry. Or maybe I was projecting from past experience with men. Man. The one who used to leave me feeling that something was my fault even when I couldn't have controlled someone else's actions or thoughts or opinions.

"Did she tell you the location? Can you show me the alleged body?"

I had just given him an eyeball. How alleged could the body be? "I—"

"Caw."

I looked at the crow—or Crow—perched in a tree a couple of yards down one of the bridle paths, of which The Jumble has many.

"Yes, I can." I set off down the path and hoped really hard that I was following Aggie and not someone else.

The second time I tripped and would have landed face-first in the dirt if the officer hadn't grabbed my arm and kept me upright, he grumbled, "You might do better watching where you're walking than looking at the trees."

Sound advice. I wished I could take it, but I didn't want to explain that our guide was in the trees, because that would require explaining the nature of our guide.

"Stop," he said after we had been walking awhile. It felt like forever, and since I hadn't gone back inside the house to get my wristwatch before we headed out, time was measured by how it felt. "Do you have any idea where you're going?"

"Of course I do, Officer . . ." I realized he hadn't told me his name. Maybe that wasn't required?

"Grimshaw."

"Really?" So not the correct response, especially from someone named Vicki DeVine. "The Milfords' place is the land between The Jumble and the road that leads to Sproing. The body was found near the farm track between the Milfords' land and mine."

"So we should be heading east?"

I was about to agree but the affirmative words stuck in my throat. *Were* we supposed to be heading east? Was this a trick question? Couldn't be heading west. The lake was to the west of the main house—could, in fact, be seen from the back of the main house. But that left two other directions unaccounted for.

"Ms. DeVine?" Officer Grimshaw was not a happy camper.

"Um . . ."

"Caw."

I breathed a sigh of relief. "This way."

Suddenly there were three crows on the same branch, making me think of the shell game where you have to figure out which shell is hiding the pea.

Three black birds were sitting in a tree. Which one was *A-G-G-I-E*?

"Caw."

Only one took off, so I followed, hoping it was a Crow, and Officer Grimshaw followed me. Big mistake. I probably should have admitted to being geographically challenged *before* I led him into the woods.

"Caw!"

Open ground. Daylight. The dirt road, aka the farm track. And the body.

"Ew." That wasn't a professional response, but I wasn't a professional and I sincerely hoped I never met this man again. Either man.

"Stay there," Grimshaw said as he moved closer to the body.

Like I was going to get closer when my knees already felt rubbery and my stomach felt swoopy.

"This body has been disturbed."

"I'd be disturbed too if I was suddenly dead," I replied.

He twisted around enough to look at me and must have decided I wasn't trying to be a smart-ass; I just wasn't quite in control of what I was saying anymore. Since I had dealt with the eyeball pretty well, the only explanation was that my brain had decided that, with someone else here to handle the problem, it no longer had to be fully functional during this stage of the crisis and could enjoy a mini anxiety attack.

"Not a lot of predation," Grimshaw said, studying the body. "I don't think he's been here long."

"Aggie said his eyeball was squooshy. That's why she wanted to warm it up in the wave-cooker. Wouldn't it take a while for the eyeball to get squooshy?"

I watched him put his sunglasses back on before he turned to face me.

"Aggie is your lodger?" Arctic Voice.

I nodded, glad I couldn't see his eyes because my insides were quivering as I braced for Arctic Voice to become Hammer Voice.

"I really need to talk to her."

My quivering insides translated his Officially Polite Voice as more encouraging than scary, so I pointed at the branch above me. "Go ahead."

His head moved, so I assumed he was looking up. Then, as he turned away, I heard him say, "Crap." It wasn't so much spoken as a breath shaped into sound.

Aggie lifted her wings in what might have been an apologetic shrug and let out a timid *caw*.

Grimshaw pulled out his mobile phone and made a call. The next couple of minutes sounded like a TV show with all the "officer needs assistance" and requests for the medical examiner and transport of the remains.

He hadn't gotten very far into explaining the situation when seven birds winged toward the body. They landed close and moved closer, despite Grimshaw waving an arm to keep them away.

"Friends of yours?" I asked, looking up at Aggie.

"Caw."

"Officer . . ."

"I heard."

Yeah. Regular crows would have been enough of a problem if you wanted to avoid having more body bits and pieces being taken away for someone's dinner. But dealing with the Crowgard? That made this a potential PR fiasco for the police department—and every other human service that could be affected by the *terra indigene*'s taking exception to someone keeping them away from the buffet.

Or *was* it the body that was so intriguing? I saw a glint of gold. A wristwatch. It looked like someone had been trying to pull it off and had been interrupted. By our arrival?

"I have to stay with the body until the Crime Investigation Unit gets here," Grimshaw said. "Can you find your way back to the house?"

"Sure."

"*Can* you find your way back?"

Could we call that a no-confidence vote for the geographically challenged?

"*Caw.*" At least Aggie was confident of getting us back to the main house.

So there, Officer Smarty-Pants.

I headed back up the path, fairly sure that I could get out of sight before getting lost.

"Ms. DeVine?"

Grimshaw's voice stopped me but I didn't turn around. "Yes, Officer?"

"I'll still need to talk to you and your lodger. Don't go anywhere."

Like I could with his big official vehicle blocking the access road that led up to the main house. Somehow I couldn't see myself taking off on my bicycle in order to escape the law. Besides, all I did was report finding a body. How much trouble could I get into for doing that?